THE ANNOTATED
Black Beauty

The cover of one of the first editions of *Black Beauty*, published in London in 1877 by Jarrold & Sons. (Paul Mellon Collection, Upperville, Virginia)

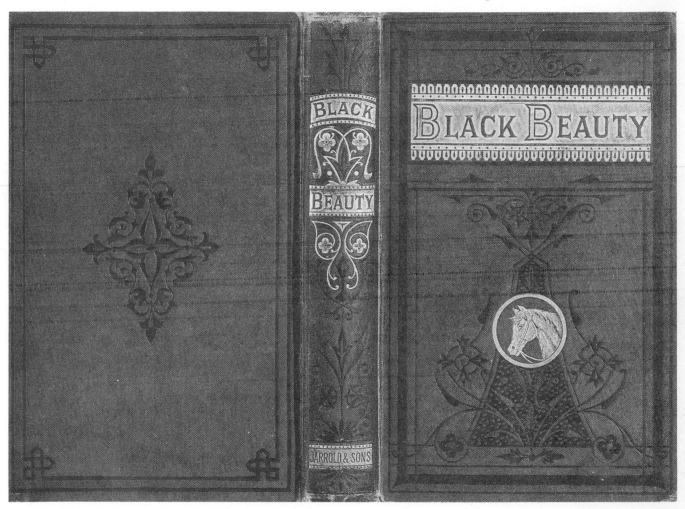

THE ANNOTATED
Black Beauty

Anna Sewell

Introduction and annotations by
Ellen B. Wells and Anne Grimshaw

J. A. Allen
London

British Library Cataloguing in Publication Data

Sewell, Anna, *1820–1878*
   The annotated Black Beauty.
   I. Title   II. Wells, Ellen B.   III. Grimshaw, Anne
823′.8 [J]

ISBN 0–85131–438–4

First published in Great Britain in 1989 by
J. A. Allen & Company Ltd
1 Lower Grosvenor Place, Buckingham Palace Road
London SW1W 0EL

Editor: Elizabeth O'Beirne-Ranelagh
Designer & Production Editor: Bill Ireson
Picture Researcher: Jane Lake

Printed in Great Britain

Contents

Acknowledgements

The mysteries and hidden meanings in Anna Sewell's moving and memorable novel *Black Beauty* may never be completely identified and verbalised. But we have enjoyed and learned from our experience with this effort, which would have been impossible without the help and encouragement of many people.

Margaret N. Coughlin, Children's Literature Center, The Library of Congress, Washington first gave encouragement to the project eight years ago and her enthusiasm never wavered.

Caroline Burt has been a support and positive help ever since she heard of the idea, encouraging us each step of the way. Elizabeth O'Beirne-Ranelagh was an editor everyone would wish for; her research and provision of additional material has made the book better than we could have ever hoped to have done by ourselves. We are very grateful to both for their constant support. Our thanks, too, go to Jane Lake for picture research and to Bill Ireson for design and production editing.

PERMISSIONS

Information, permission to publish or quote from copyrighted sources, and advice is acknowledged from the following: Adprint; American Humane Education Society; Ansonia Library, Ansonia, Conn.; Gillian Avery; B. T. Batsford Ltd, London; A. & C. Black (Publishers) Ltd; J. M. Brereton, Maj. retd; Breyer, A Division of Reeves International; Cambridge University Library; Humphrey Carpenter; Century Hutchinson Publishing Group Limited; Chancellor Press; Chapman & Hall, Publishers; Collins; Don M. Cregier, History Dept, University of Prince Edward Island, Charlottetown, P.E.I., Canada; David & Charles; Department of Mining Engineering,

University of Newcastle; Detroit Public Library; The Franklin Mint; Victor Gollancz; Grafton Books; Grosset & Dunlap Inc.; Peter Hanff, The Bancroft Library, University of California, Berkley, Calif.; Harper & Row; Harrap; Hodder & Stoughton; Houghton Mifflin Company, Boston, Mass.; Sue Jenkins; The Johns Hopkins University Press; Hutchinson; *Illustrated London News*; Institute of Agricultural History and Museum of English Rural Life, University of Reading; Jarrolds; Charles F. Kauffman; Ladybird Books Ltd, England; David Leake; Peter Lunn; Macmillan; Paul Mellon Collection, Upperville, Virginia; Modern Promotions; Col. K. R. Morgan-Jones, B.Vet. Med., MRCVS, Melton Mowbray, Leics.; Museum of London; Fred Nash, University Library, University of Illinois at Urbana–Champaign; National Army Museum, London; Octopus Books Limited, London & Artia, Prague; Puffin; Royal Society for the Prevention of Cruelty to Animals; Thomas Ryder, Salem, New Jersey; David Sharp; Shire Publications; John Speirs; John Thompson; The University of Wisconsin Press; Victoria Museum, Bath; Ward Lock; Marylian Watney; West Chester University, West Chester, Penn.

NOTE ON ILLUSTRATIONS

In order to make the captions easier to read, full publication details of the works referred to most often are omitted. The full references to these works are as follows: W. J. Gordon, *Horse World of London* (London, 1893); Edward Mayhew, *The Illustrated Horse Management* (London, 1864); Moseman's *Illustrated Guide for Purchasers of Horse Furnishing Goods* (New York, 1893); E. L. Quadekker, *Het Paardenboek*, 3 vols. (Zutphen, [1903]); Samuel Sidney, *Book of the Horse* (London, 1893; 1st edn 1874); Earl of Suffolk, *Racing and Steeplechasing* (London, 1886).

NOTE ON ORIGINAL TEXT

The original text of *Black Beauty* is reproduced here from the 1950 edition (reprinted 1966) published by J. M. Dent & Sons Limited, London, complete with the line drawings by Lucy Kemp-Welch, originally published by Dent in their 1915 edition.

List of Colour Plates

ix

Biographical Foreword

Black Beauty was Anna Sewell's only book. She wrote it during the seven years of her final illness (she died three months after it appeared in 1877) and little guessed that it was to become the sixth best seller in the English language. Its sale of forty million copies to date equals that of the entire works of Dickens.

Anna was born in Great Yarmouth, to Isaac and Mary Sewell, both descended from long lines of Quaker shopkeepers. When Anna was still a baby her father took a small drapery shop in the City of London, but he lacked business sense and went bankrupt. The family moved to the slums of Hackney. Anna by now had a brother, Philip (later to become a successful railway engineer).

Mrs Sewell was a woman of resource. She educated her children at home, instilling in them a love of nature and the strict Quaker principle, 'to seek out and alleviate suffering'. There was plenty of human suffering to be found just down the road in Shoreditch, but animal suffering affected Anna equally. There is a frequently told story of her verbal attack on the man with a gun who had brought down a blackbird in the front garden. Gripping the little feathered corpse she cried, 'Thee cruel man, thee shan't have it at all.'

Anna had loved horses since the age of two when she had begged to be carried out to the Bishopsgate cab rank to feed them. Later she was to learn to ride and drive the horses on her Uncle Wright's farm at Dudwick House in Norfolk. There she also became a passionate amateur painter of landscapes.

The longed for day of starting school in her teens proved a disaster. Running home from school in the rain she slipped and permanently damaged both ankles. She was never to walk with ease again. She became a prisoner in her parents' house, an unpaid assistant to her mother in her unrelenting good works. Her only relief was an occasional visit to a European spa in search of a cure for her increasing nervous disabilities.

The formidable Mrs Sewell by now ruled the Sewell household undisputed. Isaac Sewell did little but take orders. He had proved as ineffective in a new career as a bank manager as he had in the old one of haberdasher, moving from branch to branch with increasing velocity. However, travelling about the country had its compensations for his wife and daughter. In each new area Mrs Sewell sought out evils to rectify and Anna, now nearly forty, seemed to find new strength with which to assist her. In one Gloucestershire village she opened a Working Man's Evening Institute where she impressed her audience of labourers by dissecting a bullock's eye. It was when driving her pony cart to the Institute that she proved her ability as a first-class whip with an instinctive understanding of the animal between the shafts. Her mother's friend and biographer, Mrs Bayly, described a drive to the station with Anna.

'[Anna] seemed simply to hold the reins in her hand, trusting to her voice to give all needed directions to her horse. She evidently believed in a horse having a moral nature, if we may judge by her mode of remonstrance. "Now thee shouldn't walk up this hill – don't thee see how it rains?" "Now thee must go a little faster – thee would be sorry for us to be late at the station."'

It was probably her mother who inspired Anna to write. In late middle age Mrs Sewell became the best-selling author of *Homely and Improving Ballads for the Working Classes*. *Our Father's Care*, concerning London's street children, alone sold a million copies. Anna was the severest critic of her mother's work, and no doubt learned from it.

At the age of fifty Anna's health took an alarming plunge. By this time the Sewells had moved to their last home, The White House, near Norwich. Anna's seven years there were passed entirely between sofa and bed. It was at The White House that a 'little book' about a horse occurred to her. The horse, Black Beauty, a beast as handsome as he is wise, was almost certainly based on Anna's brother Philip's fine carriage horse, Black Bess. Now widowed, Philip was a close neighbour.

When Anna started the seven-year task of writing *Black Beauty* she was too ill even to hold a pen. She formed scenes in her head and dictated them to Mrs Sewell. Later she scribbled odd paragraphs in pencil on scraps of paper. When the manuscript was complete Mrs Sewell tidied it up and showed it to her own publisher, Jarrold of Norwich. He offered an outright fee of £30, and that was all the money the Sewell family ever made from the book.

The first edition of *Black Beauty* (now extremely rare) is dated 24 November 1877. It was a modest affair with one black and white illustration. In spite of this it was an immediate success, and this was for a very real reason. It was not a book *about* a horse, but a book *by* a horse. The title page of the first edition reads:

Black Beauty
His grooms and companions
The autobiography of a horse
Translated from the original equine
By Anna Sewell

Anna was able to think herself into the mind of a horse. She could imagine what it would feel like to have a bit forced between the teeth:

'A great piece of cold hard steel as thick as a man's finger . . . pushed into one's mouth, between one's teeth and over one's tongue, with the ends coming out at the corner of your mouth, and held fast there by straps over your head, under your throat, round your nose, and under your chin; so that no way in the world can you get rid of the nasty hard thing' (Chapter III).

Even more graphic was her description of the bearing rein:

'That day we had a steep hill to go up. Then I began to understand what I had heard of. Of course I wanted to put my head forward and take the carriage up with a will, ... but no, I had to pull with my head up now ... Day by day, hole by hole, our bearing reins were shortened' (Chapter XXII).

Anna Sewell also displayed a very practical knowledge of horses. Edward Fordham Flower, the harness expert, wrote of Anna's book, 'It is written by a veterinary surgeon, by a coachman, by a groom; there is not a mistake in the whole of it.' A modern child winning a dream pony could learn how to care for his lucky windfall tolerably well with *Black Beauty* alone as a guide.

But there is also drama in *Black Beauty*: the midnight gallops to the doctor, the fire at the inn, the miraculous escape at the flooded bridge. Even grown men admit to weeping at the death of Ginger, the spirited part-Thoroughbred flogged to death between the shafts of a London cab. Shortly before she died, Black Beauty found himself standing next to Ginger in a cab rank.

'It was Ginger! but how changed! The beautifully arched and glossy neck was now straight, ... the clean straight legs and delicate fetlocks were swelled; ... the face, that was once so full of spirit and life, was now full of suffering ... A short time after this, a cart with a dead horse in it passed our cab-stand. The head hung out of the cart tail, the lifeless tongue was slowly dropping with blood ... I believe it was Ginger' (Chapter XL).

In the United States *Black Beauty*, published on 1 April 1890, set a world record for sales. A million volumes were disposed of in the first two years, and the book was still selling at the rate of a quarter of a million a year twenty years later. George T. Angell was responsible for the publication. He was the founder of the Massachusetts Society for the Prevention of Cruelty to Animals (now, alas, moribund), and the son of a Baptist minister. By early middle age he had earned enough money as a lawyer to devote himself to philanthropy and animal welfare. Angell had been searching for some time for an equine version of *Uncle Tom's Cabin*. In *Black Beauty* he considered he had found a book that would do for horses what Harriet Beecher Stowe's book had done for slaves. A leading Boston newspaper accused him of pirating the book, selling it at a fraction of its market price and giving no royalties to Miss Sewell. This was true. Indeed, Angell went further. He gave away thousands of copies to coachmen, grooms and stable lads, or to any man who had charge of horses. And in this he would have had Anna's approval, had she not been twelve years dead. *Black Beauty* was intended as a horseman's manual, not a children's book.

To Anna only one aspect of her book would have mattered and that was its effect on the treatment of horses, and in particular on the abolition of the bearing rein. In this she succeeded. By the beginning of the present century public feeling had begun to turn so strongly against the device that only undertakers persisted in using it on funeral horses. In 1914 the RSPCA persuaded even them to do without it.

Long before that, in 1878, at least one team of funeral horses were allowed free head carriage. This was the team that pulled Anna Sewell's remains to the little Quaker burial ground at Lammas (sadly destroyed in the late 1980s). Glancing down from the window of The White House, Mrs Sewell observed that the heads of the horses were strapped up on arrival. 'Oh this will never do!' she exclaimed, and hurried downstairs. Shortly afterwards the guests observed a top-hatted gentleman moving down the line, removing the bearing reins of each animal in turn.

Susan Chitty

Introduction

It was the heyday of horse transport when *Black Beauty* was first published in 1877. True, the Golden Age of coaching was long past except in a few remote, rural areas, usurped by the railways which boosted industry, carried passengers, freight and mail. But the railways did not kill off horse transport, as is so often thought. They created a greater need than ever before for short-distance horse transport to and from the railway station for goods and passengers, as well as for a 'back-up' system for many services.

Because of the growth in the economy, the rise of the middle classes in Victorian England and the success of commercial concerns often built on a self-help basis, more people than ever before were able to afford the luxury of private transport. This ranged from governess carts to gigs and coachman-driven landaus and broughams. Even for those without private transport there were trams or the more respectable horse omnibuses, a popular form of conveyance for the new suburban commuters.

Alongside these was the increased need for services to this rising suburban population, such as road maintenance, water supplies (not all areas had piped water), building supplies for construction sites, and privy emptying, as well as the more familiar deliveries of household consumables such as milk, meat, fish and greengroceries.

Very many of these services were supplied by private enterprises, but others were large concerns such as the public transport companies (both road and rail), canal freight companies, local authorities, and the Co-operative Wholesale Society, which had been set up in Lancashire in 1844 to provide the working classes with cheap, unadulterated foodstuffs. These businesses combined to create an equine population of hundreds of thousands, if not millions, in the urban areas of Britain.

In the countryside the horse continued to be the main source of motive power on farms and it was in the country that most horses destined for town work were bred. Most of these were heavy horses, vanners and cold-blooded crossbreds. Some, however, were light horses which began life in the pleasant English countryside and, like Black Beauty, were destined to become pleasure animals of the wealthy, leisured classes who wanted hunters, hacks and elegant carriage horses, many of which ended their days on the downhill path.

Black Beauty's story covers all these aspects of equine life in the late nineteenth century. Little sentiment was attached to the horse, especially the working horse (a strange anomaly in an age now noted for its sentimentality), and he usually ended his days prematurely at the knacker's, worn out by overwork.

But the author was no soft sentimentalist looking at horses from afar. Despite a physical handicap, Anna Sewell regularly drove horses around her Norfolk home, and perhaps it was her ardent Christian upbringing which was the inspiration for her humanitarian approach to horses. It was in November 1871 that she first mentions in her diary that she was 'writing the life of a horse'.

The equine characters in the novel reflect almost the entire spectrum of the horse world: the children's pony, Merrylegs; the hunter, Sir Oliver; the fiery chestnut mare (a popular cliché) Ginger; the heavy coal wagon draught horse; the army charger, Captain, who recalls his experiences in the Crimean War. The human characters too are stereotypes with names to match: the compassionate, sensible, caring Farmer Thoroughgood; the upstanding, kind groom, John Manly; the poor but honest and considerate cabman, Jerry Barker; Filcher, a thief, and Alfred Smirk, a dishonest groom.

Anna Sewell brought sensitivity and sentiment to the horse world with her novel *Black Beauty*, written as a protest against the callous treatment of working horses, in particular the bearing rein and the docked tail – the dictates of fashion. However, she makes no reference to the operation of castration, an operation performed on the vast majority of male horses and which, at that time, did not require the use of anaesthetics. Whether the omission of this important event in Black

Beauty's life is due to Victorian delicacy in such matters or whether Anna Sewell was simply unaware that most male horses underwent this operation will probably never be known.

All through the book Anna Sewell was pleading for the humanitarian treatment of horses, usually through anecdotes or cautionary tales – all told, of course, from the horse's point of view – and almost every chapter ends with a moral. Such advice was needed, for although the horse world employed vast numbers of grooms, ostlers, nagsmen, drivers, coachmen and jobmasters, by no means all were horse lovers. Indeed many were semi-literate, unskilled, uncouth, 'of the low order' and frequently afraid of the horses in their charge, which, as a consequence, they treated badly. There was also much cruelty through ignorance rather than deliberate action.

Anna Sewell never lived to see the results of her labours for she died in 1878, the year after *Black Beauty* was published. But her campaigning had not been in vain, for along with the steps taken by the Royal Society for the Prevention of Cruelty to Animals (which, incidentally, never really appeared to appreciate the potential of Anna Sewell's missionary zeal) to alleviate cruelty and improve the lot of the working horse, it was Anna Sewell's story which appeared to have as much, if not more, influence on the men and boys who worked with horses. (There were no girl grooms in Anna Sewell's day.) Some of them considered it to be 'the best book in the world'.

Anna Sewell documented the day to day life of the working horse in London, sparing the reader nothing of the horrors of being a night cab horse, the fear of a cavalry charge in war, and street accidents and their inevitable results as befell old Captain.

Black Beauty was *not* written as a children's book, and is conspicuously absent from F. J. Harvey Darton's classic *Children's Books in England* (1932; 3rd edn 1982). It was not until the Jarrolds third edition (*c.* 1878) that it could be said to have acquired the term 'juvenile literature' (perhaps a demotion in the life of a book?), but it is a far cry from the modern pony story. Strangely, although written essentially as a moralising campaign against the mistreatment of horses, *Black Beauty* seems to have a timeless appeal even to the pony-mad teenage girl of the 1980s, as is apparent from the endless editions, revamped versions, sequels, films and television adaptations. Until recently in many of these the essentials of the story had not been lost, but sometimes only Black Beauty himself has survived.

It is perhaps a fitting tribute that on the day of Anna Sewell's funeral when the hearse pulled up, drawn, of course, by horses, Anna's mother ran out to the driver of the hearse demanding that he remove the bearing reins from all the horses in the cortège. Anna Sewell would have approved.

About the Book

Predecessors

Animal stories written in the first person singular existed long before Anna Sewell set pen to paper, the earliest to survive being Dorothy Kilner's *The Life and Perambulations of a Mouse* (1783). As was true of many such stories it was a moral tale rather than an entertaining one. In other contexts, words from animals have spoken 'wisdom' to people, for example *A Letter from A Crow to Mr. Cobden. Translated from the Original by a Northamptonshire Squire* (London, 1844), recently described by a bookseller as a 'lighthearted piece' on the Corn Laws. Another anonymous pamphlet, *The Autobiography of a Canary Bird* (© Anson D. Randolph, New York, 1866), tells the story of a bird captured when young by a sailor in Madeira, and his various owners, kind and cruel. Whereas the crow's letter was a political tract, the canary's account was an anti-slavery tract.

Anna Sewell's contribution was a compelling animal 'autobiography' with the theme of cruelty to horses, described by one writer on children's literature as 'the first real animal novel', and as 'the last of the moral tales' (Blount, *Animal Land*, New York, 1975, pp. 18, 249). According to Humphrey Carpenter, writing about the body of literature available to children:

'It was a long time since animals played any great part in English writing for children; in the late eighteenth and early nineteenth century there was a fashion for a type of moral tale in which an animal – generally a dog, a horse, or a household pet – narrated its "memoirs", really a set of moralistic observations on human (especially child) behavior. Anna Sewell's *Black Beauty* ... was really a throwback to that kind of writing' (Carpenter, *Secret Gardens*, Boston, 1985, p. 111).

The humane movement

The rise of interest in animal welfare paralleled that of interest in destitution and child welfare, reflections of the more negative aspects of the industrial revolution originating in the eighteenth century. John Lawrence's *Philosophical and Practical Treatise on Horses, and on the Moral Duties of Man towards the Brute Creation* appeared in London in 1796. He included a section 'On the Rights of Beasts' (Ch. 3, pp. 117–63), stressing the need for legislation protecting animals. In Boston, an anonymous pamphlet, *A Plea for the Horse*, was published in 1847, asking that horses be treated more kindly and considerately.

Space does not permit a history of the humane movement in England, but suffice to say that it was becoming a force to reckon with by the early 1870s, when Anna Sewell began to write. According to Susan Chitty's excellent biography, Sewell began to write the story in 1871, drawing on the wealth of knowledge about horses gained in her lifetime.

The many publications and activities of the humane movement suggest a success that perhaps was more real because of changing technology at the end of the nineteenth century than because of pressures of the societies. Certainly much publicity was given to cases of cruelty, particularly to working horses, in the British press. Such headlines as 'Disgusting cruelty to horses on the Embankment' (*The Times*, 1865), were common from the 1850s through to the 1870s. Articles on the bearing rein, on watering horses and on their treatment in the Crimean War appeared, and we may suppose were read by Sewell, in *The Times*. These reports reinforced her own conversations with cabmen and stablemen, as well as her personal experience.

The campaign against the use of the bearing rein began at least in the 1830s. William Youatt's popular and many times reprinted and re-edited *The Horse; with a Treatise on Draught* first appeared in London

xx

Royal Society for the Prevention of Cruelty to Animals sign in the High Street, Welwyn, Hertfordshire. The sign was not a declaration of law, but advisory and humanitarian. It encouraged drivers to help their horses ascending the steep hill out of Welwyn.

in 1831. In it Youatt wrote critically against improper bitting and 'the unnecessary and cruel tightness of the bearing rein'. Youatt stated that although a bearing rein was absolutely required for safety reasons, there was no excuse for overtightening. The debate heated up in the mid 1870s. Several articles appeared in *The Times* in January 1874, and with the publication of the first edition of Edward Fordham Flower's *Bits and Bearing Reins* in 1875/6 more people began to protest publicly against cruel harnessing.

The bearing rein, which in fact could really be called an 'anti-bearing' rein, is a short rein or strap supplementing the reins which go from the bit to the driver's hands. This strap connects the bit to a hook on the top of the harness on the horse's back via a ring suspended on each side of the horse's cheek, preventing the horse from lowering its

The action of the bearing rein vividly portrayed on the cover of Flower's influential tract. (Edward F. Flower, *Bits and Bearing Reins*, London: Ridgway, 1875)

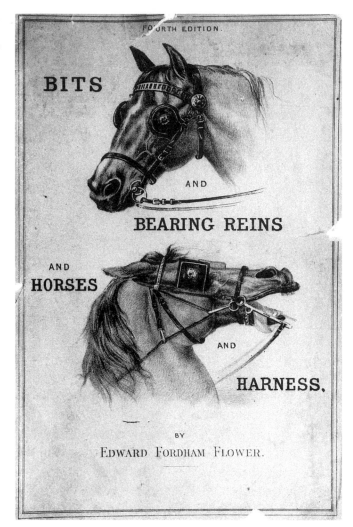

head. In the United States, reins of this type are called check reins. It was developed, apparently, to ease the fatigue coachmen suffered from the weight of horses which pulled on the reins, or hung on them (or bore on them).

The Rev. J. G. Wood (*Horse and Man: their Mutual Dependence and Duties*, London, 1885) may have been the first to suggest that bearing reins were used in antiquity, according this 'honour' to the ancient Egyptians. The earliest pictures showing real evidence of bearing reins date from the late eighteenth century. An example is George Stubbs' 'The Prince of Wales's Phaeton and Horses' dated 1793 (property of Her Majesty the Queen). An earlier Stubbs painting dated 1780–5 shows what we would call side reins, which probably served the same purpose, to fix the horses' heads and reduce driver fatigue.

In 1875, Parliament was debating two bills aimed at the control of animal experimentation. Popular middle-class parlour magazines, such as *Good Words*, ran articles against the bearing rein. It was the coming of age of a political force that is still active and working for the benefit of animal rights. And in France, a humane tract, A. Edouard Roche's *Les Martyrs du Travail*, appeared in 1876 (and that first edition is apparently even rarer than the first edition of *Black Beauty*). Anna Sewell's work appeared at a very auspicious time in a climate of growing middle-class outrage at what was often perceived as lower-class cruelty. In fact, by the mid-century, working-class England had, according to some social historians, already begun to accept animals as pets and 'fellow sufferers'.

Flower's work bore fruit, supported not only by the publication of *Black Beauty*, but by the continued hammering away at the theme by writers of the 1880s. The Rev. J. G. Wood, whose popular natural history books were read by vast numbers of people both in Britain and in the United States, mentioned Flower several times in essays on the horse. By 1881, according to the Birmingham Society for the Prevention of Cruelty to Animals, discussion of the bearing rein was not necessary in connection with cab horses because 'we have noticed that its use is not customary amongst cab drivers' (their pamphlet, *Hints to Cabmen*, p. 14).

A review of articles in *The Times* on accidents reveals a public concern and interest (somewhat morbid) in the dangers of horse-drawn vehicles in a crowded urban environment. Continual reports appeared in the British press of runaways, collisions, and falls of both persons under horses and of horses, which resulted in fatalities or horrible injuries.

It is often assumed that knowledge of the training, treatment and

The preface of *Hints to Cabmen* shows the effect of some of the anti-cruelty campaigning. (Birmingham: Birmingham Society for the Prevention of Cruelty to Animals, 1881)

HINTS TO CABMEN.

PREFACE.

A SHORT time ago the Birmingham Society for the Prevention of Cruelty to Animals offered prizes for the best essays written upon the subject of "A Cabman's Daily Duty towards his Horse," the competition being open to all cabmen within the Borough.

The substance has been gleaned from these essays, and is now, with additional information, offered for the consideration of local cabmen.

The Society hopes that the perusal of this publication may be found interesting to the cab drivers of our town, and may stimulate amongst them a deeper care and thoughtfulness for the comfort of the animals under their charge.

Birmingham, April, 1881.

handling of horses was common in the nineteenth century because they were in daily use. But in a stratified, classed urban society in mid-century, the case must have been rather different. People hired other people to attend to such chores as housekeeping, cooking, groundskeeping and horsekeeping. The latter persons may or may not have been adequately trained (as is clear in *Black Beauty*) or even had any care for their equine charges.

With ignorance on the part of owners, and ignorance on the part of stable personnel, small wonder that many horses were ill treated, often from a mixture of fear and stupidity. Reading of the many accidents that befell horse-drawn vehicles in the city, and given the concern with keeping up appearances, many people would in fact have taken up the bearing rein and gag bit not just because it was fashionable, but as a means of tying down their often well-bred and corn-fed animals. Perhaps it should not surprise us that these 'power brakes' were adopted, as they were, in crowded cities and urbanised neighbour-hoods. Perhaps they were visible symbols of man's power over their servants, horses, and evidence of man's fear of the damage caused by runaways in crowded city streets.

The text and its vicissitudes

At least 106 publishers have issued over 250 editions (some reprinted many times), translations and adaptations of *Black Beauty*. They range from the modest but many times reprinted Jarrolds editions to elegantly illustrated and produced editions such as the one used for this annotated edition, published by J. M. Dent and illustrated by Lucy Kemp-Welch, which first appeared in 1915. Many early Jarrolds editions were numbered, and 177 thousand copies had appeared by 1897 in England alone. By this time, the president of the American Humane Education Society, George T. Angell, had issued, he proclaimed, 'between one and two million' in Boston for American use.

As originally published in Britain by Jarrold and Sons in 1877, the text has been reprinted almost without change ever since. Some typographical errors have been noticed and caught; certain usages were altered in some editions, such as 'His neck is broke' to 'His neck is broken' (Chapter II), and 'when I laid down,' to 'when I lay down' (Chapter VII). Many British editions have retained all the original spellings and usages up to this day, although some changes in wording may have been on the part of the publisher or possibly Mrs Sewell (who died in 1884). Changes in language may have been with the intention of 'improving' the story, although the changes observed are so insignificant as to be unnecessary. The episodic style, each chapter almost with its separate lesson, chained together by the narrative thread of the life of the cab horse, may have been determined by the scraps of time Anna Sewell was able to use to write it.

Early British editions often carried a note on the flyleaf or verso of the title page: 'Recommended by the "Royal Society for the Prevention of Cruelty to Animals".' At the end of the text an extra page was appended, which was a suggestion by 'the Translator [i.e., Anna Sewell]' to readers to buy a pamphlet, *The Horse Book*, published by the Royal Society for the Prevention of Cruelty to Animals, as revised by George Fleming. This recommendation was dropped from most Jarrold editions by the turn of the century.

In editions of *The Horse Book* published after the appearance of *Black Beauty*, recommendations to read *Black Beauty* were included,

The cover of the *The Horse Book*, recommended reading in the early editions of *Black Beauty*. (London: RSPCA, *c.* 1877)

xxvi

and Chapter XLVIII, 'Farmer Thoroughgood and his Grandson Willie', was quoted. The author referred to Black Beauty as 'she' and described the novel as 'a very amusing and instructive autobiography of a horse'. The little pamphlet contained advice to horsemen on care and much information on the evils of the bearing rein and improper harnessing for heavy loads.

Curiously, a paragraph was added to *Black Beauty* sometime after the appearance of the first edition. At least by the fifth (1879) edition, a paragraph was inserted at the end of Chapter XXXIII which reads well and is in the spirit of the original version. At the end of that chapter, Black Beauty remarks that Jerry Barker kept his horses clean and with as much change of food as he could afford. Someone (Anna Sewell herself?) added: 'and not only that, but he always gave us plenty of clean fresh water, which he allowed to stand by us both night and day, except of course when we came in warm' and on until the original closing remarks of the chapter on the blessings of Sunday rest. Was this done because the reviewers had remarked on it, or was it done independently of criticism to make the novel even more a 'teaching tract' than it already was?

Copies of *Black Beauty* may have reached the United States before it was first issued in an American edition, but there is no evidence of such before 1890. However, the title of H. D. Minot's *The Diary of a Bird Freely Translated into Human Language* (Boston, 1880) is suggestive that the literature of the downtrodden 'captive' farmyard or household animal had found a receptive audience in the United States.

The first American edition appeared in April 1890. It was published by George T. Angell, founder of the American Humane Education Society, with various textual changes and additions. Angell had been greatly influenced by Harriet Beecher Stowe's work *Uncle Tom's Cabin* (first published in 1852 and a world bestseller). It was Angell who gave the first American edition a new subtitle: 'The Uncle Tom's Cabin of the Horse', associating it for decades in American minds with the unforgettable anti-slavery novel. Angell recognised in *Black Beauty* the same Christian message of kind and empathetic treatment of all living beings, of all God's creatures.

xxvii

The title page spread of George T. Angell's first American edition of *Black Beauty*. (Boston: American Humane Education Society, 1890)

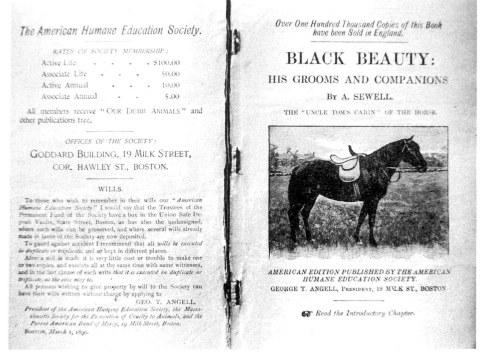

The additional text inserted by Angell related to the Society, and to kindness to animals, but included notes on methods of humane killing of horses and dogs. At the end of later editions a short essay by Captain John Codman was reprinted from a New York newspaper, in which he stated that he, like Agassiz, Cuvier and Martin Luther, believed that animals had souls. He described a dream in which deceased horses were 'dragging their carriages over the clouds [in heaven] – but the carriages were empty. Yes, there must be a place for good horses and a place for bad men.' Also appended were two essays by Angell, one on overloading horses and the other containing extracts from three of his speeches on the value and importance of humane education. The appended texts end with the constitution of the American Humane Education Society and an advertisement for its journal, *Our Dumb Animals*.

Angell's publication of the novel in America occasioned enthusiastic reviews in the American press. *Critic* (New York, 21 June 1890) is representative: 'Miss Sewell may not have a mind as powerful as that of the author of "Gulliver's Travels," but "Black Beauty: His Grooms and Companions" will do vastly more than that incomparable satire to convince mankind of the stupidity of treating the horse as an infinitely inferior animal ... It's not namby-pamby ...'

Spelling changes were designed (by Angell?) for easier reading by an American audience, apparently, such as changing whilst to while; shewed to showed, and ostler to hostler. Punctuation changes included removal of many hyphens (side-pieces to side pieces; horse-back to horseback; half-a-pint to half a pint), changes of colons to semi-colons, semi-colons to commas, and removal of commas altogether. The two exclamation points in chapter headings (A Thief! Chapter XXX and A Humbug! Chapter XXXI) were deleted, as they were in later English editions. Words which were capitalised in the original were made lower case: Nature, Market Place, Hospital, and unfortunately some which should have remained capitalised as well: 'Bridge and the Monument'. Apparently the American editor thought that 'green meat' (Chapter XXXI) was wrong and mistakenly changed it to 'green meal'. The *Oxford Universal Dictionary on Historial Principles* (3rd rev. edn. Oxford, Clarendon Press, 1955, p. 1225) defines green meat as 'grass or green vegetables used for food or fodder'. And Edward Mayhew's *Illustrated Horse Management* (first published in 1864 and reprinted steadily until 1906) recommended it for constipation along with a bran mash.

The first American edition also featured italicised or boldfaced passages throughout, emphasising the humane message strongly to readers, such as 'This steam-engine style of driving wears us out faster than any other kind. **I would far rather go twenty miles with a good, considerate driver than I would go ten with some of these; it would take less out of me**' (Chapter XXIX, 'Cockneys'). These emphases were retained in many American editions as though those who re-printed it so many times in the United States did not realise that they were not present in the original English edition.

With all these changes, it should be noted, as emphasised by Susan

Chitty and Anthony Dent in their studies of Anna Sewell, that Mr Angell had the highest regard for the authoress. For example, he was pleased to report in the journal he founded, *Our Dumb Animals*, the donation of an 'Anna Sewell Memorial Foundation' for horses. It was set up in Ansonia, Connecticut by the founder of the local public library in 1891, and remains to this day on the library property.

Translations

Many of the earliest translations were those sponsored by George T. Angell for publication by the American Humane Education Society in Boston. Angell wanted them for distribution to labouring immigrants who might not have learned English well enough to understand but who could read their native languages. These translations appeared from 1891, and few copies of them have survived. The first ones were apparently into Italian and Spanish. *Our Dumb Animals*, the monthly publication of the Society, announced in October 1891 that translations into Spanish, German, French, Italian, 'Volapük' and Swedish had been commissioned, and added that a Japanese translation was now being arranged (*Our Dumb Animals*, Oct. 1891).

According to Anthony Dent, 'By 1904, roughly in the first quarter century of the book's life, it had been translated into Italian (twice), Swedish, Arabic, Greek, Hindustani, a South Indian language called Telegu, French and Spanish, while Turkish and Armenian were on the stocks' (Dent, 'Miss Sewell', p. 546). Translations into major European languages are listed in the bibliography at the end of this book.

Not only were two early Italian translations of *Black Beauty* published, but an Italian translation of Flower's *Bits and Bearing Reins* was published in Florence in 1879, with the lithographed illustrations from an English edition. Was this to capitalise on the interest aroused in Italy by reading the Italian *Black Beauty*? According to the title page of the translation of Flower it was published by the Società Protettrice degli Animali di Firenze.

Cover of one of the Italian translations of *Black Beauty*. (Boston: American Humane Education Society, *c.* 1892)

Illustrations

No illustrator is completely identified with *Black Beauty*. Compared with *Alice in Wonderland*, or *Winnie the Pooh*, several very fine versions have appeared over the last century, but none come immediately to mind when the book is mentioned in the way that the images of Tenniel or Shepard do for *Alice* or *Pooh*.

The earliest editions of *Black Beauty* appeared with a wood-engraved frontispiece only, signed C. Hewitt. It showed a scene from Chapter XXV, 'Reuben Smith', in which Black Beauty stands by the body of Smith on the moonlit road. By 1885, Jarrolds had changed the frontispiece to a new Hewitt picture, showing, from Chapter XVIII, 'Going for the Doctor'. The Reuben Smith picture was placed as a plate in Chapter II. Decorative devices headed each chapter, and the first letter of each chapter was emphasised by a decorative initial. In the years following, a few more illustrations were added, by other artists, with no unifying style to them.

But most importantly, the 1880s editions included two illustrations based on lithographed plates published in Edward Fordham Flower's *Bits and Bearing Reins and Horses in Harness*, which had first been published in the early 1870s. They appear in Chapter VIII, 'Ginger's Story Continued', in which the bearing rein issue is first raised, and show the horse comfortably harnessed without the rein and in painful discomfort with the rein and the often accompanying gag bit. The bearing rein pictures appeared in some Jarrold editions until the end of the century, and in the American Humane Education Society editions and their pirated versions until about 1910.

In 1894, two illustrated editions appeared, one in Britain and one in the United States. The British edition was illustrated by John Beer, a well-known sporting artist who specialised in racing scenes. He is known to have worked in gouache (Sally Mitchell, *The Dictionary of British Equestrian Artists*, 1985), and many of the illustrations in this edition of *Black Beauty* seem to have been reproduced from a mix of gouache originals. Owing to the imperfect technology of halftone printing, many of these illustrations are muddy in appearance. But their design and sense of period often transcend the production. Beer's images were plagiarised on both sides of the Atlantic, and remained influential for decades.

The American 'first illustrated' edition with artistic unity as in the Beer edition was published in New York by J. Hovendon, and in-

PLATE 1
An 1880s edition of *Black Beauty* as
published by Jarrold & Sons ('35th Edition,
133rd Thousand'), in a typical trade binding.
Floral patterns were used many times in
this period for issues of the book.

PLATE 2
Cover of a nineteenth-century American
edition from the Jarrold's 1894 edition
illustrated by John Beer, probably copying
the design, if not actually using the British
cover and sheets, with the American
publisher (E. P. Dutton) on the title page.

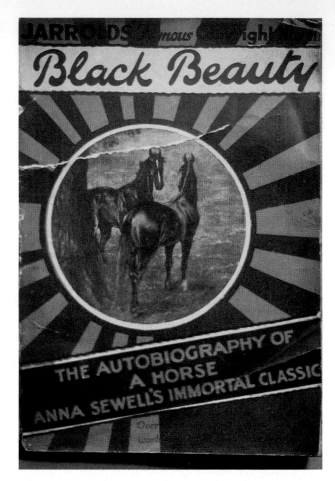

PLATE 3
The ugliest Black Beauty? Chromolithographed paper over boards cover for 'Young Folks Edition' published about 1910 by M. A. Donohue & Co., Chicago.

PLATE 4 (*top, right*)
Black Beauty and Ginger in the pasture at Birtwick Park. Early-twentieth-century 'Copyright Edition' of Jarrolds, in paper wrappers.

PLATE 5 (*right*)
Chromolithographed dust jacket for an undated but early-twentieth-century American edition published by Charles E. Graham & Co., Newark, New Jersey and New York.

Illustration by H. Toaspern of Black Beauty in his stall, from the first illustrated American edition. (*Black Beauty*, New York: J. Hovendon & Co., 1894, p. 30)

cluded twenty-two line illustrations by H. Toaspern, Jr. The Hovendon sheets were later reissued by H. M. Caldwell with the Toaspern line drawings and crude chromolithograph illustrations. One Caldwell edition included a line version of one of the Beer illustrations as a frontispiece. The Toaspern drawings are not as good as those of Beer, although a few are more than merely competent.

An undated first edition published by Donohue in Chicago is illustrated by a combination of unacknowledged reproductions from other sources. The binding and typography suggest the 1890s. The chromolithographs include one from Beer's scene of Black Beauty's first encounter with a train in a field. Several sporting pictures included 1880s-style steeplechasing and racing scenes of no relevence to the text. Throughout the second half of the volume, a series of Gustave Doré's illustrations from his *London: A Pilgrimage*, first published in 1872, are reproduced. Some are quite appropriate, for instance the London

xxxiii

Bridge scene with the crowded city traffic which so troubled Black Beauty when he first became a cab horse.

In 1912, Jarrolds brought out the next important illustrated version of *Black Beauty*, with eighteen colour plates reproducing the pastels or watercolours of Cecil Aldin. These are very stylish, beautifully designed and coloured, as was so much by this renowned sporting artist and illustrator. It is one of the finest sets of pictures for this text that has ever been done.

However, many people would probably name another significant edition as the finest version from the point of view of illustration and design. In 1915, Lucy Kemp-Welch's knowledgeable, beautiful and muscular drawings and paintings were published by J. M. Dent in a well-designed and proportioned volume. Kemp-Welch designed the headpieces and tailpieces for each chapter especially for the book. The plates glow with colour and realistic scenes, and although many show the usual incidents attempted by many of her predecessors, they take on a fresh vitality in her hands. If any one edition deserved to be identified with the book, it is probably this one. Happily, this great British animal artist's *Black Beauty* has been recently reprinted (New York: Crown Publishers, 1986), although not with all the original twenty-four colour plates. It is also the basis of this edition.

One of the most overlooked illustrated editions of quality was published in 1922 by Jarrolds, a small volume illustrated by Edmund Blampied. Many of Blampied's fine etchings and drypoints were of rural subjects, perhaps because of his rural upbringing. These small black and white line illustrations, reproduced apparently from pen and ink drawings, are very much in the design mainstream of the 1920s, yet have a knowledgeable and dramatic imagery which well matches the text. *Bookman* (April 1922) noted that this edition appeared shortly after the Vitagraph movie version of the story, stating that 'Miss Sewell's work will have more far-reaching results than ever', and praised the Blampied illustrations.

In 1945, Grosset and Dunlap of New York published an edition illustrated by international graphic artist Fritz Eichenberg. Illustrator of over sixty books, winner of many awards for his fine graphic work,

Eichenberg produced an elegant, stylised version, immediately characteristic of his work but also appropriate to the 1870s period. It included artist-designed coloured endpapers and ten colour plates as well as fine black and white line illustrations. It is still in print. Lionel Edwards illustrated two editions of *Black Beauty*. Edwards, an honoured, popular and urbane artist and hunting man, fully expressed the 'Englishness' of the hunt and the scenery of hunt country in his work. In his editions of *Black Beauty*, he showed his sensitivity to working horses as well. The first edition, published in 1946 by Peter Lunn, has a pleasant coloured frontispiece and strongly drawn pictures. The 1954 edition is even better, with twenty-four colour plates well reproduced by Ward Lock, full of period flavour.

Black Beauty as told by Uncle Mal (Malcolm Claire) (Prang Company Publishers, New York) also appeared in 1946. It was illustrated by Bernice Magnie in 1940s style, in bold black, brown and green art deco strokes which rather uneasily accompanied the much abridged and retold version. Malcolm Claire broadcast many children's stories for the National Broadcasting Corporation, which were published in the war years.

A very handsome and successful collaborative edition by Adam and Charles Black (London, 1959) brought together three British sporting artists. Racehorse artist Percy Spence provided eight colour plates, Kathleen F. Barker the black and white line drawings; and the colour dustjacket by Peter Biegel shows Black Beauty in a field and a foxhunting pack crossing another field on the other side of the rail fencing.

By the 1970s, three trends in illustration of the classic horse story had become apparent: more nostalgic and realistic interpretation, more stylising, and more colour. Few children's books appear now which are not completely illustrated in colour.

Although Victor Ambrus' pen and ink sketches are in black and white, they are very expressive and artistic in the 1973 Brockhampton Press edition. Ambrus has illustrated over sixty-five books, many of them for children, and won the Kate Greenaway Medal twice for his fine work.

A pop-up version produced in Prague by Artia appeared in 1974/5, with an English text. The artwork by J. Pavlin and G. Seda has a timeless colourful quality which would appeal to very young children. The text is reduced to perhaps the shortest version known. However, it was apparently quite popular and has been reprinted at least once.

For many pictures, the illustrators of the last hundred years have had to decide for themselves on major details. The book does not tell us, for instance, which leg on Black Beauty's off side has the white anklet. Some illustrators have chosen to ignore such details completely, and give quite false impressions. For example, one paperback abridged version (Playmore Incorporated, 1977) portrays Black Beauty on the cover as a Tennessee Walking Horse!

In about 1904, M. A. Donohue used a portrait from about 1900 by the famed American show horse artist, George Ford Morris, of a French coach stallion (reproduced later in his *Portraitures of Horses*, Fordacre Studios, 1952). The plate appeared as a black and white frontispiece and dustjacket illustration for an otherwise unillustrated edition, and also appeared in colour on the cover of Donohue's 'Young Folks' Edition' of *Black Beauty*. The horse is a splendid animal but with a docked tail and three white feet. Much later, Morris illustrated a 1950 edition of *Black Beauty*, with one double-page colour plate serving as the dust jacket design and many fine black and white illustrations, surprisingly unstylised and evidently from charcoal drawings.

A rather well-illustrated version appeared in 1979, abridged by Audry Daly and produced in England by Ladybird Books. John Bird's large-scale colour illustrations, some clearly researched from nineteenth-century photographic sources, focus on people rather than horses, and have something of a cinematic style to them. Another abridged version, this one by Robin McKinley (Random House, New York), is almost completely dominated by the striking coloured drawings by Susan Jeffers, winner of a Caldecott Honor Prize and illustrator of several children's books. They are quite realistic, although the white sock on Black Beauty's hind leg changes legs; this does not deter one from admiring the graphic qualities of the edition.

Surprisingly, perhaps, Arthur Rackham did not illustrate an edition of *Black Beauty*, but in 1982 Simon and Schuster of New York published an edition illustrated by an artist working in the Rackham idiom, John Spiers. His black and white drawings and finely coloured plates are dense with detail, and always relevant to the text. As with many illustrators, he leans on Doré for the city scene showing the traffic encountered by Black Beauty when he became a cab horse. This is an edition with great character.

From humane tract to juvenile

If we take Anna Sewell's words at face value, she wrote *Black Beauty* to describe the life of a cab horse and to exemplify the results of thoughtful treatment of working animals and in fact working people as well. Cruelty born of desperation and of ignorance are painted in broad strokes. And although apparently written as a moral novel for adults, particularly working people, it was soon promoted as a book suitable for children as well. In the Jarrolds editions of the late 1880s, advertising for the 'School Edition' appeared at the end of the text, along with the recommendation to read *The Horse Book*, published by the RSPCA. Advertising quoted *School Board*: 'Wherever children are, whether boys or girls, there this autobiography should be.'

The decades from 1890 to 1910 saw not only the appearance in the United States of *Black Beauty* as a humane tract but its publication, both full length and in abridged form, for children. In 1897, Henry Altemus published an edition in his 'Altemus' Young People's Library' with fifty illustrations, many based on the Jarrolds John Beer edition. The series also included *Swiss Family Robinson*, *Bunyan's Pilgrim's Progress*, *Water-Babies*, *Uncle Tom's Cabin*, *Tales from Shakespeare* and other classics deemed suitable for young readers. Although many in the series were abridged, *Black Beauty* was not.

As early as the 1870s, Routledge was offering 'Three-and-sixpenny one-syllable juveniles', small cloth-bound volumes with colour plates, including *Robinson Crusoe* and *Swiss Family Robinson*. One of the earliest abridgements designed for children was published in Burt's

Series of One Syllable Books. Mrs J. C. Gorham's *Black Beauty: Retold in Words of One Syllable* first appeared in 1903 and remained in print until at least the late 1920s. Names such as Ginger were printed as 'Gin-ger'. The story was shortened from forty-nine to thirty-four chapters, and diluted as follows:

> One day, during this summer, the groom cleaned and dressed me with such extraordinary care that I thought some new change must be at hand; he trimmed my fetlocks and legs, passed the tarbrush over my hoofs, and even parted my forelock. I think the harness had an extra polish. Willie seemed anxious, half-merry, as he got into the chaise with his grandfather. (original Chapter XLIX)

> One day in June, the groom cleaned and dressed me with such fine care, that I thought some new change must be at hand. Willie seemed half glad, half sad, as he took his seat in the chaise with his grand-pa. (Gorham version)

A 1908 version, published by Reilly and Britton in Chicago, was reduced to thirteen small, double spaced, large-print pages and in the same volume with 'The Little Lame Prince'. It was one of twenty-four small volumes in a series. Its significance other than its brevity is that it is an early book illustrated by John Rea Neill, a prolific book and magazine artist who later illustrated many of the Oz books of L. Frank Baum.

The abridgements of all decades tend to shorten or eliminate the 'conversational' chapters, those in which Black Beauty and his companions discuss their lives and their owners. Some reduce the accounts of pain and cruelty, and concentrate on the 'adventure' aspects of the story: going for the doctor, the stable fire, Black Beauty falling with Reuben Smith. Many children read only shortened, diluted versions of this strong tale.

In 1937 a new 'use' of *Black Beauty* appeared. The first-known issue of the story as an English language study book in non-English-speaking countries was published in Riga. It was 'provided with a vocabulary by J. Curiks' for Latvian students. In 1979, *Hungma Iyagi* appeared in Seoul, with annotations in English, apparently for use in teaching English to schoolchildren. A similar translation was published in Japanese, *Kuroma Monogatori* (Tokyo, 1982).

Appraisals of *Black Beauty*

Nineteenth-century adult readers, especially middle-class parents and church teachers, found in *Black Beauty* a tool for promoting a caring attitude to all living beings. Even though animals might not have souls, according to the church, they should receive considerate care. James Turner, an American historian, quotes from the British periodical, *Christian Intelligencer* (1847): 'There is a growing feeling of reverence for the lower creation . . . we regard them as sharers in one quality, and that the most tangible portion of our inheritance – they share in life, they are living creatures. They are in one particular our brethren.' Turner noted the belief that 'Training of the intellect alone was not sufficient. It could not teach the thing most needful, the "instinct of pity," the "only safe judge of right and wrong." But animals could fill the gap, if people would attend to their lessons, and the immense success of Anna Sewell's consciously didactic *Black Beauty* (1877) testified to the market for such instruction. Untouched by quibbling reason and unchanged by education, animals possessed a natural wisdom of their own, a "knowledge which did not depend on reason, and which was much more . . . perfect in its way" ' (Turner, *Reckoning with the Beast*, p. 75).

Since the 1930s, when educators began to re-examine what children were reading, and what some thought they should read, *Black Beauty* has invariably been in the discussion. Surveys of children's reading have until very recently shown the Sewell novel to be consistently in the canon of classics read by boys and girls aged 10–14. Frank Whitehead and others at the University of Sheffield Institute of Education pointed out that even though the technology is 'so out of date as to make little contact with current experience', it retains its appeal. Children identify with the equine hero and his animal companions (animals as children), and often equate the human characters with adults. Perhaps children see all the adults as representing 'the bad guys' and the animals as the innocent victims (Whitehead, *Children's Reading Interests*, pp. 43–4).

Not all critics look at the popularity of the novel among children with approval. Andrew Stibbs viewed *Black Beauty* with some dismay, and suggested that the 'moral complacency' and smugness he thought promoted by this Victorian tale 'add up to an ethos so passive and shortsighted, a moral complacency so infectious but unjustified, that the book does not deserve to be considered one of "quality"'. Stibbs detailed the stereotyped characters, the passivity of many human and animal characters to their fates and the class contrasts linked to good and evil ('Tales My Mother Told Me', p. 128).

Historians of the humane movement cannot ignore this novel and its influence when considering the development of legislation to protect both domestic and experimental animals. Coral Lansbury has perhaps examined *Black Beauty* most deeply in recent years in her *The Old Brown Dog: Women, Workers, and Vivisection in Edwardian England* (1985). According to Lansbury, 'Within the formal structure of a simple narrative, Anna Sewell raged against cruelty and injustice, against the nature of work, and the condition of women' (Ch. 4, 'Black Beauty and Other Horses', pp. 63–82). Black Beauty, the ever obedient worker for man (the very men against whom Ginger, the female horse, futilely rebels), was a model of the passivity or helplessness of working animals (Ch. 6, 'Riding Masters and Young Mares', pp. 96–111). Even his name symbolised slavery (Black) of women (Beauty). According to Lansbury his hapless situation also represented the condition of working man. Lansbury reminds us of Seedy Sam, the cab driver who believed he had to abuse his horses to make enough money to support himself and his family. Further, Lansbury draws a connection between the language of Sewell's account of Ginger's breaking-in and that of Edwardian pornography. In fact it is more probable that both Sewell and the pornographers drew on the language used by horse trainers of the time, but since it is clear that Sewell may not even have been aware of what gelding was (or could not bring herself to mention what obviously took place in Black Beauty's young life), Lansbury may be reading too much into this novel. But she raises important points for consideration on the inner meaning for Anna Sewell as she wrote the book.

The popularity of this long-lived story, through all its versions, lies in its powerful emotional effect on readers. Children and adults who read the story, regardless of their knowledge of the technology and traditions of the horse world, have wept over the lives of the characters since it was published. Reading the story can change attitudes towards animals, and perhaps towards poor people. The novel enjoys classic status in the minds of adults, who not only remember reading it, but enjoy the designs, colour illustrations and moral symmetry of the story, as much as children still appreciate the vivid characters, and the adventures of Black Beauty and his fellow creatures.

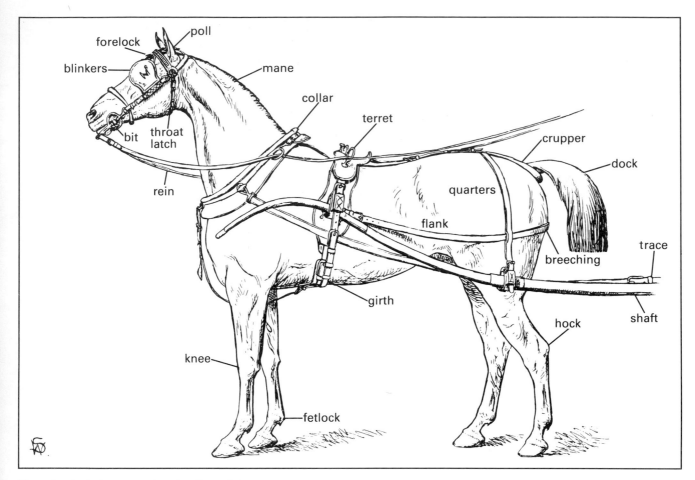

Horse in single harness, showing the points of the horse and the items of harness mentioned throughout the book. (Adapted from Sidney, *Book of the Horse*, p. 378)

Title page of the first edition of *Black Beauty*.
(London, Jarrold & Sons, 1877)

BLACK BEAUTY:

HIS GROOMS AND COMPANIONS.

THE AUTOBIOGRAPHY OF A HORSE.

Translated from the Original Equine,

BY

ANNA SEWELL.

LONDON: JARROLD AND SONS,
3, PATERNOSTER BUILDINGS.

PART I

CHAPTER I

MY EARLY HOME

THE first place that I can well remember was a large pleasant meadow with a pond of clear water in it. Some shady trees leaned over it, and rushes and water-lilies grew at the deep end. Over the hedge on one side we looked into a ploughed field, and on the other we looked over a gate at our master's house, which stood by the roadside; at the top of the meadow was a plantation of fir trees, and at the bottom a running brook overhung by a steep bank.

Whilst I was young I lived upon my mother's milk, as I could not eat grass. In the day-time I ran by her side, and at night I lay down close by her. When it was hot, we used to stand by

2

'The first place that I can well remember'. Two talented interpretations: (*top*) Lionel Edwards (*Black Beauty*, London: Peter Lunn, 1946, frontispiece); (*bottom*) Cecil Aldin (*Black Beauty*, London, Jarrolds, 1912, p. 24). It is interesting to note that these and many other artists depicted Black Beauty's mother as a chestnut, although nowhere in the text is her colour mentioned.

the pond in the shade of the trees, and when it was cold, we had a nice warm shed near the plantation.

As soon as I was old enough to eat grass, my mother used to go out to work in the day-time, and came back in the evening.

There were six young colts in the meadow besides me; they were older than I was; some were nearly as large as grown-up horses. I used to run with them, and had great fun; we used to gallop all together round and round the field, as hard as we could go. Sometimes we had rather rough play, for they would frequently bite and kick as well as gallop.

One day, when there was a good deal of kicking, my mother whinnied to me to come to her, and then she said:

'I wish you to pay attention to what I am going to say to you. The colts who live here are very good colts, but they are cart-horse colts, and, of course, they have not learned manners. You have been well bred and well born; your father has a great name in these parts, and your grandfather won the cup two years at the Newmarket races; your grandmother had the sweetest temper of any horse I ever knew, and I think you have never seen me kick or bite. I hope you will grow up gentle and good, and never learn bad ways; do your work with a good will, lift your feet up well when you trot, and never bite or kick even in play.'

I have never forgotten my mother's advice; I knew she was a wise old horse, and our master thought a great deal of her. Her name was Duchess, but he often called her Pet.

Our master was a good, kind man. He gave us good food, good lodging, and kind words; he spoke as kindly to us as he did to his little children. We were all fond of him, and my mother loved him very much. When she saw him at the gate, she would neigh with joy, and trot up to him. He would pat and stroke her and say, 'Well, old Pet, and how is your little Darkie?'

1 **Colts.** Male horses under the age of four.

2 **Rough play.** Colts especially indulge in rough play which prepares them for a time when, in the wild, they would be required to establish their position in the hierarchy and win mares for their own herds.

3 **Cart-horse colts.** The Victorian obsession with social class extended to the horse world; thus the 'working-class' horses, or crossbred heavy horses, were not expected to have the same manners and 'breeding' as high-class riding or carriage horses.

4 **Newmarket.** Centre for English racing in Suffolk. It was established in the late seventeenth century by King Charles II following his Restoration to the throne after the Civil War. He was known as the 'Merry Monarch' and one of his greatest loves was racing. He gave his nickname, 'Old Rowley', to the part of the course known as the 'Rowley Mile'. Newmarket soon became the recreational centre for the Court and was the home not only of horseracing but also of breeding horses, gambling and other pursuits. The Jockey Club was set up there in the 1750s.

5 **Duchess.** A typical example of the Victorian passion for giving characters, whether equine or human, names suited to their personality or station in life.

Racing at Newmarket. (Earl of Suffolk, *Racing and Steeplechasing*, p. 91)

I was a dull black, so he called me Darkie; then he would give me a piece of bread, which was very good, and sometimes he brought a carrot for my mother. All the horses would come to him, but I think we were his favourites. My mother always took 6 him to the town on a market day in a light gig.

There was a ploughboy, Dick, who sometimes came into our field to pluck blackberries from the hedge. When he had eaten all he wanted, he would have, what he called, fun with the colts, throwing stones and sticks at them to make them gallop. We did not much mind him, for we could gallop off; but sometimes a stone would hit and hurt us.

One day he was at this game, and did not know that the master was in the next field; but he was there, watching what was going on: over the hedge he jumped in a snap, and catching Dick by 7 the arm, he gave him such a box on the ear as made him roar with the pain and surprise. As soon as we saw the master, we trotted up nearer to see what went on.

'Bad boy!' he said, 'bad boy! to chase the colts. This is not the first time, nor the second, but it shall be the last—there—take your money and go home, I shall not want you on my farm again.' So we never saw Dick any more. Old Daniel, the man who looked after the horses, was just as gentle as our master, so we were well off.

6 **Light gig.** Driven by the owner as opposed to a coachman, gigs came in a variety of styles and designs and often took the name from the designer or place of origin, e.g. Dennett, Liverpool, Tilbury, Stanhope, Whitechapel gigs.

7 **Box on the ear.** A slap around the ears was a favourite Victorian punishment for unruly boys.

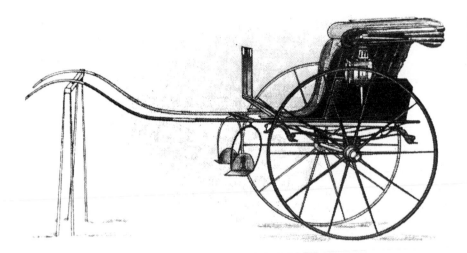

Light gig, in this case a Stanhope gig. (Nineteenth-century lithograph from the collection of Marylian Watney)

'He gave him such a box on the ear'. Illustrated by Charles Keeping. (*Black Beauty*, London: Victor Gollancz, 1988, p. 13)

CHAPTER II

THE HUNT

BEFORE I was two years old, a circumstance happened which I have never forgotten. It was early in the spring; there had been a little frost in the night, and a light mist still hung over the plantations and meadows. I and the other colts were feeding at the lower part of the field when we heard, quite in the distance, what sounded like the cry of dogs. The oldest of the colts raised his head, pricked his ears, and said, 'There are the hounds!' and immediately cantered off, followed by the rest of us to the upper part of the field, where we could look over the hedge and see several fields beyond. My mother and an old riding horse of our master's were also standing near, and seemed to know all about it.

'They have found a hare,' said my mother, 'and if they come this way, we shall see the hunt.'

And soon the dogs were all tearing down the field of young wheat next to ours. I never heard such a noise as they made.

8

1 **Hounds.** In this case harriers (i.e. chasers of hares), similar to but a little smaller than the typical white, black and tan foxhound.

2 **Hare.** One of the animals of the chase, others being the fox, stag and otter at this period.

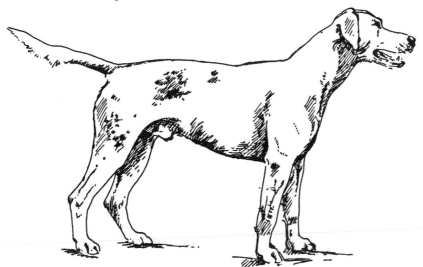

The English Foxhound (*left*) is a strong, long-legged type of hound with speed and staying power, used for hunting the fox with mounted followers. The Beagle (*bottom*) is a sturdy, short-legged type used for hunting the hare with foot followers. Unlike the fox, which runs for long distances from point to point, the hare runs in circles so staying power is not so important. A good 'nose' is essential, however, as a hare leaves a very light scent compared with a fox. Harriers, used for hunting the hare with mounted followers, are also an ancient and well-established breed, smaller than the Foxhound with whom it was interbred in the last century. Illustrated by Elaine How. (John Williams, *Riding to Hounds*, London: J. A. Allen, 1989, pp. 32, 34)

9

They did not bark, nor howl, nor whine, but kept on a 'yo! yo, o, o! yo! yo, o, o!' at the top of their voices. After them came a number of men on horseback, some of them in green

3   coats, all galloping as fast as they could. The old horse snorted and looked eagerly after them, and we young colts wanted to be galloping with them, but they were soon away into the fields lower down; here it seemed as if they had come to a stand; the dogs left off barking, and ran about every way with their noses to the ground.

'They have lost the scent,' said the old horse; 'perhaps the hare will get off.'

'What hare?' I said.

'Oh! I don't know *what* hare; likely enough it may be one of our own hares out of the plantation; any hare they can find will do for the dogs and men to run after'; and before long the dogs began their 'yo! yo, o, o!' again, and back they came altogether at full speed, making straight for our meadow at the part where the high bank and hedge overhang the brook.

'Now we shall see the hare,' said my mother; and just then a hare wild with fright rushed by, and made for the plantation. On came the dogs, they burst over the bank, leapt the stream, and came dashing across the field, followed by the huntsmen. Six or eight men leaped their horses clean over, close upon the dogs. The hare tried to get through the fence; it was too thick,

4   and she turned sharp round to make for the road, but it was too late; the dogs were upon her with their wild cries; we heard one shriek, and that was the end of her. One of the huntsmen rode up and whipped off the dogs, who would soon have torn her to pieces. He held her up by the leg torn and bleeding, and all the gentlemen seemed well pleased.

As for me, I was so astonished that I did not at first see what

3 **Green coats.** Whereas scarlet or 'hunting pink' is most frequently associated with English foxhunting, dark green is often the livery of hare hunts or harriers. Dark green is much favoured by Irish hunts.

4 **She.** Whereas the fox is usually assumed to be male (with the sobriquet 'Charles James'), the hare is invariably thought of as female and sometimes referred to as 'Puss'.

Hounds casting for scent. (Baron Karl Reille, *Hounds for a Pack*, London: J. A. Allen, 1974, p. 40)

Hounds putting up a hare. (Baron Karl Reille, *Hounds for a Pack*, London: J. A. Allen, 1974, p. 33)

was going on by the brook; but when I did look, there was a sad sight; two fine horses were down, one was struggling in the stream, and the other was groaning on the grass. One of the riders was getting out of the water covered with mud, the other lay quite still.

'His neck is broken,' said my mother.

'And serve him right too,' said one of the colts.

I thought the same, but my mother did not join with us.

'Well! no,' she said, 'you must not say that; but though I am an old horse, and have seen and heard a great deal, I never yet could make out why men are so fond of this sport; they often hurt themselves, often spoil good horses, and tear up the fields, and all for a hare or a fox, or a stag, that they could get more easily some other way; but we are only horses, and don't know.'

Whilst my mother was saying this, we stood and looked on. Many of the riders had gone to the young man; but my master, who had been watching what was going on, was the first to raise him. His head fell back and his arms hung down, and every one looked very serious. There was no noise now; even the dogs were quiet, and seemed to know that something was wrong. They carried him to our master's house. I heard afterwards that it was young George Gordon, the Squire's only son, a fine, tall young man, and the pride of his family.

There was now riding off in all directions to the doctor's, to the farrier's, and no doubt to Squire Gordon's, to let him know about his son. When Mr. Bond, the farrier, came to look at the black horse that lay groaning on the grass, he felt him all over, and shook his head; one of his legs was broken. Then someone ran to our master's house and came back with a gun; presently there was a loud bang and a dreadful shriek, and then all was still; the black horse moved no more.

5 **This sport.** From her Quaker upbringing Anna Sewell must have abhorred violence of any kind, including that towards animals. One of the Quaker codes is against hunting and the 'distressing of dumb beasts for amusement'. Indeed, she must have found it hard to accept that one of her heroes, Charles Kingsley, was extremely fond of hunting and took every possible opportunity to follow hounds. The dramatic account of the hunt given here shows how unfamiliar with the traditions and parlance of the hunting field she was, as hounds are never referred to as 'dogs' by the *cognoscente*.

6 **Farrier.** Originally farriers were horse doctors using traditional remedies and cures, as well as being shoers of horses.

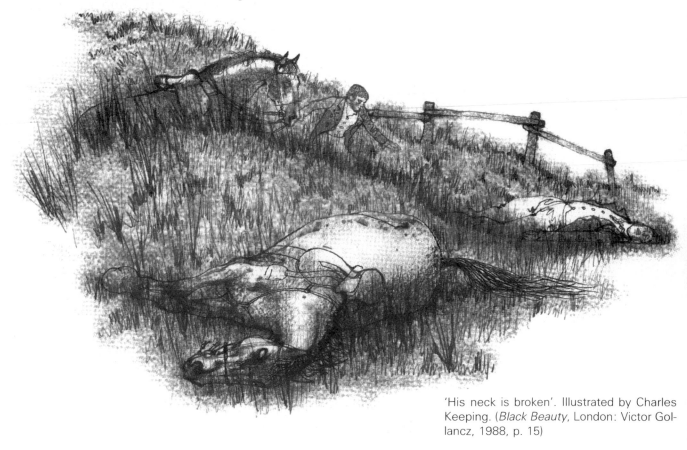

'His neck is broken'. Illustrated by Charles Keeping. (*Black Beauty*, London: Victor Gollancz, 1988, p. 15)

13

My mother seemed much troubled; she said she had known that horse for years, and that his name was Rob Roy; he was a good bold horse, and there was no vice in him. She never would go to that part of the field afterwards.

7 Not many days after, we heard the church bell tolling for a long time; and looking over the gate we saw a long strange black coach that was covered with black cloth and was drawn by black horses; after that came another and another and another, and all were black, while the bell kept tolling, tolling. They were carrying young Gordon to the churchyard to bury him. He would never ride again. What they did with Rob Roy I never knew; but 'twas all for one little hare.

14

7 **Strange black coach.** The Victorian funeral was a grand occasion, especially if the deceased was a member of the local squirearchy. The hearse would be drawn by two or more black horses, often imported Flemish stallions of noble bearing, and the mourners would follow in black-draped closed carriages drawn by black-plumed horses. The undertaker was one of the largest users of light, quality carriage horses in Victorian times.

A hearse dating from 1870. (D. J. Smith, *Discovering Horse Drawn Commercial Vehicles*, Aylesbury: Shire Publications, 1977, p. 56)

15

CHAPTER III

MY BREAKING IN

I WAS now beginning to grow handsome; my coat had grown fine and soft, and was bright black. I had one white foot, and a pretty white star on my forehead. I was thought very handsome; my master would not sell me till I was four years old; he said lads ought not to work like men, and colts ought not to work like horses till they were quite grown up.

When I was four years old, Squire Gordon came to look at me. He examined my eyes, my mouth, and my legs; he felt them all down; and then I had to walk and trot and gallop before him; he seemed to like me, and said, 'When he has been well broken in, he will do very well.' My master said he would break me in

16

1 **Colts ought not to work like horses.** A plea by Anna Sewell to the users of horses not to work them when they were too immature to take either the physical or mental stress of hard work.

The folly of a heavy man riding a colt hard all day. (Dr B. J. Kendall, *A Treatise on the Horse and his Diseases*, Enosburgh Falls, Vermont, 1887, p. 55)

17

Black Beauty in his young adulthood, as illustrated by John Beer. (*Black Beauty*, London: Jarrold & Sons, 1894, title page)

himself, as he should not like me to be frightened or hurt, and he lost no time about it, for the next day he began.

Every one may not know what breaking in is, therefore I will describe it. It means to teach a horse to wear a saddle and bridle and to carry on his back a man, woman, or child; to go just the way they wish, and to go quietly. Besides this, he has to learn to wear a collar, a crupper, and a breeching, and to stand still whilst they are put on; then to have a cart or a chaise fixed behind him, so that he cannot walk or trot without dragging it after him: and he must go fast or slow, just as his driver wishes. He must never start at what he sees, nor speak to other horses, nor bite, nor kick, nor have any will of his own; but always do his master's will, even though he may be very tired or hungry; but the worst of all is, when his harness is once on, he may neither jump for joy nor lie down for weariness. So you see this breaking in is a great thing.

I had of course long been used to a halter and a headstall, and to be led about in the field and lanes quietly, but now I was to have a bit and a bridle; my master gave me some oats as usual, and after a good deal of coaxing, he got the bit into my mouth, and the bridle fixed, but it was a nasty thing! Those who have never had a bit in their mouths cannot think how bad it feels; a great piece of cold hard steel as thick as a man's finger to be pushed into one's mouth, between one's teeth and over one's tongue, with the ends coming out at the corner of your mouth, and held fast there by straps over your head, under your throat, round your nose, and under your chin; so that no way in the world can you get rid of the nasty hard thing; it is very bad! yes, very bad! at least I thought so; but I knew my mother always wore one when she went out, and all horses did when they were grown up; and so, what with the nice oats, and what

2 **A collar, a crupper, and a breeching.** Components of harness. See illustration.

3 **Chaise.** From the French 'chaise' meaning 'chair'. A low-slung travelling carriage drawn by a single horse or a pair of horses, with an adjustable hood so that it could be used open or closed.

4 **A halter and a headstall.** A halter is usually a rudimentary head-piece made of webbing or rope and used mainly for leading horses around a stable yard or out to pasture. A headstall is similar to a halter but more substantial and made of leather (often with brass buckles), offering more control than a halter.

A leather headstall, complete with browband and brass buckles. (Moseman's *Illustrated Guide for Purchasers of Horse Furnishing Goods*, p. 33)

The collar fits around the horse's neck and rests on his shoulders. Attached to the traces it enables the horse to pull a load. A crupper passes under the horse's tail and prevents the pad (which holds up the shafts) from sliding too far forward. Breeching is a leather strap passing around the horse's buttocks which acts as a brake, preventing the vehicle from rolling into the horse. Illustrated by Charles Keeping. (*Black Beauty*, London: Victor Gollancz, 1988, p. 197)

with my master's pats, kind words, and gentle ways, I got to wear my bit and bridle.

5   Next came the saddle, but that was not half so bad; my master put it on my back very gently, whilst old Daniel held my head; he then made the girths fast under my body, patting and talking to me all the time; then I had a few oats, then a little leading about, and this he did every day till I began to look for the oats and the saddle.   At length, one morning my master got on my back and rode me round the meadow on the soft grass.   It certainly did feel queer; but must say I felt rather proud to carry my master, and as he continued to ride me a little every day, I soon became accustomed to it.

6   The next unpleasant business was putting on the iron shoes; that too was very hard at first.   My master went with me to the smith's forge, to see that I was not hurt or got any fright.   The
7 blacksmith took my feet in his hand one after the other, and cut
8 away some of the hoof.   It did not pain me, so I stood still on three legs till he had done them all.   Then he took a piece of
9 iron the shape of my foot, and clapped it on, and drove some nails through the shoe quite into my hoof, so that the shoe was firmly on. My feet felt very stiff and heavy, but in time I got used to it.

    And now having got so far, my master went on to break me to harness; there were more new things to wear.   First, a stiff heavy collar just on my neck, and a bridle with great side-pieces
10 against my eyes called blinkers and blinkers indeed they were, for I could not see on either side, but only straight in front of me; next there was a small saddle with a nasty stiff strap that went right under my tail; that was the crupper.   I hated the crupper—to have my long tail doubled up and poked through that strap was almost as bad as the bit.   I never felt more like kicking, but of course I could not kick such a good master, and

5 **Saddle.** A horse has to become accustomed to a saddle on his back as Black Beauty describes. A saddle or a pad is also an integral part of harness for draught work.

6 **Iron shoes.** Horses' hooves will usually split and crack and hence cause lameness if they are not shod for work on hard ground. In the natural state the hooves wear down with the horse's continual but gentle movement over fairly soft terrain, but when asked to work continually on paved streets the hooves wear down very quickly and hence need protection.

7 **Blacksmith.** A worker in iron, not necessarily a farrier, i.e. one who shoes horses, although the two terms are frequently interchanged.

8 **Cut away some of the hoof.** As the hoof is continually growing (like a fingernail) it has to be trimmed, and like a fingernail it has no feeling. Trimming is a skilled job and is done with a paring knife or pincers. Shoes have to be replaced every four to six weeks as they too wear, and the hoof grows over the shoe edge.

9 **Nails.** Shoes are held in place by specially designed horseshoe nails which have no definite heads. They are hammered through holes in the shoe and through the insensitive horn of the hoof to protrude through the front and sides of the hoof where the ends of the nails or 'clenches' are nipped off and made flush with the hoof wall.

10 **Blinkers.** Blinkers prevent the horse seeing sideways and to the rear. Blinkers would seem to be mainly a tradition, for often farm horses and military horses used for draught purposes carry out their work in 'open' bridles (no blinkers) without taking fright. Blinkers could be square, round, lozenge-shaped or rectangular and often decorated with brass or the owner's family crest.

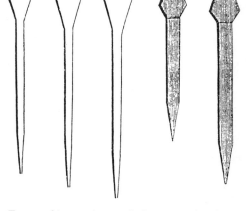

Types of horseshoe nails in use at the time: (*left*) countersunk nail; (*right*) rose-headed nail. Whereas there was some projection with the rose-headed nail, the countersunk nail was hammered in flush with the base of the shoe. The modern horseshoe nail is similar to the countersunk, having one flat side. (Lt-General Sir F. Fitzwygram, *Horses and Stables*, London: Longmans Green, 2nd edn, 1881, pl. xxxvii)

Different types of blinkers in use today. From the *left*: round; hatchet; dee; square. Illustration by Janet Johnstone. (Sallie Walrond, *Encyclopaedia of Driving*, Macclesfield: Horse Drawn Carriages, 1974, p. 287)

so in time I got used to everything, and could do my work as well as my mother.

I must not forget to mention one part of my training, which I have always considered a very great advantage. My master sent me for a fortnight to a neighbouring farmer's, who had a meadow which was skirted on one side by the railway. Here were some sheep and cows, and I was turned in amongst them.

I shall never forget the first train that ran by. I was feeding quietly near the pales which separated the meadow from the railway, when I heard a strange sound at a distance, and before I knew whence it came—with a rush and a clatter, and a puffing out of smoke—a long black train of something flew by, and was gone almost before I could draw my breath. I turned, and galloped to the further side of the meadow as fast as I could go, and there I stood snorting with astonishment and fear. In the course of the day many other trains went by, some more slowly; these drew up at the station close by, and sometimes made an awful shriek and groan before they stopped. I thought it very dreadful, but the cows went on eating very quietly, and hardly raised their heads as the black frightful thing came puffing and grinding past.

For the first few days I could not feed in peace; but as I found that this terrible creature never came into the field, or did me any harm, I began to disregard it, and very soon I cared as little about the passing of a train as the cows and sheep did.

Since then I have seen many horses much alarmed and restive at the sight or sound of a steam engine; but thanks to my good master's care, I am as fearless at railway stations as in my own stable.

Now if any one wants to break in a young horse well, that is the way.

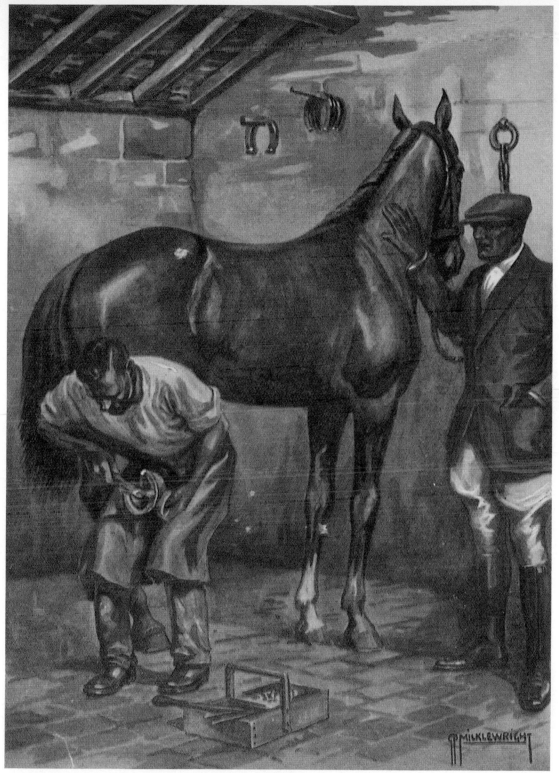

PLATE 6
Black Beauty at the forge, illustrated by G. P. Micklewright in an interwar edition
published in London by J. Coker & Co.

PLATE 7
Bucolic cover of the 1959 A. & C. Black
(London) edition, illustrated by Peter Biegel.

PLATE 8
Frontispiece from an edition published
c. 1910 by M. A. Donohue & Co., Chicago.
The designs for the colour plates were
based on illustrations by John Beer in the
first well-illustrated British edition of 1894.

'I shall never forget the first train that ran by'.
Illustrated by Lionel Edwards. (*Black Beauty*,
London: Peter Lunn, 1946, p. 6)

11   My master often drove me in double harness with my mother because she was steady, and could teach me how to go better than a strange horse. She told me the better I behaved, the better I should be treated, and that it was wisest always to do my best to please my master; 'but,' said she, 'there are a great many kinds of men; there are good, thoughtful men like our master, that any horse may be proud to serve; but there are bad, cruel men, who never ought to have a horse or dog to call their own. Beside, there are a great many foolish men, vain, ignorant, and careless, who never trouble themselves to think; these spoil more horses than all, just for want of sense; they don't mean it, but they do it for all that. I hope you will fall into good hands; but a horse never knows who may buy him, or who may drive him; it is all a chance for us, but still I say, do your best wherever it is, and keep up your good name.'

24

11 **Double harness.** Working as a pair, that is two horses side by side, as opposed to tandem, where two horses are one behind the other. See p. 217.

Driving two horses as a pair. (Sidney, *Book of the Horse*, p. 352)

CHAPTER IV

BIRTWICK PARK

AT this time I used to stand in the stable, and my coat was brushed every day till it shone like a rook's wing. It was early in May, when there came a man from Squire Gordon's, who took me away to the Hall. My master said, 'Good-bye, Darkie; be a good horse, and always do your best.' I could not say 'good-bye,' so I put my nose into his hand; he patted me kindly, and I left my first home. As I lived some years with Squire Gordon, I may as well tell something about the place.

Squire Gordon's Park skirted the village of Birtwick. It was entered by a large iron gate, at which stood the first lodge, and then you trotted along on a smooth road between clumps of large old trees; then another lodge and another gate which brought

26

1   **Lodge.** Most large houses set in several acres of land had their entrances protected by a small cottage or lodge. This was a 'tied' house occupied by an employee of the estate usually known as a lodge-keeper to whom visitors would report, although it was sometimes occupied by gardeners, grooms or others.

The labourer's cottage as imagined by a Victorian illustrator. (A. L. Barbauld, *Hymns in Prose*, 1863)

you to the house and the gardens. Beyond this lay the home paddock, the old orchard, and the stables. There was accommodation for many horses and carriages; but I need only describe the stable into which I was taken; this was very roomy, with four good stalls; a large swinging window opened into the yard, which made it pleasant and airy.

2 The first stall was a large square one, shut in behind with a wooden gate; the others were common stalls, good stalls, but not nearly so large; it had a low rack for hay and a low manger
3 for corn; it was called a loose box, because the horse that was put into it was not tied up, but left loose, to do as he liked. It
4 is a great thing to have a loose box.

Into this fine box the groom put me; it was clean, sweet, and airy. I never was in a better box than that, and the sides were not so high but that I could see all that went on through the iron rails that were at the top.

He gave me some very nice oats, he patted me, spoke kindly, and then went away.

When I had eaten my corn, I looked round. In the stall next to mine stood a little fat grey pony, with a thick mane and tail, a very pretty head, and a pert little nose.

I put my head up to the iron rails at the top of my box, and said, 'How do you do? what is your name?'

He turned round as far as his halter would allow, held up his head, and said, 'My name is Merrylegs: I am very handsome, I carry the young ladies on my back, and sometimes I take our
5 mistress out in the low chair. They think a great deal of me, and so does James. Are you going to live next door to me in the box?'

I said 'Yes.'

'Well, then,' he said, 'I hope you are good-tempered; I do not like any one next door who bites.'

2 **Stall.** Victorian stables were usually built with stalls on each side of a central aisle so that the horses were tied up facing the walls and their tails faced into the aisle. If kept in a stall a horse needed to be exercised every day, for there is only room for the horse to lie down, but not to turn around.

3 **Corn.** Generic term for grain fed to horses, usually oats but also maize (American 'corn') or barley.

4 **Loose box.** In a loose box a horse was free to lie down, walk around and perhaps look out over a half door. Victorian loose boxes often had sliding doors, and iron bars on the upper part of walls and doors to prevent the horse jumping out but affording some view of the stable interior or yard. Loose boxes were preferable to stall accommodation but took up more space.

5 **Low chair.** Low, small, sedate vehicle usually drawn by one horse or pony for gentle drives around the park or estate. Often used by the elderly.

A loose box and a good stall. (*Illustrated London News*, 1 November 1862, p. 471)

Just then a horse's head looked over from the stall beyond; the ears were laid back, and the eye looked rather ill-tempered. This was a tall chestnut mare, with a long handsome neck; she looked across to me and said:

'So it is you who have turned me out of my box; it is a very strange thing for a colt like you, to come and turn a lady out of her own home.'

'I beg your pardon,' I said, 'I have turned no one out; the man who brought me put me here, and I had nothing to do with it; and as to my being a colt, I am turned four years old, and am a grown-up horse: I never had words yet with horse or mare, and it is my wish to live at peace.'

'Well,' she said, 'we shall see; of course I do not want to have words with a young thing like you.' I said no more.

In the afternoon when she went out, Merrylegs told me all about it.

'The thing is this,' said Merrylegs, 'Ginger has a bad habit of biting and snapping; that is why they call her Ginger, and when she was in the loose box, she used to snap very much. One day she bit James in the arm and made it bleed, and so Miss Flora and Miss Jessie, who are very fond of me, were afraid to come into the stable. They used to bring me nice things to eat, an apple or a carrot, or a piece of bread, but after Ginger stood in that box, they dare not come, and I missed them very much. I hope they will now come again, if you do not bite or snap.'

I told him I never bit anything but grass, hay, and corn, and could not think what pleasure Ginger found it.

'Well, I don't think she does find pleasure,' says Merrylegs; 'it is just a bad habit; she says no one was ever kind to her, and why should she not bite? Of course it is a very bad habit; but I am sure, if all she says be true, she must have been very

30

6   **Four years old.** Generally the age at which a horse can be said to be adult, although some breeds appear to mature later than others.

'Just then a horse's head looked over from the stall beyond'. Illustrated by Charles Keeping. (*Black Beauty*, London: Victor Gollancz, 1988, p. 22)

ill-used before she came here. John does all he can to please her, and James does all he can, and our master never uses a whip if a horse acts right; so I think she might be good-tempered here; 7 you see,' he said with a wise look, 'I am twelve years old; I know a great deal, and I can tell you there is not a better place for a horse all round the country than this. John is the best groom that ever was, he has been here fourteen years; and you never saw such a kind boy as James is, so that it is all Ginger's own fault that she did not stay in that box.'

7 **Twelve years old.** A horse is said to be 'aged' at eight years old but this is usually considered a prime age. At twelve a horse would be considered fairly set in his ways but if he had been well-treated and cared for he could live to twenty or beyond.

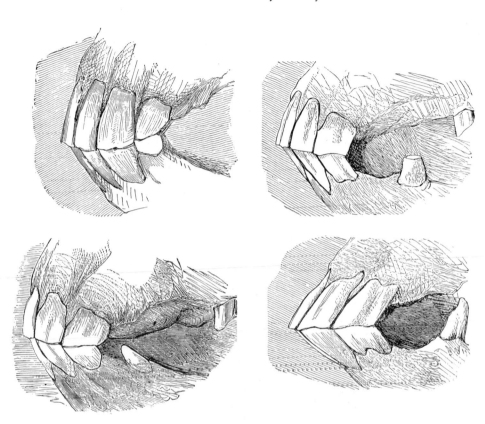

The most reliable way to assess a horse's age is by inspection of the teeth. The incisors exhibit the standard differences as the horse ages. 1st column, from top to bottom: 4½ years old; 6 years old; 2nd column, from top to bottom: 8 years old; 12 years old. (Mayhew, *The Illustrated Horse Management*, pp. 158, 168–9)

CHAPTER V

A FAIR START

I   THE name of the coachman was John Manly; he had a wife and one little child, and they lived in the coachman's cottage, very near the stables.

The next morning he took me into the yard and gave me a good grooming, and just as I was going into my box with my coat soft and bright, the Squire came in to look at me, and seemed pleased. 'John,' he said, 'I meant to have tried the new horse this morning, but I have other business. You may as well take him a round after breakfast; go by the common and the Highwood, and back by the water-mill and the river, that will show his paces.'

'I will, sir,' said John. After breakfast he came and fitted me

34

1 **John Manly.** An example of the Victorian liking for giving a character, whether good or bad, a suitable sounding name.

'Back by the water-mill and the river'. Illustrated by Mike Grimsdale. (*Black Beauty*, London: Chancellor Press, 1987, reprint of Octopus, 1984 edn, pl. opp. p. 32)

35

with a bridle. He was very particular in letting out and taking in the straps, to fit my head comfortable; then he brought the saddle, that was not broad enough for my back; he saw it in a minute and went for another, which fitted nicely. He rode me first slowly, then a trot, then a canter, and when we were on the common he gave me a light touch with his whip, and we had a splendid gallop.

'Ho, ho! my boy,' he said, as he pulled me up, 'you would like to follow the hounds, I think.'

As we came back through the Park we met the Squire and Mrs. Gordon walking; they stopped, and John jumped off.

'Well, John, how does he go?'

'First rate, sir,' answered John, 'he is as fleet as a deer, and has a fine spirit too; but the lightest touch of the rein will guide him. Down at the end of the common we met one of those travelling carts hung all over with baskets, rugs, and such like; you know, sir, many horses will not pass those carts quietly; he just took a good look at it, and then went on as quiet and pleasant as could be. They were shooting rabbits near the High-wood, and a gun went off close by; he pulled up a little and looked, but did not stir a step to right or left. I just held the rein steady and did not hurry him, and it's my opinion he has not been frightened or ill-used while he was young.'

'That's well,' said the Squire, 'I will try him myself to-morrow.'

The next day I was brought up for my master. I remembered my mother's counsel and my good old master's, and I tried to do exactly what he wanted me to do. I found he was a very good rider, and thoughtful for his horse too. When we came home, the lady was at the hall door as he rode up.

'Well, my dear,' she said, 'how do you like him?'

2 **Saddle . . . not broad enough for my back.** Horses' backs differ in width, some have a protruding spine, and others have more flesh on them. It is essential therefore that the saddle fit properly and does not rub or pinch, which would produce saddle sores and render the animal unworkable until these had healed. Saddle sores frequently resulted in white patches of hair where the saddle had rubbed the skin raw and the hairs had grown back without pigment.

3 **Common.** It had been a centuries' old right of villagers in England to graze their animals and collect firewood from land in or around their village. This land was held in common ownership until the coming of the Enclosure Acts in the late eighteenth and early nineteenth centuries, when many of these people, often casual labourers, lost these rights as common land was fenced and put into private ownership. However, some common land survived and exists until this day.

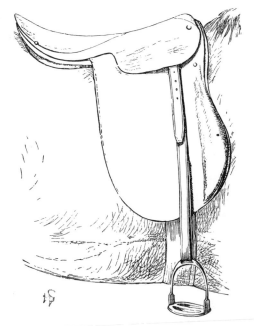

An old-fashioned English hunting saddle with a shallow seat, the deepest point of which is towards the back, tending to place the rider's weight over the horse's loins. Modern saddles are designed to bring the rider's weight further forward nearer the horse's centre of gravity. (Sidney, *Book of the Horse*, p. 261)

'Travelling carts hung all over with baskets, rugs, and such like.' Illustrated by John Beer. (*Black Beauty*, Boston: DeWolfe, Fiske & Co., [191?], p. 17)

'He is exactly what John said,' he replied; 'a pleasanter creature I never wish to mount. What shall we call him?'

'Would you like Ebony?' said she, 'he is as black as ebony.'

'No, not Ebony.'

'Will you call him Blackbird, like your uncle's old horse?'

'No, he is far handsomer than old Blackbird ever was.'

'Yes,' she said, 'he is really quite a beauty, and he has such a sweet good-tempered face and such a fine intelligent eye—what do you say to calling him Black Beauty?'

'Black Beauty—why, yes, I think that is a very good name. If you like it shall be his name,' and so it was.

When John went into the stable, he told James that master and mistress had chosen a good sensible English name for me, that meant something, not like Marengo, or Pegasus, or Abdallah. They both laughed, and James said, 'If it was not for bringing back the past, I should have named him Rob Roy, for I never saw two horses more alike.'

'That's no wonder,' said John, 'didn't you know that farmer Grey's old Duchess was the mother of them both?'

I had never heard that before, and so poor Rob Roy who was killed at that hunt was my brother! I did not wonder that my mother was so troubled. It seems that horses have no relations; at least, they never know each other after they are sold.

John seemed very proud of me: he used to make my mane and tail almost as smooth as a lady's hair, and he would talk to me a great deal; of course I did not understand all he said, but I learned more and more to know what he *meant*, and what he wanted me to do. I grew very fond of him, he was so gentle and kind, he seemed to know just how a horse feels, and when he cleaned me, he knew the tender places, and the ticklish places; when he

4 **Good sensible English name.** The insularity of the British and their position as 'top dog' in the world led them to consider anything which was not British as inferior.

5 **Marengo, or Pegasus, or Abdallah.** Marengo was the name of Napoleon's favourite charger and Pegasus was the flying horse from Greek mythology. Abdallah was probably an imported name from the British Raj in India.

'I think that is a very good name'. Illustrated by F. Milward. (*Black Beauty*, Leeds: E. J. Arnold & Son, 1928, p. 19)

brushed my head, he went as carefully over my eyes as if they were his own, and never stirred up any ill-temper.

James Howard, the stable boy, was just as gentle and pleasant in his way, so I thought myself well off.   There was another man who helped in the yard, but he had very little to do with Ginger and me.

A few days after this I had to go out with Ginger in the carriage. I wondered how we should get on together; but except laying her ears back when I was led up to her, she behaved very well. She did her work honestly, and did her full share, and I never wish to have a better partner in double harness.   When we came to a hill, instead of slackening her pace, she would throw her weight right into the collar, and pull away straight up.   We had both the same sort of courage at our work, and John had oftener to hold us in, than to urge us forward; he never had to use the whip with either of us; then our paces were much the same, and I found it very easy to keep step with her when trotting, which made it pleasant, and master always liked it when we kept step well, and so did John.   After we had been out two or three times together we grew quite friendly and sociable, which made me feel very much at home.

As for Merrylegs, he and I soon became great friends; he was such a cheerful, plucky, good-tempered little fellow, that he was a favourite with every one, and especially with Miss Jessie and Flora, who used to ride him about in the orchard, and have fine games with him and their little dog Frisky.

Our master had two other horses that stood in another stable. One was Justice, a roan cob, used for riding, or for the luggage cart; the other was an old brown hunter, named Sir Oliver; he was past work now, but was a great favourite with the master, who gave him the run of the Park; he sometimes did a little light

6 **Full share.** When working as a pair it is important that each horse literally pulls his weight.

7 **Easy to keep step.** A pair of horses working in harness must match in height, build and manner of 'going', i.e. their paces and steps must be the same. Otherwise it is difficult to ensure an even pull on the vehicle, and it usually results in one horse doing more work than the other.

8 **Miss Jessie.** Often a diminutive of Jessica, but Jessie was itself a popular name at that time.

9 **Roan cob.** Roan is a basic coat colour mixed with white hairs; thus chestnut hairs mixed with white results in a strawberry roan, black hairs mixed with white, a blue roan. A cob was not a breed but a type – a smallish, stocky animal of about fifteen hands. In Victorian times a cob would usually have had its mane hogged (clipped close to the neck) and its tail docked (the bone amputated about ten inches from the body) to emphasise its chunkiness.

10 **Hunter.** A hunter is usually part-Thoroughbred. It must have plenty of stamina and be capable of galloping and jumping well.

A typical late-nineteenth-century hunter. (Sidney, *Book of the Horse*, p. 394)

carting on the estate, or carried one of the young ladies when they rode out with their father; for he was very gentle, and could be trusted with a child as well as Merrylegs. The cob was a strong, well-made, good-tempered horse, and we sometimes had a little chat in the paddock, but of course I could not be so intimate with him as with Ginger, who stood in the same stable.

A typical strongly made cob. (William Cook, *Horse: its Keep and Management*, London, 1891, frontispiece)

CHAPTER VI

LIBERTY

I WAS quite happy in my new place, and if there was one thing that I missed, it must not be thought I was discontented; all who had to do with me were good, and I had a light airy stable and the best of food. What more could I want? Why, liberty! For three years and a half of my life I had had all the liberty I could wish for; but now, week after week, month after month, and no doubt year after year, I must stand up in a stable night and day except when I am wanted, and then I must be just as steady and quiet as any old horse who has worked twenty years. Straps here and straps there, a bit in my mouth, and blinkers over my eyes. Now, I am not

44

1 **Light airy stable.** Many Victorian stables were dark and dank, especially those used for heavy draught horses on farms or in towns. Privately owned horses for riding or carriage work usually had better stables with wide stalls or even loose boxes. In *Stable Architecture* (1862), Thomas E. Knightley stated that 'It is now generally admitted that close and confined and badly-ventilated stables produce most of the diseases to which the horse is liable.' However, it was a long time before many horses benefited from this realisation.

An advertisement for a ventilation shaft to ensure proper air circulation in the stable. (In T. E. Coleman, *Stable Sanitation and Construction*, London: E. & F. N. Spon, 1897, p. 217)

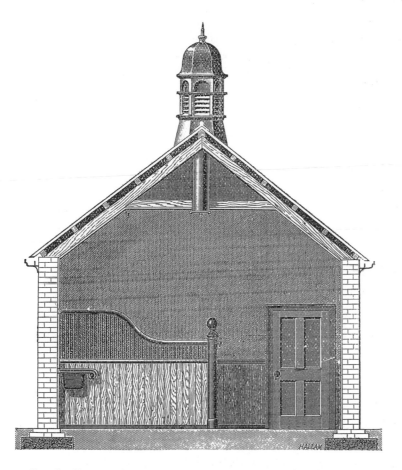

THE ST. PANCRAS IRONWORK COMPANY, LIMITED, have had a long practical experience in ventilating Stables and other buildings, and have studied the subject so closely that they are in a position to advise what arrangement will be best according to the circumstances of each case. The above illustration represents the Syphon Tube system of ventilation. It is fitted with valves to regulate the upward and downward draughts. For full particulars of various systems of ventilation, apply at

THE ST. PANCRAS IRONWORKS, ST. PANCRAS ROAD,
LONDON, N.W.
Close to St. Pancras, King's Cross and Euston Railway Stations.

complaining, for I know it must be so. I only mean to say that for a young horse full of strength and spirits who has been used to some large field or plain, where he can fling up his head, and toss up his tail and gallop away at full speed, then round and back again with a snort to his companions—I say it is hard never to have a bit more liberty to do as you like. Sometimes, when I have had less exercise than usual, I have felt so full of life and spring, that when John has taken me out to exercise, I really could not keep quiet; do what I would, it seemed as if I must jump, or dance, or prance, and many a good shake I know I must have given him, specially at the first; but he was always good and patient.

'Steady, steady, my boy,' he would say; 'wait a bit, and we 'll have a good swing, and soon get the tickle out of your feet.' Then as soon as we were out of the village, he would give me a few miles at a spanking trot, and then bring me back as fresh as before, only clear of the fidgets, as he called them. Spirited horses, when not enough exercised, are often called skittish, when it is only play; and some grooms will punish them, but our John did not, he knew it was only high spirits. Still, he had his own ways of making me understand by the tone of his voice or the touch of the rein. If he was very serious and quite determined, I always knew it by his voice, and that had more power with me than anything else, for I was very fond of him.

I ought to say, that sometimes we had our liberty for a few hours; this used to be on fine Sundays in the summer-time. The carriage never went out on Sundays, because the church was not far off.

It was a great treat to us to be turned out into the home paddock or the old orchard. The grass was so cool and soft to

2 **I always knew it by his voice.** One of the 'natural' aids a horseman possesses is the voice (others being hands, body and legs), and the importance of the voice in training and at all times cannot be overestimated. The horse is very sensitive to sound and is soon upset by loud noises, including shouting. Conversely, a horse can be reassured, given confidence and pacified by a calm voice.

A spanking trot. (Sidney, *Book of the Horse*, p. 196)

47

our feet; the air so sweet, and the freedom to do as we liked was so pleasant; to gallop, to lie down, and roll over on our backs, or to nibble the sweet grass.   Then it was a very good time for talking, as we stood together under the shade of the large chestnut
3   tree.

3 **Chestnut tree.** Either the horse chestnut with large palmate leaves, white 'candles', and 'conkers', or possibly the sweet or Spanish chestnut with pink flowers.

'As we stood together under the chestnut tree.' Illustrated by John Beer. (*Black Beauty*, London: Jarrold & Sons, 1894, p. 28)

49

CHAPTER VII

GINGER

ONE day when Ginger and I were standing alone in the shade we had a great deal of talk; she wanted to know all about my bringing up and breaking in, and I told her.

'Well,' said she, 'if I had had your bringing up I might have been as good a temper as you are, but now I don't believe I ever shall.'

'Why not?' I said.

'Because it has been all so different with me,' she replied; 'I never had any one, horse or man, that was kind to me, or that I cared to please; for in the first place I was taken from my mother as soon as I was weaned, and put with a lot of other young colts: none of them cared for me, and I cared for none of them. There

50

1 **Weaned.** A foal is separated from its mother when it is able to eat grass, oats, hay etc. and is no longer dependent on the mare's milk, usually at the age of about six months.

Two studies of Ginger: (*left*) Charles Keeping (*Black Beauty*, London: Victor Gollancz, 1988, p. 38); (*bottom*) W. Austen (*Black Beauty*, Boston: L. C. Page, 1902, pl. opp. p. 41)

was no kind master like yours to look after me, and talk to me, and bring me nice things to eat. The man that had the care of us never gave me a kind word in my life. I do not mean that he ill-used me, but he did not care for us one bit further than to see that we had plenty to eat and shelter in the winter.

'A footpath ran through our field, and very often the great boys passing through would fling stones to make us gallop. I was never hit, but one fine young colt was badly cut in the face, and I should think it would be a scar for life. We did not care for them, but of course it made us more wild, and we settled it in our minds that boys were our enemies.

'We had very good fun in the free meadows, galloping up and down and chasing each other round and round the field; then standing still under the shade of the trees. But when it came to breaking in, that was a bad time for me; several men came to catch me, and when at last they closed me in at one corner of the field, one caught me by the forelock, another caught me by the nose, and held it so tight I could hardly draw my breath; then another took my under jaw in his hard hand and wrenched my mouth open, and so by force they got on the halter and the bar into my mouth; then one dragged me along by the halter, another flogging behind, and this was the first experience I had of men's kindness, it was all force; they did not give me a chance to know what they wanted. I was high bred and had a great deal of spirit, and was very wild, no doubt, and gave them I dare say plenty of trouble, but then it was dreadful to be shut up in a stall day after day instead of having my liberty, and I fretted and pined and wanted to get loose. You know yourself, it's bad enough when you have a kind master and plenty of coaxing, but there was nothing of that sort for me.

'There was one—the old master, Mr. Ryder, who I think

2 **Nose.** Either the horse's head just above the nostrils, where pressure would constrict the air passages, or the rubbery, almost prehensile, skin between the nostrils with which the horse investigates his surroundings. Holding tightly to this part of the nose acts as a form of control. A more extreme form of control, usually for veterinary purposes, is the twitch. It has been discovered that by applying pressure to this part of the nose the horse's biochemical system produces a type of morphine which has the effect of mildly sedating the animal.

3 **Bar.** As a bit is normally attached to a bridle, not a halter, it is difficult to know exactly what it was that Ginger was forced to wear.

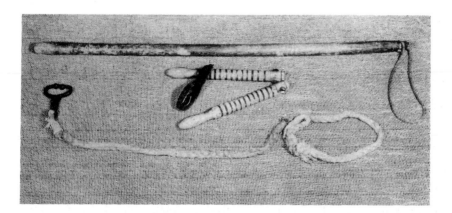

The twitch (*top*), consisting of a wooden pole with a loop of rope to twist around the horse's top lip. A mouth cramp (*centre*) was also attached to the horse's lip, also to enable the animal to be restrained. (Arthur Ingram, *The Country Animal Doctor*, Shire Album 40, Aylesbury: Shire Publications, 1979, p. 5)

Showing the twitch in use. (Arthur Ingram, *The Country Animal Doctor*, Shire Album 40, Aylesbury: Shire Publications, 1979, p. 6)

could soon have brought me round, and could have done anything with me, but he had given up all the hard part of the trade to his son and to another experienced man, and he only came at times to oversee. His son was a strong, tall, bold man; they called him Samson, and he used to boast that he had never found a horse that could throw him. There was no gentleness in him as there was in his father, but only hardness, a hard voice, a hard eye, a hard hand, and I felt from the first that what he wanted was to wear all the spirit out of me, and just make me into a quiet, humble, obedient piece of horse-flesh. ''Horse-flesh!'' Yes, that is all that he thought about,' and Ginger stamped her foot as if the very thought of him made her angry.

She went on: 'If I did not do exactly what he wanted, he would get put out, and make me run round with that long rein in the training field till he had tired me out. I think he drank a good deal, and I am quite sure that the oftener he drank the worse it was for me. One day he had worked me hard in every way he could, and when I laid down I was tired and miserable and angry; it all seemed so hard. The next morning he came for me early, and ran me round again for a long time. I had scarcely had an hour's rest, when he came again for me with a saddle and bridle and a new kind of bit. I could never quite tell how it came about; he had only just mounted me on the training ground, when something I did put him out of temper, and he chucked me hard with the rein. The new bit was very painful, and I reared up suddenly, which angered him still more, and he began to flog me. I felt my whole spirit set against him, and I began to kick, and plunge, and rear as I had never done before, and we had a regular fight: for a long time he stuck to the saddle and punished me cruelly with his whip and spurs, but my blood was thoroughly up, and I cared for nothing he could do if only I could get him

54

PLATE 9
Ginger's ill-treatment, one of the vivid illustrations which Lionel Edwards provided
for two editions, in this case Ward Lock's 1954 publication.

PLATE 10
Art Deco dust jacket designed by Bernice Magnie for a drastically abridged edition based on a radio reading by 'Uncle Mal' and published by Prang Company Publishers in 1946.

PLATE 11
Victor Ambrus provided some very fine illustrations for a 1973 edition published by Brockhampton Press (Leicester), with this lively horse on the dust jacket.

4 **Long rein.** Lunge (or longe) rein attached to a special noseband (cavesson) by which the trainer encourages the horse to circle him to the left and then right at various paces until the horse is obedient to the voice. The lunge rein is a single rein but long reins are, as their name implies, similar to driving reins but longer. Long reins are particularly used in training horses for harness work; the trainer walks behind the horse, making him obedient to the voice and control through the reins without actually pulling a vehicle.

5 **Drank a good deal.** Anna Sewell makes several references to 'the Demon Drink' and the terrible outcome of its excesses. This was a major theme in many Victorian moralising novels.

6 **Chucked me hard.** Shaking or jerking the reins roughly so that the horse is jabbed in the mouth by the bit. Here the intention was to hurt, but it is often done unintentionally by a poor rider or driver.

7 **Whip and spurs.** These are amongst the 'artificial aids' by which a rider can convey his wishes to a horse. Used properly they are simply extensions of the hand and leg, but used improperly they can cause pain and fear.

Spurs: (*top*) men's; (*centre*) ladies'; the shield was on a spring and moved to expose the spike when the spur was applied; (*bottom*) a spur which fitted into the heel of the rider's boot. (Moseman's *Illustrated Guide for Purchasers of Horse Furnishing Goods*, p. 270)

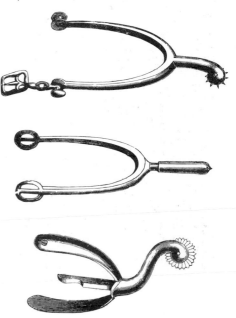

Long reins. The horse in the background is being lunged. (Earl of Suffolk, *Racing and Steeplechasing*, p. 137)

off. At last, after a terrible struggle, I threw him off backwards. I heard him fall heavily on the turf, and without looking behind me, I galloped off to the other end of the field; there I turned round and saw my persecutor slowly rising from the ground and going into the stable. I stood under an oak tree and watched, but no one came to catch me. The time went on, the sun was very hot, the flies swarmed round me, and settled on my bleeding flanks where the spurs had dug in. I felt hungry, for I had not eaten since the early morning, but there was not enough grass in that meadow for a goose to live on. I wanted to lie down and rest, but with the saddle strapped tightly on, there was no comfort, and there was not a drop of water to drink. The afternoon wore on, and the sun got low. I saw the other colts led in, and I knew they were having a good feed.

'At last, just as the sun went down, I saw the old master come out with a sieve in his hand. He was a very fine old gentleman with quite white hair, but his voice was what I should know him by amongst a thousand. It was not high, nor yet low, but full, and clear, and kind, and when he gave orders it was so steady and decided, that every one knew, both horses and men, that he expected to be obeyed. He came quietly along, now and then shaking the oats about that he had in the sieve, and speaking cheerfully and gently to me, "Come along, lassie, come along, lassie; come along, come along." I stood still and let him come up; he held the oats to me and I began to eat without fear; his voice took all my fear away. He stood by, patting and stroking me whilst I was eating, and seeing the clots of blood on my side he seemed very vexed; "Poor lassie! it was a bad business, a bad business!" then he quietly took the rein and led me to the stable; just at the door stood Samson. I laid my ears back and snapped at him. "Stand back," said the master, "and

56

8   Sieve. A usually circular container or pan, sometimes with a handle, for feedstuffs.

9   Laid my ears back. Often a sign of aggression or, at the very least, unfriendliness.

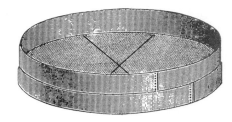

A sieve for grain. (Moseman's *Illustrated Guide for Purchasers of Horse Furnishing Goods*, p. 21)

Two interpretations of Ginger's struggle: (*left*) Cecil Aldin (*Black Beauty*, London: Jarrolds, 1912, p. 73); (*below*) Lionel Edwards (*Black Beauty*, London: Peter Lunn, 1946, p. 14)

57

keep out of her way; you 've done a bad day's work for this
10 filly.'' He growled out something about a vicious brute. ''Hark
ye,'' said the father, ''a bad-tempered man will never make a
good-tempered horse. You 've not learned your trade yet,
11 Samson.'' Then he led me into my box, took off the saddle and
bridle with his own hands and tied me up; then he called for a
pail of warm water and a sponge, took off his coat, and while the
stable man held the pail, he sponged my sides a good while so
tenderly that I was sure he knew how sore and bruised they were.
''Whoa! my pretty one,'' he said, ''stand still, stand still.''
His very voice did me good, and the bathing was very comfortable. The skin was so broken at the corners of my mouth that
I could not eat the hay, the stalks hurt me. He looked closely at
12 it, shook his head, and told the man to fetch a good bran mash
13 and put some meal into it. How good that mash was! and so
soft and healing to my mouth. He stood by all the time I was
eating, stroking me and talking to the man. ''If a high-mettled
creature like this,'' said he, ''can't be broken in by fair means,
she will never be good for anything.''

'After that he often came to see me, and when my mouth was
healed, the other breaker, Job they called him, went on training
me; he was steady and thoughtful, and I soon learned what he
wanted.'

10 **Filly.** A female horse under the age of four.

11 **Box.** Loose box. See p. 29.

12 **Bran mash.** Easily digested feed made from bran softened with hot water. Sometimes salt, carrots, apple or molasses was added for extra taste. See p. 435.

13 **Meal.** Grain ground to a coarse powder; here it could possibly mean maize.

Meal being measured into an iron feeding dish or movable manger. (Mayhew, *The Illustrated Horse Management*, p. 203)

A recipe for meal, based heavily on 'indian corn' or maize. (J. H. Walsh, *The Horse in the Stable and the Field*, London: Routledge, 1861, p. 232)

"TO MAKE ONE TON OF MEAL.	Cwt.	qrs.	lb.		Price.		
Locust Bean, finely ground, at 6*l*. a ton . . .	6	0	0	—	£1	16	0
Indian Corn, at 7*l*. a ton	9	0	0	—	3	3	0
Best Linseed Cake, at 10*l*. a ton . . °. . . .	3	0	0	—	1	10	0
Powdered turmeric, at 8*d*. a lb.	0	0	40	—	1	6	8
Sulphur, at 2*d*. a lb.	0	0	40	—	0	6	8
Saltpetre, at 5*d*. a lb.	0	0	20	—	0	8	4
Liquorice, at 1*s*. a lb.	0	0	27	—	1	7	0
Ginger, at 6*d*. a lb.	0	0	3	—	0	1	6
Aniseed, at 9*d*. a lb.	0	0	4	—	0	3	0
Coriander, at 9*d*. a lb.	0	0	10	—	0	7	6
Gentian, at 8*d*. a lb.	0	0	10	—	0	6	8
Cream of Tartar, at 1*s*. 8*d*. a lb.	0	0	2	—	0	3	4
Carbonate of Soda, at 4*d*. a lb.	0	0	6	—	0	2	0
Levigated Antimony, at 6*d*. a lb.	0	0	6	—	0	3	0
Common Salt, at ½*d*. a lb.	0	0	30	—	0	1	3
Peruvian Bark, at 4*s*. a lb.	0	0	4	—	0	16	0
Fenugreek, at 9*d*. a lb.	0	0	22	—	0	16	6
Total	20	0	0	—	12	18	5

CHAPTER VIII

GINGER'S STORY CONTINUED

THE next time that Ginger and I were together in the paddock, she told me about her first place.

1 'After my breaking in,' she said, 'I was bought by a
2 dealer to match another chestnut horse. For some
weeks he drove us together, and then we were sold to a
3 fashionable gentleman, and were sent up to London. I had
4 been driven with a bearing rein by the dealer, and I hated it
worse than anything else; but in this place we were reined far
5 tighter; the coachman and his master thinking we looked more
6 stylish so. We were often driven about in the Park and other

60

1 **Breaking in.** Black Beauty was fortunate to experience a sympathetic breaking in – the process of accustoming a horse to saddle and bridle for riding or harness for driving. He describes his breaking in as an extension of the continual training he had been receiving since he was a foal, and thus *his* breaking in was not the sudden traumatic experience which poor Ginger underwent, as she describes in Chapter VII.

2 **Chestnut.** Horse colour ranging from almost gold to deep reddish brown. Variations include sorrel, liver and light chestnut. An older, alternative spelling is 'chesnut'.

3 **Up to London.** Particularly at this time it was considered correct to speak about travelling 'up' to London even if, geographically, the journey would be 'down', say, from the North of England.

4 **Bearing rein.** Extra thin rein, with its own bit, attached to the pad or saddle of the harness (which encircles the horse's body) via a loop on the headpiece or throat-latch of the bridle. The bearing rein can be tightened at its attachment to the pad to force the horse's head higher. In American editions it was termed a 'check rein'. One of Anna Sewell's main campaigns and purposes in writing *Black Beauty* was to draw attention to the folly of using the restrictive but fashionable bearing rein, which made it impossible for the horse to put his head down to employ maximum pulling power. See pp. 63, 93, 96–9, 187, 199, 419–21.

5 **Coachman.** One who drives privately owned (as opposed to commercial) vehicles; the topmost rank of the hierarchy of stable servants.

6 **Park.** Hyde Park in London. This was the place to 'see and be seen', most notably in Rotten Row, where the fashionable hours were, for riding, the late morning and, for carriage driving, the afternoon.

Breaking tackle. The 'dumb jockey' on the horse's back was meant to imitate the hands of the rider. (Moseman's *Illustrated Guide for Purchasers of Horse Furnishing Goods*, p. 87)

fashionable places.   You who never had a bearing rein on, don't
know what it is, but I can tell you it is dreadful.

'I like to toss my head about, and hold it as high as any horse;
but fancy now yourself, if you tossed your head up high and were
obliged to hold it there, and that for hours together, not able to
move it at all, except with a jerk still higher, your neck aching
till you did not know how to bear it.   Beside that, to have two
bits instead of one; and mine was a sharp one, it hurt my tongue
and my jaw, and the blood from my tongue coloured the froth
that kept flying from my lips, as I chafed and fretted at the bits
and rein; it was worse when we had to stand by the hour waiting
for our mistress at some grand party or entertainment; and if I
fretted or stamped with impatience the whip was laid on.   It
was enough to drive one mad.'

'Did not your master take any thought for you?' I said.

'No,' said she, 'he only cared to have a stylish turn-out, as
they call it; I think he knew very little about horses, he left that
to his coachman, who told him I was an irritable temper; that
I had not been well broken to the bearing rein, but I should soon
get used to it; but *he* was not the man to do it, for when I was
in the stable, miserable and angry, instead of being soothed and
quieted by kindness, I got only a surly word or a blow.   If he
had been civil, I would have tried to bear it.   I was willing to
work, and ready to work hard too; but to be tormented for
nothing but their fancies angered me.   What right had they to
make me suffer like that?   Besides the soreness in my mouth
and the pain in my neck, it always made my windpipe feel bad,
and if I had stopped there long, I know it would have spoiled my
breathing; but I grew more and more restless and irritable, I
could not help it; and I began to snap and kick when any one
came to harness me; for this the groom beat me, and one day,

62

7 **Two bits.** The bearing rein's bit fitted above the bridle bit and was somewhat lighter and thinner. See p. 187.

8 **Sharp one.** Bits came in a wide variety of shapes and sizes. Generally speaking, the thicker and smoother the mouthpiece the milder the bit, but many bits had twisted mouthpieces so that, when made into a twist, the corners of the metal bar could, in the wrong hands, inflict severe pain on the horse's mouth.

9 **Spoiled my breathing.** By keeping the head up, a tight bearing rein obviously caused great discomfort. When expected to pull a load, a horse wearing a bearing rein would no doubt grunt and strain under the discomfort. Whether the bearing rein actually interfered with the horse's breathing so as to cause permanent respiratory damage was a topic of discussion. In a letter to *The Times* in 1867, Professor Pritchard of the Royal Veterinary College said that the bearing rein caused 'distortion of the windpipe to such a degree as to impede the respiration ever afterward'. James Irving Lupton, in *Horses: Sound and Unsound* (1893), believed that the use of the bearing rein caused the horse to become a 'roarer' (laryngeal hemiplegia, or paralysis of the larynx caused by degeneration of the nerve). He wrote: 'The bearing-rein is an instrument of torture which the fashionable world contemplates with delight; but it does so, it is hoped, in ignorance. In nineteen cases out of twenty roaring is a preventible disease; the suppression of two-year-old racing, and the abolition of the bearing-rein, would soon reduce to a minimum cases of this formidable affection.'

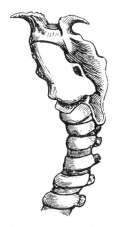

The trachea deformed: 'By the use of the bearing-rein the larynx is forced out of place, and the weight of the head is brought in violent contact with it; the action of the part is destroyed, and muscles of important use are denied their functions... and the horse becomes a confirmed roarer.' (James Irvine Lupton, *Horses: Sound and Unsound*, London: Ballière, 1893, p. 184)

'It hurt my tongue and my jaw, and the blood from my tongue coloured the froth'. Illustrated by G. Vernon Stokes and Alan Wright. (*Black Beauty*, London: Jarrold & Sons, 190?, pl. opp. p. 50)

as they had just buckled us into the carriage, and were straining my head up with that rein, I began to plunge and kick with all my might. I soon broke a lot of harness, and kicked myself clear; so that was an end of that place.

10
11 'After this, I was sent to Tattersall's to be sold; of course I could not be warranted free from vice, so nothing was said about that. My handsome appearance and good paces soon brought a gentleman to bid for me, and I was bought by another dealer; he tried me in all kinds of ways and with different bits, and soon found out what I could bear. At last he drove me quite without a bearing rein, and then sold me as a perfectly quiet horse to a gentleman in the country; he was a good master, and I was getting on very well, but his old groom left him and a new one came. This man was as hard-tempered and hard-handed as Samson; he always spoke in a rough, impatient voice, and if I did not move in the stall the moment he wanted me, he would
12 hit me above the hocks with his stable broom or the fork, which-ever he might have in his hand. Everything he did was rough, and I began to hate him; he wanted to make me afraid of him but I was too high-mettled for that; and one day when he had aggravated me more than usual, I bit him, which of course put him in a great rage, and he began to hit me about the head with a riding whip. After that, he never dared to come into my stall again, either my heels or my teeth were ready for him, and he knew it. I was quite quiet with my master, but of course he listened to what the man said, and so I was sold again.

'The same dealer heard of me, and said he thought he knew one place where I should do well. "''Twas a pity," he said, "that such a fine horse should go to the bad, for want of a real good chance," and the end of it was that I came here not long before you did; but I had then made up my mind, that men were

64

10 **Tattersall's.** London repository in Knightsbridge for the sale of high-class riding and carriage horses; this closed in 1939 but sales of Thoroughbreds and bloodstock for the racing world moved to Newmarket in Suffolk. Other London salerooms in Black Beauty's time, such as Aldridges and the Elephant and Castle, specialised in draught horses.

11 **Warranted free from vice.** A guarantee from the seller that the horse had none of the recognised equine vices, e.g. kicking, biting, rearing, bolting, shying, crib biting, windsucking, weaving.

12 **Fork.** Stable forks were usually two-pronged pitch forks designed for handling hay and straw.

A sale at Tattersall's. (Gustav Doré and Blanchard Jerrold, *London: A Pilgrimage*, London: Grants, 1872; David & Charles reprints, 1971, pl. opp. p. 66)

my natural enemies, and that I must defend myself. Of course it is very different here, but who knows how long it will last? I wish I could think about things as you do; but I can't after all I have gone through.'

'Well,' I said, 'I think it would be a real shame if you were to bite or kick John or James.'

'I don't mean to,' she said, 'while they are good to me. I did bite James once pretty sharp, but John said, "Try her with kindness," and instead of punishing me as I expected, James came to me with his arm bound up, and brought me a bran mash and stroked me; and I have never snapped at him since, and I won't either.'

I was sorry for Ginger, but of course I knew very little then, and I thought most likely she made the worst of it; however, I found that as the weeks went on, she grew much more gentle and cheerful, and had lost the watchful, defiant look that she used to turn on any strange person who came near her; and one day James said, 'I do believe that mare is getting fond of me, she quite whinnied after me this morning when I had been rubbing her forehead.'

13 'Aye, aye, Jim, 'tis the Birtwick balls,' said John, 'she 'll be as good as Black Beauty by and by; kindness is all the physic she wants, poor thing!' Master noticed the change too, and one day when he got out of the carriage and came to speak to us as he often did, he stroked her beautiful neck, 'Well, my pretty one, well, how do things go with you now? you are a good bit happier than when you came to us, I think.'

She put her nose up to him in a friendly, trustful way, while he rubbed it gently.

'We shall make a cure of her, John,' he said.

'Yes, sir, she 's wonderfully improved, she 's not the same

13 **Birtwick balls.** The only methods of administering medicine internally to a horse were by 'drenches', dry powder or liquid in the food, or solid 'balls', although the latter were often cylindrical in shape, about two inches long and three-quarters of an inch in diameter. They were often administered by a balling gun – a long, tube-like appliance, one end of which was thrust to the back of the horse's throat while the groom pressed a plunger to propel the ball down the horse's throat. Alternatively, a more primitive version involved the groom blowing down the tube of the balling gun. This gave rise to the many music hall jokes about the groom swallowing the ball – the horse having blown first! Other methods included holding the horse's tongue and pushing the ball to the back of the throat, or the use of a balling iron to keep the mouth open while the ball was placed inside.

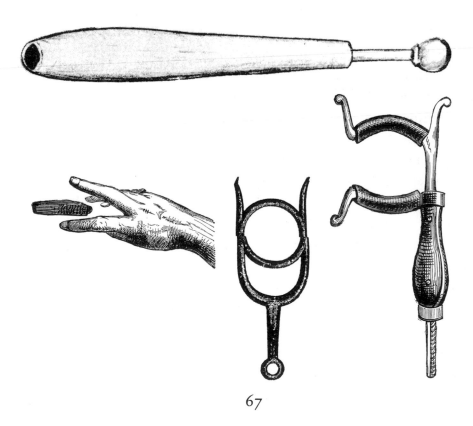

Ways and means of administering a horse ball: (*top*) a balling gun (Arthur Ingram, *The Country Animal Doctor*, Shire Album 40, Aylesbury: Shire Publications, 1979, p. 12); (*right*) a balling iron designed to open the horse's mouth (Mayhew, *The Illustrated Horse Management*, p. 54); (*centre*) an ordinary balling iron (Moseman's *Illustrated Guide for Purchasers of Horse Furnishing Goods*, p. 69); (*left*) how to hold a ball when delivering it manually (Mayhew, *The Illustrated Horse Management*, p. 58)

creature that she was; it 's the Birtwick balls, sir,' said John, laughing.

This was a little joke of John's; he used to say that a regular course of the Birtwick horse-balls would cure almost any vicious horse; these balls, he said, were made up of patience and gentleness, firmness and petting, one pound of each to be mixed up with half a pint of common sense, and given to the horse every day.

Holding the horse's tongue in the 'usual manner of giving a ball'. (Mayhew, *The Illustrated Horse Management*, p. 55)

Administering a ball. (Mayhew, *The Illustrated Horse Management*, p. 60)

CHAPTER IX

MERRYLEGS

MR. BLOMEFIELD, the Vicar, had a large family of boys and girls; sometimes they used to come and play with Miss Jessie and Flora. One of the girls was as old as Miss Jessie; two of the boys were older, and there were several little ones. When they came, there was plenty of work for Merrylegs, for nothing pleased them so much as getting on him by turns and riding him all about the orchard and the home paddock, and this they would do by the hour together.

One afternoon he had been out with them a long time, and when James brought him in and put on his halter, he said:

'There, you rogue, mind how you behave yourself, or we shall get into trouble.'

'What have you been doing, Merrylegs?' I asked.

'Oh!' said he, tossing his little head, 'I have only been giving those young people a lesson, they did not know when they had had enough, nor when I had had enough, so I just pitched

70

'I just pitched them off backwards'. Illustrated by Percy F. Spence. (*Black Beauty*, London: A. & C. Black, 1959, p. 40)

them off backwards, that was the only thing they could understand.'

'What?' said I, 'you threw the children off? I thought you did know better than that! Did you throw Miss Jessie or Miss Flora?'

He looked very much offended, and said:

'Of course not, I would not do such a thing for the best oats that ever came into the stable; why, I am as careful of our young ladies as the master could be, and as for the little ones, it is I who teach them to ride. When they seem frightened or a little unsteady on my back, I go as smooth and as quiet as old pussy when she is after a bird; and when they are all right, I go on again faster, you see, just to use them to it; so don't you trouble yourself preaching to me; I am the best friend and the best riding master those children have. It is not them, it is the boys; boys,' said he, shaking his mane, 'are quite different; they must be broken in, as we were broken in when we were colts, and just be taught what 's what. The older children had ridden me about for nearly two hours, and then the boys thought it was their turn, and so it was, and I was quite agreeable. They rode me by turns, and I galloped them about up and down the fields and all about the orchard for a good hour. They had each cut a great hazel stick for a riding whip, and laid it on a little too hard; but I took it in good part, till at last I thought we had had enough, so I stopped two or three times by way of a hint. Boys, you see, think a horse or pony is like a steam engine or a thrashing machine, and can go on as long and as fast as they please; they never think that a pony can get tired, or have any feelings; so as the one who was whipping me could not understand, I just rose up on my hind legs and let him slip off behind—that was all; he mounted me again, and I did the same. Then the other

1 **Hazel**. This tree's twigs and branches have a springy quality and are therefore ideal for whips. Hazel switches are used as whips at the Spanish Riding School in Vienna to this day.

2 **Steam engine**. Steam locomotives had been used since the early nineteenth century for industrial purposes, but by the mid-century, and certainly by Black Beauty's time (1877), the steam engine was a common sight and the passenger rail network had killed off stagecoaches in all but the most rural areas.

3 **Thrashing machine**. This too would have been steam-powered, built to separate the grains of wheat from the straw by threshing (or thrashing) the ears, a laborious process which had originally been done by hand with flails and later by animal- (usually horse-) powered machinery.

Steam engine and thrashing machine, in use in north Berkshire about 1900. (University of Reading, Institute of Agricultural History and Museum of English Rural Life, Nalder Collection)

boy got up, and as soon as he began to use his stick I laid him on the grass, and so on, till they were able to understand, that was all. They are not bad boys; they don't wish to be cruel. I like them very well; but you see I had to give them a lesson. When they brought me to James and told him, I think he was very angry to see such big sticks. He said they were only fit for drovers or gipsies, and not for young gentlemen.'

4, 5

'If I had been you,' said Ginger, 'I would have given those boys a good kick, and that would have given them a lesson.'

'No doubt you would,' said Merrylegs, 'but then I am not quite such a fool (begging your pardon) as to anger our master or make James ashamed of me; besides, those children are under my charge when they are riding; I tell you they are entrusted to me. Why, only the other day I heard our master say to Mrs. Blomefield, ''My dear madam, you need not be anxious about the children, my old Merrylegs will take as much care of them as you or I could: I assure you I would not sell that pony for any money, he is so perfectly good-tempered and trustworthy''; and do you think I am such an ungrateful brute as to forget all the kind treatment I have had here for five years, and all the trust they place in me, and turn vicious because a couple of ignorant boys used me badly? No! no! you never had a good place where they were kind to you; and so you don't know, and I 'm sorry for you, but I can tell you good places make good horses. I wouldn't vex our people for anything; I love them, I do,' said Merrylegs, and he gave a low 'ho, ho, ho,' through his nose, as he used to do in the morning when he heard James's footstep at the door.

'Besides,' he went on, 'if I took to kicking, where should I be? Why, sold off in a jiffy, and no character, and I might find

6

4 Drovers. Men who drove cattle, sheep and even geese to market along the public highway or specially developed grassy 'drove' roads or lanes from rural areas where the animals had been bred and fattened. Drovers generally had a reputation for being a fairly rough crowd.

5 Gipsies. Many 'gipsies' were often not true Romanies but tinkers, petty thieves and crooks. Consequently, all travelling folk were labelled 'gipsies' and were often not well received by the local population.

6 Character. Reference or testimonial from employer – usually given to a servant rather than a horse!

'I laid him on the grass'. Illustrated by G. Vernon Stokes and Alan Wright. (*Black Beauty*, London: Jarrold & Sons, 190?, p. 57)

7 myself slaved about under a butcher's boy, or worked to death
8 at some seaside place where no one cared for me, except to find
out how fast I could go, or be flogged alone in some cart with
three or four great men in it going out for a Sunday spree, as
I have often seen in the place I lived in before I came here; no,'
said he, shaking his head, 'I hope I shall never come to that.'

7 **Butcher's boy**. Because of the perishable nature of the goods butchers' boys often had to drive fast to get the meat to the customer before it went bad. Hence they gained a reputation for fast and furious driving. See pp. 369–72.

8 **Seaside place**. By the mid-nineteenth century many working-class people could afford to visit the seaside for a day, thanks to the cheap third-class fares on the railways. Apart from the attractions of the sea and sand, other amusements quickly sprang up including donkey rides on the beach and carriage rides along the promenade for those who were not 'carriage folk'. It was during this period that such popular resorts as Margate, Blackpool, Scarborough, Southend, Weston-Super-Mare and Weymouth became established.

The butcher's cart from the Bristol Wagon and Carriage Works catalogue, 1894. (Reproduced in *Horse-Drawn Trade Vehicles*, compiled by John Thompson, Fleet, Hampshire, 1980, p. 21)

77

CHAPTER X

A TALK IN THE ORCHARD

GINGER and I were not of the regular tall carriage horse breed, we had more of the racing blood in us. We stood about fifteen and a half hands high; we were therefore just as good for riding as we were for driving, and our master used to say that he disliked either horse or man that could do but one thing; and as he did not want to show off in London parks, he preferred a more active and useful kind of horse. As for us, our greatest pleasure was when we were saddled for a riding party; the master on Ginger, the mistress on me, and the young ladies on Sir Oliver and Merrylegs. It

ANNOTATIONS

1   **Carriage horse breed**. Not really a unique breed, although the Cleveland Bay, the Yorkshire Coach and the Hackney horse were the main British carriage horses of the time. Breeds imported from the Continent included Flemish, Hanoverian and Gelderlander, but most carriage horses were crossbreds of the right conformation, style, height and paces to make them imposing and elegant for private carriage work.

2   **Racing blood**. Thoroughbred blood, i.e. a horse whose ancestors can be traced back to the three Arabian and Barb stallions imported into England in the seventeenth and eighteenth centuries: the Byerley Turk, Godolphin Arabian and Darley Arabian.

3   **Fifteen and a half hands high**. The height of a horse is measured from the ground to the highest point of the withers. A hand is four inches and therefore 15.2 hh, as it is styled, would be a good average height for a ride and drive horse.

A typical nineteenth-century carriage horse. (Sidney, *Book of the Horse*, London: Cassell, 1874, p. 209)

was so cheerful to be trotting and cantering all together, that it always put us in high spirits. I had the best of it, for I always carried the mistress; her weight was little, her voice was sweet, and her hand was so light on the rein, that I was guided almost without feeling it.

Oh! if people knew what a comfort to horses a light hand is, and how it keeps a good mouth and a good temper, they surely would not chuck, and drag, and pull at the rein as they often do. Our mouths are so tender, that where they have not been spoiled or hardened with bad or ignorant treatment, they feel the slightest movement of the driver's hand, and we know in an instant what is required of us. My mouth had never been spoiled, and I believe that was why the mistress preferred me to Ginger, although her paces were certainly quite as good. She used often to envy me, and said it was all the fault of breaking in, and the gag bit in London, that her mouth was not so perfect as mine; and then old Sir Oliver would say, 'There, there! don't vex yourself; you have the greatest honour; a mare that can carry a tall man of our master's weight, with all your spring and sprightly action, does not need to hold her head down because she does not carry the lady; we horses must take things as they come, and always be contented and willing so long as we are kindly used.'

I had often wondered how it was, that Sir Oliver had such a very short tail; it really was only six or seven inches long, with a tassel of hair hanging from it; and on one of our holidays in the orchard I ventured to ask him by what accident it was that he had lost his tail. 'Accident!' he snorted with a fierce look, 'it was no accident! it was a cruel, shameful, cold-blooded act! When I was young I was taken to a place where these cruel things were done; I was tied up, and made fast so that I could

4 **Gag bit.** One where the rein from the rider's hand (or from the pad if the horse is in harness) threads through holes in the ring of the bit and goes over the top of the horse's head (poll) behind the ears. It has a strong pull and raises the bit in the mouth at the same time as exerting a downward pressure on the poll. See p. 187.

5 **Very short tail.** Docking, or cutting off the tail bone so that the hairs of the tail cannot grow long, was *de rigeur* for almost all horses, solely, as Sir Oliver explains, because of the dictates of fashion, although some people claimed that it was a safety measure to prevent the reins becoming caught under the tail when the horse was being driven. In practice this rarely happens. Docking was made illegal in Britain in 1949.

'Trotting and cantering all together'. Illustrated by Frank R. Grey. (*Black Beauty*, London: Collins, 1953, p. 57)

not stir, and then they came and cut off my long beautiful tail, through the flesh, and through the bone, and took it away.'

'How dreadful!' I exclaimed.

'Dreadful! ah! it was dreadful; but it was not only the pain, though that was terrible and lasted a long time; it was not only the indignity of having my best ornament taken from me, though that was bad; but it was this, how could I ever brush the flies off my sides and my hind legs any more? You who have tails just whisk the flies off without thinking about it, and you can't tell what a torment it is to have them settle upon you and sting and sting, and have nothing in the world to lash them off with. I tell you it is a life-long wrong, and a life-long loss; but thank Heaven! they don't do it now.'

'What did they do it for then?' said Ginger.

'For fashion!' said the old horse with a stamp of his foot; 'for fashion! if you know what that means; there was not a well-bred young horse in my time that had not his tail docked in that shameful way, just as if the good God that made us did not know what we wanted and what looked best.'

'I suppose it is fashion that makes them strap our heads up with those horrid bits that I was tortured with in London,' said Ginger.

'Of course it is,' said he; 'to my mind, fashion is one of the wickedest things in the world. Now look, for instance, at the way they serve dogs, cutting off their tails to make them look plucky, and shearing up their pretty little ears to a point to make them look sharp, forsooth. I had a dear friend once, a brown terrier—'Skye,' they called her; she was so fond of me that she never would sleep out of my stall; she made her bed under the manger, and there she had a litter of five as pretty little puppies

6 **Pretty little ears to a point**. Once again, for the sake of fashion, various breeds of dog were mutilated; those with cropped ears were intended to look alert, e.g. Great Danes, Boxers and some terriers. It began to go out of fashion in 1895 when the Kennel Club prohibited dogs with cropped ears being eligible to be shown under Kennel Club rules. Ear cropping is now illegal in Britain, although certain breeds of dog still have their tails docked. In the eighteenth century horses' ears were also cropped to make them fashionably small. It is said that this practice originated in the cavalry to prevent the normal-sized ears being accidentally sliced off during mounted sabre drill!

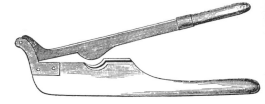

Tools for use in docking: (*top*) a docking knife; the tail bone was laid in the groove and the knife brought down forcibly so that the end of the bone was removed in one chop (J. H. Walsh, *The Horse in the Stable and the Field*, London: Routledge, 1861, p. 580); (*left*) the cauterising iron for searing the arteries at the end of the tail (Arthur Ingram, *The Country Animal Doctor*, Shire Album 40, Aylesbury: Shire Publications, 1979, p. 12)

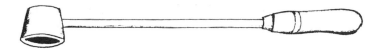

A coach horse from about 1780, with docked tail and cropped ears. (Sidney, *Book of the Horse*, p. 252)

83

7 as need be; none were drowned, for they were a valuable kind,
and how pleased she was with them! and when they got their
eyes open and crawled about, it was a real pretty sight, but one
day the man came and took them all away; I thought he might
be afraid I should tread upon them. But it was not so; in the
evening poor Skye brought them back again, one by one in her
mouth; not the happy little things that they were, but bleeding
and crying pitifully; they had all had a piece of their tails cut off,
and the soft flap of their pretty little ears was cut quite off. How
their mother licked them, and how troubled she was, poor thing!
I never forgot it. They healed in time, and they forgot the pain,
but the nice soft flap that of course was intended to protect the
delicate part of their ears from dust and injury, was gone for
ever. Why don't they cut their own children's ears into points
to make them look sharp? why don't they cut the end off their
noses to make them look plucky? One would be just as sensible
as the other. What right have they to torment and disfigure
God's creatures?'

Sir Oliver, though he was so gentle, was a fiery old fellow, and
what he said was all so new to me and so dreadful, that I found
a bitter feeling toward men rise up in my mind that I had never
had before. Of course Ginger was much excited; she flung up
her head with flashing eyes, and distended nostrils, declaring that
men were both brutes and blockheads.

'Who talks about blockheads?' said Merrylegs, who just came
up from the old apple tree, where he had been rubbing himself
against the low branch; 'who talks about blockheads? I believe
that is a bad word.'

'Bad words were made for bad things,' said Ginger, and she
told him what Sir Oliver had said. 'It is all true,' said Merrylegs
sadly, 'and I've seen that about the dogs over and over again

7 Drowned. In the late nineteenth century it was not the standard practice to neuter or spay pet animals, so the usual fate of unwanted offspring was drowning at birth.

'A talk in the orchard'. Illustrator unacknowledged in the book, although the illustration is signed. (*Black Beauty*, 48th edn. London: Jarrold & Sons, 1899, plate opp. p. 50)

85

where I lived first; but we won't talk about it here. You know that master, and John, and James are always good to us, and talking against men in such a place as this doesn't seem fair or grateful, and you know there are good masters and good grooms besides ours, though of course ours are the best.' This wise speech of good little Merrylegs, which we knew was quite true, cooled us all down, specially Sir Oliver, who was dearly fond of his master; and to turn the subject I said, 'Can any one tell me the use of blinkers?'

'No!' said Sir Oliver, shortly, 'because they are no use.'

'They are supposed,' said Justice in his calm way, 'to prevent horses from shying and starting and getting so frightened as to cause accidents.'

'Then what is the reason they do not put them on riding horses; especially on ladies' horses?' said I.

'There is no reason at all,' said he quietly, 'except the fashion; they say that a horse would be so frightened to see the wheels of his own cart or carriage coming behind him, that he would be sure to run away, although of course when he is ridden, he sees them all about him if the streets are crowded. I admit they do sometimes come too close to be pleasant, but we don't run away; we are used to it, and understand it, and if we had never blinkers put on, we should never want them; we should see what was there, and know what was what, and be much less frightened than by only seeing bits of things, that we can't understand.'

Of course there may be some nervous horses who have been hurt or frightened when they were young, and may be the better for them, but as I never was nervous, I can't judge.

'I consider,' said Sir Oliver, 'that blinkers are dangerous things in the night; we horses can see much better in the dark than man can, and many an accident would never have happened

PLATE 12
Black Beauty is named by Mrs Gordon at Birtwick Park. Illustration by Susan Jeffers for Robin McKinley's adaptation, published by Random House (New York) in 1986.

PLATE 13
Black Beauty at Birtwick Park. Stylised, but fully sympathetic and artistic illustrations were contributed by Fritz Eichenberg for the 1945 Grosset & Dunlap (New York) 'Illustrated Junior Library' version.

8 No reason at all. Although the army abandoned blinkers for its draught horses in the late nineteenth century, civilian harness horses usually wore them. Occasionally horses working in agriculture are worked in 'open bridles' (no blinkers) and appear to suffer no ill effects. Virtually all horses used in driving today are driven in bridles with blinkers and drivers are warned not to take off the bridle before the horse has been unharnessed, as accidents have resulted from the horse taking fright at the sight of the vehicle 'following' him which he has never seen. It would appear that blinkers are a tradition and, as Justice says, if a horse is trained in an open bridle from the start he will not necessarily be prone to shying at vehicles coming from behind or attempt to run away from the vehicle he is pulling assuming that he is being chased. Blinkers used in racing are apparently useful to a minority of horses in directing their attention to the front; whether they are afraid of the horses following them or merely distracted by sights around them is difficult to know, but evidently wearing blinkers on these occasions does have the desired result. See pp. 21, 89.

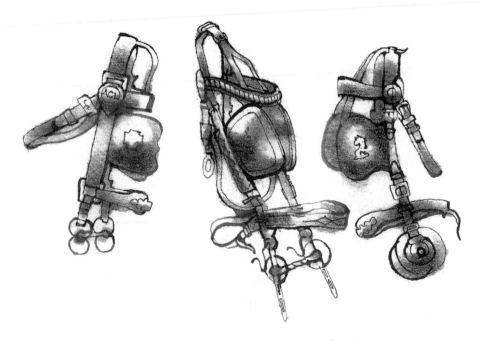

Bridles with blinkers, Illustrated by Charles Keeping. (*Black Beauty*, London: Victor Gollancz, 1988, p. 48)

87

if horses might have had the full use of their eyes. Some years ago, I remember, there was a hearse with two horses returning one dark night, and just by Farmer Sparrow's house, where the pond is close to the road, the wheels went too near the edge, and the hearse was overturned into the water; both the horses were drowned, and the driver hardly escaped. Of course after this accident a stout white rail was put up that might be easily seen, but if those horses had not been partly blinded, they would of themselves have kept farther from the edge, and no accident would have happened. When our master's carriage was over-turned, before you came here, it was said, that if the lamp on the left side had not gone out, John would have seen the great hole that the road makers had left; and so he might, but if old Colin had not had blinkers on, he would have seen it, lamp or no lamp, for he was far too knowing an old horse to run into danger. As it was, he was very much hurt, the carriage was broken, and how John escaped nobody knew.'

'I should say,' said Ginger, curling her nostril, 'that these men, who are so wise, had better give orders, that in future all foals should be born with their eyes set just in the middle of their foreheads, instead of on the side; they always think they can improve upon Nature and mend what God has made.'

Things were getting rather sore again, when Merrylegs held up his knowing little face and said, 'I'll tell you a secret; I believe John does not approve of blinkers; I heard him talking with master about it one day. The master said, that "if horses had been used to them, it might be dangerous in some cases to leave them off," and John said he thought it would be a good thing if all colts were broken in without blinkers, as was the case in some foreign countries; so let us cheer up, and have a run to the other end of the orchard; I believe the wind has blown

9 **Their eyes set just in the middle of their foreheads.** As the horse is a grazing animal and in the wild is prey to carnivorous attackers, it has to be able to see as much as possible around it, even while grazing, so that it is not crept up on from behind. Thus the horse's eyes are set in the sides of its head so that it has almost all-round vision.

10 **John does not approve of blinkers.** Neither did George Fleming, MRCVS, who wrote in his *Practical Horse Keeper* (1886): 'The advantage of *blinkers* is very questionable. There can be no doubt whatever that fashion and custom alone sanction their use. Horses can be utilised better without than with them, and all horses should be trained to harness without them. They are not worn on harness horses in the army, and in civil life hundreds of horses are worked without them. They make the bridles heavier and more expensive, require more cleaning, cause the horse's head to be hotter, injure the eyes, and are certainly unsightly to anyone who admires the noble animal. Blinkers ought to be abolished.' Fleming did, however, approve of the use of the bearing rein in certain circumstances.

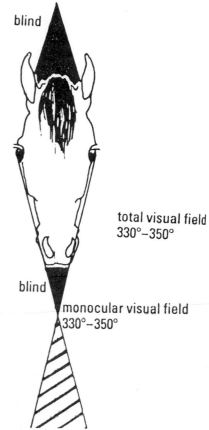

blind

total visual field
330°–350°

blind

monocular visual field
330°–350°

binocular visual field
30°–70°

The visual field of the horse. (Marthe Kiley-Worthington, *The Behaviour of Horses*, London: J. A. Allen, 1987, p. 32)

'John does not approve of blinkers'. Illustrated by Charles Keeping. (*Black Beauty*, London: Victor Gollancz, 1988, p. 39)

89

down some apples, and we might just as well eat them as the slugs.'

Merrylegs could not be resisted, so we broke off our long conversation, and got up our spirits by munching some very sweet apples which lay scattered on the grass.

'The wind has blown down some apples'.
Illustrated by Michael Rios. (*Black Beauty*,
New York: Modern Promotions, 1979, p. 40)

CHAPTER XI

PLAIN SPEAKING

THE longer I lived at Birtwick, the more proud and happy I felt at having such a place. Our master and mistress were respected and beloved by all who knew them; they were good and kind to everybody and everything; not only men and women, but horses and donkeys, dogs and cats, cattle and birds; there was no oppressed or ill-used creature that had not a friend in them, and their servants took the same tone. If any of the village children were known to treat any creature cruelly, they soon heard about it from the Hall.

The Squire and Farmer Grey had worked together, as they said, for more than twenty years, to get bearing reins on the cart-horses done away with, and in our parts you seldom saw them; but sometimes if mistress met a heavily laden horse, with his

92

1 **Bearing reins on the cart-horses**. Some advocates of the bearing rein agreed that they should not be used on cart horses. Thus George Fleming (*Practical Horse Keeper*, 1886) recommended the use of the bearing rein 'to relieve the strain on the driver's hands when the horse is impetuous through high feeding and insufficient work, knocks his head about, and is inclined to be fidgety and unmanageable'. Instructing that the bearing rein should be adjusted so as to be slack when trotting, he believed that 'Such a bearing-rein, so far from being an inconvenience or torment to the horse, if high-spirited will prove of assistance, and will certainly help the driver in averting accidents.' However, he added categorically: 'Horses doing hard work do not require bearing-reins; for heavy draught horses they should never be employed, as they hinder them in working properly, and are of no advantage whatever.'

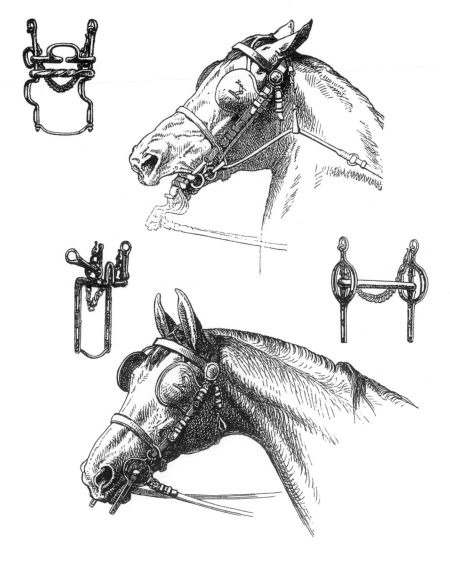

The bearing rein: 'the horse in torture' and 'the horse at ease'. The fitting of the bearing rein bit can be seen, and the difference between the narrow and twisted mouthpieces with sharp edges and the thicker, smoother one is evident. (Sidney, *Book of the Horse*, p. 361)

head strained up, she would stop the carriage and get out, and reason with the driver in her sweet serious voice, and try to show him how foolish and cruel it was.

I don't think any man could withstand our mistress. I wish all ladies were like her. Our master too used to come down very heavy sometimes. I remember he was riding me towards home one morning, when we saw a powerful man driving towards us in a light pony chaise, with a beautiful little bay pony, with slender legs, and a high-bred sensitive head and face. Just as he came to the Park gates, the little thing turned towards them; the man, without word or warning, wrenched the creature's head round with such a force and suddenness, that he nearly threw it on its haunches: recovering itself, it was going on when he began to lash it furiously; the pony plunged forward, but the strong heavy hand held the pretty creature back with force almost enough to break its jaw, whilst the whip still cut into him. It was a dreadful sight to me, for I knew what fearful pain it gave that delicate little mouth; but master gave me the word, and we were up with him in a second.

'Sawyer,' he cried in a stern voice, 'is that pony made of flesh and blood?'

'Flesh and blood and temper,' he said; 'he's too fond of his own will, and that won't suit me.' He spoke as if he was in a strong passion; he was a builder who had often been to the Park on business. 'And do you think,' said master sternly, 'that treatment like this will make him fond of your will?'

'He had no business to make that turn: his road was straight on!' said the man roughly.

'You have often driven that pony up to my place,' said master; 'it only shows the creature's memory and intelligence; how did he know that you were not going there again? but that has little

2 **Bay**. Ranging from a warm, bright brown to deep mahogany for the main body colour, but the 'points', i.e. mane, tail and legs to the knee, are black.

'Is that pony made of flesh and blood?' Illustrated by John Beer. (*Black Beauty*, Boston: DeWolfe, Fiske & Co., 191?, p. 105)

to do with it. I must say, Mr. Sawyer, that more unmanly, brutal treatment of a little pony it was never my painful lot to witness; and by giving way to such passions you injure your own character as much, nay more, than you injure your horse, and remember, we shall all have to be judged according to our works, whether they be towards man or towards beast.'

Master rode me home slowly, and I could tell by his voice how the thing had grieved him. He was just as free to speak to gentlemen of his own rank as to those below him; for another day, when we were out, we met a Captain Langley, a friend of our master's; he was driving a splendid pair of greys in a kind of brake. After a little conversation the Captain said:

'What do you think of my new team, Mr. Douglas? you know you are the judge of horses in these parts, and I should like your opinion.'

The master backed me a little, so as to get a good view of them.

'They are an uncommonly handsome pair,' he said, 'and if they are as good as they look, I am sure you need not wish for anything better; but I see you get hold of that pet scheme of yours for worrying your horses and lessening their power.'

'What do you mean,' said the other, 'the bearing reins? Oh, ah! I know that's a hobby of yours; well, the fact is, I like to see my horses hold their heads up.'

'So do I,' said master, 'as well as any man, but I don't like to see them *held up*: that takes all the shine out of it. Now you are a military man, Langley, and no doubt like to see your regiment look well on parade, "Heads up," and all that; but you would not take much credit for your drill, if all your men had their heads tied to a backboard! It might not be much harm on parade, except to worry and fatigue them, but how would it be in a bayonet charge against the enemy, when they want the free use of every muscle, and all their strength thrown forward?

3 **Brake**. A four-wheeled vehicle which came into use in the 1860s, usually drawn by a pair or by four horses. It can be a variety of styles depending on its purpose, such as the skeleton brake, which was often fitted with extra long shafts and used for breaking a horse to harness, so that if the horse kicked its hooves would not come into contact with the front of the vehicle and inflict damage. The shooting brake was a sporting vehicle accommodating four passengers on seats at the back, and two on the high box seat. Dogs were carried in ventilated compartments under the driver's seat and the rear seats. The wagonette brake was a general purpose vehicle accommodating several people on informal country outings such as picnics. Sometimes an awning was fixed to protect passengers from the sun. Other designs included the roof seat brake, built-up brake and body brake.

4 **Hold their heads up**. The most frequent argument in favour of the bearing rein at the time was on the grounds of safety. Thus E. Gough, who described himself on the cover of his book *Centaur: or the Turn Out* (1878) as 'a Member of the RSPCA', stated: 'That there are times and circumstances which demand to the harness the application of the bearing rein for the general safety of the "Turn Out" there can be no doubt or legitimate question raised. The fact is well-known that it should not be (and the author believes it is not) as a rule attached for appearance sake only, as some arguers would have it understood.' However, he called for discretion in the application of the rein, and warned that it should always be slackened when going uphill. Like Black Beauty's master, Gough also uses a military example for his argument, but to the opposite purpose: 'A friend's simile in conversation respecting the use and abuse of the bearing rein was, that with restive and over-fresh horses it held much the same position as a drill-sergeant to the raw recruit.' His final word on the subject is that if 'the animal is a very hard and excitable puller, or stumbles and throws its head about as though having business on both sides of the road at one time, then the bearing rein cannot, and must not be dispensed with.'

Brake. (Quadekker, *Het Paardenboek*, Part III, p. 137)

would not give much for their chance of victory, and it is just the same with horses; you fret and worry their tempers, and decrease their power; you will not let them throw their weight against their work, and so they have to do too much with their joints and muscles, and of course it wears them up faster. You may depend upon it, horses were intended to have their heads free, as free as men's are; and if we could act a little more according to common sense, and a good deal less according to fashion, we should find many things work easier; besides, you know as well as I, that if a horse makes a false step, he has much less chance of recovering himself if his head and neck are fastened back. And now,' said the master, laughing, 'I have given my hobby a good trot out, can't you make up your mind to mount him too, Captain? your example would go a long way.'

'I believe you are right in theory,' said the other, 'and that 's rather a hard hit about the soldiers, but—well—I 'll think about it,' and so they parted.

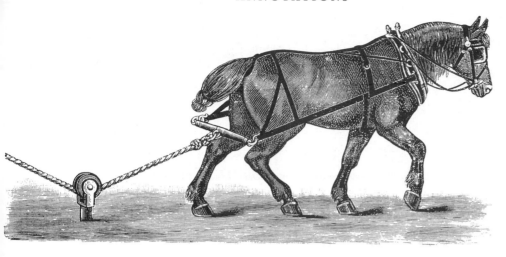

Cart horses working without bearing reins, able to throw their weight into their work: (*top*) Moseman's *Illustrated Guide for Purchasers of Horse Furnishing Goods*, p. 117; (*bottom*) Sidney, *Book of the Horse*, p. 119.

CHAPTER XII

A STORMY DAY

1 ONE day late in the autumn, my master had a long journey to go on business. I was put into the dog-cart, and John went with his master. I always liked to go in the dog-cart, it was so light, and the high wheels ran along so pleasantly. There had been a great deal of rain, and now the wind was very high, and blew the dry leaves across the road in a shower. We went along merrily

2 till we came to the toll-bar, and the low wooden bridge. The river banks were rather high, and the bridge, instead of rising, went across just level, so that in the middle, if the river was full, the water would be nearly up to the woodwork and planks; but as there were good substantial rails on each side, people did not mind it.

The man at the gate said the river was rising fast, and he feared it would be a bad night. Many of the meadows were under water, and in one low part of the road the water was half-way up to my knees; the bottom was good, and master drove gently, so it was no matter.

1 **Dog-cart**. Two- or four-wheeled vehicle originally designed for taking dogs to a shoot or greyhounds and lurchers to a race or coursing meeting. It had slatted or louvred sides to allow ventilation in the compartment under the seat where the dogs were kept.

2 **Toll-bar**. Bar or gate across a road or turnpike where a toll was required to be paid. The toll was collected by a toll-keeper who lived in an adjacent cottage. The toll usually depended upon the type or weight of vehicle – those with fashionable, narrow wheels did more damage to the road surface than wagons and carts with wider wheels, and hence were charged more. People and animals were charged individually.

The toll-bar and toll-keeper's cottage. Illustrated by John Beer. (*Black Beauty*, London: Jarrold & Sons, 1894, p. 58 (detail))

3   When we got to the town, of course, I had a good bait, but as the master's business engaged him a long time, we did not start for home till rather late in the afternoon.   The wind was then much higher, and I heard the master say to John, he had never been out in such a storm; and so I thought, as we went along the skirts of a wood, where the great branches were swaying about like twigs, and the rushing sound was terrible.

'I wish we were well out of this wood,' said my master.

'Yes, sir,' said John, 'it would be rather awkward if one of these branches came down upon us.'

The words were scarcely out of his mouth, when there was a groan, and a crack, and a splitting sound, and tearing crashing down amongst the other trees, came an oak, torn up by the roots, and it fell right across the road just before us.   I will never say I was not frightened, for I was.   I stopped still, and I believe I trembled; of course I did not turn round or run away; I was not brought up to that.   John jumped out and was in a moment at my head.

'That was a very near touch,' said my master.   'What 's to be done now?'

'Well, sir, we can't drive over that tree nor yet get round it; there will be nothing for it, but to go back to the four cross-ways, and that will be a good six miles before we get round to the wooden bridge again; it will make us late, but the horse is fresh.'

So back we went, and round by the cross-roads; but by the time we got to the bridge, it was very nearly dark, we could just see that the water was over the middle of it; but as that happened sometimes when the floods were out, master did not stop.   We were going along at a good pace, but the moment my
4   feet touched the first part of the bridge, I felt sure there was

3 **Bait**. Fodder or feed.

4 **I felt sure there was something wrong.** This ability to sense danger ahead is one of the horse's built-in survival mechanisms. Relying on being able to run fast from danger rather than staying to fight, the horse needs to ascertain that where he is about to run to is safe. The instinct is particularly strong in moorland ponies which rarely stray into bogs and become trapped.

'It fell right across the road just before us'. Illustrated by Tom Gill. (*Black Beauty*, Golden Picture Classics, New York: Simon & Schuster, 1956, p. 23)

'I felt sure there was something wrong'. Illustrated by Honor C. Appleton. (*Black Beauty*, London: Harrap, 1936, p. 27)

something wrong. I dare not go forward, and I made a dead stop. 'Go on, Beauty,' said my master, and he gave me a touch with the whip, but I dare not stir; he gave me a sharp cut, I jumped, but I dare not go forward.

'There 's something wrong, sir,' said John, and he sprang out of the dog-cart and came to my head and looked all about. He tried to lead me forward, 'Come on, Beauty, what 's the matter?' Of course I could not tell him, but I knew very well that the bridge was not safe.

Just then, the man at the toll-gate on the other side ran out of the house, tossing a torch about like one mad.

'Hoy, hoy, hoy, halloo, stop!' he cried.

'What 's the matter?' shouted my master.

'The bridge is broken in the middle and part of it is carried away; if you come on you 'll be into the river.'

'Thank God!' said my master. 'You Beauty!' said John, and took the bridle and gently turned me round to the right-hand road by the riverside. The sun had set some time, the wind seemed to have lulled off after that furious blast which tore up the tree. It grew darker and darker, stiller and stiller. I trotted quietly along, the wheels hardly making a sound on the soft road. For a good while neither master nor John spoke, and then master began in a serious voice. I could not understand much of what they said, but I found they thought, if I had gone on as the master wanted me, most likely the bridge would have given way under us, and horse, chaise, master, and man would have fallen into the river; and as the current was flowing very strongly, and there was no light and no help at hand, it was more than likely we should all have been drowned. Master said, God had given men reason, by which they could find out things for themselves, but He had given animals knowledge which did not depend on reason,

5 **Torch**. Possibly a lighted flare made from rags wrapped around a
stick and soaked in an inflammable liquid, or maybe simply an oil
lantern.

Dog-cart. (Sidney, *Book of the Horse*, p. 542)

and which was much more prompt and perfect in its way, and by which they had often saved the lives of men. John had many stories to tell of dogs and horses, and the wonderful things they had done; he thought people did not value their animals half enough, nor make friends of them as they ought to do. I am sure he makes friends of them if ever a man did.

At last we came to the Park gates, and found the gardener looking out for us. He said that mistress had been in a dreadful way ever since dark, fearing some accident had happened, and that she had sent James off on Justice, the roan cob, towards the wooden bridge to make inquiry after us.

We saw a light at the hall door and at the upper windows, and as we came up, mistress ran out, saying, 'Are you really safe, my dear? Oh! I have been so anxious, fancying all sorts of things. Have you had no accident?'

6 'No, my dear; but if your Black Beauty had not been wiser than we were, we should all have been carried down the river at the wooden bridge.' I heard no more, as they went into the house, and John took me to the stable. Oh! what a good supper 7 he gave me that night, a good bran mash and some crushed beans with my oats, and such a thick bed of straw, and I was glad of it, for I was tired.

6   **Wiser than we were.** According to her biographer, Susan Chitty, one of the horses in Anna Sewell's life, her brother's black mare Bessie, was attributed with much wisdom and foresight by the Sewell family, and it is possible that the event described here bore some resemblance to a real incident experienced by Bessie (*The Woman Who Wrote Black Beauty*, 1971).

7   **Crushed beans with my oats.** Beans are a protein food to give a horse energy, but lack the exciting and 'heating' effect of oats, which can act on a horse like alcohol on a human and, therefore, need to be fed with caution. Beans are not so popular today, having been largely replaced by manufactured concentrates such as cubes or 'nuts' containing a balanced mixture of proteins, minerals and so on.

Examples of beans of different qualities. (*Top*) good quality; (*bottom*) bad quality. (Mayhew, *The Illustrated Horse Management*, pp. 199–200)

CHAPTER XIII

THE DEVIL'S TRADE MARK

ONE day when John and I had been out on some business of our master's, and were returning gently on a long straight road, at some distance we saw a boy trying to leap a pony over a gate; the pony would not take the leap, and the boy cut him with the whip, but he only turned off on one side; he whipped him again, but the pony turned off on the other side. Then the boy got off and gave him a hard thrashing, and knocked him about the head; then he got up again and tried to make him leap the gate, kicking him all the time shamefully, but still the pony refused. When we were nearly at the spot, the pony put down his head and threw up his heels and sent the boy neatly over into a broad quickset hedge, and with the rein dangling from his head, he set off home at a full gallop. John laughed out quite loud. 'Served him right,' he said.

ANNOTATIONS

1 **Quickset hedge**. One made of striplings or specifically planted cuttings, often of hawthorn or other thorny or bushy shrub suitable for growing into a stock-proof hedge.

'Then the boy got off and gave him a hard thrashing'. Illustrated by Cecil Aldin. (*Black Beauty*, London: Jarrolds, 1912, p. 105)

'Oh! oh! oh!' cried the boy, as he struggled about amongst the thorns; 'I say, come and help me out.'

'Thank ye,' said John, 'I think you are quite in the right place, and maybe a little scratching will teach you not to leap a pony over a gate that is too high for him,' and so with that John rode off. 'It may be,' said he to himself, 'that young fellow is a liar as well as a cruel one; we'll just go home by Farmer Bushby's, Beauty, and then if anybody wants to know, you and I can tell 'em, ye see'; so we turned off to the right, and soon came up to the stack yard and within sight of the house. The farmer was hurrying out into the road, and his wife was standing at the gate, looking very frightened.

'Have you seen my boy?' said Mr. Bushby, as we came up, 'he went out an hour ago on my black pony, and the creature is just come back without a rider.'

'I should think, sir,' said John, 'he had better be without a rider, unless he can be ridden properly.'

'What do you mean?' said the farmer.

'Well, sir, I saw your son whipping, and kicking, and knocking that good little pony about shamefully because he would not leap a gate that was too high for him. The pony behaved well, sir, and showed no vice; but at last he just threw up his heels, and tipped the young gentleman into the thorn hedge: he wanted me to help him out; but I hope you will excuse me, sir, I did not feel inclined to do so. There's no bones broken, sir, he'll only get a few scratches. I love horses, and it roiles me to see them badly used; it is a bad plan to aggravate an animal till he uses his heels; the first time is not always the last.'

During this time the mother began to cry, 'Oh! my poor Bill, I must go and meet him, he must be hurt.'

'You had better go into the house, wife,' said the farmer;

2 **A gate that is too high for him**. Even the most willing jumper will stop when it knows that it cannot take a jump with safety. Nanny Power O'Donoghue wrote: 'Most riders ... seem to have a firmly rooted conviction that horses only refuse from vice, and consequently they form an idea that to whip it out of them will be the very best method of procedure that they can possibly adopt. A more ignorant theory could not by any possibility be acted upon' (*Riding for Ladies*, 1887).

3 **Roiles**. Riles.

'At last he just threw up his heels'. Illustrated by Frank Grey. (*Black Beauty*, London: Collins, 1953, p. 75)

'Bill wants a lesson about this, and I must see that he gets it; this is not the first time nor the second that he has ill-used that pony, and I shall stop it. I am much obliged to you, Manly. Good evening.'

So we went on, John chuckling all the way home, then he told James about it, who laughed and said, 'Serve him right. I knew that boy at school; he took great airs on himself because he was a farmer's son; he used to swagger about and bully the little boys; of course we elder ones would not have any of that nonsense, and let him know that in the school and the play-ground, farmers' sons and labourers' sons were all alike. I well remember one day, just before afternoon school, I found him at the large window catching flies and pulling off their wings. He did not see me, and I gave him a box on the ears that laid him sprawling on the floor. Well, angry as I was, I was almost frightened, he roared and bellowed in such a style. The boys rushed in from the playground, and the master ran in from the road to see who was being murdered. Of course I said fair and square at once what I had done, and why; then I showed the master the poor flies, some crushed and some crawling about helpless, and I showed him the wings on the window sill. I never saw him so angry before; but as Bill was still howling and whining, like the coward that he was, he did not give him any more punishment of that kind, but set him up on a stool for the rest of the afternoon, and said that he should not go out to play for that week. Then he talked to all the boys very seriously about cruelty, and said how hard-hearted and cowardly it was to hurt the weak and the helpless; but what stuck in my mind was this, he said that cruelty was the devil's own trade mark, and if we saw any one who took pleasure in cruelty, we might know who he belonged to, for the devil was a murderer from the beginning.

4 Because he was a farmer's son. In the hierarchy of the country-side, the status of the farmer depended upon whether he rented land to farm, in which case he was some way down the social scale, or whether he actually owned the land himself. The more land he owned the higher up he was, but however much he owned he would never be of the same social standing as the squirearchy or landed gentry, who formed the lower echelons of the aristocracy.

Plans for a Victorian village schoolhouse. (Design by William Butterfield published in 1852 in *Instrumenta Ecclesiastica* (second series), 1856)

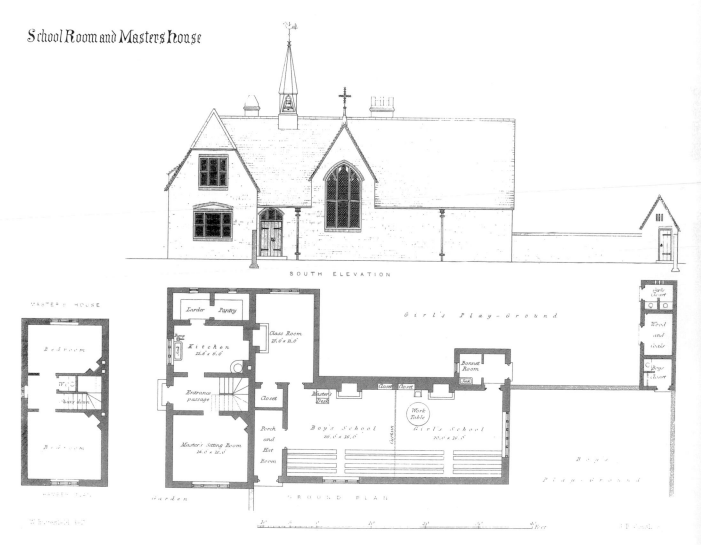

and a tormentor to the end.   On the other hand, where we saw people who loved their neighbours, and were kind to man and beast, we might know that was God's mark, for ''God is Love.'''

'Your master never taught you a truer thing,' said John; 'there is no religion without love, and people may talk as much as they like about their religion, but if it does not teach them to be good and kind to man and beast, it is all a sham—all a sham, James, and it won't stand when things come to be turned inside out and put down for what they are.'

Illustration of the boy in the hedge by Charles Keeping. (*Black Beauty*, London: Victor Gollancz, 1988, p. 57)

CHAPTER XIV

JAMES HOWARD

ONE morning early in December, John had just led me into my box after my daily exercise, and was strapping my cloth on, and James was coming in from the corn chamber with some oats, when the master came into the stable; he looked rather serious, and held an open letter in his hand. John fastened the door of my box, touched his cap, and waited for orders.

'Good morning, John,' said the master; 'I want to know if you have any complaint to make of James?'

'Complaint, sir? No, sir.'

'Is he industrious at his work and respectful to you?'

'Yes, sir, always.'

'You never find he slights his work when your back is turned?'

'Never, sir.'

'That's well; but I must put another question; have you any

1 **Cloth**. Probably a rug used for warmth in the winter, or a cotton sheet to prevent dust settling on a well-groomed coat.

2 **Corn chamber**. Feed room where oats, beans, barley, bran, maize etc. would be kept in large vermin-proof bins. Usually in the main stable building.

3 **Touched his cap**. Mark of respect for employer or to other of higher rank. A 'watered-down' version of raising or even sweeping off the hat.

A well-fitting rug for warmth. (Nanny Power O'Donoghue, *Riding for Ladies*, London: W. Thacker & Co., 1887, new edn 1905, p. 305)

reason to suspect that when he goes out with the horses to exercise them, or to take a message, he stops about talking to his acquaintances, or goes into houses where he has no business, leaving the horses outside?'

'No, sir, certainly not, and if anybody has been saying that about James, I don't believe it, and I don't mean to believe it unless I have it fairly proved before witnesses; it 's not for me to say who has been trying to take away James's character, but I will say this, sir, that a steadier, pleasanter, honester, smarter young fellow I never had in this stable. I can trust his word and I can trust his work; he is gentle and clever with the horses, and I would rather have them in his charge, than in that of half the young fellows I know in laced hats and liveries; and whoever wants a character of James Howard,' said John, with a decided jerk of his head, 'let them come to John Manly.'

The master stood all this time grave and attentive, but as John finished his speech, a broad smile spread over his face, and looking kindly across at James, who, all this time had stood still at the door, he said, 'James, my lad, set down the oats and come here; I am very glad to find that John's opinion of your character agrees so exactly with my own. John is a cautious man,' he said, with a droll smile, 'and it is not always easy to get his opinion about people, so I thought if I beat the bush on this side, the birds would fly out, and I should learn what I wanted to know quickly; so now we will come to business. I have a letter from my brother-in-law, Sir Clifford Williams, of Clifford Hall; he wants me to find him a trustworthy young groom, about twenty or twenty-one, who knows his business. His old coachman, who has lived with him twenty years, is getting feeble, and he wants a man to work with him and get into his ways, who would be able, when the old man was pensioned off, to step into his place.

4 Laced hats and liveries. Fancy uniform or livery in which stable servants and coachmen of the aristocracy were dressed.

Stable livery. (Sir Walter Gilbey, *The Harness Horse*, London: Vinton, 1905, pl. opp. p. 25 (detail))

119

He would have eighteen shillings a week at first, a stable suit, a driving suit, a bedroom over the coach-house, and a boy under him. Sir Clifford is a good master, and if you could get the place, it would be a good start for you. I don't want to part with you, and if you left us, I know John would lose his right hand.'

'That I should, sir,' said John, 'but I would not stand in his light for the world.'

'How old are you, James?' said master.

'Nineteen next May, sir.'

'That 's young; what do you think, John?'

'Well, sir, it is young: but he is as steady as a man, and is strong, and well grown, and though he has not had much experience in driving, he has a light firm hand, and a quick eye, and he is very careful, and I am quite sure no horse of his will be ruined for want of having his feet and shoes looked after.'

'Your word will go the furthest, John,' said the master, 'for Sir Clifford adds in a postscript, "If I could find a man trained by your John, I should like him better than any other"; so James, lad, think it over, talk to your mother at dinner-time, and then let me know what you wish.'

In a few days after this conversation, it was fully settled that James should go to Clifford Hall in a month or six weeks, as it suited his master, and in the meantime he was to get all the practice in driving that could be given to him. I never knew the carriage go out so often before: when the mistress did not go out, the master drove himself in the two-wheeled chaise; but now, whether it was master or the young ladies, or only an errand, Ginger and I were put into the carriage and James drove us. At the first, John rode with him on the box, telling him this and that, and after that James drove alone.

5 **Eighteen shillings**. There were 20 shillings in one pound sterling before Britain adopted decimal coinage in 1971. A wage of 18 shillings a week was good pay for a nineteenth-century coachman.

6 **A stable suit, a driving suit**. Working clothes – the first to be worn when working in the stables, and the second to be worn when in public driving the employers' horses, especially on formal occasions.

7 **Stand in his light**. Stand in his way, prevent him from making his way in the world or bettering himself.

8 **Box**. Originally, the box under the driver's seat on a coach, in which valuables were carried, but by the 1870s had come to mean the seat on which the coachman sits. It is designed to slope from the back to the front, giving the driver or whip maximum control through greater purchase and balance. If the seat is flat the knees are bent and the driver is in no position to control pulling horses. If the slope is too great the driver is almost standing and in danger of being pulled forward should the horse(s) take a strong hold.

The box seat on a coach. (Sidney, *Book of the Horse*, p. 373 (detail))

Then it was wonderful what a number of places the master would go to in the city on Saturday, and what queer streets we were driven through.   He was sure to go to the railway station just as the train was coming in, and cabs and carriages, carts and omnibuses were all trying to get over the bridge together; that bridge wanted good horses and good drivers when the railway 9 bell was ringing, for it was narrow, and there was a very sharp turn up to the station, where it would not have been at all difficult for people to run into each other, if they did not look sharp and keep their wits about them.

9 **Railway bell**. Warning bell sounded when a train was about to leave the station.

'What queer streets we were driven through'. Imaginative illustration by Tom Gill showing Black Beauty and Ginger attached to the wheels of the vehicle and driven without recourse to reins. Many illustrators of *Black Beauty* had scant regard for technical accuracy. (*Black Beauty*, Golden Picture Classics, New York: Simon & Schuster, 1956, p. 9)

CHAPTER XV

THE OLD OSTLER

AFTER this, it was decided by my master and mistress to pay a visit to some friends who lived about forty-six miles from our home, and James was to drive them. The first day we travelled thirty-two miles; there were some long heavy hills, but James drove so carefully and thoughtfully that we were not at all harassed. He never forgot to put on the drag as we went downhill, nor to take it off at the right place. He kept our feet on the smoothest part of the road, and if the uphill was very long, he set the carriage wheels a little across the road, so as not to run back, and gave us a breathing. All these little things help a horse very much, particularly if he gets kind words into the bargain.

We stopped once or twice on the road, and just as the sun was going down, we reached the town where we were to spend the

1 **Drag**. Brakeshoe – curved, U-shaped metal plate attached to the vehicle by a chain and placed under the wheel when descending a steep hill to prevent the wheels from turning and the vehicle gaining momentum and running into the horse. The friction of wheel, drag and road could create sparks and make the metal drag almost redhot. The advice given by C. Morley Knight (*Hints on Driving*, 1894) for coping with a steep hill was as follows: 'Always check the pace before reaching the crest of a hill which you are about to descend, as when once on the downward slope this may not be possible, whereas to increase the pace is easy enough.'

2 **Set the carriage wheels a little across the road**. Slightly alter the angle at which the wheels were set on the axle so that if the vehicle stopped when going uphill, it would not immediately begin to roll backwards, as the wheels would be facing in a slightly diagonal direction across the road surface.

Brakeshoes and drags: (*top*) Wiltshire cart with a brakeshoe under the rear wheel, and (*below left*) an Oxfordshire cart with a 'roller scotch' connected to the hub and bodywork to prevent the vehicle running backwards down a slope (John Vince, *Discovering Carts and Wagons*, Aylesbury: Shire Publications, 1970, p. 41); (*below right*) the roller scotch acting as a brake (D. J. Smith, *Discovering Horse Drawn Commercial Vehicles*, Aylesbury: Shire Publications, 1977, p. 70)

night. We stopped at the principal hotel, which was in the Market Place; it was a very large one; we drove under an archway into a long yard, at the further end of which were the stables and coach-houses. Two ostlers came to take us out. The head ostler was a pleasant, active little man, with a crooked leg, and a yellow striped waistcoat. I never saw a man unbuckle harness so quickly as he did, and with a pat and a good word he led me to a long stable, with six or eight stalls in it, and two or three horses. The other man brought Ginger; James stood by whilst we were rubbed down and cleaned.

I never was cleaned so lightly and quickly as by that little old man. When he had done, James stepped up and felt me over, as if he thought I could not be thoroughly done, but he found my coat as clean and smooth as silk.

'Well,' he said, 'I thought I was pretty quick, and our John quicker still, but you do beat all I ever saw for being quick and thorough at the same time.'

'Practice makes perfect,' said the crooked little ostler, 'and 'twould be a pity if it didn't; forty years' practice, and not perfect! ha, ha! that would be a pity; and as to being quick, why, bless you! that is only a matter of habit; if you get into the habit of being quick, it is just as easy as being slow; easier, I should say; in fact, it don't agree with my health to be hulking about over a job twice as long as it need take. Bless you! I couldn't whistle if I crawled over my work as some folks do! You see, I have been about horses ever since I was twelve years old, in hunting stables, and racing stables; and being small, ye see, I was jockey for several years; but at the Goodwood, ye see, the turf was very slippery and my poor Larkspur got a fall, and I broke my knee, and so of course I was of no more use there; but I could not live without horses, of course I couldn't, so I took to

3 Ostlers. Inn servants who have care of the horses, e.g. they bring out fresh horses and unharness, stable and feed tired ones.

4 Hulking about. Moving or working clumsily and unnecessarily slowly.

5 Goodwood. Racecourse in Sussex, which today holds a prestigious late summer meeting.

'I never was cleaned so lightly and quickly'. Illustrated by Lucy Kemp-Welch. (*Black Beauty*, London: J. M. Dent, 1915, pl. opp. p. 63)

the hotels, and I can tell ye it is a downright pleasure to handle an animal like this, well bred, well mannered, well cared for; bless ye! I can tell how a horse is treated. Give me the handling of a horse for twenty minutes, and I 'll tell you what sort of a groom he has had; look at this one, pleasant, quiet, turns about just as you want him, holds up his feet to be cleaned out, or anything else you please to wish; then you 'll find another, fidgety, fretty, won't move the right way, or starts across the stall, tosses up his head as soon as you come near him, lays his ears, and seems afraid of you; or else squares about at you with his heels. Poor things! I know what sort of treatment they have had. If they are timid, it makes them start or shy; if they are high-mettled, it makes them vicious or dangerous; their tempers are mostly made when they are young. Bless you! they are like children, train 'em up in the way they should go, as the good book says, and when they are old they will not depart from it, if they have a chance, that is.'

'I like to hear you talk,' said James, 'that 's the way we lay it down at home, at our master's.'

'Who is your master, young man? if it be a proper question. I should judge he is a good one, from what I see.'

'He is Squire Gordon, of Birtwick Park, the other side the Beacon hills,' said James.

'Ah! so, so, I have heard tell of him; fine judge of horses, ain't he? the best rider in the county?'

'I believe he is,' said James, 'but he rides very little now, since the poor young master was killed.'

'Ah! poor gentleman; I read all about it in the paper at the time; a fine horse killed too, wasn't there?'

'Yes,' said James, 'he was a splendid creature, brother to this one, and just like him.'

128

6 **Squares about at you with his heels**. To kick properly with both hind hooves a horse has to present his hindquarters squarely at his 'target'. When doing this the horse 'means business' – it is not a half-hearted warning as may be the case if he simply lifts a hind leg in a threatening way.

7 **High-mettled**. Highly strung, courageous or brave.

8 **The Beacon hills**. Possibly the Brecon Beacons, which would place Birtwick Park in the Monmouth/Gloucester area. The Sewell family lived for some years in 'a remote corner of Gloucestershire, on the boundaries of the Beaufort Hunt country ... probably the happiest of [Anna's] adult life' (Chitty, *The Woman who Wrote Black Beauty*, p. 129). It would not be surprising if Anna Sewell placed Black Beauty's happiest years in the same area.

Threatening to kick. Illustrator unidentified. (*Black Beauty*, New York: Modern Promotions, 1979, p. 64)

129

'Pity! pity!' said the old man, ''twas a bad place to leap, if I remember; a thin fence at top, a steep bank down to the stream, wasn't it? no chance for a horse to see where he is going. Now, I am for bold riding as much as any man, but still there are some leaps that only a very knowing old huntsman has any right to take; a man's life and a horse's life are worth more than a fox's tail, at least I should say they ought to be.'

During this time the other man had finished Ginger, and had brought our corn, and James and the old man left the stable together.

'A bad place to leap'; here a hunter is depicted taking off from sticky ground over a blind hedge. The author warns of the danger of a sprained back in such circumstances. (*Elliman's First Aid Book: Horses, Dogs, Birds and Cattle*, Slough: Elliman's, *c.* 1900, p. 26)

CHAPTER XVI

THE FIRE

1 LATER on in the evening, a traveller's horse was brought in by the second ostler, and whilst he was cleaning him, a young man with a pipe in his mouth lounged into the stable to gossip.

'I say, Towler,' said the ostler, 'just run up the ladder
2 into the loft and put some hay down into this horse's rack, will you? only lay down your pipe.'

'All right,' said the other, and went up through the trap-door; and I heard him step across the floor overhead and put down the hay. James came in to look at us the last thing, and then the door was locked.

I cannot say how long I had slept, nor what time in the night it was, but I woke up very uncomfortable, though I hardly knew why. I got up, the air seemed all thick and choking. I heard Ginger coughing, and one of the other horses moved about

1 **Traveller**. A commercial traveller often drove some type of gig with room in a special compartment for boxes and cases of samples of goods to show to potential retailers.

2 **Rack**. Victorian stables often had the hay rack fitted above the manger. It was filled by dropping hay from the loft above through a trapdoor – a bad practice which created dust and often resulted in the hayseeds lodging in the horses' eyes. In *Stable Architecture* (1862), Thomas E. Knightley states: 'In improved stables the old method of pushing hay down into the racks from the lofts above will not be available, indeed should not be adopted.'

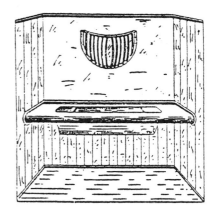

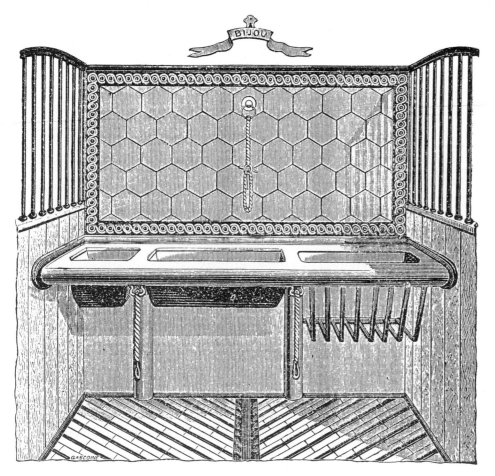

(*Left*) The recommended arrangement of manger and hay rack in the late nineteenth century (W. Procter, *The Management of the Horse*, London, 1883, p. 10); and (*above*) an overhead rack (T. E. Coleman, *Stable Sanitation and Construction*, London: E. & F. N. Spon, 1897, p. 159)

restlessly; it was quite dark, and I could see nothing, but the stable was very full of smoke, and I hardly knew how to breathe.

The trap-door had been left open, and I thought that was the place it came through. I listened and heard a soft rushing sort of noise, and a low crackling and snapping. I did not know what it was, but there was something in the sound so strange, that it made me tremble all over. The other horses were now all awake; some were pulling at their halters, others were stamping.

At last I heard steps outside, and the ostler who had put up the traveller's horse burst into the stable with a lantern, and began to untie the horses, and try to lead them out; but he seemed in such a hurry, and so frightened himself, that he frightened me still more. The first horse would not go with him; he tried the second and third, they too would not stir. He came to me next and tried to drag me out of the stall by force; of course that was no use. He tried us all by turns and then left the stable.

No doubt we were very foolish, but danger seemed to be all round, and there was nobody we knew to trust in, and all was strange and uncertain. The fresh air that had come in through the open door made it easier to breathe, but the rushing sound overhead grew louder, and as I looked upward, throught the bars of my empty rack, I saw a red light flickering on the wall. Then I heard a cry of 'Fire' outside, and the old ostler quietly and quickly came in; he got one horse out, and went to another, but the flames were playing round the trap-door, and the roaring overhead was dreadful.

The next thing I heard was James's voice, quiet and cheery, as it always was.

'Come, my beauties, it is time for us to be off, so wake up and

3 **Put up the traveller's horse.** Put away or took care of a horse after work.

4 **Horse would not go with him.** When horses are terrified, as in the case of fire, they will refuse to leave the stable, or if removed from a burning stable will return there, seeing it as familiar territory regardless of the danger therein.

'Fire'. Illustrated by Douglas Relf. (*Black Beauty*, London: Thomas Nelson & Sons, 1937, p. 81)

135

come along.' I stood nearest the door, so he came to me first, patting me as he came in.

'Come, Beauty, on with your bridle, my boy, we 'll soon be out of this smother.' It was on in no time; then he took the scarf off his neck, and tied it lightly over my eyes, and patting and coaxing he led me out of the stable. Safe in the yard, he slipped the scarf off my eyes, and shouted, 'Here, somebody! take this horse while I go back for the other.'

A tall broad man stepped forward and took me, and James darted back into the stable. I set up a shrill whinny as I saw him go. Ginger told me afterwards, that whinny was the best thing I could have done for her, for had she not heard me outside, she would never have had courage to come out.

There was much confusion in the yard; the horses being got out of other stables, and the carriages and gigs being pulled out of houses and sheds, lest the flames should spread further. On the other side the yard, windows were thrown up, and people were shouting all sorts of things; but I kept my eye fixed on the stable door, where the smoke poured out thicker than ever, and I could see flashes of red light; presently I heard above all the stir and din a loud clear voice, which I knew was master's:

'James Howard! James Howard! are you there?' There was no answer, but I heard a crash of something falling in the stable, and the next moment I gave a loud joyful neigh, for I saw James coming through the smoke leading Ginger with him; she was coughing violently and he was not able to speak.

'My brave lad!' said master, laying his hand on his shoulder, 'are you hurt?'

James shook his head, for he could not yet speak.

'Aye,' said the big man who held me, 'he is a brave lad, and no mistake.'

5 **Tied it lightly over my eyes**. Horses which refuse to be led for various reasons, such as fear, will often willingly follow a human leader if they are blindfolded.

'I gave a loud joyful neigh'. Illustrated by Frank Grey. (*Black Beauty*, London: Collins, 1953, p. 90)

137

'And now,' said master, 'when you have got your breath, James, we'll get out of this place as quickly as we can,' and we were moving towards the entry, when from the Market Place there came a sound of galloping feet and loud rumbling wheels.

6 ''Tis the fire engine! the fire engine!' shouted two or three voices, 'stand back, make way!' and clattering and thundering over the stones two horses dashed into the yard with the heavy engine behind them. The firemen leaped to the ground; there was no need to ask where the fire was—it was torching up in a great blaze from the roof.

We got out as fast as we could into the broad quiet Market Place; the stars were shining, and except the noise behind us, all was still. Master led the way to a large hotel on the other side, and as soon as the ostler came, he said, 'James, I must now hasten to your mistress; I trust the horses entirely to you, order whatever you think is needed,' and with that he was gone. The master did not run, but I never saw mortal man walk so fast as he did that night.

There was a dreadful sound before we got into our stalls; the shrieks of those poor horses that were left burning to death in the stable—it was very terrible! and made both Ginger and me feel very bad. We, however, were taken in and well done by.

The next morning the master came to see how we were and to speak to James. I did not hear much, for the ostler was rubbing me down, but I could see that James looked very happy, and I thought the master was proud of him. Our mistress had been so much alarmed in the night, that the journey was put off till the afternoon, so James had the morning on hand, and went first to the inn to see about our harness and the carriage, and then to hear more about the fire. When he came back, we heard him tell the ostler about it. At first no one could guess how the fire

6 **Fire engine**. Fire engines were often drawn by grey horses, which could be seen more easily in a crowded street than bay or brown horses. Grey was particularly favoured in London, where the London Fire Brigade hired horses from a certain Thomas Tilling, who at one time was the largest hirer of commercial horses in the world. Fire horses' harness was often suspended above the horses in their stalls so that it could be dropped on to them when the alarm sounded. Such harness was especially made to be strong and light, but with fewer straps than normal so that it was quick and easy to adjust. Sometimes bells were attached for warning as the horses galloped to the fire. Other vehicles accompanied the fire engine itself, including tenders carrying extra equipment such as a manual pump and extending ladders.

Nineteenth-century fire engine drawn by two horses. (Gordon, *Horse World of London*, frontispiece)

had been caused, but at last a man said he saw Dick Towler go into the stable with a pipe in his mouth, and when he came out he had not one, and went to the tap for another. Then the under ostler said he had asked Dick to go up the ladder to put down some hay, but told him to lay down his pipe first. Dick denied taking the pipe with him, but no one believed him. I remember our John Manly's rule, never to allow a pipe in the stable, and thought it ought to be the rule everywhere.

James said the roof and floor had all fallen in, and that only the black walls were standing; the two poor horses that could not be got out, were buried under the burnt rafters and tiles.

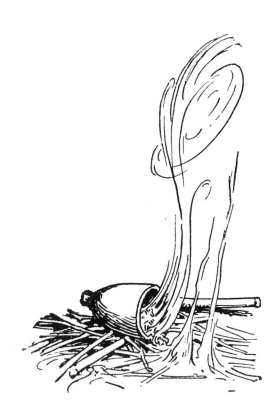

7 **Tap**. The tap room in a public house, i.e. the room where beer and other liquors were served. The term originated from the barrels or casks from which drinks were served direct by means of a tap.

A Victorian tavern. Illustrated by George Cruikshank. (Charles Dickens, *Sketches by Boz*, London: Macmillan, 1892, reprint of 1836 edn, p. 170)

CHAPTER XVII

JOHN MANLY'S TALK

THE rest of our journey was very easy, and a little after sunset we reached the house of my master's friend. We were taken into a clean snug stable; there was a kind coachman, who made us very comfortable, and who seemed to think a good deal of James when he heard about the fire.

'There is one thing quite clear, young man,' he said, 'your

'We were taken into a clean snug stable'.
Illustrator unknown. (*Black Beauty*, New
York: McLoughin Bros, 190?, p. 129)

horses know who they can trust; it is one of the hardest things in the world to get horses out of a stable, when there is either fire or flood. I don't know why they won't come out, but they won't—not one in twenty.'

We stopped two or three days at this place and then returned home. All went well on the journey; we were glad to be in our own stable again, and John was equally glad to see us.

Before he and James left us for the night, James said, 'I wonder who is coming in my place.'

'Little Joe Green at the Lodge,' said John.

'Little Joe Green! why he 's a child!'

'He is fourteen and a half,' said John.

'But he is such a little chap.'

'Yes, he is small, but he is quick, and willing, and kind-hearted too, and then he wishes very much to come, and his father would like it; and I know the master would like to give him the chance. He said, if I thought he would not do, he would look out for a bigger boy; but I said I was quite agreeable to try him for six weeks.'

'Six weeks!' said James, 'why, it will be six months before he can be of much use! it will make you a deal of work, John.'

'Well,' said John with a laugh, 'work and I are very good friends; I never was afraid of work yet.'

'You are a very good man,' said James, 'I wish I may ever be like you.'

'I don't often speak of myself,' said John, 'but as you are going away from us out into the world, to shift for yourself, I 'll just tell you how I look on these things. I was just as old as Joseph when my father and mother died of the fever, within ten days of each other, and left me and my crippled sister Nelly alone in the world, without a relation that we could look to for help. I was

1 **Nelly**. Popular girl's name in the Victorian period but now out of fashion. It figured in several songs of the time, e.g. 'Nellie Dean', 'Nellie Gray'.

'One of the hardest things'. Illustrated by John Beer. (*Black Beauty*. London: Jarrold & Sons, 1894, p. 72)

John Manly (*left*), illustrated by Lionel Edwards (*Black Beauty*, London: Peter Lunn, 1946, p. 10); and Little Joe Green (*far left*), illustrated by Honor C. Appleton (*Black Beauty*, London: Harrap, 1936, p. 34)

a farmer's boy, not earning enough to keep myself, much less both of us, and she must have gone to the workhouse, but for our mistress (Nelly calls her, her angel, and she has good right to do so). She went and hired a room for her with old widow Mallet, and she gave her knitting and needlework, when she was able to do it; and when she was ill, she sent her dinners and many nice comfortable things, and was like a mother to her. Then the master, he took me into the stable under old Norman, the coachman that was then. I had my food at the house, and my bed in the loft, and a suit of clothes and three shillings a week, so that I could help Nelly. Then there was Norman; he might have turned round and said that at his age he could not be troubled with a raw boy from the plough-tail, but he was like a father to me, and took no end of pains with me. When the old man died some years after, I stepped into his place, and now of course I have top wages, and can lay by for a rainy day or a sunny day as it may happen, and Nelly is as happy as a bird. So you see, James, I am not the man that should turn up his nose at a little boy, and vex a good, kind master. No! no! I shall miss you very much, James, but we shall pull through, and there 's nothing like doing a kindness when 'tis put in your way, and I am glad I can do it.'

'Then,' said James, 'you don't hold with that saying, "Everybody look after himself, and take care of number one."'

'No, indeed,' said John, 'where should I and Nelly have been, if master and mistress and old Norman had only taken care of number one? Why—she in the workhouse and I hoeing turnips! Where would Black Beauty and Ginger have been if you had only thought of number one? why, roasted to death! No, Jim, no! that is a selfish, heathenish saying, whoever uses it, and any man who thinks he has nothing to do but take care of number one,

2 **Workhouse**. A local authority-run institution for the poor, destitute, needy and infirm of the town or parish. It was a place to be dreaded: married couples and families were separated, men ate together and women ate together and never had the opportunity to meet. Conditions in the workhouse were spartan to act as a deterrent to malingerers and the work-shy. See p. 231.

3 **But for our mistress**. Mrs Gordon was clearly in the same tradition of helping others as Anna Sewell and in particular her mother Mary. Mary began visiting the poor when Anna was a small child and she wrote that 'The great secret of help is encouragement.'

4 **Plough-tail**. A back marker, as in the rear part or handle of a plough.

5 **Number one**. Colloquial expression meaning 'oneself'. The first reference, according to the *Oxford English Dictionary*, was by T. Pitt in Hedge's diary (1704–5).

Horse-drawn plough. (Isaac Philips Roberts, *The Horse*, New York: The Macmillan Company, 1913, p. 349)

why, it 's a pity but what he had been drowned like a puppy or a kitten, before he got his eyes open, that 's what I think,' said John, with a very decided jerk of his head.

James laughed at this; but there was a thickness in his voice when he said, 'You have been my best friend except my mother; I hope you won't forget me.'

'No, lad, no!' said John, 'and if ever I can do you a good turn, I hope you won't forget me.'

The next day Joe came to the stables to learn all he could before James left. He learned to sweep the stable, to bring in the straw and hay; he began to clean the harness, and helped to wash the carriage. As he was quite too short to do anything in the way of grooming Ginger and me, James taught him upon Merrylegs, for he was to have full charge of him; under John. He was a nice little bright fellow, and always came whistling to his work.

Merrylegs was a good deal put out, at being 'mauled about,' as he said, 'by a boy who knew nothing'; but towards the end of the second week, he told me confidentially that he thought the boy would turn out well.

At last the day came when James had to leave us; cheerful as he always was, he looked quite downhearted that morning.

'You see,' he said to John, 'I am leaving a great deal behind; my mother and Betsy, and you, and a good master and mistress, and then the horses, and my old Merrylegs. At the new place, there will not be a soul that I shall know. If it were not that I shall get a higher place, and be able to help my mother better, I don't think I should have made up my mind to it; it is a real pinch, John.'

'Aye, James, lad, so it is, but I should not think much of you, if you could leave your home for the first time and not feel it; cheer up, you 'll make friends there, and if you get on well,

ANNOTATIONS

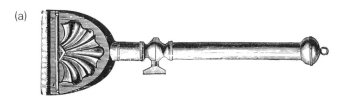

<table>
<tr><td></td><td></td><td>£ s. d.</td></tr>
</table>

	£ s. d.		x. d.
Currycomb, best 4 knocker .	1 3	Leathers, each . 1s. 6d. to	2 0
Mane comb	1 0	Rubbers, or dusters, each 1s. to	1 6
Body brush	5 0	Buckets, each	6 0
Picker for pocket	1 6	Corn sieve	2 6
Scraper	1 0	Measures, each	1 6
Water-brush	4 0	Trimming scissors, bent and	
Pitchfork	1 6	straight	5 6
Shovel	2 6	Singeing lamp	10 6
Stable besoms, each . 6d. to	2 0	Oil brushes, each	1 6
Sponges, per lb. . 1l. 1s. to 1	5 0	Bandages, woollen, per set .	6 6
Manure basket	2 0	Ditto, linen, ditto .	6 6
Stopping box	2 0		

Price list from the 1860s (J. H. Walsh, *The Horse in the Stable and the Field*, London: Routledge, 1861, p. 217); together with stable implements and grooming tools: (a) singeing lamps burned alcohol or oil and were used to burn off whiskers and long 'cat hairs' from the clipped coat. Singeing lamps are still in use today in some stables; (b) zinc-lined stall basket used to remove droppings; (c) linen bandages, since entirely replaced by the stockinette 'Newmarket' type of bandage or the elasticated variety; (d) Fentons Patent hair shedder helped remove loose hair from the coat; (e) steel mane drag with buckthorn handle. (Moseman's *Illustrated Guide for Purchasers of Horse Furnishing Goods*, pp. 8, 13, 15, 17, 18)

149

as I am sure you will, it will be a fine thing for your mother, and she will be proud enough that you have got into such a good place as that.'

So John cheered him up, but every one was sorry to lose James; as for Merrylegs, he pined after him for several days, and went quite off his appetite. So John took him out several mornings with a leading rein, when he exercised me, and trotting and galloping by my side, got up the little fellow's spirits again, and he was soon all right.

Joe's father would often come in and give a little help, as he understood the work, and Joe took a great deal of pains to learn, and John was quite encouraged about him.

Merrylegs. Illustrated by John Beer. (*Black Beauty*, London: Jarrold & Sons, 1894, p. 40)

CHAPTER XVIII

GOING FOR THE DOCTOR

ONE night, a few days after James had left, I had eaten my hay and was laid down in my straw fast asleep, when I was suddenly awoke by the stable bell ringing very loud. I heard the door of John's house open, and his feet running up to the Hall. He was back again in no time; he unlocked the stable door, and came in, calling out, 'Wake up, Beauty, you must go well now, if ever you did'; and almost before I could think, he had got the saddle on my back and the bridle on my head; he just ran round for his coat, and then took me at a quick trot up to the Hall door. The Squire stood there with a lamp in his hand.

'Now, John,' he said, 'ride for your life, that is, for your mistress's life; there is not a moment to lose; give this note to

152

1 **Stable bell.** Communication from the house to summon stable servants, in the same way that rooms in the house had bells wired to the servants' hall.

Although most horses will spend some part of their sleep lying down, they can also sleep quite happily standing up. There is a locking mechanism in the legs that prevents the horse falling over while asleep. (Mayhew, *The Illustrated Horse Management*, p. 282)

'Ride for your life'. Illustrated by Tom Gill. (*Black Beauty*, Golden Picture Classics, New York: Simon & Schuster, 1956, p. 33)

153

Dr. White; give your horse a rest at the inn, and be back as soon as you can.'

John said, 'Yes, sir,' and was on my back in a minute. The gardener who lived at the lodge had heard the bell ring, and was ready with the gate open, and away we went through the Park and through the village, and down the hill till we came to the toll-gate. John called very loud and thumped upon the door: the man was soon out and flung open the gate.

'Now,' said John, 'do you keep the gate open for the Doctor; here 's the money,' and off we went again.

There was before us a long piece of level road by the riverside; John said to me, 'Now, Beauty, do your best,' and so I did; I wanted no whip nor spur, and for two miles I galloped as fast as I could lay my feet on the ground; I don't believe that my old grandfather who won the race at Newmarket, could have gone faster. When we came to the bridge, John pulled me up a little and patted my neck. 'Well done, Beauty! good old fellow,' he said. He would have let me go slower, but my spirit was up, and I was off again as fast as before. The air was frosty, the moon was bright, it was very pleasant; we came through a village, then through a dark wood, then uphill, then downhill, till after an eight miles run we came to the town, through the streets and into the Market Place. It was all quite still except the clatter of my feet on the stones—everybody was asleep. The church clock struck three as we drew up at Dr. White's door. John rang the bell twice, and then knocked at the door like thunder. A window was thrown up, and Dr. White, in his nightcap, put his head out and said, 'What do you want?'

'Mrs. Gordon is very ill, sir; master wants you to go at once, he thinks she will die if you cannot get there—here is a note.'

'Wait,' he said, 'I will come.'

154

2 **Nightcap.** Most Victorian bedrooms were cold and draughty and it was common for both men and women to wear some kind of head covering in bed. An exaggerated modesty may also have contributed to the fashion. Men's nightcaps were often conical and sometimes decorated with a tassle; women's caps were similar to mob caps.

'Master wants you to go at once'. Illustrated by Lionel Edwards. (*Black Beauty*, London: Ward Lock, 1954, pl. opp. p. 82)

He shut the window, and was soon at the door.

'The worst of it is,' he said, 'that my horse has been out all day and is quite done up; my son has just been sent for, and he has taken the other. What is to be done? Can I have your horse?'

'He has come at a gallop nearly all the way, sir, and I was to give him a rest here; but I think my master would not be against it if you think fit, sir.'

'All right,' he said, 'I will soon be ready.'

John stood by me and stroked my neck, I was very hot. The Doctor came out with his riding whip.

'You need not take that, sir,' said John, 'Black Beauty will go till he drops; take care of him, sir, if you can, I should not like any harm to come to him.'

'No! no! John,' said the Doctor, 'I hope not,' and in a minute we had left John far behind.

I will not tell about our way back; the Doctor was a heavier man than John, and not so good a rider; however, I did my very best. The man at the toll-gate had it open. When we came to the hill, the Doctor drew me up. 'Now, my good fellow, he said, 'take some breath.' I was glad he did, for I was nearly spent, but that breathing helped me on, and soon we were in the Park. Joe was at the lodge gate, my master was at the Hall door, for he had heard us coming. He spoke not a word; the Doctor went into the house with him, and Joe led me to the stable. I was glad to get home, my legs shook under me, and I could only stand and pant. I had not a dry hair on my body, the water ran down my legs, and I steamed all over—Joe used to say, like a pot on the fire. Poor Joe! he was young and small, and as yet he knew very little, and his father, who would have helped him, had been sent to the next village; but I am sure he did the very best he knew. He rubbed my legs and my chest, but he did not

156

3 **Water**. Sweat. After hard exercise a horse sweats profusely, particularly on the neck, shoulder and flanks. The heat from the body combined with sweat causes steam.

'Black Beauty will go till he drops'. Illustrated by Percy F. Spence. (*Black Beauty*, London: A. & C. Black, 1959, p. 84)

put my warm cloth on me; he thought I was so hot I should not like it. Then he gave me a pail full of water to drink; it was cold and very good, and I drank it all; then he gave me some hay and some corn, and thinking he had done right, he went away. Soon I began to shake and tremble, and turned deadly cold, my legs ached, my loins ached, and my chest ached, and I felt sore all over. Oh! how I wished for my warm thick cloth as I stood and trembled. I wished for John, but he had eight miles to walk, so I lay down in my straw and tried to go to sleep. After a long while I heard John at the door; I gave a low moan, for I was in great pain. He was at my side in a moment stooping down by me; I could not tell him how I felt; but he seemed to know it all; he covered me up with two or three warm cloths, and then ran to the house for some hot water; he made me some

4 warm gruel which I drank, and then I think I went to sleep.

John seemed to be very much put out. I heard him say to himself, over and over again, 'Stupid boy! stupid boy! no cloth put on, and I dare say the water was cold too; boys are no good,' but Joe was a good boy after all.

5 I was now very ill; a strong inflammation had attacked my lungs, and I could not draw my breath without pain. John nursed me night and day, he would get up two or three times in the night to come to me; my master, too, often came to see me. 'My poor Beauty,' he said one day, 'my good horse, you saved your mistress's life, Beauty! yes, you saved her life.' I was very glad to hear that, for it seems the Doctor had said if we had been a little longer it would have been too late. John told my master he never saw a horse go so fast in his life, it seemed as if the horse knew what was the matter. Of course I did, though John thought not; at least I knew as much as this, that John and I must go at the top of our speed, and that it was for the sake of the mistress.

4 **Gruel**. Thin, porridge-like, but easily digested and sustaining food often given as a 'pick-me-up'.

5 **Ill**. It is difficult to give an exact diagnosis from the symptoms displayed by Black Beauty. Often too much cold water drunk when too hot can result in colic, but the illness described would appear to be of a respiratory, rather than intestinal, nature. It might have been pneumonia.

A horse showing typical symptoms of pneumonia. (Edward Mayhew, *Illustrated Horse Doctor*, London, 1860, p. 132)

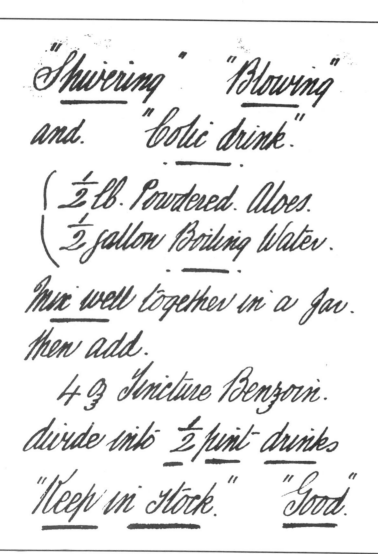

"Shivering"   "Blowing"
and   "Colic drink".

(½ lb. Powdered. Aloes.
(½ gallon Boiling Water.

Mix well together in a Jar.
then add.
    4 ℥ Tincture Benzoin.
divide into ½ pint drinks
"Keep in Stock."   "Good".

Recipe for a draught. (MS, private collection, *c.* 1900)

CHAPTER XIX

ONLY IGNORANCE

1 I DO not know how long I was ill. Mr. Bond, the horse
2 doctor, came every day. One day he bled me; John held a
pail for the blood; I felt very faint after it, and thought I
should die, and I believe they all thought so too.

Ginger and Merrylegs had been moved into the other
stable, so that I might be quiet, for the fever made me very quick
3 of hearing; any little noise seemed quite loud, and I could tell
every one's footstep going to and from the house. I knew all
4 that was going on. One night John had to give me a draught;
Thomas Green came in to help him. After I had taken it and
John had made me as comfortable as he could, he said he should
stay half an hour to see how the medicine settled. Thomas said
he would stay with him, so they went and sat down on a bench
that had been brought into Merryleg's stall, and put down the
lantern at their feet, that I might not be disturbed with the light.

For a while both men sat silent, and then Tom Green said in
a low voice,

'I wish, John, you 'd say a bit of a kind word to Joe; the boy
is quite broken-hearted, he can't eat his meals, and he can't

1 **Horse doctor**. Equine veterinary medicine was in its infancy in Black Beauty's day, as was the training of veterinary surgeons. Much of the treatment given to horses was based on tradition rather than sound, scientific reasoning.

2 **Bled me**. The practice of bleeding, particularly in cases of fever, was a common and long-established one for horses and humans, the theory being to 'let out the bad blood' and 'purify' the blood still in the body. It often did have beneficial results but the reasons why were not understood. It was carried out by use of a fleam, a multi-bladed knife with blades of different sizes for different animals, which severed a vein, usually in the neck, and a specified amount of blood was let before the flow was staunched.

3 **Quick of hearing**. Hypersensitive to sound.

4 **Draught**. Draughts or drenches were liquid medicines originally administered in a hollowed cow's horn, the sharp end having been cut off to allow the liquid to run into the horse's mouth. Later, leather-covered bottles were used or even shoulderless wine bottles, such as hock bottles, although with glass there was always the danger of it breaking. The horse's head had to be raised, sometimes by means of a rope around the upper jaw and the end pulled over a beam, while the medicine was poured slowly into the horse's mouth, but the head had to be lowered quickly when the horse swallowed otherwise choking could result. Usually more medicine ran up the groom's arm than went down the horse's gullet.

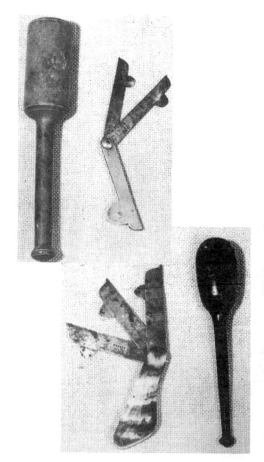

Fleams and bloodsticks. The fleam was placed on the vein and then hit with the bloodstick in order to make the cut. (Photo by Michael Harris, in Arthur Ingram. *The Country Animal Doctor*, Shire Album 40, Aylesbury: Shire Publications, 1979, p. 15)

The usual way of administering a draught. (Mayhew, *The Illustrated Horse Management*, p. 69)

smile. He says he knows it was all his fault, though he is sure he did the best he knew, and he says, if Beauty dies, no one will ever speak to him again. It goes to my heart to hear him; I think you might give him just a word, he is not a bad boy.'

After a short pause, John said slowly, 'You must not be too hard upon me, Tom. I know he meant no harm, I never said he did; I know he is not a bad boy, but you see I am sore myself; that horse is the pride of my heart, to say nothing of his being such a favourite with the master and mistress; and to think that his life may be flung away in this manner, is more than I can bear; but if you think I am hard on the boy, I will try to give him a good word to-morrow—that is, I mean if Beauty is better.'

'Well, John! thank you, I knew you did not wish to be too hard, and I am glad you see it was only ignorance.'

John's voice almost startled me as he answered, '*Only* ignorance! only *ignorance*! how can you talk about *only* ignorance? Don't you know that it is the worst thing in the world, next to wickedness?—and which does the most mischief, heaven only knows. If people can say, "Oh! I did not know, I did not mean any harm," they think it is all right. I suppose Martha Mulwash did not mean to kill that baby, when she dosed it with Dalby, and soothing syrups; but she did kill it, and was tried for manslaughter.'

'And serve her right, too,' said Tom. 'A woman should not undertake to nurse a tender little child without knowing what is good and what is bad for it.'

'Bill Starkey,' continued John, 'did not mean to frighten his brother into fits, when he dressed up like a ghost, and ran after him in the moonlight; but he did; and that bright, handsome little fellow, that might have been the pride of any mother's heart, is just no better than an idiot, and never will be, if he

5 **Martha Mulwash.** There appears to be no evidence that such a person actually existed, nor Bill Starkey mentioned later.

6 **Dalby.** 'Dalby's carminative. Oil of peppermint 1 minim, oil of nutmegs 2, oil of aniseed 3, tincture of castor 30, tincture of assafoetida 15, tincture of opium 5, spirit of pennyroyal 15, compound tincture of cardamons 30 minims, peppermint water 2 fluid oz. Dose, half to one teaspoonful.' New Sydenham Society's *Lexicon of Medicine and the Allied Sciences*. Vol. II by Henry Power and Leonard Sedgewick (London, 1882).

Administering a draught using the 'quiet method' recommended by Mayhew. (Mayhew, *The Illustrated Horse Management*, p. 71)

John Manly administers medicine to a very receptive Black Beauty, watched closely by Tom Green. Illustrated by Tom Gill. (*Black Beauty*, Golden Picture Classics, New York: Simon & Schuster, 1956, p. 40)

live to be eighty years old.　You were a good deal cut up your-self, Tom, two weeks ago, when those young ladies left your hothouse door open, with a frosty east wind blowing right in; you said it killed a good many of your plants.'

'A good many!' said Tom, 'there was not one of the tender cuttings that was not nipped off; I shall have to strike all over again, and the worst of it is, that I don't know where to go to get fresh ones.　I was nearly mad when I came in and saw what was done.'

'And yet,' said John, 'I am sure the young ladies did not mean it; it was only ignorance!'

I heard no more of this conversation, for the medicine did well and sent me to sleep, and in the morning I felt much better: but I often thought of John's words when I came to know more of the world.

7 **Strike**. Put forth roots.

Tom Green and John Manly talk. Illustrated by John Beer. (*Black Beauty*, London: Jarrold & Sons, 1894, p. 86)

CHAPTER XX

JOE GREEN

JOE GREEN went on very well; he learned quickly, and was so attentive and careful, that John began to trust him in many things; but, as I have said, he was small for his age, and it was seldom that he was allowed to exercise either Ginger or me; but it so happened one morning that John was out with Justice in the luggage cart, and the master wanted a note to be taken immediately to a gentleman's house, about

166

Joe Green. Illustrated by W. Austen. (*Black Beauty*, Boston: L. C. Page, 1902, pl. opp. p. 98)

167

three miles distant, and sent his orders for Joe to saddle me and take it; adding the caution that he was to ride carefully.

The note was delivered, and we were quietly returning till we came to the brickfield. Here we saw a cart heavily laden with bricks; the wheels had stuck fast in the stiff mud of some deep ruts; and the carter was shouting and flogging the two horses unmercifully. Joe pulled up. It was a sad sight. There were the two horses straining and struggling with all their might to drag the cart out, but they could not move it; the sweat streamed from their legs and flanks, their sides heaved, and every muscle was strained, whilst the man, fiercely pulling at the head of the forehorse, swore and lashed most brutally.

'Hold hard,' said Joe, 'don't go on flogging the horses like that; the wheels are so stuck that they cannot move the cart.' The man took no heed, but went on lashing.

'Stop! pray stop,' said Joe; 'I'll help you to lighten the cart, they can't move it now.'

'Mind your own business, you impudent young rascal, and I'll mind mine.' The man was in a towering passion, and the worse for drink, and laid on the whip again. Joe turned my head, and the next moment we were going at a round gallop towards the house of the master brickmaker. I cannot say if John would have approved of our pace, but Joe and I were both of one mind, and so angry, that we could not have gone slower.

The house stood close by the roadside. Joe knocked at the door and shouted, 'Halloa! is Mr. Clay at home?' The door was opened, and Mr. Clay himself came out.

'Hulloa! young man! you seem in a hurry; any orders from the Squire this morning?'

'No, Mr. Clay, but there's a fellow in your brickyard flogging two horses to death. I told him to stop and he wouldn't; I said

168

1   **Brickfield**. In the Victorian period bricks were often made locally wherever suitable clay could be found, and the brickworks or brickfield provided much employment.

2   **Forehorse**. The leading horse of two driven in tandem.

3   **Mr. Clay**. Another instance of the popular nineteenth-century literary ploy of using a name to fit a character – in this case, Mr. Clay is owner of the brickworks.

'There's a fellow in your brickyard flogging two horses to death.' Illustrated by John Beer. (*Black Beauty*, Boston: DeWolfe, Fiske & Co., [191?], p. 71)

169

I'd help him to lighten the cart, and he wouldn't; so I have come to tell you; pray, sir, go.' Joe's voice shook with excitement.

'Thank ye, my lad,' said the man, running in for his hat; then pausing for a moment—'Will you give evidence of what you saw if I should bring the fellow up before a magistrate?'

'That I will,' said Joe, 'and glad to.' The man was gone, and we were on our way home at a smart trot.

'Why, what's the matter with you, Joe? you look angry all over,' said John, as the boy flung himself from the saddle.

'I am angry all over, I can tell you,' said the boy, and then in hurried, excited words he told all that had happened. Joe was usually such a quiet, gentle little fellow that it was wonderful to see him so roused.

'Right, Joe! you did right, my boy, whether the fellow gets a summons or not. Many folks would have ridden by and said 'twas not their business to interfere. Now, I say, that with cruelty and oppression it is everybody's business to interfere when they see it; you did right, my boy.'

Joe was quite calm by this time, and proud that John approved of him, and he cleaned out my feet, and rubbed me down with a firmer hand than usual.

They were just going home to dinner when the footman came down to the stable to say that Joe was wanted directly in master's private room; there was a man brought up for ill-using horses, and Joe's evidence was wanted. The boy flushed up to his forehead, and his eyes sparkled. 'They shall have it,' said he.

'Put yourself a bit straight,' said John. Joe gave a pull at his necktie and a twitch at his jacket, and was off in a moment. Our master being one of the county magistrates, cases were often brought to him to settle, or say what should be done. In the

4 **Before a magistrate**. The law transgressed by the carter was probably the 1835 act prohibiting cruelty to cattle, dogs and other domestic animals. 'Martin's Act' of 1822, on which this was based, and which prevented the cruel and improper treatment of cattle, is usually held to be the first piece of legislation aimed solely at improving the lot of animals. It was through the efforts of Richard Martin that the RSPCA was formed.

5 **Cleaned out my feet**. Horses' hooves accumulate mud, small stones, manure etc. which compact to form a mass over the sole and wedge into the inner rim of the shoe. If not cleaned out regularly it will begin to smell and set up infection, the most common of which is thrush. Stones can cause bruising which leads to lameness, hence it is very important to take care of the horse's feet, as manifested by the saying, 'No foot, no horse.'

Another interpretation of the carter ill-using his horses. Illustrated by K. F. Barker. (*Black Beauty*, London: A. & C. Black, 1959, p. 92)

stable we heard no more for some time, as it was the men's dinner hour, but when Joe came next into the stable I saw he was in high spirits; he gave me a good-natured slap and said, 'We won't see such things done, will we, old fellow?' We heard afterwards that he had given his evidence so clearly, and the horses were in such an exhausted state, bearing marks of such brutal usage, that the carter was committed to take his trial, and might possibly be sentenced to two or three months in prison.

It was wonderful what a change had come over Joe. John laughed, and said he had grown an inch taller in that week, and I believe he had. He was just as kind and gentle as before, but there was more purpose and determination in all that he did—as if he had jumped at once from a boy into a man.

Joe Green and the carter. Illustrated by Frank Grey. (*Black Beauty*, London: Collins, 1953, p. 109)

173

CHAPTER XXI

THE PARTING

1   I HAD now lived in this happy place three years, but sad
changes were about to come over us. We heard from time
to time that our mistress was ill. The Doctor was often at
the house, and the master looked grave and anxious. Then
we heard that she must leave her home at once and go to a
2 warm country for two or three years. The news fell upon the
household like the tolling of a death-bell. Everybody was sorry;
but the master began directly to make arrangements for breaking
up his establishment and leaving England. We used to hear it
talked about in our stable; indeed, nothing else was talked
about.

John went about his work silent and sad, and Joe scarcely
whistled. There was a great deal of coming and going; Ginger
and I had full work.

The first of the party who went were Miss Jessie and Flora

174

1   **Three years**. This would mean that Black Beauty is now aged seven – in his prime of life.

2   **Go to a warm country**. For the mysterious illnesses which plagued Anna Sewell for most of her adult life, foreign spas were often recommended. Anna visited Marienbad in Bohemia and spent a year at Marienburg in Germany. She also stayed with her brother at a fashionable resort in Spain.

'The first of the party who went were Miss Jessie and Flora'. Illustrated by John Beer. (*Black Beauty*, Boston: DeWolfe, Fiske & Co. 191?, p. 74)

175

3 with their governess. They came to bid us good-bye. They hugged poor Merrylegs like an old friend, and so indeed he was. Then he heard what had been arranged for us. Master had sold

4 Ginger and me to his old friend, the Earl of W——, for he thought we should have a good place there. Merrylegs he had given to the Vicar, who was wanting a pony for Mrs. Blomefield, but it was on the condition that he should never be sold, and when he was past work that he should be shot and buried.

Joe was engaged to take care of him, and to help in the house, so I thought that Merrylegs was well off. John had the offer of several good places, but he said he should wait a little and look round.

The evening before they left, the master came into the stable to give some directions and to give his horses the last pat. He seemed very low-spirited; I knew that by his voice. I believe we horses can tell more by the voice than many men can.

'Have you decided what to do, John?' he said. 'I find you have not accepted any of those offers.'

'No, sir, I have made up my mind that if I could get a situation

5 with some first-rate colt-breaker and horse-trainer, that it would be the right thing for me. Many young animals are frightened and spoiled by wrong treatment which need not be, if the right man took them in hand. I always get on well with horses, and if I could help some of them to a fair start, I should feel as if I was doing some good. What do you think of it, sir?'

'I don't know a man anywhere,' said master, 'that I should think so suitable for it as yourself. You understand horses, and somehow they understand you, and in time you might set up for yourself; I think you could not do better. If in any way I can help you, write to me; I shall speak to my agent in London, and leave your character with him.'

3 **Governess**. As a private tutor employed to teach the children of a family – boys up to the age of about nine (after which they were sent to boarding school) and girls up to the age of about fourteen, the governess held a somewhat uneasy position in the hierarchy of the household. She was considered 'above' the domestic servants, largely isolated in the nursery and schoolroom where she ate her meals with the children, and yet was not considered on a par with the family of the house. Governesses were often the daughters of middle-class, but not wealthy, parents and it was one of the few respectable careers open to educated women.

4 **Earl of W—**. Common ploy of Victorian authors; the suggestion is that a real title is being protected when in fact it is a fictional character.

5 **Colt-breaker**. Man who bought young, unbroken horses (not only colts but fillies as well) to train for work in harness and under saddle before they could be sold at a profit to anyone wanting a working horse. Heavy horses were usually broken to harness on the farm where they were bred by being introduced to draught work in the somewhat easier environment of the farm rather than the city streets.

Gentling a foal. (Mayhew, *The Illustrated Horse Management*, p. 512)

Master gave John the name and address, and then he thanked
him for his long and faithful service; but that was too much for
John. 'Pray don't, sir, I can't bear it; you and my dear mistress
have done so much for me that I could never repay it; but we
shall never forget you, sir, and please God we may some day see
mistress back again like herself; we must keep up hope, sir.'
Master gave John his hand, but he did not speak, and they both
left the stable.

The last sad day had come; the footman and the heavy luggage
had gone off the day before, and there was only master and
6 mistress and her maid. Ginger and I brought the carriage up to
the Hall for the last time. The servants brought out cushions and
rugs and many other things, and when all were arranged, master
came down the steps carrying the mistress in his arms (I was
on the side next the house and could see all that went on); he
placed her carefully in the carriage, while the house servants
stood round crying.

'Good-bye again,' he said, 'we shall not forget any of you,'
and he got in—'Drive on, John.'

Joe jumped up, and we trotted slowly through the Park, and
through the village, where the people were standing at their
doors to have a last look and to say, 'God bless them.'

When we reached the railway station, I think mistress walked
7 from the carriage to the waiting room. I heard her say in her
own sweet voice, 'Good-bye, John, God bless you.' I felt the
rein twitch, but John made no answer, perhaps he could not
speak. As soon as Joe had taken the things out of the carriage,
John called him to stand by the horses, while he went on the
platform. Poor Joe! he stood close up to our heads to hide his
tears. Very soon the train came puffing up into the station;
then two or three minutes, and the doors were slammed to; the

6 Maid. A lady's maid was responsible for her mistress's personal needs, such as hairdressing, toiletries, jewellery, clothes, accessories, travelling arrangements, cleaning of clothes, nightwear etc.

7 Waiting room. Most stations had special 'Ladies Only' waiting rooms on the platform to protect a lady from the unwelcome attentions of strange men.

A lady's maid, as depicted in *Punch*, 6 April 1867, p. 142.

guard whistled and the train glided away, leaving behind it only clouds of white smoke, and some very heavy hearts.

When it was quite out of sight, John came back—

'We shall never see her again,' he said—'never.' He took the reins, mounted the box, and with Joe drove slowly home; but it was not our home now.

Railway carriages, *c.* 1847. First, second and third class. The Gordons would certainly have travelled first class. (*Illustrated London News*, 22 May 1847, p. 328)

PART II

CHAPTER XXII

EARLSHALL

THE next morning after breakfast Joe put Merrylegs into the mistress's low chaise to take him to the vicarage; he came first and said good-bye to us, and Merrylegs neighed to us from the yard.   Then John put the saddle on Ginger and the leading rein on me, and rode us across the country about fifteen miles to Earlshall Park, where the Earl of W—— lived.   There was a very fine house and a great deal of stabling; we went into the yard through a stone gateway, and John asked for Mr. York.   It was some time before he came.   He was a fine-looking, middle-aged man, and his voice said at once that he expected to be obeyed.   He was very friendly and polite to John, and after giving us a slight look, he called a groom to take us to our boxes, and invited John to take some refreshment.

We were taken to a light airy stable, and placed in boxes

PLATE 16
Arrival of the fire engine at the inn, illustrated by Lucy Kemp-Welch for the 1915
Dent edition.

PLATE 17
Ginger fights the bearing rein at Earlshall Park, illustrated by Lucy Kemp-Welch for the 1915 Dent edition.

'A very fine house'. Illustrated by Lionel Edwards. (*Black Beauty*, London: Ward Lock, 1954, p. 97)

adjoining each other, where we were rubbed down and fed. In about half an hour John and Mr. York, who was to be our new coachman, came in to see us.

'Now, Mr. Manly,' he said, after carefully looking at us both, 'I can see no fault in these horses, but we all know that horses have their peculiarities as well as men, and that sometimes they need different treatment; I should like to know if there is anything particular in either of these, that you would like to mention.'

'Well,' said John, 'I don't believe there is a better pair of horses in the country, and right grieved I am to part with them, but they are not alike. The black one is the most perfect temper I ever knew; I suppose he has never known a hard word or a blow since he was foaled, and all his pleasure seems to be to do what you wish; but the chestnut I fancy must have had bad treatment; we heard as much from the dealer. She came to us snappish and suspicious, but when she found what sort of place ours was, it all went off by degrees; for three years I have never seen the smallest sign of temper, and if she is well treated there is not a better, more willing animal than she is; but she is naturally a more irritable constitution than the black horse; flies tease her more; anything wrong in the harness frets her more; and if she were ill-used or unfairly treated, she would not be unlikely to give tit for tat; you know that many high-mettled horses will do so.'

'Of course,' said York, 'I quite understand, but you know it is not easy in stables like these to have all the grooms just what they should be; I do my best, and there I must leave it. I'll remember what you have said about the mare.'

They were going out of the stable, when John stopped and said, 'I had better mention that we have never used the "bearing

ANNOTATIONS

1 **Anything wrong in the harness**. The collar is one item of harness which needs special attention. In his *Handy Horse Book* (1865), 'Magenta' wrote: 'More care and judgement are necessary in shaping the stuffing of the collar to fit a horse than for any other part of the harness . . . Any collar, be it ever so well shaped, should be tried on the horse's neck before it is taken into wear, to make sure that it is neither too large nor too small.' He also pointed out that care should be taken in putting the collar on, so that the horse's head was not knocked as the collar went over it. He recommended that a horse with a big head but a relatively narrow neck should be provided with a collar which could be opened at the top, for though this was a weaker design the horse would be saved much distress when being harnessed.

2 **Tit for tat**. Retaliation, give as good as received. Apparently a variation of 'Tip for tap' and 'Tap for tap', i.e. blow for blow.

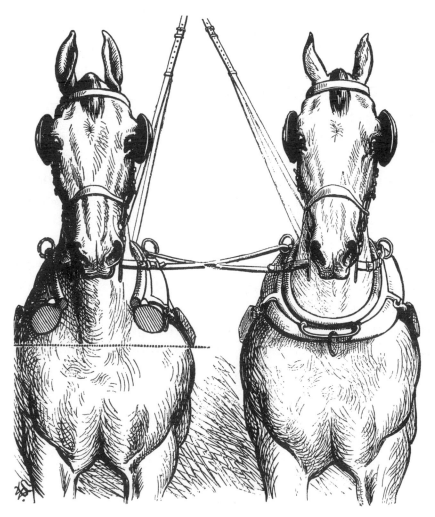

The collar, shown in section (*left*) to indicate its proper position on the horse. (Sidney, *Book of the Horse*, p. 353)

rein'' with either of them; the black horse never had one on, and the dealer said it was the gag-bit that spoiled the other's temper.'

3

'Well,' said York, 'if they come here, they must wear the bearing rein. I prefer a loose rein myself, and his lordship is always very reasonable about horses; but my lady—that's another thing, she will have style; and if her carriage horses are not reined up tight, she wouldn't look at them. I always stand out against the gag-bit, and shall do so, but it must be tight up when my lady rides!'

'I am sorry for it, very sorry,' said John; 'but I must go now, or I shall lose the train.'

He came round to each of us to pat and speak to us for the last time; his voice sounded very sad.

I held my face close to him, that was all I could do to say good-bye; and then he was gone, and I have never seen him since.

The next day Lord W—— came to look at us; he seemed pleased with our appearance.

'I have great confidence in these horses,' he said, 'from the character my friend Mr. Gordon has given me of them. Of course they are not a match in colour, but my idea is, that they will do very well for the carriage whilst we are in the country. Before we go to London I must try to match Baron; the black horse, I believe, is perfect for riding.'

York then told him what John had said about us.

'Well,' said he, 'you must keep an eye to the mare, and put the bearing rein easy; I dare say they will do very well with a little humouring at first. I'll mention it to her ladyship.'

In the afternoon we were harnessed and put in the carriage, and as the stable clock struck three we were led round to the

3 The gag-bit. In *The Encyclopaedia of the Stable* (1909), V. K. Shaw defined the gag-bit as 'a severe and totally unnecessary development of the bearing-rein . . . It consists of a bit attached to a round rein passing from the cheek upwards through rings near the browband to the pad-hook, and drawn so tightly that the corners of the lips are dragged upwards.' George Fleming, the Principal Veterinary Surgeon of the Army, who approved of bearing reins in normal circumstances, wrote that 'the "gag" bearing-rein, and its usual mode of application, is an abomination and a cruelty to horses' (*Practical Horse Keeper*, 1886).

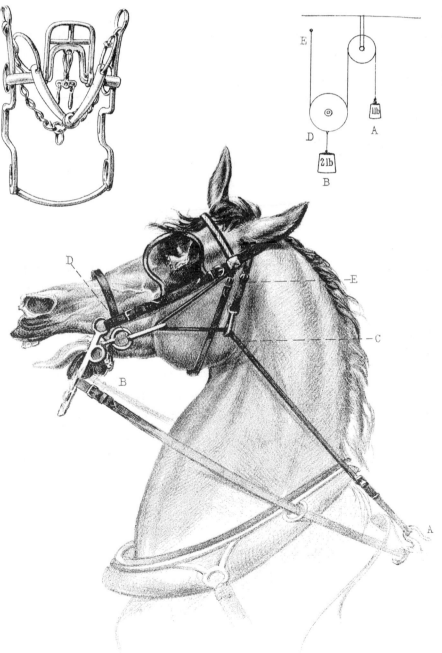

The torture of the gag bearing rein, together with diagrams showing the mechanics of its use. (Edward Fordham Flower, *Bits and Bearing Reins*, London: W. Ridgway, 1875, pl. 3)

front of the house.   It was all very grand, and three or four times as large as the old house at Birtwick, but not half so pleasant, if a horse may have an opinion.   Two footmen were standing ready, 4 dressed in drab livery, with scarlet breeches and white stockings.

Presently we heard the rustling sound of silk as my lady came down the flight of stone steps.   She stepped round to look at us; she was a tall, proud-looking woman, and did not seem pleased about something, but she said nothing, and got into the carriage. This was the first time of wearing a bearing rein, and I must say, though it certainly was a nuisance not to be able to get my head down now and then, it did not pull my head higher than I was accustomed to carry it.   I felt anxious about Ginger, but she seemed to be quiet and content.

The next day at three o'clock we were again at the door, and the footmen as before; we heard the silk dress rustle, and the lady came down the steps, and in an imperious voice she said, 'York, you must put those horses' heads higher, they are not fit to be seen.'

York got down and said very respectfully, 'I beg your pardon, my lady, but these horses have not been reined up for three years, and my lord said it would be safer to bring them to it by degrees; but if your ladyship pleases, I can take them up a little more.'

'Do so,' she said.

York came round to our heads and shortened the rein himself, one hole, I think; every little makes a difference, be it for better or worse, and that day we had a steep hill to go up.   Then I began to understand what I had heard of.   Of course I wanted to put my head forward and take the carriage up with a will, as we had been used to do; but no, I had to pull with my head up now, and that took all the spirit out of me, and the strain came on my back

4 **Drab livery**. Uniform made from a thick, strong woollen cloth of grey or dull brown colour.

'My lady came down the flight of stone steps'. Illustrated by Charles Keeping. (*Black Beauty*, London: Victor Gollancz, 1988, p. 92)

and legs. When we came in, Ginger said, 'Now you see what it is like, but this is not bad, and if it does not get much worse than this, I shall say nothing about it, for we are very well treated here; but if they strain me up tight, why, let 'em look out! I can't bear it, and I won't.'

Day by day, hole by hole, our bearing reins were shortened, and instead of looking forward with pleasure to having my harness put on as I used to do, I began to dread it. Ginger too seemed restless, though she said very little. At last I thought the worst was over; for several days there was no more shortening, and I determined to make the best of it and do my duty, though it was now a constant harass instead of a pleasure; but the worst was not come.

'Our bearing reins were shortened'. Illustrated by Lionel Edwards. (*Black Beauty*, London: Peter Lunn, 1946, p. 41)

CHAPTER XXIII

A STRIKE FOR LIBERTY

ONE day my lady came down later than usual, and the silk rustled more than ever.

'Drive to the Duchess of B——'s,' she said, and then after a pause—'Are you never going to get those horses' heads up, York? Raise them at once, and let us have no more of this humouring and nonsense.'

York came to me first, whilst the groom stood at Ginger's head. He drew my head back and fixed the rein so tight that it was almost intolerable; then he went to Ginger, who was impatiently jerking her head up and down against the bit, as was her way now. She had a good idea of what was coming, and the moment York took the rein off the terret in order to shorten it, she took her opportunity, and reared up so suddenly that York had his nose roughly hit, and his hat knocked off; the groom was nearly thrown off his legs. At once they both flew to her head, but she was a match for them, and went on plunging, rearing,

192

ANNOTATIONS

1 **Terret**. Rings in the saddle or pad of the harness through which the reins pass. Here it would seem that the bearing rein was attached to the terret rings rather than the bearing hook, and adjusted by means of a buckle.

2 **Reared**. Normally regarded as a vice in horses as it is extremely dangerous. When balancing on its hind legs the horse may fall over backwards crushing its rider, or if in harness, fall back on to the vehicle and passengers. It is a natural movement used in play, fighting and defence but is discouraged in the domesticated horse.

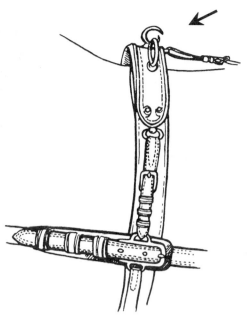

The terret. Illustrated by Janet Johnstone. (Sallie Walrond, *Encyclopaedia of Driving*, Macclesfield: Horse Drawn Carriages, 1974, p. 200)

'Reared up so suddenly'. Illustrated by Frank Grey. (*Black Beauty*, London: Collins, 1953, p. 121)

and kicking in a most desperate manner; at last she kicked right over the carriage pole and fell down, after giving me a severe blow on my near quarter.   There is no knowing what further mischief she might have done, had not York promptly sat himself down flat on her head, to prevent her struggling, at the same time calling out, 'Unbuckle the black horse! run for the winch and unscrew the carriage pole; cut the trace here, somebody, if you can't unhitch it.'   One of the footmen ran for the winch, and another brought a knife from the house.   The groom soon set me free from Ginger and the carriage, and led me to my box. He just turned me in as I was, and ran back to York.   I was much excited by what had happened, and if I had ever been used to kick or rear, I am sure I should have done it then; but I never had, and there I stood angry, sore in my leg, my head still strained up to the terret on the saddle, and no power to get it down.   I was very miserable, and felt much inclined to kick the first person who came near me.

Before long, however, Ginger was led in by two grooms, a good deal knocked about and bruised.   York came with her and gave his orders, and then came to look at me.   In a moment he let down my head.

'Confound these bearing reins!' he said to himself; 'I thought we should have some mischief soon—master will be sorely vexed; but there—if a woman's husband can't rule her, of course a servant can't; so I wash my hands of it, and if she can't get to the Duchess's garden party, I can't help it.'

York did not say this before the men; he always spoke respect-fully when they were by.   Now, he felt me all over, and soon found the place above my hock where I had been kicked.   It was swelled and painful; he ordered it to be sponged with hot water, and then some lotion was put on.

194

3 **Pole**. When a pair of horses are driven side by side they are separated from each other by a thick, usually wooden, pole which runs from underneath the front part of the carriage and is secured there by means of a pin. The pole extends to a little beyond the horses' breasts. The horses are placed alongside and attached to the pole by means of pole straps or chains from their collars to a metal hook on the front of the pole. The pole acts as a steering mechanism and brake via the harness.

4 **Sat himself down flat on her head.** A traditional way of preventing a fallen horse from struggling to rise, as it will bang its head and eye on the ground in its efforts to stand up. It was common practice to sit on the horse's head while the harness was released, and perhaps a sack or other padding was placed under the head to prevent injury.

5 **Trace**. Thick leather strap forming part of the harness which attaches the horse to the vehicle. When hitched in pairs each horse has a trace on either side of him, keeping him parallel to the pole. The ends of the traces are attached to the collar at one end and fixed around hooks on the front part of the carriage at the other end, to act as the main source of pulling power.

6 **Unhitch**. Unfasten the traces from their hooks on the carriage. If pulled tight, such as when the horse falls, the traces are almost impossible to release as they need to be slackened and twisted to release them from the hooks. Thus in this case they had to be cut.

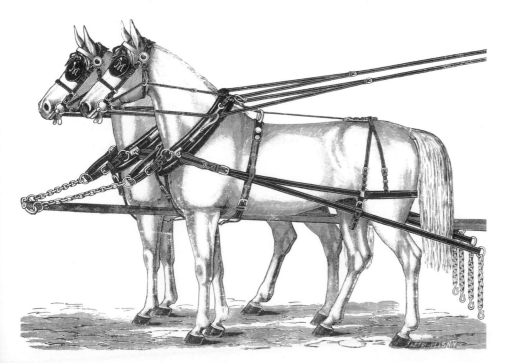

Pair harness, showing clearly the pole and the traces. (Moseman's *Illustrated Guide for Purchasers of Horse Furnishing Goods*, p. 184)

Lord W—— was much put out when he learned what had happened; he blamed York for giving way to his mistress, to which he replied, that in future he would much prefer to receive his orders only from his lordship; but I think nothing came of it, for

things went on the same as before.   I thought York might have stood up better for his horses, but perhaps I am no judge.

Ginger was never put into the carriage again, but when she was well of her bruises, one of Lord W——'s younger sons said he should like to have her; he was sure she would make a good hunter.   As for me, I was obliged still to go in the carriage, and had a fresh partner called Max; he had always been used to the tight rein.   I asked him how it was he bore it.

'Well,' he said, 'I bear it because I must, but it is shortening

A gentleman following hounds. (Sidney, *Book of the Horse*, p. 424)

'I was obliged still to go in the carriage'. Illustrator unidentified. (*Black Beauty*, New York: Modern Promotions, 1979, p. 217)

197

my life, and it will shorten yours too, if you have to stick to it.'

'Do you think,' I said, 'that our masters know how bad it is for us?'

7 'I can't say,' he replied, 'but the dealers and the horse doctors know it very well. I was at a dealer's once, who was training me and another horse to go as a pair; he was getting our heads up, as he said, a little higher and a little higher every day. A gentleman who was there asked him why he did so. "Because," said he, "people won't buy them unless we do. The London people always want their horses to carry their heads high, and to step high; of course it is very bad for the horses, but then it is good for trade. The horses soon wear up, or get diseased, and they come for another pair." That,' said Max, 'is what he said in my hearing and you can judge for yourself.'

What I suffered with that rein for four long months in my lady's carriage, it would be hard to describe; but I am quite sure 8 that, had it lasted much longer, either my health or my temper would have given way. Before that, I never knew what it was to foam at the mouth, but now the action of the sharp bit on my tongue and jaw, and the constrained position of my head, and throat, always caused me to froth at the mouth more or less. Some people think it very fine to see this, and say, 'What fine, spirited creatures!' But it is just as unnatural for horses as for men, to foam at the mouth: it is a sure sign of some discomfort, and should be attended to. Besides this, there was a pressure on my windpipe, which often made my breathing very uncomfortable; when I returned from my work, my neck and chest were 9 strained and painful, my mouth and tongue, tender, and I felt worn and depressed.

In my old home, I always knew that John and my master were

7 **The dealers and the horse doctors know it very well**. The dealer's conversation is based on a real incident quoted by Edward Fordham Flower in *Horse and Harness* (1876). He also quoted the opinion of a well-known horse dealer on the effect of the gag bearing rein on 'horses standing for a long time gagged up, it alters their natural position so much that they stretch out their fore legs, while waiting at doors, throwing all their weight on their heels, causing inflammation, and eventually navicular lameness, naturally also putting such a strain upon the back sinews, that they often give way from that cause only'. A vet was quoted on his opinion that the gag bearing rein caused various wind problems and 'megrim, staggers and softening of the brain'.

8 **My health or my temper would have given way**. In *Bits and Bearing Reins* (1875), Flower wrote: 'The pain thus occasioned to the horse is intense. The action of every muscle is impeded. If a false step is taken, recovery is rendered difficult. Discomfort makes the poor animal restless.' Anna Sewell sent a copy of her book to Flower, who responded enthusiastically.

9 **Mouth and tongue, tender**. Through continued rough handling and severe bitting, the bars of the horse's mouth are finally made insensitive and the horse becomes hard-mouthed. Signalling the horse to stop or turn increasingly results in no response. As a result, more severe bits are often employed and thus the vicious circle continues.

'Torture in harness': the horse stands with legs outstretched and back hollow to avoid the pain of the bearing rein. (*The Horse Book*, London: RSPCA, *c.* 1877, p. 63)

my friends; but here, although in many ways I was well treated, I had no friend.   York might have known, and very likely did know, how that rein harassed me; but I suppose he took it as a matter of course that could not be helped; at any rate, nothing was done to relieve me.

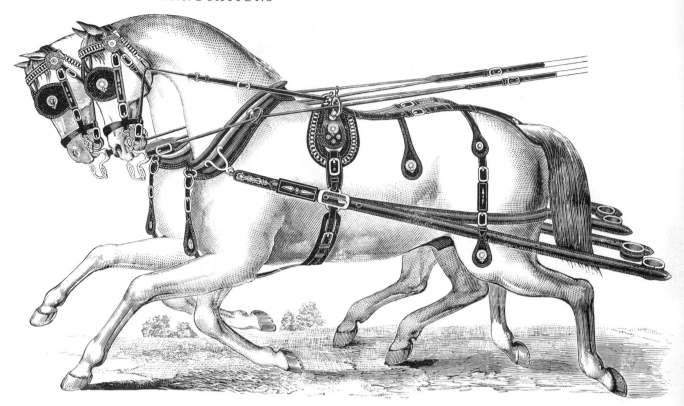

Coach horses working with the bearing rein in place. (Moseman's *Illustrated Guide for Purchasers of Horse Furnishing Goods*, p. 178)

CHAPTER XXIV

THE LADY ANNE

EARLY in the spring, Lord W—— and part of his family went up to London, and took York with them. I and Ginger and some other horses were left at home for use, and the head groom was left in charge.

The Lady Harriet, who remained at the Hall, was a great invalid, and never went out in the carriage, and the Lady Anne preferred riding on horseback with her brother, or cousins. She was a perfect horse-woman, and as gay and gentle as she was beautiful. She chose me for her horse, and named me 'Black Auster.' I enjoyed these rides very much in the clear cold air, sometimes with Ginger, sometimes with Lizzie. This Lizzie was a bright bay mare, almost thorough-bred, and a great favourite with the gentlemen, on account of her fine action and lively spirit; but Ginger, who knew more of her than I did, told me she was rather nervous.

There was a gentleman of the name of Blantyre staying at the Hall; he always rode Lizzie, and praised her so much, that one

1 **Black Auster**. Auster, the south wind.

2 **Almost thorough-bred**. Although Black Beauty and Ginger had some Thoroughbred blood, too much Thoroughbred would make them unsuitable for carriage horses. Hunters also would normally be only half or three-quarter Thoroughbred. See p. 79.

The type of horse suitable for a lady. Notice the balance strap which helps to keep the saddle in position. (Sidney, *Book of the Horse*, p. 318)

203

3   day Lady Anne ordered the side-saddle to be put on her, and the other saddle on me.   When we came to the door, the gentleman seemed very uneasy.

'How is this?' he said, 'are you tired of your good Black Auster?'

'Oh! no, not at all,' she replied, 'but I am amiable enough to let you ride him for once, and I will try your charming Lizzie. You must confess that in size and appearance she is far more like

4   a lady's horse than my own favourite.'

'Do let me advise you not to mount her,' he said; 'she is a charming creature, but she is too nervous for a lady.   I assure you she is not perfectly safe; let me beg you to have the saddles changed.'

'My dear cousin,' said Lady Anne, laughing, 'pray do not trouble your good careful head about me; I have been a horse-woman ever since I was a baby, and I have followed the hounds a great many times, though I know you do not approve of ladies

5   hunting; but still that is the fact, and I intend to try this Lizzie

6   that you gentlemen are all so fond of; so please help me to mount like a good friend as you are.'

There was no more to be said; he placed her carefully on the

7   saddle, looked to the bit and curb, gave the reins gently into her hand, and then mounted me.   Just as we were moving off, a footman came out with a slip of paper and message from the Lady Harriet—'Would they ask this question for her at Dr. Ashley's, and bring the answer?'

The village was about a mile off, and the Doctor's house was the last in it.   We went along gaily enough till we came to his gate.   There was a short drive up to the house between tall ever-greens.   Blantyre alighted at the gate, and was going to open it for Lady Anne, but she said, 'I will wait for you here, and you can hang Auster's rein on the gate.'

3 **Side-saddle**. A lady riding in a habit sits facing forwards with both legs on the left side of the horse. The side-saddle is said to be very secure because the thighs and knees are hooked around pommels riveted to the saddle.

4 **Lady's horse**. Small, neat, attractive, elegant, lightly built horse about 15–15.2hh, with perfect manners and smooth paces suitable for carrying a lady side-saddle.

5 **Ladies hunting.** Up to about the middle of the nineteenth century, few women rode to hounds, partly because it was considered unladylike and 'fast' and partly because the design of the side-saddle did not allow for jumping and was not particularly safe. Side-saddle riding habits were very long and almost trailed on the ground; in the event of a fall the rider was likely to be dragged. By the 1870s the design of side-saddles was modified so that they became safer and fashion called for shorter habits. The combination of these two factors encouraged more women to ride to hounds. When the 'leaping head' pommel on the side-saddle was perfected women were able to remain secure even when jumping.

6 **Help me to mount**. It was difficult for a woman to mount a horse unaided when riding side-saddle. A groom or helper would stoop slightly and offer her his hands locked together to form a step. Once her foot was placed in his hands she sprang and he lifted her simultaneously so that she alighted on the saddle. He then had to adjust the hem of her habit to cover the toes of her boots after she had arranged her legs around the pommels.

7 **Bit and curb.** A double bridle with two bits, a curb and a snaffle, which was *de rigeur* for riding. A snaffle alone, as frequently used nowadays, was considered very sloppy and quite incorrect. The curb, due to leverage action and pressure on the chin groove via the curb chain, offered better control, although it could be tortuous in the wrong hands. See p. 261.

205

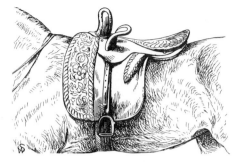

Side-saddle, showing the single stirrup and the double pommel. (Sidney, *Book of the Horse*, p. 324)

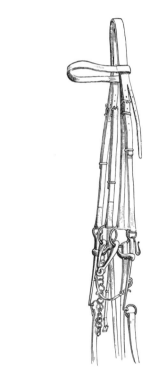

A double bridle shown with the snaffle bit hanging in front of the curb bit. In the horse's mouth the snaffle lies behind the curb. (Sidney, *Book of the Horse*, p. 307)

He looked at her doubtfully—'I will not be five minutes,' he said.

'Oh, do not hurry yourself; Lizzie and I shall not run away from you.'

8   He hung my rein on one of the iron spikes, and was soon hidden amongst the trees.   Lizzie was standing quietly by the side of the road a few paces off with her back to me.   My young mistress was sitting easily with a loose rein, humming a little song.   I listened to my rider's footsteps until they reached the house, and heard him knock at the door.   There was a meadow on the opposite side of the road, the gate of which stood open; just then, some cart-horses and several young colts came trotting out in a very disorderly manner, whilst a boy behind was cracking a great whip.   The colts were wild and frolicsome, and one of them bolted across the road, and blundered up against Lizzie's hind legs; and whether it was the stupid colt, or the loud cracking of the whip, or both together, I cannot say, but she gave a violent kick, and dashed off into a headlong gallop.   It was so sudden, that Lady Anne was nearly unseated, but she soon recovered herself.   I gave a loud shrill neigh for help: again and again I neighed, pawing the ground impatiently, and tossing my head to get the rein loose.   I had not long to wait.   Blantyre came running to the gate; he looked anxiously about, and just caught sight of the flying figure, now far away on the road.   In an instant he sprang into the saddle.   I needed no whip, or spur, for I was as eager as my rider; he saw it, and giving me a free

9   rein, and leaning a little forward, we dashed after them.

For about a mile and a half the road ran straight, and then bent to the right, after which it divided into two roads.   Long before we came to the bend, she was out of sight.   Which way had she turned?   A woman was standing at her garden gate, shading her

8 Hung my rein on one of the iron spikes. Present-day riders are always advised never to tie up their horses by the reins, for fear of breaking the reins or other parts of the bridle or hurting the horse's mouth. They are advised instead to tie up only with a headcollar and rope. Perhaps in Black Beauty's day the well-to-do expected a groom to be on hand, but for whatever reason Anna Sewell did not give a lesson in tying up a horse. In some parts of the country, notably Lancashire, harness horses wore a halter complete with tethering rope under the bridle as a sign that they were for sale and the purchaser could take the horse away there and then!

9 Leaning a little forward. The riding style of the late nineteenth century was to sit upright or even lean slightly back, certainly so when jumping. Leaning forward when galloping and jumping was introduced in 1897 by the American jockey, Tod Sloane, and later through the theories and practice of the Italian cavalry officer, Federico Caprilli. This style was adopted by the British army about 1910 but was not widely adopted by civilians until the 1930s, so Black Beauty's rider appeared to be ahead of his time as regards equestrian practice.

The forward seat and the backward seat: (*top*) K. F. Barker's illustration for *Black Beauty* (London: A. & C. Black, 1959), p. 117; (*bottom*) Sidney, *Book of the Horse*, p. 427.

eyes with her hand, and looking eagerly up the road. Scarcely drawing the rein, Blantyre shouted, 'Which way?' 'To the right,' cried the woman, pointing with her hand, and away we went up the right-hand road; then for a moment we caught sight of her; another bend and she was hidden again. Several times we caught glimpses, and then lost them. We scarcely seemed to gain ground upon them at all. An old road-mender was standing near a heap of stones—his shovel dropped, and his hands raised. As we came near he made a sign to speak. Blantyre drew the rein a little. 'To the common, to the common, sir; she has turned off there.' I knew this common very well; it was for the most part very uneven ground, covered with heather and dark green furze bushes, with here and there a scrubby old thorn tree; there were also open spaces of fine short grass, with ant-hills and mole turns everywhere; the worst place I ever knew for a headlong gallop.

We had hardly turned on the common, when we caught sight again of the green habit flying on before us. My lady's hat was gone, and her long brown hair was streaming behind her. Her head and body were thrown back, as if she were pulling with all her remaining strength, and as if that strength were nearly exhausted. It was clear that the roughness of the ground had very much lessened Lizzie's speed, and there seemed a chance that we might overtake her.

Whilst we were on the high road, Blantyre had given me my head; but now with a light hand and a practised eye, he guided me over the ground in such a masterly manner, that my pace was scarcely slackened, and we were decidedly gaining on them.

About half-way across the heath there had been a wide dyke recently cut, and the earth from the cutting was cast up roughly on the other side. Surely this would stop them! but no; with

10 **Road-mender**. Road maintenance was often carried out on a somewhat haphazard basis and potholes and ruts only filled in when absolutely necessary. Road maintenance had long been a bone of contention and originally it was the responsibility of individual parishes to secure the service of each able-bodied man living within the parish to spend a certain amount of time each year on road repairs. When local government began to get organised in the mid-nineteenth century, road maintenance was transferred to the local authorities and paid for from household rates.

11 **Green habit**. Fashionable colours for a lady's riding costume were bottle green, navy blue and black. Sometimes other colours such as fawn or pastel shades were permitted for town wear, especially riding in Rotten Row in Hyde Park during the London Season in the summer.

12 **Given me my head**. Allowed him to find his own way and choose his own pace.

A hunting lady, showing the shorter riding habit suitable for jumping. (Nanny Power O'Donoghue, *Riding for Ladies*, London: W. Thacker, 1887, p. 157)

scarcely a pause Lizzie took the leap, stumbled among the rough clods, and fell. Blantyre groaned. 'Now, Auster, do your best!'   He gave me a steady rein, I gathered myself well together, and with one determined leap cleared both dyke and bank.

Motionless among the heather, with her face to the earth, lay my poor young mistress.   Blantyre kneeled down and called her name—there was no sound; gently he turned her face upward, it was ghastly white, and the eyes were closed. 'Annie, dear Annie, do speak!' but there was no answer.   He unbuttoned her habit, loosened her collar, felt her hands and wrists, then started up and looked wildly round him for help.

13   At no great distance there were two men cutting turf, who seeing Lizzie running wild without a rider had left their work to catch her.

14   Blantyre's halloo soon brought them to the spot.   The foremost man seemed much troubled at the sight, and asked what he could do.

'Can you ride?'

'Well, sir, I bean't much of a horseman, but I 'd risk my neck for the Lady Anne; she was uncommon good to my wife in the winter.'

'Then mount this horse, my friend; your neck will be quite safe, and ride to the Doctor's and ask him to come instantly—then on to the Hall—tell them all that you know, and bid them send me the carriage with Lady Anne's maid and help.   I shall stay here.'

'All right, sir, I 'll do my best, and I pray God the dear young lady may open her eyes soon.'   Then seeing the other man, he called out, 'Here, Joe, run for some water, and tell my missis to come as quick as she can to the Lady Anne.'

He then somehow scrambled into the saddle, and with a 'Gee

13 **Cutting turf**. Digging out sections of peat-like deposits for burning as fuel.

14 **Halloo**. Shout or cry used (normally in the hunting field) to attract attention.

'Lizzie took the leap'. Illustrated by Lionel Edwards. (*Black Beauty*, London: Ward Lock, 1954, pl. opp. p. 113)

15 up' and a clap on my sides with both his legs, he started on his journey, making a little circuit to avoid the dyke. He had no whip, which seemed to trouble him, but my pace soon cured that difficulty, and he found the best thing he could do was to stick to the saddle, and hold me in, which he did manfully. I shook him as little as I could help, but once or twice on the rough ground he called out, 'Steady! Woah! Steady.' On the high road we were all right; and at the Doctor's and the Hall, he did his errand like a good man and true. They asked him in to take a drop of something. 'No! no,' he said, 'I'll be back to 'em again by a short cut through the fields, and be there afore the carriage.'

There was a great deal of hurry and excitement after the news became known. I was just turned into my box, the saddle and bridle were taken off, and a cloth thrown over me.

Ginger was saddled and sent off in great haste for Lord George, and I soon heard the carriage roll out of the yard.

It seemed a long time before Ginger came back and before we were left alone; and then she told me all that she had seen.

'I can't tell much,' she said; 'we went a gallop nearly all the way, and got there just as the Doctor rode up. There was a woman sitting on the ground with the lady's head in her lap. The Doctor poured something into her mouth, but all that I heard was "She is not dead." Then I was led off by a man to a little distance. After a while she was taken to the carriage, and we came home together. I heard my master say to a gentleman who stopped him to inquire, that he hoped no bones were broken, but that she had not spoken yet.'

When Lord George took Ginger for hunting, York shook his head; he said it ought to be a steady hand to train a horse for

16 the first season, and not a random rider like Lord George.

15 **Gee up**. Popular command or encouragement to a horse to go forward. It was originally used by ploughmen in various parts of the country to mean either 'go forward' or more specifically 'turn right'. Other local variations include 'Come up', 'Come over', 'Gee back' and 'Wug off'.

16 **Random rider**. One who rides occasionally or irregularly, possibly an unskilled rider.

Two interpretations of Lady Anne's flight; (*left*) Percy F. Spence (*Black Beauty*, London, A. & C. Black, 1959, p. 111); (*above*) Charles Keeping (*Black Beauty*, London: Victor Gollancz, 1988, p. 101)

Ginger used to like it very much, but sometimes when she came back, I could see that she had been very much strained, and now and then she gave a short cough. She had too much spirit to complain but I could not help feeling anxious about her.

Two days after the accident, Blantyre paid me a visit: he patted me and praised me very much, he told Lord George that he was sure the horse knew of Annie's danger as well as he did. 'I could not have held him in, if I would,' said he; 'she ought never to ride any other horse.' I found by their conversation, that my young mistress was now out of danger, and would soon be able to ride again. This was good news to me, and I looked forward to a happy life.

PLATE 18

Although Black Beauty had little to do with women in his 'workplace', he encountered many friendly and kind ones in his life. Here one visits him on one of his
infrequent periods in a pasture after he grew up. Printed paper panel designed by
John M. Burke in cover of the 1911 Platt & Peck (New York) edition.

PLATE 19
Colour plates by Cecil Aldin for the 1912
Jarrolds edition: (*right*) foxhunt witnessed
by Black Beauty when a colt, and (*bottom*)
the farmer finding a stone in his shoe.

Black Beauty's leap. Illustrated by Cecil Aldin. (*Black Beauty*, London: Jarrolds, 1912, pl. opp. p. 169)

CHAPTER XXV

REUBEN SMITH

I MUST now say a little about Reuben Smith, who was left in charge of the stables when York went to London. No one more thoroughly understood his business than he did, and when he was all right, there could not be a more faithful or valuable man. He was gentle and very clever in his management of horses, and could doctor them almost as well as a farrier, for he had lived two years with a veterinary surgeon. He was a first-rate driver; he could take a four-in-hand, or a tandem, as easily as a pair. He was a handsome man, a good scholar, and had very pleasant manners. I believe everybody liked him; certainly the horses did; the only wonder was, that he should be in an under situation, and not in the place of a head coachman like York: but he had one great fault, and that was the love of drink. He was not like some men, always at it; he used to keep steady for weeks or months together; and then he would break out and have a 'bout' of it, as York called it, and be a disgrace

216

1 **Four-in-hand**. Team of four horses driven as two wheelers (side by side immediately in front of the vehicle) and two leaders (side by side in front of the wheelers).

2 **Tandem**. Two horses harnessed one in front of the other, a leader and a wheeler. This style of driving originated from the practice of harnessing a hunter as leader (the position using least energy) to go to a meet. Tandem harness is often employed for extra pulling up steep hills, in snow, and so on.

Four-in-hand harnessed to a coach. (Duke of Beaufort, *Driving*, London: Longmans Green, 1889, p. 12)

Two horses pulling in tandem. (Moseman's *Illustrated Guide for Purchasers of Horse Furnishing Goods*, p. 107)

217

to himself, a terror to his wife, and a nuisance to all that had to
do with him. He was, however, so useful, that two or three
times York had hushed the matter up, and kept it from the Earl's
knowledge; but one night, when Reuben had to drive a party
home from a ball, he was so drunk that he could not hold the
reins, and a gentleman of the party had to mount the box and
drive the ladies home. Of course this could not be hidden, and
Reuben was at once dismissed; his poor wife and little children
3 had to turn out of the pretty cottage by the Park gate and go
where they could. Old Max told me all this, for it happened
a good while ago; but shortly before Ginger and I came Smith
had been taken back again. York had interceded for him with
the Earl, who is very kind-hearted, and the man had promised
faithfully that he would never taste another drop as long as he
lived there. He had kept his promise so well that York thought
he might be safely trusted to fill his place whilst he was away,
and he was so clever and honest, that no one else seemed so well
fitted for it.

It was now early in April, and the family was expected home
4 some time in May. The light brougham was to be fresh done
5 up, and as Colonel Blantyre was obliged to return to his regiment,
it was arranged that Smith should drive him to the town in it,
and ride back; for this purpose he took the saddle with him, and
I was chosen for the journey. At the station the Colonel put
some money into Smith's hand and bid him good-bye, saying,
'Take care of your young mistress, Reuben, and don't let Black
Auster be hacked about by any random young prig that wants to
ride him—keep him for the lady.'

We left the carriage at the maker's, and Smith rode me to the
6 White Lion, and ordered the ostler to feed me well and have me
ready for him at four o'clock. A nail in one of my front shoes

218

3 **Turn out of the pretty cottage**. Employees on a large estate were usually provided with accommodation. This was a 'tied' house or cottage or room and if the employee left or was dismissed, he had to give up the accommodation.

4 **Brougham**. (Pronounced 'broom'). Four-wheeled, closed, coachman-driven carriage seating two or four passengers and drawn by one horse. Named after Lord Brougham who had such a carriage built to his specification. Broughams became extremely popular for town transport.

5 **Fresh done up**. Refurbished and cleaned, probably repainted and axles greased – work which a coachbuilder must do as opposed to the stable staff.

6 **White Lion**. A very common name for public houses all over the country, said to originate from the armorial bearings or coats of arms of local aristocratic families.

A fashionable brougham. Notice the adjustment of the bearing rein on the horse. (Sidney, *Book of the Horse*, p. 524)

7 had started as I came along, but the ostler did not notice it till just about four o'clock. Smith did not come into the yard till five, and then he said he should not leave till six, as he had met with some old friends. The man then told him of the nail, and asked if he should have the shoe looked to.

'No,' said Smith, 'that will be all right till we get home.'

He spoke in a very loud off-hand way, and I thought it very unlike him, not to see about the shoe, as he was generally wonderfully particular about loose nails in our shoes. He did not come at six, nor seven, nor eight, and it was nearly nine o'clock before he called for me, and then it was with a loud rough voice. He seemed in a very bad temper, and abused the ostler, though I could not tell what for.

The landlord stood at the door and said, 'Have a care, Mr. Smith!' but he answered angrily with an oath; and almost before he was out of the town he began to gallop, frequently giving me a sharp cut with his whip, though I was going at full speed. The moon had not yet risen, and it was very dark. The roads were stony, having been recently mended; going over them at this pace, my shoe became looser and when we were near the turnpike gate it came off.

If Smith had been in his right senses, he would have been sensible of something wrong in my pace; but he was too madly drunk to notice anything.

Beyond the turnpike was a long piece of road, upon which fresh stones had just been laid; large sharp stones, over which no horse could be driven quickly without risk of danger. Over this road, with one shoe gone, I was forced to gallop at my utmost speed, my rider meanwhile cutting into me with his whip, and with wild curses urging me to go still faster. Of course my

8 shoeless foot suffered dreadfully; the hoof was broken and split

220

7 **Started.** Begun to work loose.

8 **Broken and split.** The horse's hoof being composed of keratin, a similar substance to the human nail, it will split and break if left unprotected by an iron shoe and subjected for long periods of time to rough surfaces.

A shod foot with cracked hooves. (Nanny Power O'Donoghue, *Riding for Ladies*, London: W. Thacker & Co., 1887, new edn 1905, p. 263)

Reuben Smith. Illustrated by Michael Rios. (*Black Beauty*, New York: Modern Promotions, 1979, p. 105)

9 down to the very quick, and the inside was terribly cut by the sharpness of the stones.

This could not go on; no horse could keep his footing under such circumstances, the pain was too great. I stumbled, and fell with violence on both my knees. Smith was flung off by my fall, and owing to the speed I was going at, he must have fallen with great force. I soon recovered my feet and limped to the side of the road, where it was free from stones. The moon had just risen above the hedge, and by its light I could see Smith lying a few yards beyond me. He did not rise, he made one slight effort to do so, and then there was a heavy groan. I could have groaned too, for I was suffering intense pain both from my foot and knees; but horses are used to bear their pain in silence. I uttered no sound, but I stood there and listened. One more heavy groan from Smith; but though he now lay in the full moonlight, I could see no motion. I could do nothing for him nor myself, but, oh! how I listened for the sound of horse, or wheels, or footsteps. The road was not much frequented, and at this time of the night we might stay for hours before help came to us. I stood watching and listening. It was a calm sweet April night; there were no sounds, but a few low notes of a nightingale, and nothing moved but the white clouds near the moon, and a brown owl that flitted over the hedge. It made me think of the summer nights long ago, when I used to lie beside my mother in the green pleasant meadow at Farmer Grey's.

9 Quick. Sensitive part of the hoof just inside the hard, insensitive outer covering of horn.

The dangers of a horse stumbling at speed. (E. J. Ellis, *Riding*, London: Routledge, 1896, p. 58)

CHAPTER XXVI

HOW IT ENDED

IT must have been nearly midnight, when I heard at a great distance the sound of a horse's feet. Sometimes the sound died away, then it grew clearer again and nearer. The road to Earlshall led through plantations that belonged to the Earl: the sound came in that direction, and I hoped it might be someone coming in search of us. As the sound came nearer and nearer, I was almost sure I could distinguish Ginger's step; a little nearer still, and I could tell she was in the dog-cart. I neighed loudly, and was overjoyed to hear an answering neigh from Ginger, and men's voices. They came slowly over the stones, and stopped at the dark figure that lay upon the ground.

One of the men jumped out, and stooped down over it. 'It is Reuben!' he said, 'and he does not stir.'

The other man followed and bent over him. 'He's dead,' he said; 'feel how cold his hands are.'

224

'The dark figure that lay upon the ground'.
Illustrator unknown. (*Black Beauty*, London:
Jarrold & Sons, 35th edn, 189?, p. 122)

They raised him up, but there was no life, and his hair was soaked with blood. They laid him down again, and came and looked at me. They soon saw my cut knees.

'Why, the horse has been down and thrown him! Who would have thought the black horse would have done that? Nobody thought he could fall. Reuben must have been lying here for hours! Odd, too, that the horse has not moved from the place.'

Robert then attempted to lead me forward. I made a step, but almost fell again.

'Hallo! he 's bad in his foot as well as his knees; look here —his hoof is cut all to pieces, he might well come down, poor fellow! I tell you what, Ned, I 'm afraid it hasn't been all right with Reuben! Just think of him riding a horse over these stones without a shoe! Why, if he had been in his right senses, he would just as soon have tried to ride him over the moon. I 'm afraid it has been the old thing over again. Poor Susan! she looked awfully pale when she came to my house to ask if he had not come home. She made believe she was not a bit anxious, and talked of a lot of things that might have kept him. But for all that, she begged me to go and meet him—but what must we do? There 's the horse to get home as well as the body—and that will be no easy matter.'

Then followed a conversation between them, till it was agreed that Robert as the groom should lead me, and that Ned must take the body. It was a hard job to get it into the dog-cart, for there was no one to hold Ginger; but she knew as well as I did what was going on, and stood as still as a stone. I noticed that, because, if she had a fault, it was that she was impatient in standing.

Ned started off very slowly with his sad load, and Robert came

1 **Knees**. The injury sustained by Black Beauty is known as 'broken knees', despite the fact that there are not usually any fractures. The skin is cut or badly grazed and depending upon the depth of the wound there is always the possibility of the horse losing synovial fluid ('joint oil'), the lubricant which ensures smooth working of the knee bones. If this joint oil is lost the knee can become stiff due to lack of lubrication. A joint injury can be slow to heal because of unavoidable movement. The hair frequently grows back white or sometimes not at all so that the blemish remains, which could indicate to a potential buyer that the horse is prone to falling and stumbling and is, therefore, unsafe.

2 **Riding a horse over these stones**. On the subject of broken knees, 'Magenta' advises: 'For prevention, avoid the use of bearing-reins in harness . . . keep out of the way of ruts and stones upon the road, and be very careful of your beast when the work you are giving him is calculated to make him leg-weary' (*The Handy Horse Book*, 1865). In *The Practical Horse Keeper* (1886), George Fleming adds that broken knees 'very often arise from the horse falling while trotting down hill, and most frequently when he is being ridden by a servant or groom'!

3 **The old thing over again**. Anna Sewell and her mother formed a temperance brotherhood for the working men in their area when they lived in Gloucestershire. At one point 120 local men had signed the pledge against drinking and attended their meetings, where Bible readings and prayers took place and coffee and cakes were served.

4 **Impatient in standing**. This was a fault shared by Bessie, the black mare belonging to Anna Sewell's brother Philip and which may be one of the models for Black Beauty. Susan Chitty writes: 'She was a restless horse . . . and would not allow social calls to last beyond the prescribed fifteen minutes. When she brought Anna's nieces to see her they would put their heads out of the window and plead with her to wait an extra five minutes, but Philip found it hard to hold her and the carriage was usually moving away down the road before the last one had climbed in' (*The Woman who Wrote Black Beauty*, 1971).

and looked at my foot again; then he took his handkerchief and bound it closely round, and so he led me home. I shall never forget that night walk; it was more than three miles. Robert led me on very slowly, and I limped and hobbled on as well as I could with great pain. I am sure he was sorry for me, for he often patted and encouraged me, talking to me in a pleasant voice.

At last I reached my own box, and had some corn, and after Robert had wrapped up my knees in wet cloths, he tied up my foot in a bran poultice to draw out the heat, and cleanse it before the horse doctor saw it in the morning, and I managed to get myself down on the straw, and slept in spite of the pain.

The next day, after the farrier had examined my wounds, he said he hoped the joint was not injured, and if so, I should not be spoiled for work, but I should never lose the blemish. I believe they did the best to make a good cure, but it was a long and painful one; proud flesh, as they called it, came up in my knees, and was burnt out with caustic, and when at last it was healed, they put a blistering fluid over the front of both knees to bring all the hair off; they had some reason for this, and I suppose it was all right.

As Smith's death had been so sudden, and no one was there to see it, there was an inquest held. The landlord and ostler at the White Lion, with several other people, gave evidence that he was intoxicated when he started from the inn. The keeper of the toll-gate said he rode at a hard gallop through the gate; and my shoe was picked up amongst the stones, so that the case was quite plain to them, and I was cleared of all blame.

Everybody pitied Susan; she was nearly out of her mind: she kept saying over and over again, 'Oh! he was so good—so good! it **was all** that cursed drink; why will they sell that cursed drink?

5 **Bran poultice**. A soft mass of hot, wet bran was smeared on to a cloth and applied against the skin to reduce swelling and pain. The bran helped conserve heat.

Blistering ointment: a commercial preparation. (Moseman's *Illustrated Guide for Purchasers of Horse Furnishing Goods*, p. 61)

6 **A good cure**. The description of Black Beauty's cure accords reasonably well with that recommended by 'Magenta' in *The Handy Horse Book* (1865). After washing the wound in warm water he suggests a lotion of chloride of zinc (made with a ratio of one grain to one ounce of water). Once the wound is healed, his remedy for promoting the growth of hair is the application of an ointment made of hog's lard mixed with finely powdered burnt leather or a weak mercurial ointment. However, he also advised that the horse should not be allowed to lie down until the wound was healed, and he recommended one or two mild purges during the period of healing.

7 **Proud flesh**. Horses are very prone to this over-production of granulation tissue (lumpy flesh) around the edges of an open wound. It was not a result of ignorance about veterinary matters in Black Beauty's day.

8 **Burnt out with caustic**. Cauterisation or burning using a solid or liquid corrosive agent to destroy the tissue would have been used in Black Beauty's day. Today copper sulphate is often used to dry up and reduce the growth of proud flesh.

9 **Blistering fluid**. Traditionally oil of cantharides, a popular counter-irritant as treatment for sprains, injuries etc. and also used 'to harden the legs', the idea being to create irritation which would encourage blood to flow more strongly in that area and hence aid the healing process. Little used nowadays, if at all.

229

Oh, Reuben, Reuben!' So she went on till after he was buried, and then, as she had no home or relations, she, with her six little children, were obliged once more to leave the pleasant home by the tall oak trees, and go into that great gloomy Union
10 House.

10 **Union House**. Workhouse.

A ward in the Marylebone workhouse, regarded as a model of its kind. (*Illustrated London News, c.* 1847)

231

CHAPTER XXVII

RUINED, AND GOING DOWNHILL

AS soon as my knees were sufficiently healed, I was turned into a small meadow for a month or two; no other creature was there, and though I enjoyed the liberty and the sweet grass, yet I had been so long used to society that I felt very lonely. Ginger and I had become fast friends, and now I missed her company extremely. I often neighed when I heard horses' feet passing in the road, but I seldom got an answer; till one morning the gate was opened, and who should come in but dear old Ginger. The man slipped off her halter and left her there. With a joyful whinny I trotted up to her; we were both glad to meet, but I soon found that it was not for our pleasure that she was brought to be with me. Her story would be too long to tell, but the end of it was that she

232

Black Beauty is led away from Ginger after their reunion. Illustrated by Lucy Kemp-Welch. (*Black Beauty*, London: J. M. Dent, 1915, pl. opp. p. 118)

had been ruined by hard riding, and was now turned off to see what rest would do.

Lord George was young and would take no warning; he was a hard rider, and would hunt whenever he could get the chance, quite careless of his horse.   Soon after I left the stable there was a steeplechase, and he determined to ride.   Though the groom told him she was a little strained, and was not fit for the race, he did not believe it, and on the day of the race urged Ginger to keep up with the foremost riders.   With her high spirit, she strained herself to the utmost; she came in with the first three horses, but her wind was touched, beside which, he was too heavy for her, and her back was strained.   'And so,' she said, 'here we are—ruined in the prime of our youth and strength— you by a drunkard, and I by a fool; it is very hard.'   We both felt in ourselves that we were not what we had been.   However, that did not spoil the pleasure we had in each other's company; we did not gallop about as we once did, but we used to feed, and lie down together, and stand for hours under one of the shady lime trees with our heads close to each other; and so we passed our time till the family returned from town.

One day we saw the Earl come into the meadow, and York was with him.   Seeing who it was, we stood still under our lime tree, and let them come up to us.   They examined us carefully. The Earl seemed much annoyed.

'There is three hundred pounds flung away for no earthly use,' said he; 'but what I care most for is, that these horses of my old friend, who thought they would find a good home with me, are ruined.   The mare shall have a twelvemonth's run, and we shall see what that will do for her; but the black one, he must be sold; 'tis a great pity, but I could not have knees like these in my stables.'

1 **Steeplechase**. Originally a race run over natural countryside, often of several miles, which involved jumping any fence, gate, wall or ditch *en route*. It was so named because the course ran from one village to the next using the church steeples as markers. By Black Beauty's time steeplechases had moved to racecourses with specially built fences, usually of brushwood, and some ditches.

2 **Wind was touched**. It used to be thought that over-strenuous exercise when unfit made a horse 'broken winded', i.e. it no longer inhaled and exhaled smoothly. Such a horse would have less stamina and be more prone to exhaustion. It was classified as 'unsound'. Nowadays, research has shown 'broken wind' to be an allergic condition.

3 **Three hundred pounds**. This was a good price to pay for two horses. In 1886, Fleming (*Practical Horse Keeper*) suggests a price of 200 to 400 guineas for a first-class, weight-carrying hunter. A carriage horse of the best type would fetch £200–300. See p. 283 for the decline in Black Beauty's value.

4 **Knees like these**. Although Black Beauty has escaped without permanent injury, the fact that he carries a blemish is enough to bar him for life from a gentleman's stable.

Nineteenth-century steeplechasing. (Earl of Suffolk, *Racing and Steeplechasing*, p. 339)

'No, my lord, of course not,' said York; 'but he might get a place where appearance is not of much consequence, and still be well treated. I know a man in Bath, the master of some livery stables, who often wants a good horse at a low figure; I know he looks well after his horses. The inquest cleared the horse's character, and your lordship's recommendation, or mine, would be sufficient warrant for him.'

'You had better write to him, York. I should be more particular about the place than the money he would fetch.'

After this they left us.

'They 'll soon take you away,' said Ginger, 'and I shall lose the only friend I have, and most likely we shall never see each other again. 'Tis a hard world!'

About a week after this, Robert came into the field with a halter, which he slipped over my head, and led me away. There was no leave-taking of Ginger; we neighed to each other as I was led off, and she trotted anxiously along by the hedge calling to me as long as she could hear the sound of my feet.

Through the recommendation of York, I was bought by the master of the livery stable. I had to go by train, which was new to me, and required a good deal of courage the first time; but as I found the puffing, rushing, whistling, and more than all, the trembling of the horse-box in which I stood did me no real harm, I soon took it quietly.

When I reached the end of my journey, I found myself in a tolerably comfortable stable and well attended to. These stables were not so airy and pleasant as those I had been used to. The stalls were laid on a slope instead of being level, and as my head was kept tied to the manger, I was obliged always to stand on the slope, which was very fatiguing. Men do not seem to know yet that horses can do more work if they can stand comfortably and

236

5 Train. Travelling by train was the only method of transporting horses long distances over land, the only other alternatives being either to ride, drive or lead the horse or, in the case of valuable racehorses, take them by road in a horse-drawn horse box which was, of course, very slow. Rail carriage service for horses continued well into the twentieth century, but was finally withdrawn by British Rail in the 1960s.

6 Tied. In a stall such as described, the horse had to be restrained otherwise it could simply back out into the aisle (see p. 29). The manger would have been a permanent fixture at the opposite end of the stall from the aisle. Near to the manger or in the wall would have been a ring through which a rope from the horse's headcollar would have been passed. The end of this rope would normally have passed through a wooden ball (known as a log) about four inches in diameter, and knotted so it did not pull through the log, thus allowing the horse a certain freedom of movement, enough to lie down and get up. The idea of this weighted rope was that as the horse moved the rope was kept taut by gravity acting on the log and thus did not form dangerous loops in which the horse could get entangled. Sometimes, of course, the horse was merely tied to a ring in the wall and had far less ease of movement.

7 Stand on the slope. Drains were a big issue in nineteenth-century stable management. Stalls in late-eighteenth- and early-nineteenth-century Britain were built with a slope to the rear so as to drain urine and spilled water towards the central aisle. Thus the horse was effectively standing with its front feet higher than its hind feet, putting unnecessary strain on leg and back muscles. The pitch of this slope was frequently more than ten degrees – a pitch of two degrees would have served equally well. Some (mostly from the newly developing profession of veterinary surgeons) declared: 'too rapid a slope strains the back sinews'. On the other hand, a much reprinted writer, John Stewart, in his *Stable Economy* of 1849, disagreed: 'No one has ever seen a horse harmed in this way.'

Tied in a stall. (Robert Jennings, *The Horse and Other Live Stock*, Philadelphia: John E. Potter, [1886], p. 126)

Horse in a stall secured by a log and rope. Boredom often led to stable vices such as crib-biting, where the horse swallowed air while gripping any solid object, such as a manger, with its teeth. (Vero Shaw, *The Encyclopaedia of the Stable*, London: George Routledge, 1909, p. 94)

can turn about: however, I was well fed and well cleaned, and, on the whole, I think our master took as much care of us as he could. He kept a good many horses and carriages of different 8 kinds, for hire. Sometimes his own men drove them; at others, the horse and chaise were let to gentlemen or ladies who drove themselves.

8 **For hire.** Stables where horses and carriages were kept for hire were originally termed livery stables, which now usually refers to stables looking after privately owned horses. It was usual for the hirer to drive, although it was also possible to hire a driver.

Black Beauty enters the special horse carriage on the train. Illustrated by John Beer. (*Black Beauty*, London: Jarrold & Sons, [191?], p. 135)

CHAPTER XXVIII

A JOB-HORSE AND HIS DRIVERS

HITHERTO I had always been driven by people who at least knew how to drive; but in this place I was to get my experience of all the different kinds of bad and ignorant driving to which we horses are subjected; for

1 I was a 'job-horse,' and was let out to all sorts of people, who wished to hire me; and as I was good-tempered and gentle, I think I was oftener let out to the ignorant drivers than some of the other horses, because I could be depended upon. It would take a long time to tell of all the different styles in which I was driven, but I will mention a few of them.

2 First, there were the tight-rein drivers—men who seemed to

240

1 **Job-horse**. A horse for public hire which was rented or leased complete with harness and carriage or other vehicle. Men who owned such horses and ran these businesses were known as job-masters.

2 **Tight-rein drivers**. When riding or driving it is essential to keep a contact with the horse's mouth via the bit and the reins so that the horse can immediately feel any signals given by the rider or driver as to whether to turn left or right or to stop. If the contact is too tight such delicate communication lines are lost, as well as being painful for the horse. If too slack, the horse cannot pick up the signals quickly and accurately.

Driving with a tight and uneven rein. (Duke of Beaufort, *Driving*, London: Longmans Green, 1889, p. 4)

think that all depended on holding the reins as hard as they could, never relaxing the pull on the horse's mouth, or giving him the liberty of movement. They are always talking about 'keeping the horse well in hand,' and 'holding a horse up,' just as if a horse was not made to hold himself up.

Some poor broken-down horses, whose mouths have been made hard and insensible by just such drivers as these, may, perhaps, find some support in it; but for a horse who can depend upon its own legs, and who has a tender mouth, and is easily guided, it is not only tormenting, but it is stupid.

Then there are the loose-rein drivers, who let the reins lie easily on our backs, and their own hand rest lazily on their knees. Of course, such gentlemen have no control over a horse, if anything happens suddenly. If a horse shies, or starts, or stumbles, they are nowhere and cannot help the horse or themselves, till the mischief is done. Of course, for myself, I had no objection to it, as I was not in the habit either of starting or stumbling, and had only been used to depend on my driver for guidance and encouragement; still, one likes to feel the rein a little in going downhill, and likes to know that one's driver is not gone to sleep.

Besides, a slovenly way of driving gets a horse into bad, and often lazy habits; and when he changes hands, he has to be whipped out of them with more or less pain and trouble. Squire Gordon always kept us to our best paces, and our best manners. He said that spoiling a horse, and letting him get into bad habits, was just as cruel as spoiling a child, and both had to suffer for it afterwards.

Besides these drivers are often careless altogether, and will attend to anything else rather than their horses. I went out in the phaeton one day with one of them; he had a lady, and two

3 Manners. A discipline imposed on the horse, usually when young, to control its behaviour in the stable and out, when being led, ridden or driven. Good manners are vital for safety's sake. A horse should stop, walk, trot, canter or gallop immediately it is asked to do so, but not too fast nor lazily. A horse should also be taught to obey commands to move to one side, pick up its feet and so on.

4 Phaeton. An open, four-wheeled carriage often driven by the owner rather than a coachman. It can be large enough to require a team of four horses or small enough for a single pony or even a donkey. There are many varieties of phaeton depending upon various aspects of its construction (e.g. the spider phaeton, with its fine lines and delicate springing, or the high flyer phaeton with its large wheels and driver's seat perched precariously above the centre of gravity), or named after the coachbuilder (e.g. the Tilbury phaeton), or named after the person commissioning such a vehicle to be built (e.g. the Stanhope phaeton). The vehicle is said to be named after the mythological Greek god, Phaethon, son of Helios, the sun god, who drove his father's sun chariot but the horses bolted and almost set fire to the earth.

A park phaeton. Again, the bearing reins are fashionably tight. (Sidney, *Book of the Horse*, p. 536)

children behind. He flopped the reins about as we started, and of course gave me several unmeaning cuts with the whip, though I was fairly off. There had been a good deal of road-mending going on, and even where the stones were not freshly laid down there were a great many loose ones about. My driver was laughing and joking with the lady and the children, and talking about the country to the right and the left; but he never thought it worth while to keep an eye on his horse, or to drive on the smoothest parts of the road; and so it easily happened that I got a stone in one of my fore feet.

Now, if Mr. Gordon, or John, or in fact any good driver had been there he would have seen that something was wrong before I had gone three paces. Or even if it had been dark, a practised hand would have felt by the rein that there was something wrong in the step, and they would have got down and picked out the stone. But this man went on laughing and talking, whilst at every step the stone became more firmly wedged between my shoe and the frog of my foot. The stone was sharp on the inside and round on the outside, which, as every one knows, is the most dangerous kind that a horse can pick up; at the same time cutting his foot, and making him most liable to stumble and fall.

Whether the man was partly blind, or only very careless, I can't say; but he drove me with that stone in my foot for a good half-mile before he saw anything. By that time I was going so lame with the pain, that at last he saw it and called out, 'Well, here 's a go! Why, they have sent us out with a lame horse! What a shame!'

He then chucked the reins and flipped about with the whip, saying, 'Now, then, it 's no use playing the old soldier with me; there 's the journey to go and it 's no use turning lame and lazy.'

5 **Frog**. The triangular-shaped, rubbery part on the underside of the horse's hoof which acts as a shock absorber. Stones and other objects are liable to wedge themselves near the heel and press on the sensitive parts of the foot, causing bruising or even an open wound.

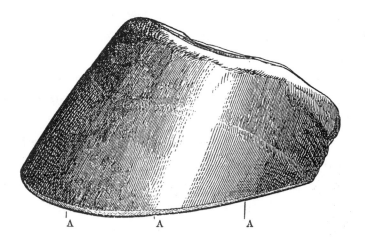

The horse's foot from the side and underneath, showing the frog. Stones can easily get wedged in the area marked D when the foot is shod. (Lt-General Sir F. Fitzwygram, *Horses and Stables*, London: Longmans Green, 2nd edn, 1881, pl. xxxvi)

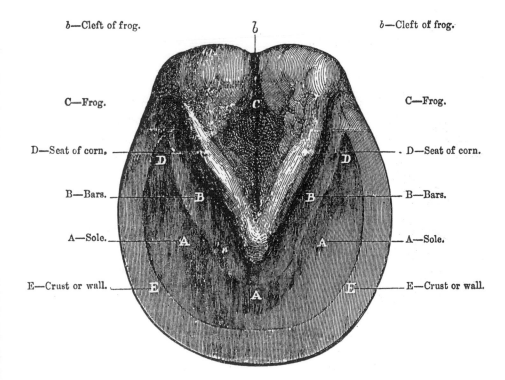

Just at this time a farmer came riding up on a brown cob; he lifted his hat and pulled up.

'I beg your pardon, sir,' he said, 'but I think there is something the matter with your horse, he goes very much as if he had a stone in his shoe. If you will allow me, I will look at his feet; these loose scattered stones are confounded dangerous things for the horses.'

'He 's a hired horse,' said my driver; 'I don't know what 's the matter with him, but it 's a great shame to send out a lame beast like this.'

The farmer dismounted, and slipping his rein over his arm, at once took up my near foot.

'Bless me, there 's a stone! Lame! I should think so!'

At first he tried to dislodge it with his hand, but as it was now very tightly wedged, he drew a stone-pick out of his pocket, and very carefully, and with some trouble, got it out. Then holding it up, he said, 'There, that 's the stone your horse had picked up; it is a wonder he did not fall down and break his knees into the bargain!'

'Well, to be sure!' said my driver, 'that is a queer thing! I never knew that horses picked up stones before.'

'Didn't you?' said the farmer, rather contemptuously; 'but they do, though, and the best of them will do it, and can't help it sometimes on such roads as these. And if you don't want to lame your horse, you must look sharp and get them out quickly. This foot is very much bruised,' he said, setting it gently down and patting me. 'If I might advise, sir, you had better drive him gently for a while; the foot is a good deal hurt, and the lameness will not go off directly.'

Then mounting his cob and raising his hat to the lady, he trotted off.

6 **Stone-pick**. More commonly called a hoof-pick, it is a strong metal implement small enough to be carried in the pocket (sometimes it will fold for more convenience) with a blunt hook at one end. It is specifically for prising stones and other foreign bodies out of horses' hooves.

7 **Break his knees**. See p. 227.

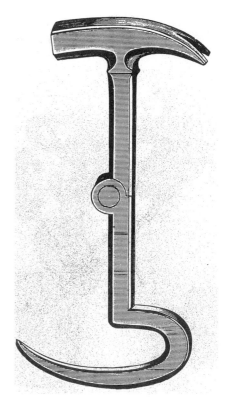

Folding stone-pick or hoof-pick. (Moseman's *Illustrated Guide for Purchasers of Horse Furnishing Goods*, p. 19)

Picking up a horse's foot. Illustrated by Mike Grimsdale. (*Black Beauty*, London: Chancellor Press, 1987, reprint of Octopus, 1984 edn, pl. opp. p. 113)

When he was gone, my driver began to flop the reins about, and whip the harness, by which I understood that I was to go on, which of course I did, glad that the stone was gone, but still in a good deal of pain.

This was the sort of experience we job-horses often came in for.

'I don't know what's the matter with him'. Illustrated by Lucy Kemp-Welch. (*Black Beauty*, London: J. M. Dent, 1915, pl. opp. p. 123)

CHAPTER XXIX

COCKNEYS

THEN there is the steam-engine style of driving; these drivers were mostly people from towns, who never had a horse of their own, and generally travelled by rail.

They always seemed to think that a horse was something like a steam-engine, only smaller. At any rate, they think that if only they pay for it, a horse is bound to go just as far, and just as fast, and with just as heavy a load as they please. And be the roads heavy and muddy, or dry and good; be they stony or smooth, uphill or downhill, it is all the same—on, on, on, one must go at the same pace, with no relief, and no consideration.

These people never think of getting out to walk up a steep hill. Oh, no, they have paid to ride, and ride they will! The horse? Oh, he 's used to it! What were horses made for, if not to drag people uphill? Walk! A good joke indeed! And so the whip is plied and the rein is chucked, and often a rough scolding voice

'The steam-engine style of driving': (*top*)
Gordon, *Horse World of London*, p. 114;
(*bottom*) Duke of Beaufort, *Driving*, London:
Longmans Green, 1889, p. 142

cries out, 'Go along, you lazy beast!' And then another slash of the whip, when all the time we are doing our very best to get along, uncomplaining and obedient, though often sorely harassed and down-hearted.

This steam-engine style of driving wears us up faster than any other kind. I would far rather go twenty miles with a good considerate driver, than I would go ten with some of these; it would take less out of me.

Another thing—they scarcely ever put on the drag, however steep the downhill may be, and thus bad accidents sometimes happen; or if they do put it on, they often forget to take it off at the bottom of the hill; and more than once I have had to pull half-way up the next hill, with one of the wheels lodged fast in the drag-shoe, before my driver chose to think about it; and that is a terrible strain on a horse.

Then these Cockneys, instead of starting at an easy pace as a gentleman would do, generally set off at full speed from the very stable yard; and when they want to stop, they first whip us and then pull up so suddenly, that we are nearly thrown on our haunches, and out mouths jagged with the bit; they call that pulling up with a dash! and when they turn a corner, they do it as sharply as if there were no right side or wrong side of the road.

I well remember one spring evening I and Rory had been out for the day. (Rory was the horse that mostly went with me when a pair was ordered, and a good honest fellow he was.) We had our own driver, and as he was always considerate and gentle with us, we had a very pleasant day. We were coming home at a good smart pace about twilight; our road turned sharp to the left; but as we were close to the hedge on our own side, and there was plenty of room to pass, our driver did not pull us in. As we neared the corner I heard a horse and two wheels coming

1 **A good considerate driver**. Such a driver might be familiar with the rhyme set out by 'Magenta' (*Handy Horse Book*, 1865):

> Walk me a mile out and a mile in;
> Up the hill spur me not,
> Down the hill I'll walk or trot;
> On the plain spare me not;
> In the stable forget me not.

2 **Cockneys**. Working-class Londoners from the East End with a very strong sense of community. Strictly speaking, true Cockneys are those born within the sound of Bow bells, i.e. within the area in which the 'Great Bell of Bow' of the nursery rhyme 'Oranges and Lemons' could be heard. Bow Churchyard is just to the east of St Paul's Cathedral in the City of London.

Two interpretations of the thoughtlessness of drivers: (*left*) 'Pulling up with a dash', illustrated by Pauline Baynes (*Black Beauty*, Harmondsworth: Puffin, 1984, p. 125); (*bottom*); 'Go along, you lazy beast', illustrated by Charlotte Hough (*Black Beauty*, Harmondsworth: Puffin, 1983, p. 116).

rapidly down the hill towards us. The hedge was high and I could see nothing, but the next moment we were upon each other. Happily for me, I was on the side next the hedge. Rory was on the right side of the pole, and had not even a shaft to protect him. The man who was driving was making straight for the corner, and when he came in sight of us he had no time to pull over to his own side. The whole shock came upon Rory. The gig shaft ran right into the chest, making him stagger back with a cry that I shall never forget. The other horse was thrown upon his haunches, and one shaft broken. It turned out that it was a horse from our own stables, with the high-wheeled gig, that the young men were so fond of.

The driver was one of those random, ignorant fellows, who don't even know which is their own side of the road, or if they know, don't care. And there was poor Rory with his flesh torn open and bleeding, and the blood streaming down. They said if it had been a little more to one side, it would have killed him; and a good thing for him, poor fellow, if it had.

As it was, it was a long time before the wound healed, and then he was sold for coal-carting; and what that is, up and down those steep hills, only horses know. Some of the sights I saw there, where a horse had to come downhill with a heavily loaded two-wheel cart behind him, on which no drag could be placed, make me sad even now to think of.

After Rory was disabled, I often went in the carriage with a mare named Peggy, who stood in the next stall to mine. She was a strong, well-made animal, of a bright dun colour, beautifully dappled, and with a dark-brown mane and tail. There was no high breeding about her, but she was very pretty, and remarkably sweet-tempered and willing. Still, there was an anxious look about her eye, by which I knew that she had some trouble.

3 Shaft. When a single horse is being driven it is placed between shafts (shaped parallel poles fixed to the front of the vehicle). These are usually made of lancewood, which is springy, or ash, which can be steam-bent into an elegant curve for a fashionable carriage, although most shafts on carts and wagons were straight. The shafts keep the horse pointing forwards and act as steering and brakes.

4 Dun. A term applied to a horse whose basic coat colour ranges from yellow-fawn through golden brown to mouse grey, but has black or brown 'points', i.e. muzzle, ears, mane, tail, legs to the knee and nearly always an eel stripe – a black or brown line running the length of the spine.

5 Dappled. This pattern of darker circular markings about an inch and a half in diameter can be seen in duns and bays, but is most often seen in greys.

Dappled coat. (E. Dillon, *Catalogue of Norman French Horses*, Bloomington, Ill.: Pantagraph Stock Printing Establishment, 1882, p. 29)

The first time we went out together I thought she had a very odd pace; she seemed to go partly in a trot, partly in a canter—three or four paces, and then to make a little jump forward.

It was very unpleasant for any horse who pulled with her, and made me quite fidgety. When we got home, I asked her what made her go in that odd, awkward way.

'Ah,' she said in a troubled manner, 'I know my paces are very bad, but what can I do? It really is not my fault, it is just because my legs are so short. I stand nearly as high as you, but your legs are a good three inches longer above your knees than mine, and of course you can take a much longer step, and go much faster. You see I did not make myself; I wish I could have done so, I would have had long legs then; all my troubles come from my short legs,' said Peggy, in a desponding tone.

'But how is it,' I said, 'when you are so strong and good-tempered and willing?'

'Why you see,' said she, 'men will go so fast, and if one can't keep up to other horses, it is nothing but whip, whip, whip, all the time. And so I have had to keep up as I could, and have got into this ugly shuffling pace. It was not always so; when I lived with my first master I always went a good regular trot, but then he was not in such a hurry. He was a young clergyman in the country, and a good kind master he was. He had two churches a good way apart, and a great deal of work, but he never scolded or whipped me for not going faster. He was very fond of me. I only wish I was with him now; but he had to leave and go to a large town, and then I was sold to a farmer.

'Some farmers, you know, are capital masters; but I think this one was a low sort of man. He cared nothing about good horses, or good driving; he only cared for going fast. I went as fast as I could, but that would not do, and he was always

A well-matched pair which would have no trouble keeping in stride. (Gordon, *The Horse World of London*, p. 103)

whipping; so I got into this way of making a spring forward to keep up. On market nights he used to stay very late at the inn, and then drive home at a gallop.

'One dark night he was galloping home as usual, when all on a sudden the wheel came against some great heavy thing in the road, and turned the gig over in a minute. He was thrown out and his arm broken, and some of his ribs, I think. At any rate, it was the end of my living with him, and I was not sorry. But you see it will be the same everywhere for me, if men *must* go so fast. I wish my legs were longer!'

Poor Peggy! I was very sorry for her, and I could not comfort her, for I knew how hard it was upon slow-paced horses to be put with fast ones; all the whipping comes to their share, and they can't help it.

She was often used in the phaeton, and was very much liked by some of the ladies, because she was so gentle; and some time after this she was sold to two ladies who drove themselves, and wanted a safe good horse.

I met her several times out in the country, going a good steady pace, and looking as gay and contented as a horse could be. I was very glad to see her, for she deserved a good place.

After she left us, another horse came in her stead. He was young, and had a bad name for shying and starting, by which he had lost a good place. I asked him what made him shy.

'Well, I hardly know,' he said; 'I was timid when I was young, and was a good deal frightened several times, and if I saw anything strange, I used to turn and look at it—you see, with our blinkers one can't see or understand what a thing is unless one looks round; and then my master always gave me a whipping, which of course made me start on, and did not make me less afraid. I think if he would have let me just look at things quietly, and see

6 **Shying**. The horse is essentially a nervous animal. Because its eyes are set at the sides of its head it can see well laterally and to a certain extent to the rear, although close forward vision is limited. When frightened, the horse's first instinct is flight and shying results from seeing potential 'enemies' to the side and swinging round to avoid them. Horses sometimes shy out of habit or high spirits rather than fear. It is disconcerting for the rider or driver and a horse which habitually shies is considered to be dangerous. In *The Handy Horse Book* (1865) 'Magenta' writes: '*Shying* may proceed from various causes, such as defective sight, nervousness, or tricks; thus it may be the result of either constitutional infirmity or vice. From whatever cause proceeding, the proper way to manage a shying horse is to turn his head *away from* the object at which he shies ... but if it is particularly desirable that the animal should become familiarised with anything of which he is shy, let him be brought to a standstill, and coaxed gradually to it, that he may assure himself of its harmlessness by smelling and feeling it with his nose and lips, if possible.'

Shying. (Mayhew, *The Illustrated Horse Management*, p. 320)

Shying. (Wood engraving by W. S. Herrick for an edition of Maria Edgeworth's *The Parent's Assistant; or, Stories for Children*, c. 1860)

that there was nothing to hurt me, it would have been all right, and I should have got used to them.   One day an old gentleman was riding with him, and a large piece of white paper or rag blew across just on one side of me; I shied and started forward —my master as usual whipped me smartly, but the old man cried out, ''You 're wrong! you 're wrong! you should never whip a horse for shying: he shies because he is frightened, and you only frighten him more, and make the habit worse.''   So I suppose all men don't do so.   I am sure I don't want to shy for the sake of it; but how should one know what is dangerous and what is not, if one is never allowed to get used to anything?   I am never afraid of what I know.   Now I was brought up in a park where there were deer; of course, I knew them as well as I did a sheep or a cow, but they are not common, and I know many sensible horses who are frightened at them, and who kick up quite a shindy before they will pass a paddock where there are deer.'

I knew what my companion said was true, and I wished that every young horse had as good a master as Farmer Grey and Squire Gordon.

Of course we sometimes came in for good driving here.   I remember one morning I was put into the light gig, and taken to a house in Pulteney Street.   Two gentlemen came out; the taller of them came round to my head, he looked at the bit and bridle, and just shifted the collar with his hand, to see if it fitted comfortably.

7   'Do you consider this horse wants a curb?' he said to the ostler.

'Well,' said the man, 'I should say he would go just as well without, he has an uncommon good mouth, and though he has a fine spirit, he has no vice; but we generally find people like the curb.'

7　**Curb.** A type of bit usually used in driving with a mouthpiece and metal shanks (called cheeks) on either side of the horse's mouth to which the reins are threaded through slots. The reference here is probably to the curb chain, which passes from the bit under the horse's chin, and can easily be removed. It acts in a pincer movement with the bit when the rein is pulled, and the greater the leverage of the bit, the more pressure is brought to bear on the horse's lower jaw. A curb bit of a different design is used in conjunction with a snaffle bit in the double bridle for riding, but it also has a curb chain. See p. 263.

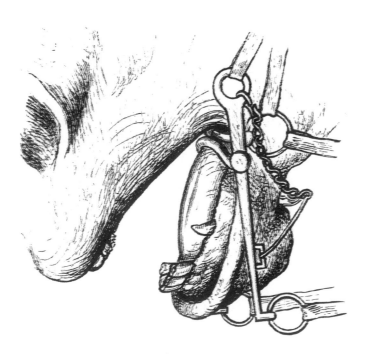

Curb chains (*above*) for riding and driving bits (Moseman's *Illustrated Guide for Purchasers of Horse Furnishing Goods*, p. 167); and (*left*) the bits of a double bridle, where the snaffle bit is placed above the curb bit (L. von Heydebrand und der Lasa, *Die Amazone*, Leipzig: Otto Spamer, 1884, p. 86)

261

'I don't like it,' said the gentleman: 'be so good as to take it
off, and put the rein in at the cheek; an easy mouth is a great
thing on a long journey, is it not, old fellow?' he said, patting
my neck.

Then he took the reins, and they both got up. I can remember
now how quietly he turned me round, and then with a light feel
of the rein, and drawing the whip gently across my back, we
were off.

I arched my neck and set off at my best pace. I found I had
someone behind me who knew how a good horse ought to be
driven. It seemed like old times again, and made me feel quite
gay.

This gentleman took a great liking to me, and after trying me
several times with the saddle, he prevailed upon my master to
sell me to a friend of his, who wanted a safe pleasant horse for
riding. And so it came to pass that in the summer I was sold
to Mr. Barry.

8   **Rein in at the cheek**. Depending on the design of the bit, its severity can be increased or decreased by adjusting the position of the rein to a higher or lower hole in the cheeks, to give more or less leverage.

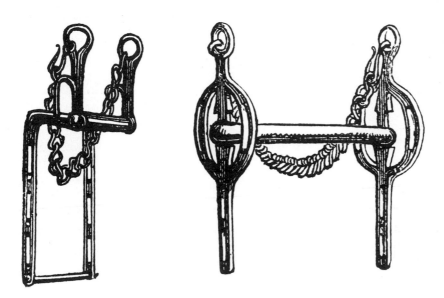

Two types of driving curbs, the Wimbush (*left*) with long shanks and so capable of a great deal of leverage, and the Liverpool. (Sidney, *Book of the Horse*, p. 361, detail)

263

CHAPTER XXX

A THIEF

1
2
MY new master was an unmarried man. He lived at Bath, and was much engaged in business. His doctor advised him to take horse exercise, and for this purpose he bought me. He hired a stable a short distance from

3, 4 his lodgings, and engaged a man named Filcher as groom. My master knew very little about horses, but he treated me well, and I should have had a good and easy place, but for circum-

5 stances of which he was ignorant. He ordered the best hay with

6 plenty of oats, crushed beans, and bran, with vetches, or rye grass, as the man might think needful. I heard the master give the order, so I knew there was plenty of good food, and I thought I was well off.

For a few days all went on well; I found that my groom understood his business. He kept the stable clean and airy, and he groomed me thoroughly; and was never otherwise than gentle. He had been an ostler in one of the great hotels in Bath. He had given that up, and now cultivated fruit and vegetables for the market; and his wife bred and fattened poultry and rabbits for

264

1   **Bath**. Roman spa town south east of Bristol. It was a very popular watering place in the eighteenth and early nineteenth centuries when fashionable society came to drink the health-giving mineral waters. It has some of the finest Georgian architecture in England. Anna Sewell lived there from 1864 to 1867. Bath is also noted for its connections with the novelist, Jane Austen.

2   **Horse exercise**. Often prescribed for a variety of complaints on the basis that 'The outside of a horse is good for the inside of a man' – a popular saying amongst fashionable physicians in the nineteenth century.

3   **Lodgings**. Until the middle of the twentieth century most people rented rather than bought their homes. Tenants had few rights and could be evicted at a moment's notice. Lodgings were not a matter of class or poverty; for example, Sherlock Holmes lived in lodgings.

4   **Filcher**. Another instance of the popular Victorian ploy for indicating the character by using a flattering or unflattering surname. Filching is a colloquial term for pilfering or stealing, hence the title of this chapter.

5   **The best hay**. Meadow hay, which includes a variety of wild flowers and herbs, or seed hay, which is cut from specially sown grass seed. Old hay is generally reckoned to be better than new hay, having had a chance to mature (for up to eighteen months) before being fed.

6   **Vetches or rye grass**. It is difficult to know whether these would have been fed fresh or as hay. Most town horses' fodder was delivered dry as it was easier to transport and could be stored for long periods. Freshly cut vetches and rye grass would have been welcomed, but there would have been difficulties in delivering it while it was still fresh and before it began to wilt and go sour.

sale. After a while it seemed to me that my oats came very short; I had the beans, but bran was mixed with them instead of oats, of which there were very few; certainly not more than a quarter of what there should have been. In two or three weeks this began to tell upon my strength and spirits. The grass food, though very good, was not the thing to keep up my condition without corn. However, I could not complain, nor make known my wants. So it went on for about two months; and I wondered
7 my master did not see that something was the matter. However, one afternoon he rode out into the country to see a friend
8 of his—a gentleman farmer, who lived on the road to Wells. This gentleman had a very quick eye for horses; and after he had welcomed his friend, he said, casting his eye over me—

'It seems to me, Barry, that your horse does not look so well as he did when you first had him; has he been well?'

'Yes, I believe so,' said my master, 'but he is not nearly so lively as he was; my groom tells me that horses are always dull and weak in the autumn, and that I must expect it.'

9 'Autumn! fiddlesticks!' said the farmer; 'why this is only August; and with your light work and good food he ought not to go down like this, even if it was autumn. How do you feed him?'

My master told him. The other shook his head slowly, and began to feel me over.

'I can't say who eats your corn, my dear fellow, but I am much mistaken if your horse gets it. Have you ridden very fast?'

'No! very gently.'

'Then just put your hand here,' said he, passing his hand over
10 my neck and shoulder; 'he is as warm and damp as a horse just come up from grass. I advise you to look into your stable a little more. I hate to be suspicious, and, thank heaven, I have

7 **Master did not see**. A popular Victorian saying was: 'The eye of the master maketh the horse fat', meaning that, although the master himself did not necessarily tend his horses, he should know enough about them to ensure that they were kept in good condition.

8 **Wells**. Town in Somerset not far from Bath and famous for its cathedral.

9 **Fiddlesticks**. A popular inoffensive expletive used at a time when cursing or forceful slang were not acceptable on the printed page – nor, one imagines, to Anna Sewell.

10 **Neck and shoulder ... warm and damp as a horse just come up from grass**. When a horse has spent time grazing and been given no protein-rich foods and exercise to build him up, he is said to be in soft condition, which can be indicated by the softness of the muscles along the top of the neck and the ease with which he sweats and becomes damp or even wet. A horse in firmly muscled condition is the opposite.

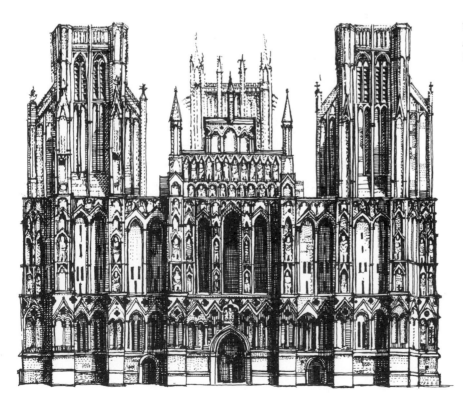

Wells Cathedral. (John B. Nellist, *British Architecture and its Background*, London: Macmillan, 1967, p. 117)

no cause to be, for I can trust my men, present or absent; but there are mean scoundrels, wicked enough to rob a dumb beast of his food; you must look into it.'   And turning to his man who had come to take me, 'Give this horse a right good feed of bruised oats, and don't stint him.'

'Dumb beasts!' yes we are; but if I could have spoken, I could have told my master where his oats went to.   My groom used to come every morning about six o'clock, and with him a little boy, who always had a covered basket with him.   He used to go with his father into the harness room where the corn was kept, and I could see them when the door stood ajar, fill a little bag with oats out of the bin and then he used to be off.

Five or six mornings after this, just as the boy had left the stable, the door was pushed open and a policeman walked in, holding the child tight by the arm; another policeman followed, and locked the door on the inside, saying, 'Show me the place where your father keeps his rabbits' food.'

The boy looked very frightened and began to cry; but there was no escape, and he led the way to the corn-bin.   Here the policeman found another empty bag like that which was found full of oats in the boy's basket.

Filcher was cleaning my feet at the time, but they soon saw him, and though he blustered a good deal, they walked him off to the 'lock-up,' and his boy with him.   I heard afterwards, that the boy was not held to be guilty, but the man was sentenced to prison for two months.

11 **Policeman**. The British police force has its origins in 1829 when it was founded by Robert Peel. Early policemen were known as 'peelers', a term which has died out, but the affectionate slang term 'Bobby' remains to this day.

12 **Lock-up**. Originally a small building in a town or village for holding one or two petty criminals, drunkards etc., but in Victorian times this would have meant the cells in the local police station.

The dishonest groom and the boy. Illustrated by John Beer. (*Black Beauty*, Boston: De-Wolfe, Fiske & Co., 191?, p. 110)

269

CHAPTER XXXI

A HUMBUG

1   **M**Y master was not immediately suited, but in a few days my new groom came. He was a tall, good-looking fellow enough; but if ever there was a humbug
2 in the shape of a groom, Alfred Smirk was the man. He was very civil to me, and never used me ill; in fact, he did
3 a great deal of stroking and patting, when his master was there to see it. He always brushed my mane and tail with water, and
4 my hoofs with oil before he brought me to the door, to make me look smart; but as to cleaning my feet, or looking to my shoes,
5 or grooming me thoroughly, he thought no more of that than if I had been a cow. He left my bit rusty, my saddle damp, and
6 my crupper stiff.

1   **Immediately suited**. Quickly found a suitable replacement employee.

2   **Alfred Smirk**. Another stereotypical name used to describe a character, in this case an unpleasant type covering his true self by outward signs of pleasantness and insincere smiles.

3   **Master was there to see it**. Nanny Power O'Donoghue, in *Riding for Ladies* (1887), writes: 'An idle groom is generally an eye-server. The wisp is oftener in his hand than the brush. When a horse does not *look* amiss on being brought to the door, and yet that his skin leaves a dirty whitish stain on the fingers when they are pressed into it, the fact is proved beyond all doubt.'

A proprietary hoof dressing. (Moseman's *Illustrated Guide for Purchasers of Horse Furnishing Goods*, p. 41)

4   **Hoofs with oil**. Hooves were, and still are, frequently oiled, partly for cosmetic reasons to make them shine and partly to promote healthy growth of horn. However, it is now thought that oiling has little effect on horn growth, although one school of thought suggests that wetting the hooves with water and then oiling them to seal in the moisture prevents the horn from splitting and cracking. See p. 447.

5   **Grooming me thoroughly**. A stabled horse should be groomed thoroughly once a day, which should take about an hour and involve vigorous brushing with a soft, close-bristled brush (body brush) which gives the coat a shine and cleans out the scurf from the skin; 'wisping', which is massaging with a straw pad to build up muscle; and finally a wiping over with a soft cloth to polish the coat. Eyes, nose and dock should also be wiped with damp sponges, hooves picked out and oiled, and mane and tail either brushed with a body brush or parted into strands with the fingers.

6   **Crupper**. A crupper is made of soft leather and stuffed with oiled padding to keep it smooth and soft, for it is in contact with the underside of the horse's dock which is sensitive and hairless. Any soreness here will lead to kicking in an effort to be rid of the irritation. See p. 19.

Alfred Smirk considered himself very handsome; he spent a great deal of time about his hair, whiskers, and necktie, before a little looking-glass in the harness room. When his master was speaking to him, it was always, 'Yes, sir; yes, sir'; touching his hat at every word; and every one thought he was a very nice young man, and that Mr. Barry was very fortunate to meet with him. I should say he was the laziest, most conceited fellow I ever came near. Of course it was a great thing not to be ill-used, but then a horse wants more than that. I had a loose box, and might have been very comfortable if he had not been too indolent to clean it out. He never took all the straw away, and the smell from what lay underneath was very bad; while the strong vapours that rose up, made my eyes smart and inflame, and I did not feel the same appetite for my food.

One day his master came in and said, 'Alfred, the stable smells rather strong; should not you give that stall a good scrub, and throw down plenty of water?'

'Well, sir,' he said, touching his cap, 'I'll do so if you please, sir, but it is rather dangerous, sir, throwing down water in a horse's box, they are very apt to take cold, sir. I should not like to do him an injury, but I'll do it if you please, sir.'

'Well,' said his master, 'I should not like him to take cold, but I don't like the smell of this stable; do you think the drains are all right?'

'Well, sir, now you mention it, I think the drain does some-times send back a smell; there may be something wrong, sir.'

'Then send for the bricklayer and have it seen to,' said his master.

'Yes, sir, I will.'

The bricklayer came and pulled up a great many bricks, and found nothing amiss; so he put down some lime and charged

272

7 **Strong vapours ... eyes smart and inflame**. The sign of a poorly maintained stable is the strong, pungent smell of ammonia from the horses' decomposing urine, which affects the breathing and eyes of both horses and humans. Mayhew comments: 'It is sad to think that the creature which lives but to toil, and whose existence is a type of such slavery that its greatest freedom is to labour, should be begrudged the bed whereon it reposes, or be doomed to stand in filth which will generate disease. The horse's foot is not very susceptible to external influences. It is encased in a hard and inorganic, yet elastic substance. Thus protected, it appears like praising the ingenuity of man when we say such a body is not proof against his neglect. The hoof is made to travel through mud and through water; it is created to canter over sand and over stones. It is capable of all its purposes; but it only seems not fitted to be soaking days and nights in the filth of a human lazar-house. The drainage of the stable is too often clogged, the ventilation bad, the bedding rotten, and more than half composed of excrement. All that passes through the body, from the inclination of the flooring, tends towards the hind feet. Over this muck the animal breathes. In it the creature stands, and on it the victim reposes.

'No wonder the horn rots, when implanted in a mass of fermenting filth. The fleshy, secreting parts, which it is the office of the hoof to protect, ultimately become affected. They take on a peculiar form of irritation. From the cleft of the frog a discharge issues; it becomes coloured and offensive through being mixed with the decaying horn; the smell is most abhorrent – frequently it taints the interior of the place, and to the educated nose thus makes known its presence.' (*Illustrated Horse Doctor*, London, 1904, pp. 385–6)

8 **Lime**. Calcium oxide or calcium hydroxide to counteract the presence of ammonia and act as a general disinfectant.

Grooming tools. (Mayhew, *Illustrated Horse Management*, p. 561)

the master five shillings, and the smell in my box was as bad as ever: but that was not all—standing as I did on a quantity of moist straw, my feet grew unhealthy and tender, and the master used to say—

'I don't know what is the matter with this horse, he goes very fumble-footed. I am sometimes afraid he will stumble.'

'Yes, sir,' said Alfred, 'I have noticed the same myself, when I have exercised him.'

Now the fact was, that he hardly ever did exercise me, and when the master was busy, I often stood for days together without stretching my legs at all, and yet being fed just as high as if I were at hard work. This often disordered my health, and made me sometimes heavy and dull, but more often restless and feverish. He never even gave me a meal of green meat, or a bran mash, which would have cooled me, for he was altogether as ignorant as he was conceited; and then, instead of exercise or change of food, I had to take horse-balls and draughts; which, beside the nuisance of having them poured down my throat, used to make me feel ill and uncomfortable.

One day my feet were so tender, that trotting over some fresh stones with my master on my back, I made two such serious stumbles, that as he came down Lansdown into the city, he stopped at the farrier's, and asked him to see what was the matter with me. The man took up my feet one by one and examined them; then standing up and dusting his hands one against the other, he said—

'Your horse has got the "thrush," and badly too; his feet are very tender; it is fortunate that he has not been down. I wonder your groom has not seen to it before. This is the sort of thing we find in foul stables, where the litter is never properly cleared out. If you will send him here to-morrow, I will attend to the

9 **Unhealthy and tender**. By standing on wet, dirty straw day after day the chemicals in the uncleared urine and manure in the stable cause infection on the underside of the horse's hoof, particularly in the horny triangular pad, the frog. This disease, known as thrush, is characterised by a foul smell.

10 **Fumble-footed**. Moving clumsily and prone to stumbling.

11 **Fed just as high ... restless and feverish**. Being 'corned up' with rich protein foods and with no opportunity to work off the energy created is very bad for the horse's digestion and constitution. Changes to the routine, whether preparing for hard work or 'letting down' for less strenuous work, should be done gradually. The horse should be fed according to the work he is asked to do, so that the quantity of feed is reduced and the type of feed changed when the work is less.

12 **Green meat, or a bran mash**. Grass or fresh produce such as sliced carrots, apples or other vegetables. Bran mash was dampened bran which was thought to act as a digestive aid and a laxative. See pp. 59 and 435.

13 **Lansdown**. District in Bath between The Circus and the River Avon to the north of the town.

14 **Thrush**. Fungal infection of a horse's feet as described above.

The Royal Crescent, Bath. Watercolour by Robert Woodroffe, 1828. (Victoria Art Gallery, Bath)

15   hoof, and I will direct your man how to apply the liniment which I will give him.'

     The next day I had my feet thoroughly cleansed and stuffed
16   with tow, soaked in some strong lotion; and a very unpleasant business it was.

     The farrier ordered all the litter to be taken out of my box day by day, and the floor kept very clean. Then I was to have bran mashes, a little green meat, and not so much corn, till my feet were well again. With this treatment I soon regained my spirits, but Mr. Barry was so much disgusted at being twice deceived by his grooms, that he determined to give up keeping a horse, and to hire when he wanted one. I was therefore kept till my feet were quite sound, and was then sold again.

15 **Liniment.** Embrocation, lotion or ointment, usually to soothe and ease rather than to heal an affected part.

16 **Tow.** Usually a coarse lump of hemp or flax but could be cotton rags soaked in a solution such as chloride of zinc lotion as described by Edward Mayhew in his *Illustrated Horse Doctor* of 1860, or a paste of blue vitriol, tar and lard as recommended by William Youatt in his *Horse: With a Treatise on Draught*, published in 1865.

A recipe for thrush. (MS, private collection, *c.* 1900)

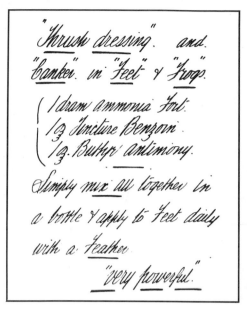

"Thrush dressing". and. "Canker". in "Feet" & "Frogs".
(1 dram ammonia Fort.
/ ½ Tincture Benzoin
/ ½. Butter antimony.
Simply mix all together in a bottle & apply to Feet daily with a Feather.
"very powerful."

DR. O. T. PATT'S
VETERINARY OINTMENT
—— FOR ——
SCRATCHES, Thrush, Quarter Cracks, Sore, Brittle an
Contracted Hoofs, Shoe Boils, Galls and Sores of a

have used it to be far superior to anything of the kind
condition It is warranted to grow an entire new Hoof
parts with a dry cloth. Then apply the Ointment and
ecial *Directions for Scratches.* — Be very particular N
have been strictly followed, it has never known to fail

A veterinary ointment suitable for thrush, as well as other conditions. (Moseman's *Illustrated Guide for Purchasers of Horse Furnishing Goods*, p. 65)

277

PART III

CHAPTER XXXII

A HORSE FAIR

1 NO doubt a horse fair is a very amusing place to those who have nothing to lose; at any rate, there is plenty to see.

2 Long strings of young horses out of the country, fresh from the marshes; and droves of shaggy little 3 Welsh ponies, no higher than Merrylegs; and hundreds of cart-horses of all sorts, some of them with their long tails braided up, 4 and tied with scarlet cord; and a good many like myself, handsome and high-bred, but fallen into the middle class, through some 5 accident or blemish, unsoundness of wind, or some other complaint. There were some splendid animals quite in their prime, 6 and fit for anything; they were throwing out their legs and showing off their paces in high style, as they were trotted out

1   **Horse fair**. Horse fairs were common and almost every town and village held such a fair, often in its main street. Some of the larger, more famous fairs have survived to the present day, such as Appleby Fair in Cumbria and Stow Fair in the Cotswolds. Such fairs were (and still are) notorious places for unwary buyers to be duped.

2   **Young horses out of the country**. Britain has never had a government-sponsored horse-breeding programme, even when her need for horses was at its peak in the second half of the nineteenth century. Horses of all types were bred in small numbers by farmers who had a mare or two and wished to make a few pounds by breeding a foal. These offspring were sometimes broken in by the farmer, who took them to the fair himself or sold them to dealers who toured the countryside buying young horses. Such horses were generally of no particular breed but of types: hunters, hacks or saddle horses, vanners, light or heavy draught horses, or light harness horses such as Black Beauty.

3   **Welsh ponies**. Wales was a great breeding area for ponies for the coal mines. The Welsh Mountain pony, the smallest, was ideal for the purpose when crossed with small, stocky, strong Shetlands. Welsh cobs were larger and sometimes used in mines but their flashy action was liked by butchers and other tradesmen.

4   **Scarlet cord**. Putting a red ribbon round a horse's tail is usually meant to signify that it is a kicker, but in this case the scarlet cord was probably just a decoration.

5   **Unsoundness of wind**. Generally regarded as a major fault in a horse, meaning that its respiratory tract is affected in some way, making it less than one hundred per cent fit for work and hence reducing its value.

6   **Throwing out their legs**. Implying flashy, extravagant action as shown by high-stepping hackneys and some Welsh cobs.

279

High, round action (*top*) and (*bottom*) low, free action. (Vero Shaw, *The Encyclopaedia of the Stable*, London: George Routledge, 1909, pp. 280 and 141)

with a leading rein, the groom running by the side. But round in the background there were a number of poor things, sadly broken down with hard work, with their knees knuckling over, and their hind legs swinging out at every step; and there were some very dejected-looking old horses, with the under lip hanging down, and the ears laying back heavily, as if there was no more pleasure in life, and no more hope; there were some so thin, you might see all their ribs, and some with old sores on their backs and hips; these were sad sights for a horse to look upon, who knows not but he may come to the same state.

There was a great deal of bargaining; or running up and beating down, and if a horse may speak his mind so far as he understands, I should say, there were more lies told, and more trickery at that horse fair than a clever man could give an account of. I was put with two or three other strong, useful-looking horses, and a good many people came to look at us. The gentlemen always turned from me when they saw my broken knees; though the man who had me swore it was only a slip in the stall.

The first thing was to pull my mouth open, then to look at my eyes, then feel all the way down my legs, and give me a hard feel of the skin and flesh, and then try my paces. It was wonderful what a difference there was in the way these things were done. Some did it in a rough off-hand way, as if one was only a piece of wood; while others would take their hands gently over one's body, with a pat now and then, as much as to say, 'by your leave.' Of course I judged a good deal of the buyers by their manners to myself.

There was one man, I thought, if he would buy me, I should be happy. He was not a gentleman, nor yet one of the loud flashy sort that called themselves so. He was rather a small man, but well made, and quick in all his motions. I knew in a moment

7 **Knees knuckling over**. A sign of age, over-work, lack of care leading to poor condition, or poor conformation indicating a weakness in the tendons below the knee. See p. 429.

8 **Lip hanging down**. A pendulous lower lip often accompanies old age in horses, and although it does not affect performance gives the horse a rather 'dopey' expression.

9 **Old sores on their backs and hips**. When harness has been badly fitting over a long period of time it will rub the skin so much that it removes the hair and eventually creates an open wound. Even if this is allowed to heal the hair follicles will often have been badly damaged so that future hair will grow white at the site of the original injury. Similarly, harness can cause galls which eventually become like callouses or raised scars.

10 **Running up and beating down**. Haggling over the price was an expected part of horse dealing. When a price was finally agreed it was settled by the vendor and purchaser slapping hands.

11 **Pull my mouth . . . try my paces**. When buying a horse a prospective purchaser will examine the teeth from which the age of the horse can be roughly ascertained – if they have not been tampered with to make the horse appear younger or older than he really is. A purchaser also feels the horse's legs for any lumps, tenderness or heat which might indicate unsoundness in the limbs. In trying a horse's paces a purchaser could see if the horse moved easily and fluently without limping, stumbling or striking his own legs.

12 **Loud flashy sort**. An aspiring working-class man lacking 'good breeding', especially one who assumed the airs and outward signs but not the social graces, would never be mistaken for a real gentleman – not even by a horse!

by the way he handled me, that he was used to horses; he spoke gently, and his grey eye had a kindly, cheery look in it. It may seem strange to say—but it is true all the same—that the clean fresh smell there was about him made me take to him; no smell of old beer and tobacco, which I hated, but a fresh smell as if he had come out of a hayloft. He offered twenty-three pounds for me; but that was refused, and he walked away. I looked after him, but he was gone, and a very hard-looking, loud-voiced man came; I was dreadfully afraid he would have me; but he walked off. One or two more came who did not mean business. Then the hard-faced man came back again and offered twenty-three pounds. A very close bargain was being driven, for my sales-man began to think he should not get all he asked, and must come down; but just then the grey-eyed man came back again. I could not help reaching out my head towards him. He stroked my face kindly.

'Well, old chap,' he said, ' I think we should suit each other. I 'll give twenty-four for him.'

'Say twenty-five and you shall have him.'

'Twenty-four ten,' said my friend, in a very decided tone, 'and not another sixpence—yes or no?'

'Done,' said the salesman, 'and you may depend upon it there 's a monstrous deal of quality in that horse, and if you want him for cab work, he 's a bargain.'

The money was paid on the spot, and my new master took my halter, and led me out of the fair to an inn, where he had a saddle and bridle ready. He gave me a good feed of oats, and stood by whilst I ate it, talking to himself, and talking to me. Half an hour after we were on our way to London, through pleasant lanes and country roads, until we came into the great London thoroughfare, on which we travelled steadily, till in the twilight

13 **Beer and tobacco**. Beer was a working-class drink and alcohol was seen as the scourge of the working classes, hence the growth of the Temperance Movement in Victorian times. Tobacco also had its class divisions: cigar smoking was for gentlemen, roll-your-owns for the working class. However, this is an example of Anna Sewell's own morals being attributed to Black Beauty, as race-horses drink stout quite happily, and horses are said to like the smell of 'twist' or pipe tobacco.

14 **Chap**. Generally fairly affectionate slang term for 'man', especially when phrased in 'old chap' as here. Originally *c*. 1715 – abbreviation of 'chapman', meaning customer/buyer/seller.

15 **Twenty-four ten**. Twenty-four pounds and ten shillings. Ten shillings is the pre-decimalisation equivalent of fifty pence. This was an enormous fall from the price of £300 given for Black Beauty and Ginger by the Earl of W—. See p. 235.

16 **Sixpence**. The smallest silver coin before decimalisation, worth half a shilling.

17 **Cab work**. In this case probably a Hansom cab – the 'gondola of London' – or a four-wheeled Clarence. Cab is generally thought to be a shortened form of 'cabriolet' – a two-wheeled vehicle of French origin which became extremely popular with 'gentlemen-about-town' after improvements were made to the original design of the early 1800s. The Hansom cab, invented by J. A. Hansom in 1834, underwent various modifications until by 1880 it had reached perfect proportions and balance. It was considered a somewhat dashing vehicle for the man-about-town and a lady would hesitate to use one. See p. 289.

18 **On our way to London**. We are not told where the horse fair took place, or how Black Beauty travelled there, but the journey from Bath to London of approximately 100 miles would take a fit horse used to long journeys a good fifteen hours, so it seems that some story-teller's licence was used here.

25   'Sausage dumpling and apple turnover,' shouted the boy, which
set them all laughing. I was led into a comfortable clean-
smelling stall with plenty of dry straw, and after a capital supper,
I lay down, thinking I was going to be happy.

25 **Sausage dumpling and apple turnover.** Cheap, filling working-class dishes using a minimum of the more expensive foods (meat and apples) and a maximum of the cheap filling ones (flour, suet, sugar).

Showing his paces at the horse sale. Illustrated by Cecil Aldin. (*Black Beauty*, London: Jarrolds, 1912, pl. opp. p. 181)

287

CHAPTER XXXIII

A LONDON CAB HORSE

1
2
MY new master's name was Jeremiah Barker, but as every-one called him Jerry, I shall do the same. Polly, his wife, was just as good a match as a man could have. She was a plump, trim, tidy little woman, with smooth dark hair, dark eyes, and a merry little mouth. The boy was nearly twelve years old: a tall, frank, good-tempered lad; and little Dorothy (Dolly, they called her) was her mother over again, at eight years old. They were all wonderfully fond of each other; I never knew such a happy, merry family before,
3 or since. Jerry had a cab of his own, and two horses, which he

288

ANNOTATIONS

1 **Jeremiah Barker**. Jerry, short for Jeremiah, is a Biblical name, a popular source of Christian names in the Victorian period.

2 **Polly, his wife**. In a Victorian working-class home the wife was housekeeper, cook and several other 'domestics' all rolled into one.

3 **A cab of his own, and two horses.** Jerry Barker had a four-wheeled cab, probably a Clarence, which for use as a public carriage had to be inspected and licensed annually. It seated two or four passengers and was known as a 'growler' because of the noise its iron-rimmed wheels made on the street surface. It was a closed cab, based on the design of a private carriage owned by the Duke of Clarence, more sedate than a Hansom Cab and afforded luggage storage on the roof. See p. 339.

A Hansom cab, photographed in 1877. (T. C. Barker and Michael Robbins, *A History of London Transport*, vol. 1: *The Nineteenth Century*, London: George Allen & Unwin, 1975, plate 100)

drove and attended to himself. His other horse was a tall, white, rather large-boned animal, called Captain; he was old now, but when he was young he must have been splendid; he had still a proud way of holding his head and arching his neck; in fact, he was a high-bred, fine-mannered, noble old horse, every inch of him. He told me that in his early youth he went to the Crimean War; he belonged to an officer in the cavalry, and used to lead the regiment; I will tell more of that hereafter.

The next morning, when I was well groomed, Polly and Dolly came into the yard to see me, and make friends. Harry had been helping his father since the early morning, and had stated his opinion that I should turn out 'a regular brick.' Polly brought me a slice of apple, and Dolly a piece of bread, and made as much of me as if I had been the 'Black Beauty' of olden time. It was a great treat to be petted again, and talked to in a gentle voice, and I let them see as well as I could that I wished to be friendly. Polly thought I was very handsome, and a great deal too good for a cab, if it was not for the broken knees.

'Of course, there 's no one to tell us whose fault that was,' said Jerry, 'and as long as I don't know, I shall give him the benefit of the doubt; for a firmer, neater stepper I never rode; we 'll call him Jack, after the old one—shall we, Polly?'

'Do,' she said, 'for I like to keep a good name going.'

Captain went out in the cab all the morning. Harry came in after school to feed me and give me water. In the afternoon I was put into the cab. Jerry took as much pains to see if the collar and bridle fitted comfortably, as if he had been John Manly over again. When the crupper was let out a hole or two, it all fitted well. There was no bearing rein—no curb—nothing but a plain ring snaffle. What a blessing that was!

After driving through the side street we came to the large cab

290

4 White . . . animal, called Captain. On the whole grey or white was not a preferred colour for a cab horse, it being difficult and time-consuming to keep clean. White hairs tended to blow back on the passengers and stick to dark clothing. However, one advantage was that they did stand out and were more easily seen by anyone wishing to hail a cab. But grey horses were often used by regimental trumpeters, as in today's Household Cavalry. The most famous regiment to use grey horses was the Royal Scots Dragoon Guards or, as they were more popularly known, the Scots Greys. At the time of writing (1870s), Captain would have been over twenty years old if he had been in the Crimean War of 1854–6.

5 Brick. A good fellow, slang from the 1840s.

Snaffle bridle. (L. von Heydebrand und der Lasa, *Die Amazone*, Leipzig: Otto Spamer, 1884, p. 83)

How to measure a horse for a collar. (Moseman's *Illustrated Guide for Purchasers of Horse Furnishing Goods*, p. 169)

291

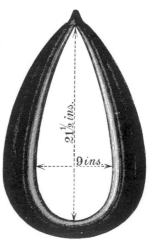

6 stand where Jerry had said 'Good night.' On one side of this wide street were high houses with wonderful shop fronts, and on the other was an old church and churchyard surrounded by iron palisades. Alongside these iron rails a number of cabs were drawn up, waiting for passengers: bits of hay were lying about on the ground; some of the men were standing together, some were sitting on their boxes reading the newspaper; and one or two were feeding their horses with bits of hay, and a drink of water. We pulled up in the rank at the back of the last cab. Two or three men came round and began to look at me and pass their remarks.

7 'Very good for a funeral,' said one.

'Too smart-looking,' said another, shaking his head in a very wise way; 'you'll find out something wrong one of these fine mornings, or my name isn't Jones.'

'Well,' said Jerry pleasantly, 'I suppose I need not find it out till it finds me out; eh? and if so, I'll keep up my spirits a little longer.'

Then came up a broad-faced man, dressed in a great grey coat with great grey capes, and great white buttons, a grey hat, and a blue comforter loosely tied round his neck; his hair was grey too, but he was a jolly-looking fellow, and the other men made way for him. He looked me all over, as if he had been going to buy me; and then straightening himself up with a grunt, he said, 'He's the right sort for you, Jerry; I don't care what you gave for him, he'll be worth it.' Thus my character was established on the stand.

This man's name was Grant, but he was called 'Grey Grant,' or 'Governor Grant.' He had been the longest on that stand of any of the men, and he took it upon himself to settle matters, and stop disputes He was generally a good-humoured, sensible

292

6 **Cab stand**. Place where cabs were authorised to stand while waiting for hire, a convention developed in the eighteenth century.

7 **Very good for a funeral**. Cab horses were by preference bay or chestnut. London's funeral horses, known as 'The Black Brigade', were mostly imported black Flemish stallions. This was one of the very few instances in the British horse world when stallions were preferred to geldings or mares.

A Victorian funeral coach, drawn by 'The Black Brigade'. (Gordon, *Horse World of London*, p. 138)

293

man; but if his temper was a little out, as it was sometimes, when 8 he had drunk too much, nobody liked to come too near his fist, for he could deal a very heavy blow.

The first week of my life as a cab horse was very trying; I had never been used to London, and the noise, the hurry, the crowds 9 of horses, carts, and carriages, that I had to make my way through made me feel anxious and harassed; but I soon found that I could perfectly trust my driver, and then I made myself easy, and got used to it.

Jerry was as good a driver as I had ever known; and what was better, he took as much thought for his horses as he did for himself. He soon found out that I was willing to work, and do my best; and he never laid the whip on me, unless it was gently drawing the end of it over my back, when I was to go on; but generally I knew this quite well by the way in which he took 10 up the reins; and I believe his whip was more frequently stuck up by his side than in his hand.

In a short time I and my master understood each other, as well as horse and man can do. In the stable, too, he did all that he 11 could for our comfort. The stalls were the old-fashioned style, too much on the slope; but he had two movable bars fixed across the back of our stalls, so that at night, and when we were resting, he just took off our halters, and put up the bars, and thus we could turn about and stand whichever way we pleased, which is a great comfort.

Jerry kept us very clean, and gave us as much change of food as he could, and always plenty of it; and not only that, but he always gave us plenty of clean fresh water, which he allowed to stand by us both night and day, except of course when we came 12 in warm. Some people say that a horse ought not to drink all he likes; but I know if we are allowed to drink when we want it,

8   **Drunk too much**. Here rises the vexed question of alcoholism amongst the working classes. The period of the 1870s is memorable as the annual per capita consumption of alcohol (beer, spirits and wine in that rank order) rose to an all-time high, about 32 gallons for every person in Britain.

9   **Crowds of horses, carts and carriages.** The population of London had reached about four million by this time, and the necessary volume of horse-drawn vehicles must have been immense during daylight hours, not to mention the pedestrians, men pushing handcarts, herds of cattle, flocks of sheep and other livestock being driven to market.

10   **Stuck up**. Set in position in a whip socket next to the driver's seat.

11   **Stalls were the old-fashioned style.** See p. 237.

12   **Ought not to drink all he likes.** Fresh, clean water, present at all times in a horse's stall, was a controversial idea. By the 1860s it was just becoming accepted, with the caveat (still valid) that heated horses should be restricted in water intake until cool and rested, otherwise colic could result.

The usual problems caused by a stall which is too much on a slope; the groom tries to prevent the horse from easing his hind legs by standing in the passageway. (Mayhew, *The Illustrated Horse Management*, p. 278)

we drink only a little at a time, and it does us a great deal more good than swallowing down half a bucketful at a time, because we have been left without till we are thirsty and miserable. Some grooms will go home to their beer and leave us for hours with our dry hay and oats and nothing to moisten them; then of course we gulp down too much at once, which helps to spoil our breathing and sometimes chills our stomachs. But the best thing that we had here was our Sundays for rest; we worked so hard in the week, that I do not think we could have kept up to it, but for that day; besides, we had then time to enjoy each other's company. It was on these days that I learned my companion's history.

13 Sundays for rest. Hackney carriages had been permitted to ply for hire on Sundays since the 1830s.

The drinking horse. The diagrams show how water (a) is drawn into the mouth and forced upwards by the alternate compression and enlargement of the tongue (dd). The larynx (c) lowers to admit the water, then moves upwards to force the water down the gullet (bb). The soft palate (e) floats upwards and closes off the nasal passages. (Mayhew, *The Illustrated Horse Management*, pp. 64 and 65)

CHAPTER XXXIV

AN OLD WAR HORSE

APTAIN had been broken in and trained for an army horse; his first owner was an officer of cavalry going out to the Crimean War. He said he quite enjoyed the training with all the other horses, trotting together, turning together, to the right hand or to the left, halting at the word of command, or dashing forward at full speed at the sound of the trumpet, or signal of the officer. He was, when young, a dark, dappled iron grey, and considered very handsome. His master, a young, high-spirited gentleman, was very fond of him, and treated him from the first with the greatest care and kindness. He told me he thought the life of an army horse was very pleasant; but when he came to being sent abroad, over the sea in a great ship, he almost changed his mind.

'That part of it,' said he, 'was dreadful! Of course we could not walk off the land into the ship; so they were obliged to put strong straps under our bodies, and then we were lifted off our

298

ANNOTATIONS

1   **Officer of cavalry.** An officer's horse or charger was generally a quality horse with some Thoroughbred blood, good looking and full of presence as befitted the status of its rider.

2   **Dark, dappled iron grey.** Grey horses are born any solid colour and lighten with age. A grey horse in the Crimean War could have been a troop horse of the Royal Scots Greys or any other regimental officer's charger, or even a trumpeter's horse.

3   **Lifted off our legs.** Slings, usually of canvas, were used to hoist horses from the dockside on to the deck of the ship. Gangplanks were not used as was the case when transporting the more phlegmatic cattle, for fear the horses might panic and fall overboard. Also, horses do not like to walk over insecure floors such as a gangplank would offer.

Using slings to hoist horses on board ship. (*Illustrated London News*, 26 January 1862, p. 99)

legs in spite of our struggles, and were swung through the air over the water, to the deck of the great vessel. There we were

4 placed in small close stalls, and never for a long time saw the sky, or were able to stretch our legs. · The ship sometimes rolled about in high winds, and we were knocked about, and felt bad

5 enough. However, at last it came to an end, and we were hauled up, and swung over again to the land; we were very glad, and

6 snorted, and neighed for joy, when we once more felt firm ground under our feet.

'We soon found that the country we had come to was very

7 different to our own, and that we had many hardships to endure besides the fighting; but many of the men were so fond of their horses, that they did everything they could to make them comfortable, in spite of snow, wet, and all things out of order.'

'But what about the fighting?' said I; 'was not that worse than anything else?'

'Well,' said he, 'I hardly know; we always liked to hear the trumpet sound, and to be called out, and were impatient to start off, though sometimes we had to stand for hours, waiting for the word of command; and when the word was given, we used to spring forward as gaily and eagerly as if there were no cannon balls, bayonets, or bullets. I believe so long as we felt our rider firm in the saddle, and his hand steady on the bridle, not one of us gave way to fear, not even when the terrible bombshells whirled through the air and burst into a thousand pieces.

'I, with my noble master, went into many actions together without a wound; and though I saw horses shot down with bullets, pierced through with lances, and gashed with fearful sabre cuts; though we left them dead on the field, or dying in the agony of their wounds, I don't think I feared for myself. My master's cheery voice, as he encouraged his men, made me

4 **Stalls**. The conditions under which the horses were kept were cramped, dark and unhygienic. Officers' chargers were kept in better accommodation on the upper decks, troop horses below in the hold. Baggage and pack animals had the worst accommodation as they were the lowest on the military equine social scale.

5 **Knocked about, and felt bad enough**. Once a horse had fallen he could not easily rise in the cramped conditions. Lord George Paget, in his *Journal of the Crimean War* (1881), described how the fallen horses became stuck under the stall divisions, which were open for two feet at the bottom, and in kicking and struggling would also bring down the horse in the neighbouring stall. He also described how on his first night at sea two horses went mad, 'in the lower deck, from the heat of the boiler. They get a sort of mad staggers, but are generally relieved by a bucket or two of water thrown over their heads.' Dead horses had to be manhandled and the carcasses thrown overboard. Horses are unable to vomit so their seasickness could not be physically expressed.

6 **Snorted, and neighed for joy.** The horses would probably be too weak to do much capering about after the voyage to the Crimea. Eye-witness reports such as those from William Russell, war correspondent of *The Times*, commented on 'emaciated horses'. For him to make such a comment at all, the horses must have been in a very poor state, for horses were regarded as expendable and were not usually mentioned by war correspondents.

7 **Hardships**. Horse management in the field was abysmal. It followed the English routine regardless of local conditions; thus many horses were cold, or weak through lack of food, and some so weak that their troopers had to walk and carry the saddles. Despite ships moored at Sebastopol filled with grain many officers considered it beneath their (and their horses') dignity to use their horses as pack animals to transport the grain to camps.

301

feel as if he and I could not be killed. I had such perfect trust in him, that whilst he was guiding me, I was ready to charge up to the very cannon's mouth. I saw many brave men cut down, many fall mortally wounded from their saddles. I had heard the cries and groans of the dying, I had cantered over ground slippery with blood, and frequently had to turn aside to avoid trampling on wounded man or horse, but, until one dreadful day, I had never felt terror; that day I shall never forget.'

Here old Captain paused for a while and drew a long breath; I waited, and he went on.

'It was one autumn morning, and as usual, an hour before daybreak our cavalry had turned out, ready caparisoned for the day's work, whether it might be fighting or waiting. The men stood by their horses waiting, ready for orders. As the light increased, there seemed to be some excitement among the officers; and before the day was well begun, we heard the firing of the enemy's guns.

'Then one of the officers rode up and gave the word for the men to mount, and in a second, every man was in his saddle, and every horse stood expecting the touch of the rein, or the pressure of his rider's heels, all animated, all eager; but still we had been trained so well, that, except by the champing of our bits, and the restive tossing of our heads from time to time, it could not be said that we stirred.

'My dear master and I were at the head of the line, and as all sat motionless and watchful, he took a little stray lock of my mane which had turned over on the wrong side, laid it over on the right, and smoothed it down with his hand; then patting my neck, he said, "We shall have a day of it to-day, Bayard, my beauty; but we 'll do our duty as we have done." He stroked my neck that morning, more, I think, than he had ever done

8 **Turn aside**. Horses will not tread on fallen riders if they can help it – not through any altruistic motives but because they dislike anything insecure underfoot.

9 **One autumn morning**. The Battle of Balaclava took place on 25 October 1854.

10 **Bayard**. A name often given to valuable or prized horses. It can also mean bay coloured, i.e. brown with black points. The origin of the name derives from the swift horse given by Charlemagne to the four sons of Aymon. If all four rode him he increased in size to accommodate them all.

Lord George Paget, an officer in the Crimean War. Although somewhat the worse for wear, his horse's general type suggests it was well bred. (National Army Museum, London)

before; quietly on and on, as if he were thinking of something else. I loved to feel his hand on my neck, and arched my crest proudly, and happily; but I stood very still, for I knew all his moods, and when he liked me to be quiet, and when gay.

'I cannot tell all that happened on that day, but I will tell of the last charge that we made together: it was across a valley right in front of the enemy's cannon. By this time we were well used to the roar of heavy guns, the rattle of musket fire, and the flying of shot near us; but never had I been under such a fire as we rode through on that day. From the right, from the left, and from the front, shot and shell poured in upon us. Many a brave man went down, many a horse fell, flinging his rider to the earth; many a horse without a rider ran wildly out of the ranks: then terrified at being alone with no hand to guide him, came pressing in amongst his old companions, to gallop with them to the charge.

'Fearful as it was, no one stopped, no one turned back. Every moment the ranks were thinned, but as our comrades fell, we closed in to keep them together; and instead of being shaken or staggered in our pace, our gallop became faster and faster as we neared the cannon, all clouded in white smoke, while the red fire flashed through it.

'My master, my dear master, was cheering on his comrades with his right arm raised on high, when one of the balls, whizzing close to my head, struck him. I felt him stagger with the shock, though he uttered no cry; I tried to check my speed, but the sword dropped from his right hand, the rein fell loose from the left, and sinking backward from the saddle he fell to the earth; the other riders swept past us, and by the force of their charge I was driven from the spot where he fell.

'I wanted to keep my place by his side, and not leave him

11 **The last charge that we made together**. Description of the Charge of the Light Brigade led by Lord Cardigan (1797–1868). It involved regiments of Hussars, Lancers and Light Dragoons who were given orders to attack the Russian gun positions. Whether it was the orders that were at fault, or whether they were disobeyed, misinterpreted or misunderstood is still open to question. It was a magnificent but futile and suicidal charge – so much so that the Russians were said to have thought the Light Brigade was drunk! The British cavalry was raked by Russian artillery fire the full length of the valley. Out of the initial 600 or more men only 195 came back, and 500 horses lay dead or wounded on the battlefield. Alfred Lord Tennyson commemorated the event in his poem 'The Charge of the Light Brigade':

> Half a league, half a league, half a league onward,
> Into the Valley of Death rode the Six Hundred...

12 **Shot and shell.** Probably canister, grapeshot and shrapnel as well as solid shot cannonballs. Such artillery wreaked havoc amongst the cavalry, effectively spraying them, shotgun-like, with fragments of metal, small iron balls and other scattered missiles.

The Light Brigade at the battle of Balaclava. (National Army Museum, London)

under that rush of horses' feet, but it was in vain; and now, without a master or a friend, I was alone on that great slaughter ground; then fear took hold on me, and I trembled as I had never trembled before; and I too, as I had seen other horses do, tried to join in the ranks and gallop with them; but I was beaten off by the swords of the soldiers. Just then, a soldier whose horse had been killed under him, caught at my bridle and mounted me; and with this new master I was again going forward: but our gallant company was cruelly overpowered, and those who remained alive after the fierce fight for the guns, came galloping back over the same ground. Some of the horses had been so badly wounded that they could scarcely move from the loss of blood; other noble creatures were trying on three legs to drag themselves along, and others were struggling to rise on their fore feet, when their hind legs had been shattered by shot. Their groans were piteous to hear, and the beseeching look in their eyes as those who escaped passed by, and left them to their fate, I shall never forget. After the battle the wounded men were brought in, and the dead were buried.'

'And what about the wounded horses?' I said, 'were they left to die?'

'No, the army farriers went over the field with their pistols, and shot all that were ruined; some that had only slight wounds were brought back and attended to, but the greater part of the noble willing creatures that went out that morning, never came back! In our stables there was only about one in four that returned.

'I never saw my dear master again. I believe he fell dead from the saddle. I never loved any other master so well. I went into many other engagements, but was only once wounded, and then not seriously; and when the war was over, I came back again to England, as sound and strong as when I went out.'

13 **Join in the ranks**. Horses are gregarious and will usually try to run with their companions, as can be seen in steeplechases when loose horses will stay with the others, apparently galloping and jumping in enjoyment but in reality wanting the security of the herd.

14 **Army farriers**. Apart from shoeing and treating sick or wounded horses, army farriers also had the duty of dispatching badly wounded horses after the battle. Lord George Paget wrote: 'The farriers' pistols were soon brought into requisition, to shoot such of the poor beasts as were too mutilated for further service (a repetition of which task was enacted for many mornings after)' (*Journal of the Crimean War*, 1881). It was quite common for the farriers to use an axe to kill the horses rather than a pistol as bullets cost money. It was also standard practice to cut off a hoof bearing an army brand to prove that the horse had indeed been killed and not sold illegally.

15 **When the war was over**. The Crimean War lasted from 1854 to 1856. It would have been unusual for an army horse to be shipped back from the Crimea. Captain was exceptional in this respect – maybe he was the favourite charger of an officer who paid for the return voyage out of his own pocket. Most horses were simply left – they were expendable and could be replaced in England.

'The army farriers went over the field with their pistols.' Illustrated by Edmund Blampied. (*Black Beauty*, London: Jarrolds, 1922, p. 177)

I said, 'I have heard people talk about war as if it was a very fine thing.'

'Ah!' said he, 'I should think they never saw it. No doubt it is very fine when there is no enemy, when it is just exercise and parade, and sham-fight. Yes, it is very fine then; but when thousands of good brave men and horses are killed, or crippled for life, it has a very different look.'

16 'Do you know what they fought about?' said I.

'No,' he said, 'that is more than a horse can understand, but the enemy must have been awfully wicked people, if it was right to go all that way over the sea on purpose to kill them.'

308

16 **Fought about.** The war in the Crimea was a conflict of the great powers of the time: Britain, France, Turkey and Russia, in the Near East. In 1853 Russia invaded the Balkans, but was forced to withdraw by Austria. In 1854 an alliance was struck between France and Britain and war declared on Russia. The war was ostensibly brought about by Russia's quarrel with Turkey – the 'Sick Man of Europe' – over Russia's demands to exercise protection over the Orthodox subjects of the Ottoman Sultan and the dispute over privileges of Russian Orthodox and Roman Catholic monks in holy places in Palestine. But Russia chiefly wanted to gain influence in the Black Sea area and the Balkans which would give her access to the Mediterranean via the Dardanelles. The British, whose ambassador in Turkey was suspicious of and disliked the Russians, saw this move as a threat to the British hold in India. Napoleon III in France regarded war as a means to strengthen his position on the throne and a conflict with Russia in particular would have the added attraction of revenge for Napoleon Bonaparte's defeat in the Moscow Campaign of 1812. It could also be said that both Britain and France were spoiling for a fight and hungry for military glory. The war ended in the Peace of Paris which placed restrictions on Russia's expansion.

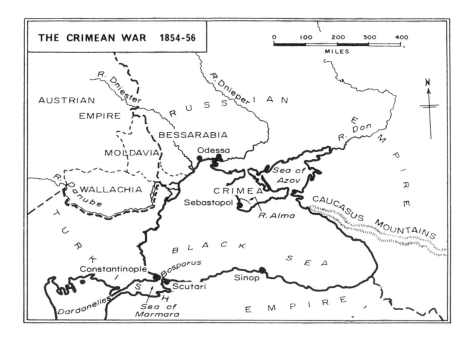

Map of Crimea. (From E. K. Milliken, *The Victorian Era*, London: Harrap, 1963, p. 154)

CHAPTER XXXV

JERRY BARKER

I NEVER knew a better man than my new master; he was kind and good, and as strong for the right as John Manly; and so good-tempered and merry, that very few people could pick a quarrel with him. He was very fond of making little songs, and singing them to himself. One, he was very fond of, was this—

¶

Come, father and mother,
And sister and brother,
Come, all of you, turn to
And help one another.

And so they did; Harry was as clever at stablework as a much older boy, and always wanted to do what he could. Then Polly and Dolly used to come in the morning to help with the cab—

1 **Come, father and mother.** No evidence has been found of this or other verses quoted existing as songs at the time, so it is likely that it was not Jerry Barker who was 'fond of making little songs', but Anna Sewell herself.

Two studies of Jerry Barker: (*left*) by K. F. Barker (*Black Beauty*, London: A. & C. Black, 1959, p. 160); (*above*) by John Beer (*Black Beauty*, London: Jarrold & Sons, 1894, p. 166)

311

to brush and beat the cushions, and rub the glass, while Jerry was giving us a cleaning in the yard, and Harry was rubbing the harness. There used to be a great deal of laughing and fun between them, and it put Captain and me in much better spirits than if we had heard scolding and hard words. They were always early in the morning, for Jerry would say—

'If you in the morning
Throw minutes away
You can't pick them up
In the course of the day.
You may hurry and skurry,
And flurry and worry,
You 've lost them for ever,
For ever and aye.'

He could not bear any careless loitering, and waste of time; and nothing was so near making him angry, as to find people who were always late, wanting a cab horse to be driven hard, to make up for their idleness.

One day, two wild-looking young men came out of a tavern close by the stand, and called Jerry.

2 'Here, cabby! look sharp, we are rather late; put on the
3 steam, will you, and take us to the Victoria in time for the one o'clock train? You shall have a shilling extra.'

'I will take you at the regular pace, gentlemen; shillings don't pay for putting on the steam like that.'

Larry's cab was standing next to ours; he flung open the door, and said, 'I 'm your man, gentlemen! take my cab, my horse will get you there all right'; and as he shut them in, with a wink towards Jerry, said, 'It 's against his conscience to go beyond a
4, 5 jog-trot ' Then slashing his jaded horse, he set off as hard as he could. Jerry patted me on the neck—'No, Jack, a shilling would not pay for that sort of thing, would it, old boy?'

312

2 **Put on the steam**. Meaning 'Hurry up', it originated with the development of steam locomotives in the 1840s.

3 **Victoria**. Station in southwest London, built *c*.1859 to serve passengers travelling to the south and southwestern parts of the country.

4 **Jog-trot**. A pace faster than a walk but not a full trot.

5 **Jaded**. Tired. The term 'jade' was sometimes used for an old or worn-out horse.

The new Victoria railway station, serving Kent and the South Coast. (*The Illustrated London News*, 4 May 1861, p. 418)

313

Although Jerry was determinately set against hard driving, to please careless people, he always went a good fair pace, and was not against putting on the steam, as he said, if only he knew *why*.

6   I well remember one morning, as we were on the stand waiting for a fare, that a young man, carrying a heavy portmanteau, trod on a piece of orange peel which lay on the pavement, and fell down with great force.

Jerry was the first to run and lift him up. He seemed much stunned, and as they led him into a shop, he walked as if he were in great pain. Jerry of course came back to the stand, but in about ten minutes one of the shopmen called him, so he drew up to the pavement.

7   'Can you take me to the South-Eastern Railway?' said the young man; 'this unlucky fall has made me late, I fear; but it is of great importance that I should not lose the twelve o'clock train. I should be most thankful if you could get me there in time, and will gladly pay you an extra fare.'

'I 'll do my very best,' said Jerry heartily, 'if you think you are well enough, sir,' for he looked dreadfully white and ill.

'I *must* go,' he said, earnestly, 'please to open the door, and let us lose no time.'

8   The next minute Jerry was on the box; with a cheery chirrup to me, and a twitch of the rein that I well understood.

'Now then, Jack, my boy,' said he, 'spin along, we 'll show them how we can get over the ground, if we only know why.'

It is always difficult to drive fast in the city in the middle of the day, when the streets are full of traffic, but we did what could be done; and when a good driver and a good horse, who understand each other, are of one mind, it is wonderful what they can

9   do. I had a very good mouth—that is, I could be guided by the slightest touch of the rein, and that is a great thing in London,

6 Stand. Cab rank – a place where cabs waited for customers. There were approximately 500 such cabstands in London. See p. 293.

7 South-Eastern Railway. The South-Eastern Railway Company was one of a network of railway companies in Britain serving different parts of the country. Others included the Great Western Railway, the Lancashire and Yorkshire Railway, the London and North Eastern Railway, and the London, Midland and Scottish Railway.

8 Chirrup. Either vocal encouragement or clicking with the tongue to urge the horse faster.

9 Very good mouth. A horse's mouth which has not been made insensitive by harsh use of the bit. Such abuse, over time, deadens the nerves in the horse's mouth and makes him less responsive to the action of the reins and bit.

Various ways of abusing a horse's mouth. (Edward Mayhew, *Illustrated Horse Doctor*, London, 1860, p. 55)

10 amongst carriages, omnibuses, carts, vans, trucks, cabs, and great wagons creeping along at a walking pace; some going one

11 way, some another, some going slowly, others wanting to pass them, omnibuses stopping short every few minutes to take up a passenger, obliging the horse that is coming behind to pull up too, or to pass, and get before them: perhaps you try to pass, but just then, something else comes dashing in through the narrow opening, and you have to keep in behind the omnibus again; presently you think you see a chance, and manage to get to the front, going so near the wheels on each side, that half an inch nearer and they would scrape. Well—you get along for a bit, but soon find yourself in a long train of carts and carriages all obliged to go at a walk; perhaps you come to a regular block-up, and have to stand still for minutes together, till something clears out into a side street, or the policeman interferes: you have to be ready for any chance—to dash forward if there

12 be an opening, and be quick as a rat dog to see if there be room, and if there be time, lest you get your own wheels locked, or

13 smashed, or the shaft of some other vehicle run into your chest or shoulder. All this is what you have to be ready for. If you want to get through London fast in the middle of the day, it wants a deal of practice.

Jerry and I were used to it, and no one could beat us at getting through when we were set upon it. I was quick and bold, and could always trust my driver; Jerry was quick, and patient at the same time, and could trust his horse, which was a great thing too. He very seldom used the whip; I knew by his voice, and his click, click, when he wanted to get on fast, and by the rein where I was to go; so there was no need for whipping; but I must go back to my story.

The streets were very full that day, but we got on pretty well

10 **Carriages, omnibuses, carts, vans, trucks, cabs, and great wagons.** Carriage was the generic term for private four-wheeled vehicles which could be open or closed, for single horse or a pair. They came in a multitude of designs and styles. Omnibuses were public vehicles for town use, the first of which were known as Shillibeers after their proprietor who started the service in 1829; other companies started up but the largest was the London General Omnibus Company. Omnibuses could be of several designs, the most popular being the knifeboard omnibus with longitudinal seating, and later the garden seat omnibus with transverse seating. They were usually drawn by a pair of horses but sometimes three abreast. For carts see p. 417. 'Van' was a general term for a lightweight four-wheeled trade or goods vehicle which was usually covered. It could be drawn by a single horse or a pair. Trucks were open or flat carts. For cabs see pp. 283, 289, 339. Wagon was a general term for a heavyweight four-wheeled vehicle which could be open or covered, drawn by a single horse, a pair, a tandem, or a team of four or even six.

11 **Going one way, some another.** There was little 'lane discipline' and although most drivers attempted to drive on the left-hand side of the road there were no rules in the form of a 'Highway Code'.

12 **Rat dog.** Terrier or mongrel with much terrier blood adept at catching rats. Had to be quick, alert and aggressive.

13 **Shaft of some other vehicle run into your chest or shoulder.** This was a common cause of accidents when rounding a corner too fast or too sharply and colliding head on with another horse-drawn vehicle. 'Magenta' recommended: 'In driving through crowded streets or in a narrow way, especially with vehicles coming rapidly towards you, and every prospect of a collision, take a stronger hold of your horses, and moderate your pace, remembering that, if you cannot avoid grief, the less the impetus the less the crash, if it should come' (*Handy Horse Book*, 1865). See the accident to Rory described in Chapter XXIX.

14 as far as the bottom of Cheapside, where there was a block for three or four minutes. The young man put his head out, and said anxiously, 'I think I had better get out and walk, I shall never get there if this goes on.'

'I 'll do all that can be done, sir,' said Jerry, 'I think we shall be in time; this block-up cannot last much longer, and your luggage is very heavy for you to carry, sir.'

Just then the cart in front of us began to move on, and then we had a good turn. In and out—in and out we went, as fast as horse-flesh could do it, and for a wonder had a good clear time 15 on London Bridge, for there was a whole train of cabs and carriages, all going our way at a quick trot—perhaps wanting to catch that very train; at any rate, we whirled into the station with many more, just as the great clock pointed to eight minutes to twelve o'clock.

'Thank God! we are in time,' said the young man, 'and thank you too, my friend, and your good horse; you have saved me more 16 than money can pay for, take this extra half-crown.'

'No, sir, no, thank you all the same; so glad we hit the time, sir, but don't stay now, sir, the bell is ringing. Here, porter! take this gentleman's luggage—Dover line—twelve o'clock train —that 's it,' and without waiting for another word, Jerry wheeled me round to make room for other cabs that were dashing up at the last minute, and drew up on one side till the crush was past.

'So glad!' he said, 'so glad! poor young fellow! I wonder what it was that made him so anxious!'

Jerry often talked to himself quite loud enough for me to hear, when we were not moving.

On Jerry's return to the rank, there was a good deal of laughing and chaffing at him, for driving hard to the train for an extra fare,

14 Cheapside. Street in the East End of London.

15 London Bridge. Bridge over the River Thames between South-wark Bridge and Tower Bridge, made famous in the nursery rhyme 'London Bridge is falling down'. The London Bridge of Anna Sewell's time is now a tourist attraction in Arizona.

16 Half-crown. A silver coin worth two shillings and sixpence.

Traffic on London Bridge as seen by Gustave Doré. (Gustave Doré and Blanchard Jerrold, *London: A Pilgrimage*, London: Grant, 1872; David & Charles reprints, 1971, p. 11)

as they said, all against his principles; and they wanted to know how much he had pocketed.

'A good deal more than I generally get,' said he, nodding slyly; 'what he gave me will keep me in little comforts for several days.'

'Gammon!' said one.

'He's a humbug,' said another, 'preaching to us, and then doing the same himself.'

'Look here, mates,' said Jerry, 'the gentleman offered me half a crown extra, but I didn't take it; 'twas quite pay enough for me, to see how glad he was to catch that train; and if Jack and I choose to have a quick run now and then, to please ourselves, that's our business and not yours.'

'Well,' said Larry, '*you 'll* never be a rich man.'

'Most likely not,' said Jerry, 'but I don't know that I shall be the less happy for that. I have heard the commandments read a great many times, and I never noticed that any of them said, "Thou shalt be rich"; and there are a good many curious things said in the New Testament about rich men, that I think would make me feel rather queer if I was one of them.'

'If you ever do get rich,' said Governor Grant, looking over his shoulder across the top of his cab, 'you 'll deserve it, Jerry, and you won't find a curse come with your wealth. As for you, Larry, you 'll die poor, you spend too much in whipcord.'

'Well,' said Larry, 'what is a fellow to do if his horse won't go without it?'

'You never take the trouble to see if he will go without it; your whip is always going as if you had the St. Vitus's dance in your arm; and if it does not wear you out, it wears your horse out; you know you are always changing your horses, and why? because you never give them any peace or encouragement.'

17 **Gammon.** Old-fashioned expression meaning to deceive with lies while talking plausibly.

18 **Commandments.** The Ten Commandments (Book of Exodus, Chapter 20).

19 **Whipcord.** The very end of the thong of the whip, usually a few inches of knotted cord.

20 **St. Vitus's dance.** A nervous disease causing involuntary movements in the limbs.

The crowded streets of London. (*Illustrated London News*, 17 December 1864, p. 604)

'Well, I have not had good luck,' said Larry, 'that's where it is.'

21   'And you never will,' said the Governor. 'Good Luck is rather particular who she rides with, and mostly prefers those who have got common sense and a good heart; at least, that is my experience.'

Governor Grant turned round again to his newspaper, and the other men went to their cabs.

322

21 **Good Luck ...** Victorian homily implying that 'God helps those who help themselves', that good will triumph over adversity and that 'fate' is very much in the hands of the individual through the notion of self-help. This was a popular idea in the nineteenth century begun by Samuel Smiles (1812–1904), a social reformer and champion of the working classes, and author of *Self Help* in 1859.

The cab stand. Illustrated by Tom Gill. (*Black Beauty*, Golden Picture Classics, New York: Simon & Schuster, 1956, p. 69)

323

CHAPTER XXXVI

THE SUNDAY CAB

ONE morning, as Jerry had just put me into the shafts and was fastening the traces, a gentleman walked into the yard. 'Your servant, sir,' said Jerry.

'Good morning, Mr. Barker,' said the gentleman. 'I should be glad to make some arrangements with you for taking Mrs. Briggs regularly to church on Sunday mornings. We go to the new church now, and that is rather further than she can walk.'

'Thank you, sir,' said Jerry, 'but I have only taken out a six days' licence,[1] and therefore I could not take a fare on a Sunday, it would not be legal.'

'Oh!' said the other, 'I did not know yours was a six days'

[1] A few years since the annual charge for a cab licence was very much reduced, and the difference between the six and seven days' cabs was abolished.

324

1 **Six days' licence.** All cabs which plied for hire had to be licensed annually, as did the driver himself. On passing the required standard of knowledge of London and payment of five shillings, he was issued with a licence and a badge which had to be displayed. For many years there was a big difference between the cost of a six and a seven days' licence.

'I could not take a fare on a Sunday'. Illustrated by Lionel Edwards. (*Black Beauty*, London: Ward Lock, 1954, p. 156)

cab; but of course it would be very easy to alter your licence. I would see that you did not lose by it; the fact is, Mrs. Briggs very much prefers you to drive her.'

2 'I should be glad to oblige the lady, sir, but I had a seven days' licence once, and the work was too hard for me, and too hard for my horses. Year in and year out, not a day's rest, and never a Sunday with my wife and children, and never able to go to a place of worship, which I had always been used to do before I took to the driving box; so for the last five years I have only taken a six days' licence, and I find it better all the way round.'

'Well, of course,' replied Mr. Briggs, 'it is very proper that every person should have rest, and be able to go to church on Sundays, but I should have thought you would not have minded such a short distance for the horse, and only once a day; you would have all the afternoon and evening for yourself, and we are very good customers, you know.'

3 'Yes, sir, that is true, and I am grateful for all favours, I am sure, and anything that I could do to oblige you, or the lady, I should be proud and happy to do; but I can't give up my Sundays, sir, indeed I can't. I read that God made man, and He made horses and all the other beasts, and as soon as He had made them, He made a day of rest, and bade that all should rest one day in seven; and I think, sir, He must have known what was good for them, and I am sure it is good for me; I am stronger and healthier altogether, now that I have a day of rest; the horses are fresh too, and do not wear up nearly so fast. The six-day drivers all tell 4 me the same, and I have laid by more money in the savings bank than ever I did before; and as for the wife and children, sir— why, heart alive! they would not go back to the seven days for all they could see.'

326

2   **I should be glad to oblige the lady.** Jerry Barker's arguments are based on a real incident in Anna Sewell's life. During the years in which she wrote *Black Beauty*, she was confined to her house in Norwich, whose windows overlooked the street. Her mother's biographer found the following note in Anna's hand. 'Some weeks ago I had a conversation at my open window with an intelligent Cabman who was waiting at our door, which has deeply impressed me. He led the conversation to the Sunday question, after telling me that he never plied on the Sabbath. I found there was a sore, even a bitter feeling against the religious people, who, by their use of cabs on Sunday, practically deny the Sabbath to the drivers. "Even ministers do it, Ma'am," he said, "and I say it's a shame upon religion." Then he told me of one of the London drivers who had driven a lady to church – as she stepped from the cab, she handed the driver a tract on the observance of the Sabbath. This naturally thoroughly disgusted the man. "Now, Ma'am," said my friend, "I call that hypocrisy – don't you?" I suppose most of us agree with him, and yet it might not have been done hypocritically – so few Christians apparently realise the responsibility of taking a cab on Sunday' (quoted by Susan Chitty, *The Woman Who Wrote Black Beauty*, 1971).

3   **Yes, sir, that is true.** The whole paragraph exudes typically Victorian morals, religious ideals and a growing concern that Sunday should be observed. Saturday was considered a working day, the average person had only one day free in seven and according to the Bible, he should rest on the seventh day – and go to church.

4   **Savings bank.** Most banks were privately owned and run and had largely been used by the upper and rising middle classes. However, towards the end of the nineteenth century various financial institutions were set up to help the working man invest and save. Some banks advertised that only one penny was needed to open an account. Thriftiness was a favourite Victorian virtue.

'Oh, very well,' said the gentleman. 'Don't trouble yourself, Mr. Barker, any further; I will inquire somewhere else,' and he walked away.

'Well,' says Jerry to me, 'we can't help it, Jack, old boy, we must have our Sundays.'

'Polly!' he shouted, 'Polly! come here.'

She was there in a minute.

'What is it all about, Jerry?'

'Why, my dear Mr Briggs wants me to take Mrs. Briggs to church every Sunday morning. I say, I have only a six days' licence. He says "Get a seven days' licence, and I'll make it worth your while"; and you know, Polly, they are very good customers to us. Mrs. Briggs often goes out shopping for hours, or making calls, and then she pays down fair and honourable like a lady; there's no beating down, or making three hours into two hours and a half, as some folks do; and it is easy work for the horses; not like tearing along to catch trains for people that are always a quarter of an hour too late; and if I don't oblige her in this matter, it is very likely we shall lose them altogether. What do you say, little woman?'

'I say Jerry,' says she, speaking very slowly, 'I say, if Mrs. Briggs would give you a sovereign every Sunday morning, I would not have you a seven days' cabman again. We have known what it was to have no Sundays; and now we know what it is to call them our own. Thank God, you earn enough to keep us, though it is sometimes close work to pay for all the oats and hay, the licence, and the rent besides; but Harry will soon be earning something, and I would rather struggle on harder than we do, than go back to those horrid times, when you hardly had a minute to look at your own children, and we never could go to a place of worship together, or have a happy, quiet day. God forbid

328

The type of turn-out used for church-going in Victorian England: (*top*) a Landau and (*bottom*) a wagonette. (Sidney, *Book of the Horse*, pp. 528 and 530)

that we should ever turn back to those times: that 's what I say, Jerry.'

'And that is just what I told Mr. Briggs, my dear,' said Jerry, 'and what I mean to stick to; so don't go and fret yourself, Polly —for she had begun to cry—'I would not go back to the old times if I earned twice as much, so that is settled, little woman. Now cheer up, and I 'll be off again to the stand.'

Three weeks had passed away after this conversation, and no order had come from Mrs. Briggs; so there was nothing but taking jobs from the stand. Jerry took it to heart a good deal, for of course the work was harder for horse and man; but Polly would always cheer him up and say, 'Never mind, father, never mind—

> 'Do your best,
> And leave the rest,
> 'Twill all come right,
> Some day or night.'

It soon became known that Jerry had lost his best customer, and for what reason; most of the men said he was a fool, but two or three took his part.

'If working men don't stick to their Sunday,' said Truman, 'they 'll soon have none left; it is every man's right and every beast's right. By God's law we have a day of rest, and by the law of England we have a day of rest; and I say we ought to hold to the rights these laws give us, and keep them for our children.'

'All very well for you religious chaps to talk so,' said Larry, 'but I 'll turn a shilling when I can. I don't believe in religion, for I don't see that your religious people are any better than the rest.'

'If they are not better,' put in Jerry, 'it is because they are *not* religious. You might as well say that our country's laws are

5 **Father.** Common term of endearment used by wife to her husband. Similarly, husbands frequently used 'Mother' when addressing their wives. This continued in working-class and country families until well into the twentieth century.

6 **If working men don't stick to their Sunday.** The average working person had only Sunday as a day of rest. Many thought that if this was taken away their only free time would be eroded and would become the 'thin end of the wedge' with no free time at all. There were no paid holidays and strong unions to demand time off or compensation for excessive hours worked either in money or time in lieu.

Jerry Barker. Illustrated by Michael Rios. (*Black Beauty*, New York: Modern Promotions, 1979, p. 148)

not good because some people break them. If a man gives way to his temper, and speaks evil of his neighbour, and does not pay his debts, he is not religious; I don't care how much he goes to church. If some men are shams and humbugs, that does not make religion untrue. Real religion is the best and the truest thing in the world; and the only thing that can make a man really happy, or make the world any better.'

'If religion was good for anything,' said Jones, 'it would prevent your religious people from making us work on Sundays as you know many of them do, and that's why I say religion is nothing but a sham—why, if it was not for the church- and chapel-goers it would be hardly worth while our coming out on a Sunday; but they have their privileges, as they call them, and I go without. I shall expect them to answer for my soul, if I can't get a chance of saving it.'

Several of the men applauded this, till Jerry said—

'That may sound well enough, but it won't do; every man must look after his own soul; you can't lay it down at another man's door like a foundling, and expect him to take care of it; and don't you see, if you are always sitting on your box waiting for a fare, they will say, "If we don't take him, someone else will, and he does not look for any Sunday." Of course they don't go to the bottom of it, or they would see if they never came for a cab, it would be no use your standing there; but people don't always like to go to the bottom of things; it may not be convenient to do it; but if you Sunday drivers would all strike for a day of rest, the thing would be done.'

'And what would all the good people do, if they could not get to their favourite preachers?' said Larry.

''Tis not for me to lay down plans for other people,' said Jerry, 'but if they can't walk so far, they can go to what is nearer; and

7 Church- and chapel-goers. Since the time of Henry VIII (1491–1547) and the establishment of the Church of England, this brand of Protestantism had been the religion of the land. Eventually, Catholicism became accepted and in the eighteenth century varieties of Protestantism grew up, notably Non-Conformity, Wesleyan Methodism (established by John Wesley, 1703–91) and the like, for which chapels were built. Methodism was considered the religion of the working classes and 'inferior' to the Church of England. Its strongholds were Yorkshire and Wales but by the end of the nineteenth century it was very widespread.

8 If they never came for a cab. See p. 327.

An early Victorian chapel. (Isaac Watts, *Divine and Moral Songs for Children*, 1849)

if it should rain they can put on their mackintoshes as they do on a week-day.   If a thing is right, it *can* be done, and if it is wrong, it *can be done without*; and a good man will find a way; and that is as true for us cabmen as it is for the church-goers.'

Family church-going. (*The Children's Friend* (London), 1881, p. 29)

335

CHAPTER XXXVII

THE GOLDEN RULE

TWO or three weeks after this, as we came into the yard rather late in the evening, Polly came running across the road with the lantern (she always brought it to him if it was not very wet).

'It has all come right, Jerry; Mrs. Briggs sent her servant this afternoon, to ask you to take her out to-morrow at eleven o'clock. I said, "Yes, I thought so, but we supposed she employed someone else now."

'"Well," says he, "the real fact is, master was put out because Mr. Barker refused to come on Sundays, and he has been trying other cabs, but there 's something wrong with them all; some drive too fast, and some too slow, and the mistress says, there is

336

1 **Lantern.** In these pre-electricity days working-class houses and commercial premises were lit by gas, oil or paraffin lamps. Stables frequently had no lighting at all or simply portable oil lamps and lanterns, which were easily knocked over with the risk of fire spreading rapidly through straw and hay.

A selection of Victorian lanterns. (Moseman's *Illustrated Guide for Purchasers of Horse Furnishing Goods*, p. 23)

337

not one of them so nice and clean as yours, and nothing will suit
her but Mr. Barker's cab again.'''

Polly was almost out of breath, and Jerry broke out into a
merry laugh—

'All come right some day or night; you were right, my dear;
you generally are. Run in and get the supper, and I'll have
Jack's harness off and make him snug and happy in no time.'

After this, Mrs. Briggs wanted Jerry's cab quite as often as
before, never, however, on a Sunday; but there came a day when
we had Sunday work, and this was how it happened. We had
all come home on the Saturday night very tired, and very glad to
think that the next day would be all rest, but so it was not to be.

On Sunday morning Jerry was cleaning me in the yard, when
Polly stepped up to him, looking very full of something.

'What is it?' said Jerry.

'Well, my dear,' she said, 'poor Dinah Brown has just had a
letter brought to say that her mother is dangerously ill, and that
she must go directly if she wishes to see her alive. The place
is more than ten miles away from here, out in the country, and
she says if she takes the train she should still have four miles to
walk; and so weak as she is, and the baby only four weeks old,
of course that would be impossible; and she wants to know if
you would take her in your cab, and she promises to pay you
faithfully as she can get the money.'

'Tut, tut, we'll see about that. It was not the money I was
thinking about, but of losing our Sunday; the horses are tired,
and I am tired too—that's where it pinches.'

'It pinches all round, for that matter,' said Polly, 'for it's
only half Sunday without you, but you know we should do to
other people as we should like they should do to us; and I know
very well what I should like if my mother was dying; and, Jerry

338

2 Mr. Barker's cab. Jerry Barker, who worked his own cab and his own two horses exclusively, took a pride in their turn-out and welfare and his own driving standards, unlike some cabmasters who owned hundreds of horses and cabs which they hired out to other drivers.

3 We should do to other people. Here is another example of Victorian didacticism. Anna Sewell was not the only author to preach good manners and respect for others: Charles Kingsley also did so in his *Water Babies*, in which there was even a character called Mrs Doasyouwouldbedoneby. Anna Sewell would have been familiar with the book, which was published in 1863, as she was a great admirer of Kingsley.

A thorough grooming. Illustrated by John Beer. (*Black Beauty*, London: Jarrold & Sons, 1894, p. 207)

Four-wheeled cabs: (*above left*) from Henry Charles Moore, *Omnibuses and Cabs* (London: Chapman Hall, 1902, p. 225); (*left*) a Clarence, now in a museum in Leicester (D. J. Smith, *Discovering Horse Drawn Carriages*, Aylesbury: Shire Publications, 1985, pl. 6)

dear, I am sure it won't break the Sabbath; for if pulling a poor beast or donkey out of a pit would not spoil it, I am quite sure taking poor Dinah would not do it.'

'Why, Polly, you are as good as the minister, and so, as I 've had my Sunday morning sermon early to-day, you may go and tell Dinah that I 'll be ready for her as the clock strikes ten; but stop—just step round to butcher Braydon's with my compli-
4 ments, and ask him if he would lend me his light trap; I know he never uses it on the Sunday, and it would make a wonderful difference to the horse.'

Away she went, and soon returned, saying that he could have the trap and welcome.

'All right,' said he, 'now put me up a bit of bread and cheese, and I 'll be back in the afternoon as soon as I can.'
5 'And I 'll have the meat pie ready for an early tea instead of for dinner,' said Polly; and away she went, whilst he made his preparations to the tune of 'Polly, the woman and no mistake,' of which tune he was very fond.

I was selected for the journey, and at ten o'clock we started, in a light, high-wheeled gig, which ran so easily, that after the four-wheeled cab, it seemed like nothing.

It was a fine May day, and as soon as we were out of the town, the sweet air, the smell of the fresh grass, and the soft country
6 roads were as pleasant as they used to be in the old times, and I soon began to feel quite fresh.
7 Dinah's family lived in a small farmhouse, up a green lane, close by a meadow with some fine shady trees: there were two cows feeding in it. A young man asked Jerry to bring his trap into the meadow, and he would tie me up in the cowshed; he wished he had a better stable to offer.

'If your cows would not be offended,' said Jerry, 'there is

4 **Trap.** Trap is a colloquial expression for almost any two-wheeled, one-horse vehicle.

5 **Tea.** The meal 'tea', as opposed to the drink, could take two forms: 'afternoon tea', consisting of small sandwiches and cakes accompanied by tea to drink, taken at about 4 p.m. and followed by dinner, a meal of several courses with wine, at about 8 p.m. in upper- and middle-class households; or, as in this case, 'high tea', in working-class homes, usually a hot, substantial meal eaten about 6 p.m. and accompanied by tea to drink as the last large meal of the day. There might follow a light snack and beverage before going to bed which was known as 'supper'.

6 **Soft country roads.** Unlike the hard London streets, rural roads were usually unpaved; simply earth which had been compressed by wheels and hooves and were dusty in summer and muddy in winter. See p. 345.

7 **Green lane.** This may simply be a description of a lane overhung by trees and bordered by hedges, or it may indicate that the farmhouse was by one of the old drovers' roads, overgrown by grass, along which cattle, sheep, pigs and geese were driven, often long distances, to market.

A light trap (Stanhope gig). (Duke of Beaufort, *Driving*, London: Longmans, Green, 1889, p. 113)

nothing my horse would like so well as to have an hour or two in your beautiful meadow; he's quiet, and it would be a rare treat for him.'

'Do, and welcome,' said the young man; 'the best we have is at your service for your kindness to my sister; we shall be having some dinner in an hour, and I hope you'll come in, though with mother so ill we are all out of sorts in the house.'

Jerry thanked him kindly, but said as he had some dinner with him, there was nothing he should like so well as walking about in the meadow.

When my harness was taken off, I did not know what I should do first—whether to eat the grass, or roll over on my back, or lie down and rest, or have a gallop across the meadow out of sheer spirits at being free; and I did all by turns. Jerry seemed to be quite as happy as I was; he sat down by a bank under a shady tree, and listened to the birds, then he sang himself, and read out of the little brown book he is so fond of, then wandered round the meadow and down by a little brook, where he picked the flowers and the hawthorn, and tied them up with long sprays of ivy; then he gave me a good feed of the oats which he had brought with him; but the time seemed all too short—I had not been in a field since I left poor Ginger at Earlshall.

We came home gently, and Jerry's first words were as we came into the yard, 'Well, Polly, I have not lost my Sunday after all, for the birds were singing hymns in every bush, and I joined in the service; and as for Jack, he was like a young colt.'

When he handed Dolly the flowers, she jumped about for joy.

8 **Rare treat.** Most horses used in towns were never turned out to graze or had the opportunity to eat grass, gallop about freely or roll. After leaving the rural surroundings where they had been bred, at the age of three or so, most town working horses never saw the countryside again and had an average lifespan of about eight years – less in London or if worked very hard in hilly parts of the country or if their work involved much stopping and starting. Much, of course, depended upon the care a horse was afforded as to how long he could continue to work.

9 **Dinner.** Here, a working-class term for the midday meal, called lunch or luncheon in upper- and middle-class households who used the term 'dinner' to denote the evening meal. The term 'lunch' or 'luncheon' was not usually used by the working classes.

10 **Little brown book.** No doubt the Bible or a prayer book.

Rare treat. Illustrated by John Beer. (*Black Beauty*, London: Jarrold & Sons, 1894, p. 176)

343

CHAPTER XXXVIII

DOLLY AND A REAL GENTLEMAN

THE winter came in early, with a great deal of cold and wet. There was snow, or sleet, or rain, almost every day for weeks, changing only for keen driving winds, or sharp frosts. The horses all felt it very much. When it is a dry cold, a couple of good thick rugs will keep the warmth in us; but when it is soaking rain, they soon get wet through and are no good. Some of the drivers had a waterproof cover to throw over, which was a fine thing; but some of the men were so poor that they could not protect themselves or their horses, and many of them suffered very much that winter. When we horses had worked half the day we went to our dry stables, and could rest; whilst they had to sit on their boxes, sometimes staying out as late as one or two o'clock in the morning, if they had a party to wait for.

When the streets were slippery with frost or snow, that was

344

1   **The horses all felt it very much.** Horses can stand a great deal of dry cold, but constant rain, particularly when combined with wind, will soon set them shivering even when the actual temperature is not particularly low.

2   **Streets.** Road surfaces would have been either cobbled (small rounded beach or river pebbles) or paved with stone 'setts' approximately 9 inches by 6 inches laid in a brick-like pattern. Rainwater would accumulate and freeze between the setts, thus forming an almost continuous sheet of ice.

The cab stand; on the rank in all weathers. (Gordon, *Horse World of London*, p. 40)

345

the worst of all for us horses; one mile of such travelling, with a weight to draw, and no firm footing, would take more out of us than four on a good road; every nerve and muscle of our bodies is on the strain to keep our balance; and added to this, the fear of falling is more exhausting than anything else.   If the roads are very bad indeed, our shoes are roughed, but that makes us feel nervous at first.

When the weather was very bad, many of the men would go and sit in the tavern close by, and get someone to watch for them; but they often lost a fare in that way, and could not, as Jerry said, be there without spending money.   He never went to the 'Rising Sun'; there was a coffee-shop near, where he now and then went—or he bought of an old man who came to our rank with tins of hot coffee and pies.   It was his opinion that spirits and beer made a man colder afterwards, and that dry clothes, good food, cheerfulness, and a comfortable wife at home, were the best things to keep a cabman warm.   Polly always supplied him with something to eat when he could not get home and sometimes he would see little Dolly peeping from the corner of the street, to make sure if 'father' was on the stand.   If she saw him, she would run off at full speed and soon come back with something in a tin or basket—some hot soup or pudding that Polly had ready.   It was wonderful how such a little thing could get safely across the street, often thronged with horses and carriages; but she was a brave little maid, and felt it quite an honour to bring 'father's first course,' as he used to call it.   She was a general favourite on the stand, and there was not a man who would not have seen her safely across the street, if Jerry had not been able to do it.

One cold windy day, Dolly had brought Jerry a basin of something hot, and was standing by him whilst he ate it.   He had

3 **Shoes.** The surface of a horseshoe was usually flat affording little grip on slippery surfaces. Some purchase was given by roughing or rasping the shoe. The better ones had metal studs which could be screwed into extra stud holes in the shoe, or calkins built into the heel of the shoe when it was made, and these would engage in the cracks between the setts and prevent slipping.

4 **Rising Sun.** Popular name for a public house.

5 **Old man who came to our rank.** Vendors of food both hot and cold were a common sight on Victorian streets. They usually sold their (often unhygienic) wares from trays slung around their necks or, in the case of hot peas or hot soup, from cans carried on a yoke across the shoulders, with a small burner under each can to keep food hot. Others had small hand carts with a brazier of red coals for foods such as chestnuts.

A shoe with a high calkin. (Mayhew, *The Illustrated Horse Management*, p. 108)

An outdoor coffee stall. (Gustave Doré and Blanchard Jerrold, *London; A Pilgrimage*, London: Grant, 1872; David & Charles reprints, 1971, pl. opp. p. 122)

scarcely begun, when a gentleman, walking towards us very fast,
6 held up his umbrella. Jerry touched his hat in return, gave the
basin to Dolly, and was taking off my cloth, when the gentleman,
hastening up, cried out, 'No, no, finish your soup, my friend; I
have not much time to spare, but I can wait till you have done,
and set your little girl safe on the pavement.' So saying, he
seated himself in the cab. Jerry thanked him kindly, and came
back to Dolly.

'There, Dolly, that's a gentleman; that's a real gentleman,
Dolly; he has got time and thought for the comfort of a poor
cabman and a little girl.'

Jerry finished his soup, set the child across, and then took his
7 orders to drive to Clapham Rise. Several times after that, the
same gentleman took our cab. I think he was very fond of dogs
and horses, for whenever we took him to his own door, two or
three dogs would come bounding out to meet him. Sometimes
he came round and patted me, saying in his quiet, pleasant way,
'This horse has got a good master, and he deserves it.' It was
8 a very rare thing for any one to notice the horse that had been
working for him. I have known ladies do it now and then, and
this gentleman, and one or two others have given me a pat and a
kind word; but ninety-nine out of a hundred would as soon think
of patting the steam-engine that drew the train.

This gentleman was not young, and there was a forward stoop
in his shoulders as if he was always going at something. His lips
were thin, and close shut, though they had a very pleasant smile;
his eye was keen, and there was something in his jaw and the
motion of his head that made one think he was very determined
in anything he set about. His voice was pleasant and kind; any
horse would trust that voice, though it was just as decided as
everything else about him.

348

6 **Held up his umbrella.** This signal is still used today when attracting a cabbie's attention.

7 **Clapham Rise.** Clapham is an area of southwest London between Lambeth and Battersea, south of the River Thames.

8 **Rare thing.** A fact often forgotten, ignored or taken for granted not only by Black Beauty's contemporaries but also by historians today, is that without the horse the economy would have ceased, and the Industrial Revolution and the rise of the British Empire could never have taken place.

Getting safely across the street. (Gordon, *Horse World of London*, p. 87)

349

One day, he and another gentleman took our cab; they stopped
9 at a shop in R——— Street, and whilst his friend went in, he stood
at the door.   A little ahead of us on the other side of the street,
a cart with two very fine horses was standing before some wine
vaults; the carter was not with them, and I cannot tell how long
they had been standing, but they seemed to think they had waited
long enough, and began to move off.   Before they had gone
many paces, the carter came running out and caught them.   He
seemed furious at their having moved, and with whip and rein
punished them brutally, even beating them about the head.   Our
gentleman saw it all and stepping quickly across the street, said
in a decided voice—

'If you don't stop that directly, I 'll have you summoned for
10 leaving your horses, and for brutal conduct.'

The man, who had clearly been drinking, poured forth some
abusive language, but he left off knocking the horses about, and
taking the reins, got into his cart; meantime our friend had
quietly taken a note-book from his pocket, and looking at the
name and address painted on the cart, he wrote something down.

'What do you want with that?' growled the carter, as he
cracked his whip and was moving on.   A nod, and a grim smile,
was the only answer he got.

On returning to the cab, our friend was joined by his companion, who said laughingly, 'I should have thought, Wright,
you had enough business of your own to look after, without
troubling yourself about other people's horses and servants.'

Our friend stood still for a moment, and throwing his head a
little back, 'Do you know why this world is as bad as it is?'

'No,' said the other.

'Then I 'll tell you.   It is because people think *only* about
their own business, and won't trouble themselves to stand up

9 **R— street.** As with titles, the suggestion of a real street is given in order not to dilute the authentic flavour of the narrative.

10 **Brutal conduct.** Public awareness (and later public opinion) and the establishment of the police force (1829) and the Royal Society for the Prevention of Cruelty to Animals (1824) meant that actions such as this were prosecutable and punishments could be enforced in the light of various animal welfare acts being passed by Parliament.

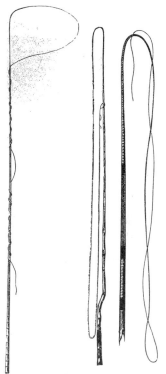

Driving whips. (Quadekker, *Het Paardenboek*, Part III, p. 219)

'Even beating them about the head'. Illustrated by H. Toaspern. (*Black Beauty*, New York: J. Hovendon & Co., 1894, p. 155)

351

for the oppressed, nor bring the wrong-doer to light. I never see a wicked thing like this without doing what I can, and many a master has thanked me for letting him know how his horses have been used.'

'I wish there were more gentlemen like you, sir,' said Jerry, 'for they are wanted badly enough in this city.'

After this we continued our journey, and as they got out of the cab, our friend was saying, 'My doctrine is this, that if we see cruelty or wrong that we have the power to stop, and do nothing, we make ourselves sharers in the guilt.'

11

352

II **And do nothing.** There are very many instances in *Black Beauty* where strangers interfere with others when they see cruelty. It is difficult to know whether this was common practice or whether it was a ploy used by Anna Sewell to encourage people to prevent cruelty. It may have been more common in the late nineteenth century, when there was considerable respect for the law and authority, and the fear of being reported to the police or employer (with the attendant risk of dismissal) may have carried more weight than it would today.

A real gentleman. Illustrated by Michael Rios. (*Black Beauty*, New York, Modern Promotions, 1979, p. 164)

CHAPTER XXXIX

SEEDY SAM

I SHOULD say, that for a cab horse I was very well off indeed; my driver was my owner, and it was his interest to treat me well, and not overwork me, even had he not been so good a man as he was; but there were a great many horses which belonged to the large cab-owners, who let them out to their drivers for so much money a day. As the horses did not belong to these men, the only thing they thought of was how to get their money out of them: first, to pay the master, and then to provide for their own living, and a dreadful time some of these horses had of it. Of course I understood but little, but it was often talked over on the stand, and the Governor, who was a kind-hearted man, and fond of horses, would sometimes speak up if one came in very much jaded or ill-used.

One day, a shabby, miserable-looking driver, who went by the name of 'Seedy Sam,' brought in his horse looking dreadfully beat, and the Governor said—

354

1 **Seedy Sam.** Another instance of using a nickname as a character description, although in this case, Sam is only seedy in appearance, not in character.

Dreadfully beat. Illustrated by Michael Rios. (*Black Beauty*, New York: Modern Promotions, 1979, p. 172)

'You and your horse look more fit for the police station than for this rank.'

The man flung his tattered rug over the horse, turned full round upon the Governor, and said, in a voice that sounded almost desperate—

'If the police have any business with the matter, it ought to be with the masters who charge us so much, or with the fares that are fixed so low. If a man has to pay eighteen shillings a day for the use of a cab and two horses, as many of us have to do in the season, and must make that up before we earn a penny for ourselves—I say, 'tis more than hard work; nine shillings a day to get out of each horse, before you begin to get your own living; you know that's true, and if the horses don't work we must starve, and I and my children have known what that is before now. I've six of 'em, and only one earns anything; I am on the stand fourteen or sixteen hours a day, and I haven't had a Sunday these ten or twelve weeks; you know, Skinner never gives a day if he can help it, and if I don't work hard, tell me who does! I want a warm coat and a mackintosh, but with so many to feed, how can a man get it? I had to pledge my clock a week ago to pay Skinner, and I shall never see it again.'

Some of the other drivers stood round nodding their heads, and saying he was right. The man went on—

'You that have your own horses and cabs, or drive for good masters, have a chance of getting on, and a chance of doing right; I haven't. We can't charge more than sixpence a mile after the first, within the four-mile radius. This very morning I had to go a clear six miles and only took three shillings. I could not get a return fare, and had to come all the way back; there's twelve miles for the horse and three shillings for me. After that I had a three-mile fare, and there were bags and boxes

2 **Cab and two horses.** It was usual to work a horse for only half a day although the driver worked a full day – in Sam's case, between fourteen and sixteen hours – hence the need to rent from the cab master two horses but only one cab.

3 **Six of 'em.** A family of six children was by no means uncommon in Victorian times and over a dozen was not considered exceptionally unusual.

4 **Skinner.** An unattractive surname for one who abuses and exploits both his equine and human workers.

5 **Pledge my clock.** Reference to the very popular and necessary (in working-class areas) pawnbroker, who would offer money against valuables and other saleable goods which could be redeemed later for payment.

6 **Bags.** Luggage was charged for if carried upon the roof or in the boot of a hired vehicle. If stowed with the passenger(s) on a seat it was carried free of charge.

Victorian pawnbroker's shop. Illustrated by George Cruikshank. (Charles Dickens, *Sketches by Boz*, London: Macmillan, 1892, reprint of 1836 edn, p. 178)

enough to have brought in a good many twopences if they had been put outside; but you know how people do; all that could be piled up inside on the front seat, were put in, and three heavy boxes went on the top, that was sixpence, and the fare one and sixpence; then I got a return for a shilling; now that makes eighteen miles for the horse and six shillings for me; there's three shillings still for that horse to earn, and nine shillings for the afternoon horse before I touch a penny. Of course it is not always as bad as that, but you know it often is, and I say 'tis a mockery to tell a man that he must not overwork his horse, for when a beast is downright tired, there's nothing but the whip that will keep his legs agoing—you can't help yourself—you must put your wife and children before the horse, the masters must look to that, we can't. I don't ill-use my horse for the sake of it; none of you can say I do. There's wrong lays somewhere—never a day's rest—never a quiet hour with the wife and children. I often feel like an old man, though I'm only forty-five. You know how quick some of the gentry are to suspect us of cheating and over-charging; why, they stand with their purses in their hands, counting it over to a penny, and looking at us as if we were pickpockets. I wish some of 'em had got to sit on my box sixteen hours a day, and get a living out of it, and eighteen shillings beside, and that in all weathers; they would not be so uncommon particular never to give us a sixpence over, or to cram all the luggage inside. Of course, some of 'em tip us pretty handsome now and then, or else we could not live, but you can't *depend* upon that.'

The men who stood round, much approved this speech, and one of them said, 'It is desperate hard, and if a man sometimes does what is wrong, it is no wonder; and if he gets a dram too much, who's to blow him up?'

7 **Lays.** Slang for laws or impositions.

8 **Dram too much.** A colloquial expression for getting drunk. A dram was a small drink of liquor, not a specific measure in this case. Drinking to excess was very common in Victorian times. Gin especially was cheap, but beer would also suffice to drown the sorrows of the working classes caught in the vicious circle of low wages, poor housing, the threat of unemployment and eviction, large families, poor food and so on. The effects of alcohol at least provided a brief refuge from it all.

'The men who stood round'. Illustrated by Charles Keeping. (*Black Beauty*, London: Victor Gollancz, 1988, p. 169)

359

Jerry had taken no part in this conversation, but I never saw his face look so sad before. The Governor had stood with both his hands in his pockets; now he took his handkerchief out of his hat, and wiped his forehead.

'You 've beaten me, Sam,' he said, 'for it 's all true, and I won't cast it up to you any more about the police; it was the look in that horse's eye that came over me. It is hard lines for man, and it is hard lines for beast, and who 's to mend it I don't know; but anyway you might tell the poor beast that you were sorry to take it out of him in that way. Sometimes a kind word is all we can give 'em, poor brutes, and 'tis wonderful that they do understand.'

A few mornings after this talk, a new man came on the stand with Sam's cab.

'Halloo!' said one, 'what 's up with Seedy Sam?'

'He 's ill in bed,' said the man; 'he was taken last night in the yard, and could scarcely crawl home. His wife sent a boy this morning to say his father was in a high fever and could not get out; so I 'm here instead.'

The next morning the same man came again.

'How is Sam?' inquired the Governor.

'He 's gone,' said the man.

'What, gone? You don't mean to say he 's dead?'

'Just snuffed out,' said the other; 'he died at four o'clock this morning; all yesterday he was raving—raving about Skinner, and having no Sundays. "I never had a Sunday's rest," these were his last words.'

No one spoke for a while, and then the Governor said, 'I tell you what, mates, this is a warning for us.'

Two very similar studies of Seedy Sam: (*left*) by Alan Wright (*Black Beauty*, London: Jarrold & Sons, 190?, pl. opp. p. 233); (*bottom*) by John Beer (*Black Beauty*, London: Jarrold & Sons, 1894, p. 182).

361

" SEEDY SAM."

CHAPTER XL

POOR GINGER

ONE day, whilst our cab and many others were waiting outside one of the parks, where a band was playing, a shabby old cab drove up beside ours. The horse was an old worn-out chestnut, with an ill-kept coat, and bones that showed plainly through it. The knees knuckled over, and the forelegs were very unsteady. I had been eating some hay, and the wind rolled a little lock of it that way, and the poor creature put out her long thin neck and picked it up, and then turned round and looked about for more. There was a hopeless look in the dull eye that I could not help noticing, and then, as I was thinking where I had seen that horse before, she looked full at me and said, 'Black Beauty, is that you?'

It was Ginger! but how changed! The beautifully arched and glossy neck was now straight and lank, and fallen in, the clean straight legs and delicate fetlocks were swelled; the joints were grown out of shape with hard work; the face, that was once so full of spirit and life, was now full of suffering, and I could tell

362

1 **Neck.** A straight, lank neck with the muscles fallen in on both sides is a sure sign of poor condition. A horse in good condition has a hard, solidly muscled crest to the neck which usually has a slight convex curve.

2 **Fetlocks.** The fetlock, the first main joint above the hoof, is very prone to strains and sprains with resulting heat and swelling due to damaged tendons over the joint.

The horse's fetlock. (Quadekker, *Het Paardenboek*. Part I, p. 426)

'It was Ginger! but how changed!' Illustrated by Lionel Edwards. (*Black Beauty*, London: Peter Lunn, 1946, p. 79)

3 by the heaving of her sides, and her frequent cough, how bad her breath was.

Our drivers were standing together a little way off, so I sidled up to her a step or two, that we might have a little quiet talk. It was a sad tale that she had to tell.

After a twelvemonth's run off at Earlshall, she was considered to be fit for work again, and was sold to a gentleman. For a little while she got on very well, but after a longer gallop than usual, the old strain returned, and after being rested and doctored she was again sold. In this way she changed hands several times, but always getting lower down.

'And so at last,' said she, 'I was bought by a man who keeps a number of cabs and horses, and lets them out. You look well off, and I am glad of it, but I could not tell you what my life has been. When they found out my weakness, they said I was not worth what they gave for me, and that I must go into one of the low cabs, and just be used up; that is what they are doing, whipping and working with never one thought of what I suffer; they paid for me, and must get it out of me, they say. The man who hires me now, pays a deal of money to the owner every day, and so he has to get it out of me too; and so it 's all the week round and round, with never a Sunday rest.'

I said, 'You used to stand up for yourself if you were ill-used.'

'Ah!' she said, 'I did once, but it 's no use; men are strongest, and if they are cruel and have no feeling, there is nothing that we can do, but just bear it, bear it on and on to the end. I wish the end was come, I wish I was dead. I have seen dead horses, and I am sure they do not suffer pain. I wish I may drop down

4 dead at my work, and not be sent off to the knacker's.'

I was very much troubled, and I put my nose up to hers, but

3 Heaving of her sides. Combined with a frequent cough this could indicate one or more respiratory complaints including 'broken wind', lungworm, allergies or virus infections of the lungs.

4 Knacker's. Professional horse slaughterers were a necessary part of the Victorian horse world and their 'turnover' was enormous, especially in cities. Dead horses provided bones for glue, hair for stuffing furniture, leather for harness and whips, tails for military plumes and lawyers' wigs, and meat for pet food with a small amount for human consumption.

Black Beauty and Ginger meet again. Illustrated by Edmund Blampied. (*Black Beauty*, London: Jarrolds, 1922, p. 209)

I could say nothing to comfort her.   I think she was pleased to see me, for she said, 'You are the only friend I ever had.'

Just then her driver came up, and with a tug at her mouth, backed her out of the line and drove off, leaving me very sad indeed.

5   A short time after this, a cart with a dead horse in it passed our cab-stand.   The head hung out of the cart tail, the lifeless tongue was slowly dropping with blood; and the sunken eyes! but I can't speak of them, the sight was too dreadful.   It was a chestnut horse with a long thin neck.   I saw a white streak down the forehead.   I believe it was Ginger; I hoped it was, for then her troubles would be over.   Oh! if men were more merciful,

6   they would shoot us before we came to such misery.

5 **Dead horse.** Street accidents were common and when a horse was killed its carcase had to be taken to the knacker's yard. It was winched on to a flat cart drawn, of course, by a horse.

6 **Shoot us.** For a long time the method of killing a horse was like that for cattle, by pole-axing, but gradually the use of the captive bolt pistol was introduced on humanitarian grounds and later by law. (Its use was promoted in some early American editions of *Black Beauty*.) The horse, not being a food animal, had a higher status than cattle, sheep and pigs in the eyes of the law and was afforded the privacy of separate stunning stalls in the abattoir out of sight of other horses. In Black Beauty's day the London abattoirs killed thousands of horses each year, usually under the most primitive conditions, although some of the large abattoirs prided themselves on the speed with which carcases could be processed and, for the time, their hygienic conditions.

The end. (Mayhew, *The Illustrated Horse Management*, p. 590)

Cold storage at the knacker's yard. (Gordon, *Horse World of London*, p. 188)

CHAPTER XLI

THE BUTCHER

I SAW a great deal of trouble amongst the horses in London, and much of it that might have been prevented by a little common sense. We horses do not mind hard work if we are treated reasonably; and I am sure there are many driven by quite poor men who have a happier life than I had, when I used to go in the Countess of W——'s carriage, with my silver-mounted harness and high feeding.

It often went to my heart to see how the little ponies were used, straining along with heavy loads, or staggering under heavy blows from some low cruel boy. Once I saw a little grey pony with a thick mane and a pretty head, and so much like Merrylegs, that if I had not been in harness, I should have neighed to him. He was doing his best to pull a heavy cart, while a strong rough boy was cutting him under the belly with his whip, and chucking cruelly at his little mouth. Could it be Merrylegs? It was just

1 **If I had not been in harness.** This is another indication of Black Beauty's excellent upbringing, for as part of a horse's training in good manners it should be discouraged from whinnying to other horses while being ridden or driven.

The butcher's cart outside his shop. (David H. Kennett, *Victorian and Edwardian Horses from Historic Photographs.* London: B. T. Batsford, 1980, pl. 74)

like him; but then Mr. Blomefield was never to sell him, and I think he would not do it; but this might have been quite as good a little fellow, and had as happy a place when he was young.

I often noticed the great speed at which butchers' horses were made to go, though I did not know why it was so, till one day when we had to wait some time in St. John's Wood. There was a butcher's shop next door, and as we were standing, a butcher's cart came dashing up at a great pace. The horse was hot, and much exhausted; he hung his head down, while his heaving sides and trembling legs showed how hard he had been driven. The lad jumped out of the cart and was getting the basket, when the master came out of the shop much displeased. After looking at the horse, he turned angrily to the lad:—

'How many times shall I tell you not to drive in this way? You ruined the last horse and broke his wind, and you are going to ruin this in the same way. If you were not my own son, I would dismiss you on the spot; it is a disgrace to have a horse brought to the shop in a condition like that; you are liable to be taken up by the police for such driving, and if you are, you need not look to me for bail, for I have spoken to you till I am tired; you must look out for yourself.'

During this speech, the boy had stood by, sullen and dogged, but when his father ceased, he broke out angrily. It wasn't his fault, and he wouldn't take the blame, he was only going by orders all the time.

'You always say, "Now be quick; now look sharp!" and when I go to the houses, one wants a leg of mutton for an early dinner, and I must be back with it in a quarter of an hour. Another cook had forgotten to order the beef; I must go and fetch it and be back in no time, or the mistress will scold; and the house-keeper says they have company coming unexpectedly and must

2   St. John's Wood. Fashionable area of London near Regent's Park.

3   Liable to be taken up by the police. The statute which set out the duties of the Metropolitan police in 1839 laid down a penalty of not more than 40 shillings for 'Every person who shall ride or drive furiously, or so as to endanger the life or limb of any person, or to the common danger of the passengers in any thoroughfare' in the Metropolitan police district. Furthermore, 'it shall be lawful for any constable belonging to the Metropolitan police force to take into custody, without warrant, any person who shall commit any such offence within view of any such constable', hence the need for bail. Other offences under this act included sitting on the shafts of a wagon, driving without proper reins, stopping for too long to load or unload, and letting a horse stand across the pavement. A number of restrictions were placed on activities between the hours of 10 a.m. and 7 p.m.; driving cattle and unloading casks with the aid of winches or pulleys was not permitted between these hours.

'A butcher's cart came dashing up'. Illustrated by Charles Keeping. (*Black Beauty*, London: Victor Gollancz, 1988, p. 174)

371

have some chops sent up directly; and the lady at No. 4, in the Crescent, *never* orders her dinner till the meat comes in for lunch, and it 's nothing but hurry, hurry, all the time. If the gentry would think of what they want, and order their meat the day before, there need not be this blow up!'

'I wish to goodness they would,' said the butcher; ''twould save me a wonderful deal of harass, and I could suit my customers much better if I knew beforehand—but there—what 's the use of talking—who ever thinks of a butcher's convenience, or a butcher's horse? Now then, take him in, and look to him well: mind, he does not go out again to-day, and if anything else is wanted, you must carry it yourself in the basket.' With that he went in, and the horse was led away.

But all boys are not cruel. I have seen some as fond of their pony or donkey as if it had been a favourite dog, and the little creatures have worked away as cheerfully and willingly for their young drivers as I work for Jerry. It may be hard work sometimes, but a friend's hand and voice make it easy.

4   There was a young coster-boy who came up our street with greens and potatoes; he had an old pony, not very handsome, but the cheerfullest and pluckiest little thing I ever saw, and to see how fond those two were of each other, was a treat. The pony followed his master like a dog, and when he got into his cart, would trot off without a whip or a word, and rattle down

5   the street as merrily as if he had come out of the Queen's stables. Jerry liked the boy, and called him 'Prince Charlie,' for he said he would make a king of drivers some day.

There was an old man, too, who used to come up our street

6   with a little coal cart; he wore a coal-heaver's hat, and looked rough and black. He and his horse used to plod together along the street, like two good partners who understood each other;

372

4 **Coster-boy.** A costermonger was a streetseller of fruit and vegetables who frequently operated from a horse- or donkey-drawn cart
or wagon. Some were very poorly kept. Others were a great pride
to their owners and were decorated with brasses, ribbons, plumes
and bells.

5 **The Queen's stables.** The Royal Mews was then situated, as now,
on Buckingham Palace Road, London. They contain the horses,
harness and vehicles used by royalty on all state occasions, including the Coronation Coach.

6 **Coal-heaver's hat.** Old-time coal delivery men, especially in London, frequently wore a close-fitting skull cap attached to which was
a flap, often of leather, to protect the back of the neck from the coal
sacks he carried on his back and to prevent as much coal dust and
particles as possible from going down his neck.

Coster-boy and coal-heaver. Illustrated by
Fritz Eichenberg. (*Black Beauty*, New York:
Grosset & Dunlap, 1945, p. 247)

373

the horse would stop of his own accord, at the doors where they took coal of him; he used to keep one ear bent towards his master. The old man's cry could be heard up the street long before he came near. I never knew what he said, but the children called him 'Old Ba-a-ar Hoo,' for it sounded like that. Polly took her coal of him, and was very friendly, and Jerry said it was a comfort to think how happy an old horse *might* be in a poor place.

PLATE 20
John Berry's illustrations for an adaptation by Audrey Daly for Ladybird Books, Loughborough, published in 1979, were bold and cheerful.

PLATE 21 (*bottom, left*)
Black Beauty as a three-gaited American Saddle Horse. Dust jacket design from the 1930s 'Art Type Edition' published by Books Inc., New York and Boston.

PLATE 22 (*bottom, right*)
Black Beauty as a Tennessee Walking Horse. Cover illustration by A. Leiner for a 1977 adaptation by Deirdre S. Laiken. (Illustrated Classic Editions, a Moby Books paperback, published by Playmore, Inc., under arrangement with I. Waldman & Son, Inc., New York.)

Beauty became a London cab horse. His first master was a kind man called Jerry. They both worked hard and Black Beauty became very fond of Jerry's happy wife and children. At first Beauty was frightened by the crowded streets and bustling people, but he soon became used to pulling the cab during the week and resting on Sundays. Just as Beauty began to think that at last he could be content, Jerry fell ill and both the cab and Beauty had to be sold.

Beauty was bought by a mean and cruel man called Skinner. He was made to work every day, never resting and never having enough to eat. One day he collapsed and since he was no longer able to work he was sent to the horse market. Beauty knew that he was ill and tired and he wondered what would happen to him.

Beauty liked his new home. Although he worked hard he was well fed and looked after. His new master was Squire Gordon and Beauty loved all the squire's children. Beauty was clever as well as gentle. Once while he was pulling a dog-cart during a terrible storm he saved the squire's life by refusing to cross a dangerous bridge. Later it was Beauty's turn to be saved. He was nearly trapped in a burning stable and was led to safety by his brave groom, James. Sadly, the squire's family had to leave England and Beauty was sold. This time his life changed completely.

PLATE 23
Pop-up illustrations by J. Pavlin and G. Seda for the abridged version by Octopus Books London, 1980 (and Prague: Artia, 1974/5).

Delivery vans in London. (Gordon, *Horse World of London*, p. 67)

375

CHAPTER XLII

THE ELECTION

1 AS we came into the yard one afternoon, Polly came out, 'Jerry! I've had Mr. B—— here asking about your vote, and he wants to hire your cab for the election; he will call for an answer.'

2 'Well, Polly, you may say that my cab will be otherwise engaged; I should not like to have it pasted over with their great bills, and as to make Jack and Captain race about to the public-houses to bring up half-drunken voters, why I think 'twould be an insult to the horses. No, I shan't do it.'

'I suppose you'll vote for the gentleman? He said he was of your politics.'

3 'So he is in some things, but I shall not vote for him, Polly; you know what his trade is?'

'Yes.'

376

1   **The election.** This could have been either the 1868 or 1874 general election. During the Victorian period franchise and suffrage were contentious issues. One of the most notable Acts of Parliament was the Reform Act of 1867 which attempted to give the working man the right to vote. Cheating, harassment, bribery and corruption had always attended elections, and this Act set out to eliminate these and most of the property-owning anomalies of previous Acts which had entitled a man to vote. The secret ballot was introduced in 1872, so if Anna Sewell is referring to the 1868 election there could have been much pressure on people as to how they should vote. The ideal of one man, one vote had to wait until the twentieth century.

2   **Bills.** Advertising posters for the candidates' campaigns.

3   **His trade.** It is a pity we are not told what the gentleman's trade was.

Electioneering. Illustrated by John Beer. (*Black Beauty*, London: Jarrold & Sons, 191?, p. 215)

377

'Well, a man who gets rich by that trade, may be all very well in some ways, but he is blind as to what working men want: I could not in my conscience send him up to make the laws. I dare say they 'll be angry, but every man must do what he thinks to be the best for his country.'

On the morning before the election, Jerry was putting me into the shafts, when Dolly came into the yard sobbing and crying, with her little blue frock and white pinafore spattered all over with mud.

'Why, Dolly, what is the matter?'

'Those naughty boys,' she sobbed, 'have thrown the dirt all over me, and called me a little ragga—ragga——'

'They called her a little blue raggamuffin, father,' said Harry, who ran in looking very angry; 'but I have given it to them, they won't insult my sister again. I have given them a thrashing they will remember; a set of cowardly rascally, orange black-guards!'

Jerry kissed the child and said, 'Run in to mother, my pet, and tell her I think you had better stay at home to-day and help her.'

Then turning gravely to Harry—

'My boy, I hope you will always defend your sister, and give anybody who insults her a good thrashing—that is as it should be; but mind, I won't have any election blackguarding on my premises. There are as many blue blackguards as there are orange, and as many white as there are purple, or any other colour, and I won't have any of my family mixed up with it. Even women and children are ready to quarrel for the sake of a colour, and not one in ten of them knows what it is about.'

'Why, father, I thought blue was for Liberty.'

'My boy, Liberty does not come from colours, they only show

378

4 **Pinafore.** It was not simply the temporary, front covering known today as a pinafore or apron but a full-length, usually cotton, garment which fastened down the back to protect the dress. It was sleeveless, often with frills over the shoulders and sometimes had a frill along the hem. It was often colloquially called a 'pinny'.

5 **Blue.** Blue was the colour associated with the Conservatives – 'true blue Tories'.

6 **Orange.** Orange or buff was the colour of the Liberal party.

Doré's illustrations of Derby Day crowds were used as the model for studies of electioneering by an unknown illustrator. (*Black Beauty*, Chicago: M. A. Donohue, 191?, pl. opp. p. 252)

party, and all the liberty you can get out of them is, liberty to get drunk at other people's expense, liberty to ride to the poll in a dirty old cab, liberty to abuse any one that does not wear your colour, and to shout yourself hoarse at what you only half understand—that 's your liberty!'

'Oh, father, you are laughing.'

'No, Harry, I am serious, and I am ashamed to see how men go on that ought to know better. An election is a very serious thing; at least it ought to be, and every man ought to vote according to his conscience, and let his neighbour do the same.'

A further study of electioneering, after Doré's Derby Day illustrations. Illustrator unknown. (*Black Beauty*, Chicago: M. A. Donohue, 191?, pl. opp. p. 248)

CHAPTER XLIII

A FRIEND IN NEED

1 2 3 A T last came the election day; there was no lack of work for Jerry and me. First came a stout puffy gentleman with a carpet bag; he wanted to go to the Bishopsgate Station; then we were called by a party who wished to be taken to the Regent's Park; and next we were wanted in a side street where a timid anxious old lady was waiting to be taken to the bank: there we had to stop to take her back again, and just as we had set her down, a red-faced gentleman with a handful of papers, came running up out of breath, and before Jerry could get down, he had opened the door, popped himself in, and called out 'Bow Street Police Station, quick!' so

4

5

382

ANNOTATIONS

1 **Carpet bag.** Large fabric bag for travelling, originally made from carpet, with two handles meeting over the top.

2 **Bishopsgate Station.** A station on the London Underground, serving the Metropolitan Railway Company. It was opened in July 1875 at the same time as the new Liverpool Street mainline station, and in November 1909 the underground station was also named Liverpool Street and the name Bishopsgate was dropped.

3 **Regent's Park.** Fashionable residential area and park of north London.

4 **Bank.** Not necessarily a specific bank, but it could refer to the area known as Bank, near the Bank of England in the City of London.

5 **Bow Street Police Station.** Originally the headquarters of the police force who were known as Bow Street Runners in the early nineteenth century.

New terminus station at Liverpool Street. (*Illustrated London News*, 24 July 1875, p. 89)

off we went with him, and when after another turn or two we came back, there was no other cab on the stand. Jerry put on my nose-bag, for as he said, 'We must eat when we can on such days as these; so munch away, Jack, and make the best of your time, old boy.'

I found I had a good feed of crushed oats wetted up with a little bran; this would be a treat any day, but was specially refreshing then. Jerry was so thoughtful and kind—what horse would not do his best for such a master? Then he took out one of Polly's meat pies, and standing near me, he began to eat it. The streets were very full, and the cabs with the candidates' colours on them were dashing about through the crowd as if life and limb were of no consequence; we saw two people knocked down that day, and one was a woman. The horses were having a bad time of it, poor things! but the voters inside thought nothing of that, many of them were half drunk, hurrahing out of the cab windows if their own party came by. It was the first election I had seen, and I don't want to be in another, though I have heard things are better now.

Jerry and I had not eaten many mouthfuls, before a poor young woman, carrying a heavy child, came along the street. She was looking this way, and that way, and seemed quite bewildered. Presently she made her way up to Jerry, and asked if he could tell her the way to St. Thomas's Hospital, and how far it was to get there. She had come from the country that morning, she said, in a market cart; she did not know about the election, and was quite a stranger in London. She had got an order for the hospital for her little boy. The child was crying with a feeble pining cry.

'Poor little fellow!' she said, 'he suffers a deal of pain; he is four years old, and can't walk any more than a baby; but the

384

6   **Nose-bag.** When working horses were away from the stables for several hours, most were provided with a canvas bag for fodder, which at the appropriate time was fastened over their heads with a leather strap so that they could feed.

7   **Knocked down.** Road accidents were very common, for there was little traffic discipline and the unpredictability of equine behaviour gave rise to many incidents involving both horses and people.

8   **St. Thomas's Hospital.** Founded in 1207 on the south bank of the Thames, one of the two oldest hospitals in London, the other being Bart's, or St Bartholomew's, founded in 1123.

9   **Market cart.** General term for any open vehicle used for carrying vegetable produce to market.

10   **Order for the hospital.** Possibly a recommendation from the local poorhouse doctor for her son to be admitted to a city hospital as a charity patient.

Feeding from a nose-bag. (Gordon, *Horse World of London*, p. 133 (detail))

doctor said if I could get him into the hospital, he might get well; pray, sir, how far is it? and which way is it?'

'Why, missis,' said Jerry, 'you can't get there walking through crowds like this! why, it is three miles away, and that child is heavy.'

'Yes, bless him, he is, but I am strong, thank God, and if I knew the way, I think I should get on somehow: please tell me the way.'

'You can't do it,' said Jerry, 'you might be knocked down and the child be run over. Now, look here, just get into this cab, and I'll drive you safe to the hospital: don't you see the rain is coming on?'

'No, sir, no, I can't do that, thank you, I have only just money enough to get back with: please tell me the way.'

'Look you here, missis,' said Jerry, 'I've got a wife and dear children at home, and I know a father's feelings: now get you into that cab, and I'll take you there for nothing; I'd be ashamed of myself to let a woman and a sick child run a risk like that.'

'Heaven bless you!' said the woman, and burst into tears.

'There, there, cheer up, my dear, I'll soon take you there; come, let me put you inside.'

As Jerry went to open the door, two men, with colours in their hats and button-holes, ran up, calling out, 'Cab!'

'Engaged,' cried Jerry; but one of the men, pushing past the woman, sprang into the cab, followed by the other. Jerry looked as stern as a policeman: 'This cab is already engaged, gentlemen, by that lady.'

'Lady!' said one of them; 'oh! she can wait: our business is very important, beside we were in first, it is our right, and we shall stay in.'

A droll smile came over Jerry's face as he shut the door upon

11 **Button-holes.** Streamers or ribbons, or nowadays rosettes or flowers, in party colours have long been worn by each party's supporters.

'I'll drive you safe to the hospital'. Illustrated by Lucy Kemp-Welch. (*Black Beauty*, London: J. M. Dent. 1915, pl. opp. p. 195)

them. 'All right, gentlemen, pray stay in as long as it suits you: I can wait whilst you rest yourselves'; and turning his back upon them, he walked up to the young woman, who was standing near me. 'They 'll soon be gone,' he said, laughing, 'don't trouble yourself, my dear.'

And they soon were gone, for when they understood Jerry's dodge, they got out, calling him all sorts of bad names, and blustering about his number, and getting a summons. After this little stoppage we were soon on our way to the hospital, going as much as possible through by-streets. Jerry rung the great bell, and helped the young woman out.

'Thank you a thousand times,' she said; 'I could never have got here alone.'

'You 're kindly welcome, and I hope the dear child will soon be better.'

He watched her go in at the door, and gently he said to himself, 'Inasmuch as ye have done it to one of the least of these.' Then he patted my neck, which was always his way when anything pleased him.

The rain was now coming down fast, and just as we were leaving the hospital the door opened again, and the porter called out, 'Cab!' We stopped, and a lady came down the steps. Jerry seemed to know her at once; she put back her veil and said, 'Barker! Jeremiah Barker! is it you? I am very glad to find you here; you are just the friend I want, for it is very difficult to get a cab in this part of London to-day.'

'I shall be proud to serve you, ma'am, I am right glad I happened to be here; where may I take you to, ma'am?'

'To the Paddington Station, and then if we are in good time, as I think we shall be, you shall tell me all about Mary and the children.'

12 **Number.** Cab licence number.

13 **By-streets.** Side streets.

14 **Inasmuch as ye.** 'Inasmuch as ye have done it unto one of the least of these, my brethren, ye have done it unto me.' (St Matthew, Chapter 25, verse 40.)

15 **Paddington Station.** London main line station for trains to the West Country.

16 **Mary.** Polly was frequently a nickname for Mary, although the reason is not clear.

Two interpretations of Jerry's kindness: (*left*) illustrated by Charles Keeping (*Black Beauty*, London: Victor Gollancz, 1988, p. 181); (*above*) illustrated by Tom Gill (*Black Beauty*, Golden Picture Classics, New York: Simon & Schuster, 1956, p. 76)

We got to the station in good time. and being under shelter, the lady stood a good while talking to Jerry. I found she had been Polly's mistress, and after many inquiries about her, she said—

'How do you find the cab-work suit you in winter? I know Mary was rather anxious about you last year.'

'Yes, ma'am, she was; I had a bad cough that followed me up quite into the warm weather, and when I am kept out late, she does worry herself a good deal. You see, ma'am, it is all hours and all weathers, and that does try a man's constitution; but I am getting on pretty well, and I should feel quite lost if I had not horses to look after. I was brought up to it, and I am afraid I should not do so well at anything else.'

'Well, Barker,' she said, 'it would be a great pity that you should seriously risk your health in this work, not only for your own, but for Mary and the children's sake: there are many places where good drivers or good grooms are wanted; and if ever you think you ought to give up this cab work, let me know.' Then sending some kind messages to Mary, she put something into his hand, saying, 'There is five shillings each for the two children; Mary will know how to spend it.'

Jerry thanked her and seemed much pleased, and turning out of the station, we at last reached home, and I, at least, was tired.

17 **Polly's mistress.** Presumably Jerry's wife, Polly, most likely before her marriage to Jerry Barker, had been in domestic service with this lady.

18 **Five shillings each.** Five shillings was over a quarter of James Howard's weekly wage (see p. 121) and, as such, was a considerable sum of money to be given as a present to Jerry Barker's children. However, it should be noted that it was suggested that their mother would know how to spend it on their behalf – it was not given directly to the children as 'pocket money'.

Driving the cab through London. Illustrated by Charles Keeping. (*Black Beauty*, London: Victor Gollancz, 1988, p. 150)

CHAPTER XLIV

OLD CAPTAIN AND HIS SUCCESSOR

CAPTAIN and I were great friends. He was a noble old fellow, and he was very good company. I never thought that he would have to leave his home and go down the hill, but his turn came; and this was how it happened. I was not there, but I heard all about it.

He and Jerry had taken a party to the great railway station over London Bridge, and were coming back, somewhere between the Bridge and the Monument, when Jerry saw a brewer's empty dray coming along, drawn by two powerful horses. The drayman was lashing his horses with his heavy whip; the dray was light, and they started off at a furious rate; the man had no control over them, and the street was full of traffic; one young girl was knocked down and run over, and the next moment they

392

1 **Monument.** Tall tower near Pudding Lane just outside the City of London, reputedly built on the site where the Great Fire of London began in a baker's shop on 2 September 1666 and which raged for three days.

2 **Brewer's empty dray.** Strongly built flat wagon for carrying heavy goods such as barrels of beer; often with a high driver's seat and a board above advertising the brewer. Usually drawn by a pair of heavy horses.

The Monument. Pencil and wash drawing by G. R. Clarke, mid nineteenth century. (Museum of London)

dashed up against our cab; both the wheels were torn off, and the cab was thrown over. Captain was dragged down, the shafts splintered, and one of them ran into his side. Jerry too was thrown, but was only bruised; nobody could tell how he escaped, he always said 'twas a miracle. When poor Captain was got up, he was found to be very much cut and knocked about. Jerry led him home gently, and a sad sight it was to see the blood soaking into his white coat, and dropping from his side and shoulder. The drayman was proved to be very drunk, and was fined, and the brewer had to pay damages to our master; but there was no one to pay damages to poor Captain.

The farrier and Jerry did the best they could to ease his pain, and make him comfortable. The fly had to be mended, and for several days I did not go out, and Jerry earned nothing. The first time we went to the stand after the accident, the Governor came up to hear how Captain was.

'He 'll never get over it,' said Jerry, 'at least not for my work, so the farrier said this morning. He says he may do for carting, and that sort of work. It has put me out very much. Carting indeed! I 've seen what horses come to at that work round London. I only wish all the drunkards could be put in a lunatic asylum, instead of being allowed to run foul of sober people. If they would break their *own* bones, and smash their *own* carts, and lame their *own* horses, that would be their own affair, and we might let them alone, but it seems to me that the innocent always suffer; and then they talk about compensation! You can't make compensation—there 's all the trouble, and vexation, and loss of time, besides losing a good horse that 's like an old friend—it 's nonsense talking of compensation! If there 's one devil that I should like to see in the bottomless pit more than another, it 's the drink devil.'

3 **Fly.** Cab or hackney carriage.

4 **Carting.** General haulage work – often heavy work with much stopping and starting which was very tiring and wearing on a horse's feet and legs, particularly on hard city streets. Quite frequently it was the 'end of the line' for working horses.

5 **Drink devil.** The Temperance Movement gained many adherents from the working classes who, like Jerry Barker, saw the error of their ways and renounced the Demon Drink. See p. 227.

A brewer's dray, from the Bristol Wagon and Carriage Works Company catalogue, 1894. (Reproduced in *Horse-Drawn Heavy Goods Vehicles*, compiled by John Thompson, Fleet, Hampshire, 1977, p. 18)

Pulling the coal cart. (Gordon, *Horse World of London*, p. 131)

'I say, Jerry,' said the Governor, 'you are treading pretty hard on my toes, you know; I 'm not so good as you are, more shame for me, I wish I was.'

'Well,' said Jerry, 'why don't you cut with it, Governor? you are too good a man to be the slave of such a thing.'

'I 'm a great fool, Jerry; but I tried once for two days, and I thought I should have died: how did you do?'

'I had hard work at it for several weeks; you see, I never did get drunk, but I found that I was not my own master, and that when the craving came on, it was hard work to say "no." I saw that one of us must knock under—the drink devil, or Jerry Barker, and I said that it should not be Jerry Barker, God helping me: but it was a struggle, and I wanted all the help I could get, for till I tried to break the habit, I did not know how strong it was; but then Polly took such pains that I should have good food, and when the craving came on, I used to get a cup of coffee, or some peppermint, or read a bit in my book, and that was a help to me: sometimes I had to say over and over to myself, "Give up the drink or lose your soul? Give up the drink or break Polly's heart?" But thanks be to God, and my dear wife, my chains were broken, and now for ten years I have not tasted a drop, and never wish for it.'

'I 've a great mind to try it,' said Grant, 'for 'tis a poor thing not to be one's own master.'

'Do, Governor, do, you 'll never repent it, and what a help it would be to some of the poor fellows in our rank if they saw you do without it. I know there 's two or three would like to keep out of that tavern if they could.'

At first Captain seemed to do well, but he was a very old horse, and it was only his wonderful constitution, and Jerry's care, that had kept him up at the cab-work so long; now he

6 Old horse. Horses can live until well into their twenties or even thirties. The oldest on record is 'Old Billy' who died aged 62. Captain, whose story of being a cavalry horse during the Crimean War is told in Chapter XXXIV, must have been over twenty.

A Victorian tavern, illustrated by Gustave Doré. (Gustave Doré and Blanchard Jerrold, *London: A Pilgrimage*, London: Grant, 1872; David & Charles reprints, 1971, p. 150)

Captain after his accident. Illustrated by G. Vernon Stokes and Alan Wright. (*Black Beauty*, London: Jarrold & Sons, 190?, p. 258)

broke down very much.   The farrier said he might mend up enough to sell for a few pounds, but Jerry said, no! a few pounds got by selling a good old servant into hard work and misery would canker all the rest of his money, and he thought the kindest thing he could do for the fine old fellow would be to put a sure bullet through his heart, and then he would never suffer more; for he did not know where to find a kind master for the rest of his days.

The day after this was decided, Harry took me to the forge for some new shoes; when I returned, Captain was gone.   I and the family all felt it very much.

Jerry had now to look out for another horse, and he soon heard of one through an acquaintance who was under-groom in a nobleman's stables.   He was a valuable young horse, but he had run away, smashed into another carriage, flung his lordship out, and so cut and blemished himself that he was no longer fit for a gentleman's stables, and the coachman had orders to look round, and sell him as well as he could.

'I can do with high spirits,' said Jerry, 'if a horse is not vicious or hard-mouthed.'

'There is not a bit of vice in him,' said the man, 'his mouth is very tender, and I think myself that was the cause of the accident; you see he had just been clipped, and the weather was bad, and he had not had exercise enough, and when he did go out, he was as full of spring as a balloon.   Our governor (the coachman, I mean) had him harnessed in as tight and strong as he could, with the martingale, and the bearing rein, a very sharp curb, and the reins put in at the bottom bar; it is my belief that it made the horse mad, being tender in the mouth and so full of spirit.'

'Likely enough; I 'll come and see him,' said Jerry.

7 **Forge.** Originally a place where horseshoes were made and horses shod. By Black Beauty's time horseshoes were being mass-produced in factories and bought in bulk by farriers, who then heated them in the fire and shaped them to fit individual horses which had to be brought to the forge to be shod.

8 **Under-groom in a nobleman's stables.** Under-groom was fairly well down the hierarchy of stable staff. In a large household there would have been coachmen at the top with grooms, horsemen and stableboys at the bottom.

9 **Clipped.** In the autumn horses which were worked hard or ridden hard were usually clipped to remove all or part of the thick winter coat to reduce excessive sweating. Newly clipped horses felt the cold and were likely to be jumpy, or shivered miserably after work and had to be rugged up to prevent chills. Depending upon the work done, the amount of coat removed could be considerable, as in a 'hunter clip' when most of the coat was removed, or just a little, as with a horse in fairly gentle work where only the hair along his throat and under his belly was removed. A half-way stage, particularly for harness horses, was 'trace clipping', when the coat was removed below the level of the traces of the harness. Clippers were either hand-worked or powered by a chain mechanism cranked by a handle, which was very hard work and usually the job of the stableboy, whereas the actual clipping required much skill. Eventually electric clippers became available.

10 **Martingale, and the bearing rein, a very sharp curb, and the reins put in at the bottom bar.** The martingale, a strap passing between the front legs and connecting the noseband to the girth, keeps the horse's head down and hence gives the driver more control. The bearing rein is of course intended to keep the head up. By connecting the reins to the bottom bar of a sharp curb, maximum leverage is obtained and effectively keeps the horse's lower jaw in a vice between the metal mouthpiece of the bit and the chain which passed behind the jaw, as well as exerting pressure on the top of the horse's head via the headpiece of the bridle. All in all, a horrendous combination.

The 'Gillette Featherweight' hand-driven clipper (*top*), and (*bottom*) a cutting head. (Moseman's *Illustrated Guide for Purchasers of Horse Furnishing Goods*, p. 222)

11 The next day, Hotspur—that was his name—came home; he was a fine brown horse, without a white hair in him, as tall as Captain, with a very handsome head, and only five years old. I gave him a friendly greeting by way of good fellowship, but did not ask him any questions. The first night he was very restless; instead of lying down, he kept jerking his halter rope up and down through the ring, and knocking the block about against the manger so that I could not sleep. However, the next day, after five or six hours in the cab, he came in quiet and sensible. Jerry patted and talked to him a good deal, and very soon they understood each other, and Jerry said that with an easy bit, and plenty of work, he would be as gentle as a lamb; and that it was an ill wind that blew nobody good, for if his lordship had lost a hundred-guinea favourite, the cabman had gained a good horse with all his strength in him.

Hotspur thought it a great come down to be a cab horse, and was disgusted at standing in the rank, but he confessed to me at the end of the week, that an easy mouth, and a free hand, made up for a great deal, and after all, the work was not so degrading 12 as having one's head and tail fastened to each other at the saddle. In fact, he settled in well, and Jerry liked him very much.

11 **Hotspur.** Nickname of Sir Henry Percy, hot-headed son of the first Earl of Northumberland. He fought for Owen Glendower, the Welshman, against Henry IV. Appears in Shakespeare's *Henry IV*.

12 **Head and tail fastened to each other at the saddle.** This rig would hold the front end of the horse while a tight crupper ran from the saddle or pad along his back under his tail, which could be tightened and would force the tail into a high, unnatural position. The muscles of the tail were often cut or 'nicked' in order for this 'smart' appearance to be achieved more easily.

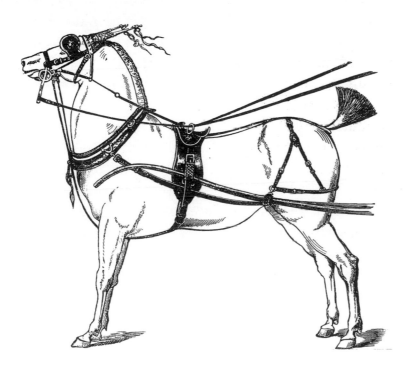

An example of the use of the martingale, bearing rein and crupper fixing the horse into position, based on one of Flower's publications. (J. G. Wood, *Horse and Man: Their Mutual Dependence and Duties*, Philadelphia: J. B. Lippincott, 1886, p. 200)

CHAPTER XLV

JERRY'S NEW YEAR

I CHRISTMAS and the New Year are very merry times for some people; but for cabmen and cabmen's horses, it is no holiday, though it may be a harvest. There are so many parties, balls, and places of amusement open, that the work is hard and often late. Sometimes driver and horse have to wait for hours in the rain or frost, shivering with cold, whilst the merry people within are dancing away to the music. I wonder if the beautiful ladies ever think of the weary cabman waiting on his box, and his patient beast standing, till his legs get stiff with cold.

I had now most of the evening work, as I was well accustomed to standing, and Jerry was also more afraid of Hotspur taking

402

1 **Christmas.** The Victorians were responsible for the beginnings of Christmas celebrations as we know them today. Prince Albert is said to have introduced the use of the fir tree into England from Germany, and the first Christmas card was designed in 1843. By 1870 the custom of sending Christmas cards was well established.

Christmas in a Victorian middle-class family. (Iris Grender, *An Old-Fashioned Christmas*, London: Hutchinson, 1979, p. 23)

403

cold.   We had a great deal of late work in the Christmas week, and Jerry's cough was bad; but however late we were, Polly sat up for him, and came out with the lantern to meet him, looking anxious and troubled.

On the evening of the New Year, we had to take two gentlemen to a house in one of the West End Squares.   We set them down at nine o'clock and were told to come again at eleven. 'But,' said one of them, 'as it is a card party, you may have to wait a few minutes, but don't be late.'

As the clock struck eleven we were at the door, for Jerry was always punctual.   The clock chimed the quarters—one, two, three, and then struck twelve, but the door did not open.

The wind had been very changeable, with squalls of rain during the day, but now it came on sharp driving sleet, which seemed to come all the way round; it was very cold, and there was no shelter.   Jerry got off his box and came and pulled one of my cloths a little more over my neck; then he took a turn or two up and down, stamping his feet; then he began to beat his arms, but that set him off coughing; so he opened the cab door and sat at the bottom with his feet on the pavement, and was a little sheltered.   Still the clock chimed the quarters, and no one came. At half-past twelve, he rang the bell and asked the servant if he would be wanted that night.

'Oh! yes, you 'll be wanted safe enough,' said the man, 'you must not go, it will soon be over,' and again Jerry sat down, but his voice was so hoarse I could hardly hear him.

At a quarter-past one the door opened, and the two gentlemen came out; they got into the cab without a word, and told Jerry where to drive, that was nearly two miles.   My legs were numb with cold, and I thought I should have stumbled.   When the men got out, they never said they were sorry to have kept us

2 **West End.** Entertainment area of London around Leicester Square, to the west of the original centre of the town.

'Pulled one of my cloths a little more over my neck'. Illustrator unknown. (*Black Beauty*, New York: Thomas Crowell, 191?, p. 222)

waiting so long, but were angry at the charge: however, as Jerry never charged more than was his due, so he never took less, and they had to pay for the two hours and a quarter waiting; but it was hard-earned money to Jerry.

At last we got home; he could hardly speak, and his cough was dreadful. Polly asked no questions, but opened the door and held the lantern for him.

'Can't I do something?' she said.

'Yes, get Jack something warm, and then boil me some gruel.'

This was said in a hoarse whisper; he could hardly get his breath, but he gave me a rub down as usual, and even went up into the hayloft for an extra bundle of straw for my bed. Polly brought me a warm mash that made me comfortable, and then they locked the door.

It was late the next morning before any one came, and then it was only Harry. He cleaned us and fed us, and swept out the stalls, then he put the straw back again as if it was Sunday. He was very still, and neither whistled nor sang. At noon he came again, and gave us our food and water: this time Dolly came with him; she was crying, and I could gather from what they said, that Jerry was dangerously ill, and the doctor said it was a bad case. So two days passed, and there was great trouble indoors. We only saw Harry, and sometimes Dolly. I think she came for company, for Polly was always with Jerry, and he had to be kept very quiet.

On the third day, whilst Harry was in the stable, a tap came at the door, and Governor Grant came in.

'I wouldn't go to the house, my boy,' he said, 'but I want to know how your father is.'

'He is very bad,' said Harry, 'he can't be much worse; they

PLATE 24
Cover of *Classics Illustrated* comic book
version of *Black Beauty*, 1949.

PLATE 25
The impossible dream! 1950s dust jacket
for Phyllis Briggs' *Son of Black Beauty*
(Dean & Son, by arrangement with Thames
Publishing Company, London). As the
publisher noted, 'the art of the storyteller
has been enlisted to produce what Black
Beauty the horse could not – a son.'

PLATE 26
Models of Black Beauty: (*top*) with a foal, Royal Doulton porcelain, 1972 (photo: David Leake), and (*bottom*) with Merrylegs, plastic by Breyer Animal Creations (a division of Reeves International), 1980.

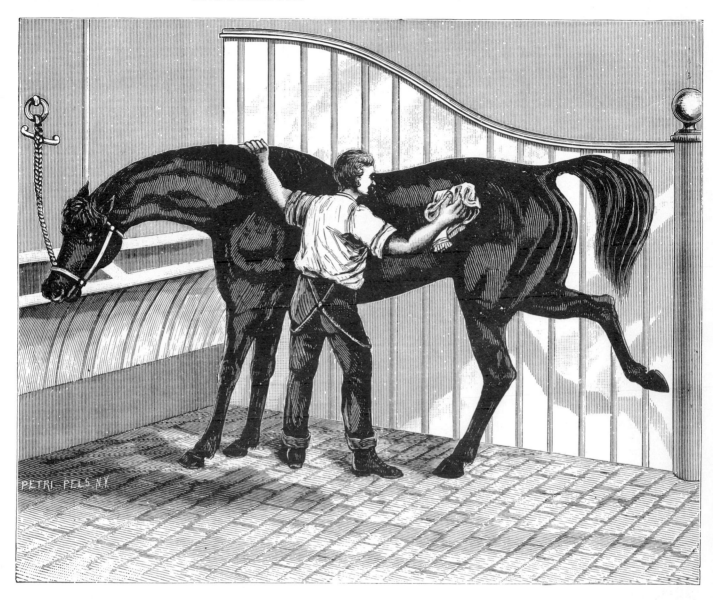

A rub down, using a soft cloth. (Moseman's *Illustrated Guide for Purchasers of Horse Furnishing Goods*, p. 17)

407

3 call it bronchitis; the doctor thinks it will turn one way or another to-night.'

'That 's bad, very bad!' said Grant, shaking his head; 'I know two men who died of that last week; it takes 'em off in no time; but whilst there 's life there 's hope, so you must keep up your spirits.'

'Yes,' said Harry quickly, 'and the doctor said that father had a better chance than most men, because he didn't drink. He said yesterday the fever was so high, that if father had been a drinking man, it would have burnt him up like a piece of paper; but I believe he thinks he will get over it; don't you think he will, Mr. Grant?'

The Governor looked puzzled.

'If there 's any rule that good men should get over these things, I am sure he will, my boy; he 's the best man I know. I 'll look in early to-morrow.'

Early next morning he was there.

'Well?' said he.

'Father is better,' said Harry. 'Mother hopes he will get over it.'

'Thank God!' said the Governor, 'and now you must keep him warm, and keep his mind easy, and that brings me to the horses; you see, Jack will be all the better for the rest of a week or two in a warm stable, and you can easily take him a turn up and down the street to stretch his legs; but this young one, if

4 he does not get work, he will soon be all up on end, as you may say, and will be rather too much for you; and when he does go out, there 'll be an accident.'

'It is like that now,' said Harry, 'I have kept him short of corn, but he 's so full of spirit I don't know what to do with him.'

'Just so,' said Grant. 'Now look here, will you tell your

3 Bronchitis. Inflammation of the bronchial tubes was and is a very common complaint in Britain, especially amongst the middle aged and elderly. It is frequently attributed to the cold, damp weather in the winter and, in Victorian times, to the soot-laden smog.

4 All up on end. So full of energy and raring to go that the horse would stand up on his hind legs or rear. See p. 193.

'All up on end.' (Mayhew, *Illustrated Horse Management*, p. 258)

mother that if she is agreeable, I will come for him every day till something is arranged, and take him for a good spell of work, and whatever he earns I 'll bring your mother half of it, and that will help with the horses' feed. Your father is in a good club, I know, but that won't keep the horses, and they 'll be eating their heads off all this time: I 'll come at noon and hear what she says,' and without waiting for Harry's thanks, he was gone.

At noon I think he went and saw Polly, for he and Harry came to the stable together, harnessed Hotspur and took him out.

For a week or more he came for Hotspur, and when Harry thanked him or said anything about his kindness, he laughed it off, saying, it was all good luck for him, for his horses were wanting a little rest which they would not otherwise have had.

Jerry grew better, steadily, but the doctor said that he must never go back to the cab-work again if he wished to be an old man. The children had many consultations together about what father and mother would do, and how they could help to earn money.

One afternoon, Hotspur was brought in very wet and dirty.

'The streets are nothing but slush,' said the Governor; 'it will give you a good warming, my boy, to get him clean and dry.'

'All right, Governor,' said Harry, 'I shall not leave him till he is; you know I have been trained by my father.'

'I wish all the boys had been trained like you,' said the Governor.

While Harry was sponging off the mud from Hotspur's body and legs, Dolly came in, looking very full of something.

'Who lives at Fairstowe, Harry? Mother has got a letter from Fairstowe; she seemed so glad, and ran upstairs to father with it.'

5 **Good club.** By the mid-Victorian period working people were paying a penny or two a week towards private insurance schemes which would ensure a small income in the case of illness or hardship. There was no welfare state, unemployment pay, sick pay or other benefits until well into the twentieth century.

6 **Sponging off the mud.** When a horse's legs are washed, it is essential that the heels are thoroughly dried. If they are not, cracked heels and lameness can result.

Recipe for an ointment for cracked heels. (MS, private collections, *c.* 1900)

'Don't you know? Why, it is the name of Mrs. Fowler's place—mother's old mistress, you know—the lady that father met last summer, who sent you and me five shillings each.'

'Oh! Mrs. Fowler; of course I know all about her. I wonder what she is writing to mother about.'

'Mother wrote to her last week,' said Harry; 'you know she told father if ever he gave up the cab-work, she would like to know. I wonder what she says; run in and see, Dolly.'

7   Harry scrubbed away at Hotspur with a huish! huish! like any old ostler.

In a few minutes Dolly came dancing into the stable.

'Oh! Harry, there never was anything so beautiful; Mrs. Fowler says, we are all to go and live near her. There is a cottage now empty that will just suit us, with a garden, and a hen house, and apple trees, and everything! and her coachman is going away in the spring, and then she will want father in his place; and there are good families round, where you can get a place in the garden, or the stable, or as a page boy; and there 's a good school for me; and mother is laughing and crying by turns, and father does look *so* happy!'

'That 's uncommon jolly,' said Harry, 'and just the right thing, I should say; it will suit father and mother both; but I don't intend to be a page boy with tight clothes and rows of buttons. I 'll be a groom or a gardener.'

It was quickly settled that as soon as Jerry was well enough, they should remove to the country, and that the cab and horses should be sold as soon as possible.

This was heavy news for me, for I was not young now, and could not look for any improvement in my condition. Since I left Birtwick I had never been so happy as with my dear master, Jerry; but three years of cab-work, even under the best conditions,

7 **Huish.** Grooms frequently whistled or hissed when grooming a
horse. This was supposed to keep the inevitable dust and hairs from
entering their mouths.

Washing the horse's legs: (*top*) how not to
do it and (*bottom*) doing it with care.
(Mayhew, *The Illustrated Horse Management*, pp. 382 and 387)

will tell on one's strength, and I felt that I was not the horse that I had been.

Grant said at once that he would take Hotspur; and there were men on the stand who would have bought me; but Jerry said I should not go to cab-work again with just anybody, and the Governor promised to find a place for me where I should be comfortable.

The day came for going away. Jerry had not been allowed to go out yet, and I never saw him after that New Year's Eve. Polly and the children came to bid me good-bye. 'Poor old Jack! dear old Jack! I wish we could take you with us,' she said, and then, laying her hand on my mane, she put her face close to my neck and kissed me. Dolly was crying and kissed me too. Harry stroked me a great deal, but said nothing, only he seemed very sad, and so I was led away to my new place.

Jerry's New Year. Illustrated by F. Milward.
(*Black Beauty*, Leeds: E. J. Arnold & Son,
1928, p. 80)

PART IV

CHAPTER XLVI

JAKES AND THE LADY

1 I WAS sold to a corn dealer and baker, whom Jerry knew, and with him he thought I should have good food and fair work. In the first he was quite right, and if my master had always been on the premises, I do not think I should have been overloaded; but there was a foreman who was always hurrying and driving every one, and frequently when I had quite a full load, he would order something else to be taken on. My
2 carter, whose name was Jakes, often said it was more than I

416

1 **Corn dealer.** Merchant specialising in the buying and selling of grain usually for animal feed. Here 'corn' is a generic term for all grains but mostly applied to wheat, oats, barley, rye and maize.

2 **Carter.** Carters were in charge of goods or agricultural vehicles, as opposed to passenger transport, when they are known as 'drivers' or, if in private employ, 'coachmen'. Others terms for carters were 'wagoners' or 'horsemen' in rural areas.

Woodcarter and cart. (*Wood Engravings of Thomas Bewick*, London: Grafton Books, 1953, p. 215)

Bread vans: (*top*) a typical van of about 1900 and (*bottom*) a van on its rounds, *c.* 1922. (D. J. Smith, *Discovering Horse Drawn Commercial Vehicles*, Aylesbury: Shire Publications, 1977, p. 21 and pl. 8)

417

ought to take, but the other always overruled him: ''Twas no use going twice when once would do, and he chose to get business forward.'

Jakes, like the other carters, always had the bearing rein up, which prevented me from drawing easily, and by the time I had been there three or four months, I found the work telling very much on my strength.

One day, I was loaded more than usual, and part of the road was a steep uphill: I used all my strength, but I could not get on, and was obliged continually to stop. This did not please my driver, and he laid his whip on badly. 'Get on, you lazy fellow,' he said, 'or I 'll make you.'

Again I started the heavy load, and struggled on a few yards; again the whip came down, and again I struggled forward. The pain of that great cart whip was sharp, but my mind was hurt quite as much as my poor sides. To be punished and abused when I was doing my very best was so hard, it took the heart out of me. A third time he was flogging me cruelly, when a lady stepped quickly up to him, and said in a sweet earnest voice—

'Oh! pray do not whip your good horse any more; I am sure he is doing all he can, and the road is very steep, I am sure he is doing his best.'

'If doing his best won't get this load up, he must do something more than his best; that 's all I know, ma'am,' said Jakes.

'But is it not a very heavy load?' she said.

'Yes, yes, too heavy,' he said, 'but that 's not my fault, the foreman came just as we were starting, and would have three hundredweight more put on to save him trouble, and I must get on with it as well as I can.'

He was raising the whip again, when the lady said—

'Pray, stop, I think I can help you if you will let me.'

418

3 Hundredweight. One hundredweight equals 112 pounds or one twentieth of a ton.

The horse drawing a cart with his head fixed up, able only to use muscle power. (*The Horse Book*, London: RSPCA, *c.* 1877, p. 87)

With the use of his head and neck, the horse can use both weight and muscle to pull the cart uphill. (*The Horse Book*, p. 89)

The man laughed.

'You see,' she said, 'you do not give him a fair chance; he cannot use all his power with his head held back as it is with that bearing rein; if you would take it off, I am sure he would do better—*do* try it,' she said persuasively, 'I should be very glad if you would.'

'Well, well,' said Jakes, with a short laugh, 'anything to please a lady of course. How far would you wish it down, ma'am?'

'Quite down, give him his head altogether.'

4 The rein was taken off, and in a moment I put my head down to my very knees. What a comfort it was! Then I tossed it up and down several times to get the aching stiffness out of my neck.

'Poor fellow! that is what you wanted,' said she, patting and stroking me with her gentle hand; 'and now if you will speak kindly to him and lead him on, I believe he will be able to do better.'

Jakes took the rein—'Come on, Blackie.' I put down my head, and threw my whole weight against the collar; I spared no strength; the load moved on, and I pulled it steadily up the hill, and then stopped to take breath.

The lady had walked along the footpath, and now came across into the road. She stroked and patted my neck, as I had not been patted for many a long day.

'You see he was quite willing when you gave him the chance; I am sure he is a fine-tempered creature, and I dare say has known better days. You won't put that rein on again, will you?' for he was just going to hitch it up on the old plan.

'Well, ma am, I can't deny that having his head has helped him up the hill, and I 'll remember it another time, and thank you, ma'am; but if he went without a bearing rein, I should be

4 Put my head down . . . The following paragraphs explain the reasons for not using the bearing rein and how much better it was for the horse, although unfashionable, if the bearing rein was not used.

'I put down my head, and threw my whole weight against the collar'. Illustrated by G. P. Micklewright. (*Black Beauty*, London: J. Coker & Co., 1933, pl. opp. p. 96)

the laughing stock of all the carters; it is the fashion, you see.'

'Is it not better,' she said, 'to lead a good fashion, than to follow a bad one? A great many gentlemen do not use bearing reins now; our carriage horses have not worn them for fifteen years, and work with much less fatigue than those who have them; besides,' she added in a very serious voice, 'we have no right to distress any of God's creatures without a very good reason; we call them dumb animals, and so they are, for they cannot tell us how they feel, but they do not suffer less because they have no words. But I must not detain you now; I thank you for trying my plan with your good horse, and I am sure you will find it far better than the whip. Good day,' and with another soft pat on my neck, she stepped lightly across the path, and I saw her no more.

'That was a real lady, I'll be bound for it,' said Jakes to himself; 'she spoke just as polite as if I was a gentleman, and I'll try her plan, uphill, at any rate'; and I must do him the justice to say, that he let my rein out several holes, and going uphill after that he always gave me my head; but the heavy loads went on. Good feed and fair rest will keep up one's strength under full work, but no horse can stand against overloading; and I was getting so thoroughly pulled down from this cause, that a younger horse was brought in my place. I may as well mention here what I suffered at this time from another cause. I had heard horses speak of it, but had never myself had experience of the evil; this was a badly lighted stable; there was only one very small window at the end, and the consequence was that the stalls were almost dark.

Besides the depressing effect this had on my spirits, it very much weakened my sight, and when I was suddenly brought out

5 **Badly lighted stable.** Victorian stables for working horses (as opposed to privately owned hunters, hacks or carriage horses) were often equine slums – the equivalent of their counterparts for the human working class. Apart from being badly lit they were often badly drained and ventilated, cramped, prone to fire hazards and difficult to keep clean. Spiders' webs were left to accumulate for years on the basis that they acted as fly traps. Darkness was sometimes used as a method of subduing a recalcitrant horse. In *General Remarks on Stables and Examples of Stable Fittings* (1860), William Miles suggested that the reason for the assertion by some that horses thrive better and become livelier in dark stables is that the horse becomes so frightened on coming out into the light and being able to see so much that it acts skittishly.

Outbreaks of kicking in the night were common when horses were kept in stalls. One horse would kick out in the dark and the noise would frighten its companion. Hysteria would spread, only to be calmed by the appearance of a familiar groom with a lantern. (Mayhew, *The Illustrated Horse Management*, p. 245)

423

of the darkness into the glare of daylight, it was very painful to my eyes.   Several times I stumbled over the threshold, and could scarcely see where I was going.

I believe, had I stayed there very long, I should have become purblind, and that would have been a great misfortune, for I have heard men say, that a stone-blind horse was safer to drive than one which had imperfect sight, as it generally makes them very timid.   However, I escaped without any permanent injury to my sight, and was sold to a large cab-owner.

6 Purblind. Partially blind or poor-sighted. It was a common assumption that horses kept in a dark environment would go blind, hence the myth which arose that ponies used in the coal mines automatically went blind. They did not.

A pit pony working underground, pulling a coal tram. (Thomas H. Hair, *The Crane for Loading the Rollies*, *c.* 1842 (etching); Department of Mining Engineering, University of Newcastle)

CHAPTER XLVII

HARD TIMES

1   I SHALL never forget my new master; he had black eyes and a hooked nose, his mouth was as full of teeth as a bull-dog's, and his voice was as harsh as the grinding of cart-wheels over gravel stones. His name was Nicholas Skinner, and I believe he was the same man that poor Seedy Sam drove for.

I have heard men say, that seeing is believing; but I should say that *feeling* is believing; for much as I had seen before, I never knew till now the utter misery of a cab horse's life.

Skinner had a low set of cabs and a low set of drivers; he was hard on the men, and the men were hard on the horses. In this place we had no Sunday rest, and it was in the heat of summer.

2   Sometimes on a Sunday morning, a party of fast men would hire the cab for the day; four of them inside and another with the driver, and I had to take them ten or fifteen miles out into the country, and back again: never would any of them get down

426

1 **I shall never forget . . .** Typical Victorian ploy of attributing to the 'bad' characters as many undesirable features as possible (especially a hooked nose!) to creating a stereotype.

2 **Fast men.** 'Gadabouts' or those intent upon having a good time in an irresponsible manner, usually drinking and gambling.

Nicholas Skinner. Illustrated by H. Toaspern. (*Black Beauty*, New York: J. Hovendon & Co., 1894, p. 188)

to walk up a hill, let it be ever so steep, or the day ever so hot—unless indeed, when the driver was afraid I should not manage it, and sometimes I was so fevered and worn that I could hardly touch my food. How I used to long for the nice bran mash with

3 nitre in it that Jerry used to give us on Saturday nights in hot weather, that used to cool us down and make us so comfortable. Then we had two nights and a whole day for unbroken rest, and on Monday morning we were as fresh as young horses again; but here, there was no rest, and my driver was just as hard as his master. He had a cruel whip with something so sharp at the end that it sometimes drew blood, and he would even whip me under the belly, and flip the lash out at my head. Indignities like these took the heart out of me terribly, but still I did my best and never hung back; for, as poor Ginger said, it was no use;

4 men are the strongest.

My life was now so utterly wretched, that I wished I might, like Ginger, drop down dead at my work, and be out of my misery; and one day my wish very nearly came to pass.

I went on the stand at eight in the morning, and had done a good share of work, when we had to take a fare to the railway. A long train was just expected in, so my driver pulled up at the back of some of the outside cabs, to take the chance of a return fare. It was a very heavy train, and as all the cabs were soon engaged, ours was called for. There was a party of four; a noisy, blustering man with a lady, a little boy, and a young girl, and a great deal of luggage. The lady and the boy got into the cab, and while the man ordered about the luggage, the young girl came and looked at me.

'Papa,' she said, 'I am sure this poor horse cannot take us and all our luggage so far, he is so very weak and worn out; do look at him.'

3 **Nitre.** Potassium or sodium nitrate – salty-tasting appetiser in the bran mash to stimulate the appetite.

4 **Men are the strongest.** Anna Sewell was strongly influenced by a work of Horace Bushnell, an American pastor, entitled *Essay on Animals*. In it he expounded the theory that man's brainpower enables him to direct the physical force found in animals, especially horses, which have been created for him by God in order to give man much more strength than he himself possesses. It is therefore man's duty to use his intellect to treat animals correctly and in such a way that their lives are happy. In turn, animals know that man is the stronger and that they must carry out man's will. Writing to her mother's biographer, who introduced her to this work, Anna said: 'the thoughts you gave me from Horace Bushnell years ago have followed me entirely through the writing of my book and have more than anything else helped me to feel it was worth a great effort to try at least to bring the thoughts of men more in harmony with the purposes of God on this subject' (quoted in Susan Chitty, *The Woman Who Wrote Black Beauty*, 1971).

An overworked and underfed cab-horse. (Gordon, *Horse World of London*, p. 43)

429

'Oh! he 's all right, miss,' said my driver, 'he 's strong enough.'

The porter, who was pulling about some heavy boxes, suggested to the gentleman, as there was so much luggage, whether he would not take a second cab.

'Can your horse do it, or can't he?' said the blustering man.

'Oh! he can do it all right, sir; send up the boxes, porter: he could take more than that,' and he helped to haul up a box so heavy that I could feel the springs go down.

'Papa, papa, do take a second cab,' said the young girl in a beseeching tone; 'I am sure we are wrong, I am sure it is very cruel.'

'Nonsense, Grace, get in at once, and don't make all this fuss; a pretty thing it would be if a man of business had to examine every cab horse before he hired it—the man knows his own business of course: there, get in and hold your tongue!'

My gentle friend had to obey; and box after box was dragged up and lodged on the top of the cab, or settled by the side of the driver.   At last all was ready, and with his usual jerk at the rein, and slash of the whip, he drove out of the station.

The load was very heavy, and I had had neither food nor rest since the morning; but I did my best, as I always had done, in spite of cruelty and injustice.

I got along fairly till we came to Ludgate Hill, but there, the heavy load and my own exhaustion were too much.   I was struggling to keep on, goaded by constant chucks of the rein and use of the whip, when, in a single moment—I cannot tell how—my feet slipped from under me, and I fell heavily to the ground on my side; the suddenness and the force with which I fell, seemed to beat all the breath out of my body.   I lay perfectly still; indeed, I had no power to move, and I thought now I was

5 Springs. There were various patterns and designs of springs depending on the type of vehicle, but all were intended to give the passengers a more comfortable ride, Overloading or uneven loading of the vehicle, especially a two-wheeled vehicle, was transmitted to the horse via the springs and shafts, which altered the balance of the vehicle and made pulling more difficult.

6 Ludgate Hill. Street in the City of London leading to St Paul's Cathedral.

'I had no power to move, and I thought now I was going to die'. Illustrated by Charles Keeping (*Black Beauty*, London: Victor Gollancz, 1988, p. 204)

going to die. I heard a sort of confusion round me, loud angry voices, and the getting down of the luggage, but it was all like a dream. I thought I heard that sweet pitiful voice saying, 'Oh! that poor horse! it is all our fault.' Someone came and loosened the throat strap of my bridle, and undid the traces which kept the collar so tight upon me. Someone said, 'He 's dead, he 'll never get up again.' Then I could hear a policeman giving orders, but I did not even open my eyes; I could only draw a gasping breath now and then. Some cold water was thrown over my head, and some cordial was poured into my mouth, and something was covered over me. I cannot tell how long I lay there, but I found my life coming back, and a kind-voiced man was patting me and encouraging me to rise. After some more cordial had been given me, and after one or two attempts, I staggered to my feet, and was gently led to some stables which were close by. Here I was put into a well-littered stall, and some warm gruel was brought to me, which I drank thankfully.

In the evening I was sufficiently recovered to be led back to Skinner's stables, where I think they did the best for me they could. In the morning Skinner came with a farrier to look at me. He examined me very closely, and said—

'This is a case of overwork more than disease, and if you could give him a run off for six months, he would be able to work again; but now there is not an ounce of strength in him.'

7 'Then he must just go to the dogs,' said Skinner, 'I have no meadows to nurse sick horses in—he might get well or he might not; that sort of thing don't suit my business. My plan is to work 'em as long as they 'll go, and then sell 'em for what they 'll fetch, at the knacker's or elsewhere.'

'If he was broken-winded,' said the farrier, 'you had better
8 have him killed out of hand, but he is not; there is a sale of

7 **Go to the dogs.** Be sold as meat for dogs. Possibly originated from the fact that most hunters, when their hunting life was over, were killed and fed to hounds.

8 **Sale.** Almost every town and even village in Britain held horse sales. It was a social event to which people came for miles around. London had several 'repositories', the most famous being Tattersalls where (generally) high-class riding and carriage horses were sold; Aldridges and the Elephant and Castle usually sold working horses of all types. See pp. 65, 279.

The sale ring at Tattersall's. (Duke of Beaufort, *Driving*, London: Longmans, Green, 1889, p. 77)

433

horses coming off in about ten days; if you rest him and feed him up, he may pick up, and you may get more than his skin is worth, at any rate.'

Upon this advice, Skinner rather unwillingly, I think, gave orders that I should be well fed and cared for, and the stable man, happily for me, carried out the orders with a much better will than his master had in giving them. Ten days of perfect
9   rest, plenty of good oats, hay, bran mashes, with boiled linseed mixed in them, did more to get up my condition than anything else could have done; those linseed mashes were delicious, and I began to think, after all, it might be better to live than go to the dogs. When the twelfth day after the accident came, I was taken to the sale, a few miles out of London. I felt that any change from my present place must be an improvement, so I held up my head, and hoped for the best.

9 **Bran mashes.** One recipe for bran mash with linseed recommended half a pint of linseed to be soaked in one quart of boiling water for four hours, then added to half a bucket of bran which had been moistened in a gallon of water ('Magenta', *Handy Horse Book*, 1865). See p. 59.

'I was taken to the sale.' Illustrated by Cecil Aldin. (*Black Beauty*, London: Jarrolds, 1912, p. 283)

435

CHAPTER XLVIII

FARMER THOROUGHGOOD AND HIS GRANDSON WILLIE

AT this sale, of course, I found myself in company with the old broken-down horses—some lame, some broken-winded, some old, and some that I am sure it would have been merciful to shoot.

The buyers and sellers too, many of them, looked not much better off than the poor beasts they were bargaining about. There were poor old men, trying to get a horse or pony for a few pounds, that might drag about some little wood or coal cart. There were poor men trying to sell a worn-out beast for two or three pounds, rather than have the greater loss of killing him. Some of them looked as if poverty and hard times had hardened them all over; but there were others that I would have willingly used the last of my strength in serving; poor and shabby, but kind and human, with voices that I could trust. There was one tottering old man that took a great fancy to me, and I to him,

1 Wood or coal cart. As all types of heating for homes or other premises were solid fuel, most notably coal in urban and suburban areas and sometimes wood in rural areas, there was always a need for the fuel merchant to keep a horse, pony or donkey (depending upon the size of his business) to pull a fuel cart.

'I found myself in company with the old broken-down horses'. Illustrated by G. P. Micklewright. (*Black Beauty*, London: J. Coker & Co., 1933, p. 113)

but I was not strong enough—it was an anxious time! Coming
from the better part of the fair, I noticed a man who looked like
a gentleman farmer, with a young boy by his side; he had a broad
back and round shoulders, a kind, ruddy face, and he wore a
broad-brimmed hat. When he came up to me and my companions, he stood still, and gave a pitiful look round upon us. I
saw his eye rest on me; I had still a good mane and tail, which did
something for my appearance. I pricked my ears and looked at him.

'There 's a horse, Willie, that has known better days.'

'Poor old fellow!' said the boy, 'do you think, grandpapa, he
was ever a carriage horse?'

'Oh yes! my boy,' said the farmer, coming closer, 'he might
have been anything when he was young; look at his nostrils and
his ears, the shape of his neck and shoulder; there 's a deal of
breeding about that horse.' He put out his hand and gave me a
kind pat on the neck. I put out my nose in answer to his kindness; the boy stroked my face.

'Poor old fellow! see, grandpapa, how well he understands
kindness. Could not you buy him and make him young again,
as you did with Ladybird?'

'My dear boy, I can't make all old horses young; besides,
Ladybird was not so very old, as she was run down and badly
used.'

'Well, grandpapa, I don't believe that this one is old; look at
his mane and tail. I wish you would look into his mouth, and
then you could tell; though he is so very thin, his eyes are not
sunk like some old horses'.'

The old gentleman laughed. 'Bless the boy! he is as horsy
as his old grandfather.'

'But do look at his mouth, grandpapa, and ask the price; I
am sure he would grow young in our meadows.'

2 **Better part of the fair.** Apart from the poor, run-down, over-worked horses mentioned, sales and fairs also had their share of good quality, sound, useful horses. Not all horses sold at fairs were suspect.

3 **Gentleman farmer.** An 'amateur' farmer who also had private income apart from that which he earned from farming. He was higher up the social scale than a 'real' farmer.

4 **Broad back . . .** Another example of attributing physical features to the character of a person. In this case they are good features worthy of a 'gentleman farmer'.

5 **Deal of breeding.** The signs of Black Beauty's Thoroughbred blood would be apparent even in his run-down condition, such as finely textured hair, thin skin, good mane and tail, finely chiselled head and legs and general upstanding bearing. See p. 79.

6 **Ladybird.** Popular name for a mare after the attractive red and black spotted flying beetle, the ladybird or ladybug.

7 **Eyes are not sunk.** In very old horses the cavity above the eye tends to be very hollow. However, the unscrupulous horse dealer could try to hide the horse's age by a trick known as 'puffing the glims': 'This is pricking the hollow above the eyes with a needle to cause local inflammation and swelling of the part. The swelling fills up the cavity above the eye, and gives the horse a younger appearance, but it only lasts for a day or two, and often ends in opthalmia, from the inflammation affecting the optic nerve' (W. Procter, *Management of the Horse*, 1883). Another description suggests that air was blown into the cavities through a hollow needle.

Trotted out at the horse sale. Illustrated by K. F. Barker. (*Black Beauty*, London: A. & C. Black, 1959, p. 247)

The head of a low-bred horse (*left*) and (*right*) a well-bred horse. (Mayhew, *The Illustrated Horse Management*, p. 590)

439

The man who had brought me for sale now put in his word.

'The young gentleman's a real knowing one, sir; now the fact is, this 'ere hoss is just pulled down with overwork in the cabs; he 's not an old one, and I heerd as·how the vetenary should say, that a six months' run off would set him right up, being as how his wind was not broken. I 've had the tending of him these ten days past, and a gratefuller, pleasanter animal I never met with, and 'twould be worth a gentleman's while to give a five-pound note for him, and let him have a chance. I 'll be bound he 'd be worth twenty pounds next spring.'

The old gentleman laughed, and the little boy looked up eagerly.

'Oh! grandpapa, did you not say, the colt sold for five pounds more than you expected? you would not be poorer if you did buy this one.'

The farmer slowly felt my legs, which were much swelled and strained; then he looked at my mouth—'Thirteen or fourteen, I should say; just trot him out, will you?'

I arched my poor thin neck, raised my tail a little, and threw out my legs as well as I could, for they were very stiff.

'What is the lowest you will take for him?' said the farmer as I came back.

'Five pounds, sir; that was the lowest price my master set.'

''Tis a speculation,' said the old gentleman, shaking his head, but at the same time slowly drawing out his purse—'quite a speculation! Have you any more business here?' he said, counting the sovereigns into his hand.

'No, sir, I can take him for you to the inn, if you please.'

'Do so, I am now going there.'

They walked forward, and I was led behind. The boy could hardly control his delight, and the old gentleman seemed to enjoy

8   **I heerd as how the vetenary . . .** The speech of a working-class character is demonstrated by incorrect spelling to indicate pronunciation and poor grammar.

Examining the horse's teeth. (Mayhew, *The Illustrated Horse Management*, p. 140)

441

his pleasure. I had a good feed at the inn, and was then gently ridden home by a servant of my new master's and turned into a large meadow with a shed in one corner of it.

9 Mr. Thoroughgood, for that was the name of my benefactor, gave orders that I should have hay and oats every night and morning, and the run of the meadow during the day, and 'you, Willie,' said he, 'must take the oversight of him; I give him in charge to you.'

The boy was proud of his charge, and undertook it in all seriousness. There was not a day when he did not pay me a visit; sometimes picking me out from amongst the other horses, and giving me a bit of carrot, or something good, or sometimes standing by me whilst I ate my oats. He always came with kind words and caresses, and of course I grew very fond of him. He called me Old Crony, as I used to come to him in the field and follow him about. Sometimes he brought his grandfather, who always looked closely at my legs—

'This is our point, Willie,' he would say; 'but he is improving so steadily that I think we shall see a change for the better in the spring.'

The perfect rest, the good food, the soft turf, and gentle exercise, soon began to tell on my condition and my spirits. I had a good constitution from my mother, and I was never strained when I was young, so that I had a better chance than many horses, who have been worked before they came to their full strength. During the winter my legs improved so much, that I began to feel quite young again. The spring came round, and one day in March, Mr. Thoroughgood determined that he would try me in the phaeton. I was well pleased, and he and Willie drove me a few miles. My legs were not stiff now, and I did the work with perfect ease.

9 **Mr. Thoroughgood.** Yet another example of a name to fit a character, along with John Manly, Nicholas Skinner, Alfred Smirk, etc.

10 **Was never strained when I was young.** Many horses never reached their full potential because they were overworked when young and their bones (and minds) had not had the chance to develop and mature. Too much work too early often resulted in weaknesses later which ultimately shortened a horse's working life.

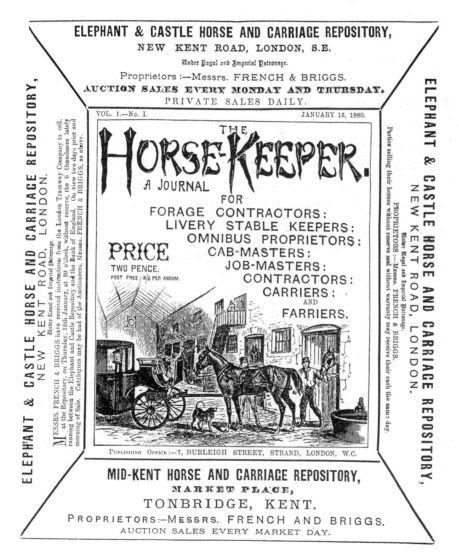

A contemporary journal advertising sales, harness etc. (*The Horse-Keeper*, 15 January 1880)

'He 's growing young, Willie; we must give him a little gentle work now, and by midsummer he will be as good as Ladybird: he has a beautiful mouth, and good paces, they can't be better.'

'Oh! grandpapa, how glad I am you bought him!'

'So am I, my boy, but he has to thank you more than me; we must now be looking out for a quiet genteel place for him, where he will be valued.'

Mr Thoroughgood and Willie. Illustrated by Frank Grey. (*Black Beauty*, London: Collins, 1953, p. 247)

CHAPTER XLIX

MY LAST HOME

ONE day during this summer, the groom cleaned and dressed me with such extraordinary care, that I thought some new change must be at hand; he trimmed my fetlocks and legs, passed the tar-brush over my hoofs, and even parted my forelock. I think the harness had an extra polish. Willie seemed half anxious, half merry as he got into the chaise with his grandfather.

'If the ladies take to him,' said the old gentleman, 'they 'll be suited, and he 'll be suited: we can but try.'

At the distance of a mile or two from the village, we came to a pretty, low house, with a lawn and shrubbery at the front, and a drive up to the door. Willie rang the bell, and asked if Miss Blomefield, or Miss Ellen was at home. Yes, they were. So, whilst Willie stayed with me, Mr. Thoroughgood went into the house. In about ten minutes he returned, followed by three ladies; one tall, pale lady, wrapped in a white shawl, leaned on a younger lady, with dark eyes and a merry face; the other, a very stately looking person, was Miss Blomefield. They all came and looked at me and asked questions. The younger lady—that

446

1 **Trimmed my fetlocks.** Depending upon a horse's breeding it would have a little or a lot of hair around its fetlocks. A lot indicated draught horse blood in its ancestry, but Black Beauty probably had very little; even so, a trim would give the legs a fine, clean-cut appearance.

2 **Tar-brush over my hoofs.** Some kind of oil, possibly neatsfoot or even a specially prepared hoof oil, or tar was brushed over the horny surface of the foot to give a smart, shiny appearance. George Armatage recommended that 'equal parts of Stockholm or Archangel tar and mutton suet are to be melted together, and a small portion brushed round the hoof each day'. He thought that grease or fats in other mixtures rendered the hoof brittle (*The Horse Owner and Stableman's Companion*, 1869).

'Followed by three ladies'. Illustrated by Lucy Kemp-Welch. (*Black Beauty*, London: J. M. Dent, 1915, pl. opp. p. 224)

was Miss Ellen—took to me very much; she said she was sure she should like me, I had such a good face. The tall, pale lady said that she should always be nervous in riding behind a horse that had once been down, as I might come down again, and if I did, she should never get over the fright.

'You see, ladies,' said Mr. Thoroughgood, 'many first-rate horses have had their knees broken through the carelessness of their drivers, without any fault of their own, and from what I see of this horse, I should say, that is his case: but of course I do not wish to influence you. If you incline, you can have him on trial, and then your coachman will see what he thinks of him.'

'You have always been such a good adviser to us about our horses,' said the stately lady, 'that your recommendation would go a long way with me, and if my sister Lavinia sees no objection, we will accept your offer of a trial, with thanks.'

It was then arranged that I should be sent for the next day.

In the morning a smart-looking young man came for me; at first he looked pleased; but when he saw my knees, he said in a disappointed voice—

'I didn't think, sir, you would have recommended my ladies a blemished horse like that.'

'Handsome is—that handsome does,' said my master; 'you are only taking him on trial, and I am sure you will do fairly by him, young man, and if he is not as safe as any horse you ever drove, send him back.'

I was led home, placed in a comfortable stable, fed, and left to myself. The next day, when my groom was cleaning my face, he said—

'That is just like the star that Black Beauty had, he is much the same height too; I wonder where he is now.'

A little further on, he came to the place in my neck where I

3 Handsome is. Proverb in Ray's *Collection* (1747) which also appears in Goldsmith's *Vicar of Wakefield* (1766).

4 Star. Small group of white hairs in the centre of the horse's forehead.

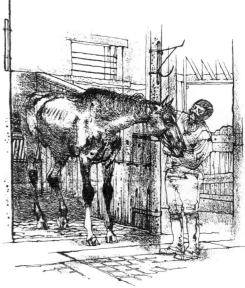

'That is just like the star that Black Beauty had'; (*left*) illustrated by Lionel Edwards (*Black Beauty*, London: Ward Lock, 1954. pl. opp. p. 220); (*top*) illustrated by Charles Keeping (*Black Beauty*, London: Victor Gollancz, 1988, p. 213)

was bled, and where a little knot was left in the skin. He almost started, and began to look me over carefully, talking to himself.

'White star in the forehead, one white foot on the off side, this little knot just in that place'; then looking at the middle of my back—'and as I am alive, there is that little patch of white hair that John used to call "Beauty's threepenny bit." It *must* be Black Beauty! Why, Beauty! Beauty! do you know me? little Joe Green, that almost killed you?' And he began patting and patting me as if he was quite overjoyed.

I could not say that I remembered him, for now he was a fine grown young fellow, with black whiskers and a man's voice, but I was sure he knew me, and that he was Joe Green, and I was very glad. I put my nose up to him, and tried to say that we were friends. I never saw a man so pleased.

'Give you a fair trial! I should think so indeed! I wonder who the rascal was that broke your knees, my old Beauty! you must have been badly served out somewhere; well, well, it won't be my fault if you haven't good times of it now. I wish John Manly was here to see you.'

In the afternoon I was put into a low park chair and brought to the door. Miss Ellen was going to try me, and Green went with her. I soon found that she was a good driver, and she seemed pleased with my paces. I heard Joe telling her about me, and that he was sure I was Squire Gordon's old Black Beauty.

When we returned, the other sisters came out to hear how I had behaved myself. She told them what she had just heard, and said—

'I shall certainly write to Mrs. Gordon, and tell her that her favourite horse has come to us. How pleased she will be!'

After this I was driven every day for a week or so, and as I appeared to be quite safe, Miss Lavinia at last ventured out in the

5 **Threepenny bit.** The Victorian threepenny piece was a small silver coin, later replaced by an eight-sided alloy coin.

6 **Park chair.** Like a low chair, for the use in particular of the elderly or infirm. See p. 29.

'I was put into a low park chair.' Illustrated by Cecil Aldin. (*Black Beauty*, London: Jarrolds, 1912, plate opp. p. 290)

451

7   small close carriage.   After this it was quite decided to keep me and call me by my old name of Black Beauty.

I have now lived in this happy place a whole year.   Joe is the best and kindest of grooms.   My work is easy and pleasant, and I feel my strength and spirits all coming back again.   Mr. Thoroughgood said to Joe the other day—

'In your place he will last till he is twenty years old—perhaps more.'

Willie always speaks to me when he can, and treats me as his special friend.   My ladies have promised that I shall never be sold, and so I have nothing to fear; and here my story ends.   My troubles are all over, and I am at home; and often before I am quite awake, I fancy I am still in the orchard at Birtwick standing with my old friends under the apple trees.

7 **Close carriage.** Any private vehicle with a hood drawn by a single horse.

'With my old friends under the apple trees'. Illustrated by Percy F. Spence. (*Black Beauty*, London: A. & C. Black, 1959, p. 254)

Major editions and selected translations

Included in the hundreds of editions, abridgements, and translations, there is a smaller group of landmark versions which could be cited. This selection seeks to name early printings, early translations, versions with significant introductions and of course important illustrated editions. Some early editions have been recently reprinted, and there continue to be finely drawn and designed new editions. This chronological list gives a hint of the variety of versions available to the reader or collector either in libraries or in the out-of-print book market.

Black Beauty: his Grooms and Companions. The Autobiography of a Horse. Translated from the original equine, by Anna Sewell. London: Jarrold & Sons, [1877].

Prince-Noir. Souvenirs d'un cheval. Traduit de l'anglais sur la 19e édition. Lausanne: G. Budel, 1888.

Black Beauty: his Grooms and Companions. By A. Sewell. The 'Uncle Tom's Cabin' of the horse. American edition. Boston: American Humane Education Society, [1890]. **Note:** At head of title: 'Over One Hundred Thousand Copies of this book have been Sold in England.'

Black Beauty. Detroit: American Horse Monthly, 1891. **Note:** Monthly instalments in vol. 1 of this periodical, which published only chapters I–XII. The only magazine serialisation?

Schön Schwarzhärchen. Lebensbeschreibung eines Pferdes. Nach des 28. Aufl. originals übertr. von Wilh. Engelbrecht. Dresden: Brandner, 1891.

Azabache (Black Beauty), sus caballerizos y compañeros. La 'Cabana del Tio Tom' del caballo. Edición publicada en América por la Sociedad Américana de Education Humanitaria. Boston: American Humane Education Society, [1892?].

Belmoro o l'autografia di un cavallo. Traduzione dall'inglese di Alaide Vanzetti, con disegni illustrative originali di A. J. Pertz. Florence: Pia Casa di Patronato, 1892.

Black Beauty: his Grooms and Companions. The 'Uncle Tom's Cabin' of the Horse ... With twenty-two original illustrations by H. Toaspern, Jr. New York: J. Hovendon & Company, [1894]. **Note:** Retains italicised passages as first published by George T. Angell. Reissued by The H. M. Caldwell Co. Publishers at a later date.

Black Beauty: the Autobiography of a Horse ... Illustrated by John Beer. London: Jarrold & Sons, 1894.

Black Beauty: the Autobiography of a Horse. By A. Sewell. Illustrated by John Beer. New York: E. P. Dutton & Company, 1894.

E Magré, oraiotes e autobiographia enos ippou. Metaphrasis ektou Agglikou. Athens, 1894.

Black Beauty: the Autobiography of a Horse. By Anna Sewell. London: Jarrold & Sons, 1899. **Note:** Paper covers, with 'Copyright Edition' on cover. John Beer illustration on cover.

Black Beauty: Retold in Words of One Syllable. By Mrs J. C. Gorham. Fully illustrated. New York: A. L. Burt Company, [1903]. **Note:** Abridged to 35 chapters. Colour plates signed E. Clark, black and white illustrations reproduced from a Beer-illustrated edition.

Black Beauty: I suoi Stallieri ed i suoi Compagni. Racconto che si puodire 'La Capanna dello Zio Tom' del Cavallo. Traduzione dall'Inglese di Elisabetta Cavazza. Rivista da Padre Atanasio da Treppio. Boston: Società Americana dell'Educazione Umanitaria, [1901?]. **Note:** At head of title: 'Quattro cento cinquanta sei miglia copie, e più, già vendute ... in America'.

Black Beauty: his Grooms and Companions. By A. Sewell. American edition ... Boston: American Humane Education Society, [1904?]. **Note:** At head of title: 'Over One Hundred Thousand Copies of this Book have been sold in England, and between One and Two Millions printed ... in America ...'.

Re Moro: Autobiografia di un cavallo. Liberamente trascritta da E. Casella, con prefazione di Fanny Zampini Salazar. 14 illustrazioni. Approvato dall'Autorità Ecclesiastica. Turin–Rome–Milan–Florence–Naples: Ditta G. B. Paravia e Comp. (Figli di I. Vigliardi–Paravia), 1904. **Note:** Paper board covers with Winifred Austen illustrations.

Black Beauty. Pictured by John R. Neill. Chicago: The Reilly & Britton Co., [1908]. **Note:** Abridged to portions of Chapters I, II, XII, XVI, XXVII, XXVIII and XLIX. With this is issued *The Little Lame Prince.* Neill was the first illustrator of the Oz books.

Black Beauty: his Grooms and Companions. By Anna Sewell. Boston: The American Humane Education Society, [1910?]. **Note:** At head of title: 'Between Two and Three Million Copies of This Book Have Been Printed'.

Black Beauty: the Autobiography of a Horse ... Illustrated by Eighteen Plates in Colour specially drawn for this edition by Cecil Aldin. London: Jarrolds, [1912?]. **Note:** Includes 'Appreciation and Life of the Author', by William T. F. Jarrold.

Black Beauty. ... With twenty-four coloured pictures and many line illustrations by Lucy Kemp-Welch. London: J. M. Dent & Sons Ltd, 1915. **Note:** Reissued many times, latest in 1986 (New York: Crown Publishers). Perhaps the finest illustrated edition.

Black Beauty: the Autobiography of a Horse. By Anna Sewell. London and Toronto [etc.]: J. M. Dent [etc.], [1921]. **Note:** Everyman edition. Introduction by Vincent Starrett (reprinted with slight variations from his *Buried Caesars*, 1923).

Black Beauty: a Story of the Ups and Downs of a Horse's Life. By Anna Sewell. Illustrated by Blampied. London: Jarrolds, [1922]. **Note:** 'Appreciation and Life of Author', pp. 9–18, by William T. F. Jarrold, is a reprint from the 1912 Jarrolds edition.

Black Beauty ... With illustrations of the late 19th century, by John Beer. New York: Dodd, Mead & Company, 1945. **Note:** The last edition to reproduce the Beer illustrations?

Black Beauty: the Autobiography of a Horse. By Anna Sewell. Illustrated by Fritz Eichenberg. (Illustrated Junior Library.) New York: Grosset & Dunlap, [1945]. **Note:** Boxed.

Black Beauty: the Autobiography of a Horse ... Illustrated by Wesley Dennis. Introduction by May Lamberton Becker. Cleveland and New York: World Publishing Company, [1946].

Black Beauty. By Anna Sewell. New York: Gilberton Company, 1949. **Note:** Classic Comics, no. 60, June 1949. Illustrated by August M. Froehlich in comic-book form.

Black Beauty: the Autobiography of a Horse ... Illustrated by George Ford Morris. Introduction by Angelo Patri. Philadelphia and New York: J. B. Lippincott Company, [1950].

Black Beauty ... With 24 colour plates by Lionel Edwards, R.I. London and Melbourne: Ward, Lock & Co., Limited, [1954]. **Note:** A 1946 edition, in oblong format, published by Peter Lunn, was illustrated by Lionel Edwards with a coloured frontispiece and black and white illustrations, different from this edition.

Black Beauty ... With an introduction by Eleanor Graham. Illustrations by Charlotte Hough. [Harmondsworth]: Penguin Books, [1954]. **Note:** Puffin paperback.

Black Beauty: the Life Story of a Horse. With sixteen plates (eight in colour). London: Adam & Charles Black, [1959]. **Note:** 'Eight colour plates by Percy F. S. Spence, eight black and white plates by K. F. Baker and a jacket by Peter Biegel', according to dustjacket.

Black Beauty ... Illustrated by John Groth. Afterword by Clifton Fadiman. New York, London: Macmillan, 1962.

Black Beauty ... Cover by Don Irwin. San Rafael, Calif.: Classics Publishing Corporation, [1970]. **Note:** At head of title: 'Illustrated by Michael Rios'. Backword, pp. 214–23. Annotated edition. Reprinted New York: Modern Promotions, Ottenheimer Publishers Inc., 1979.

Black Beauty. Introduction by Susan Chitty. Illustrations by Victor Ambrus. [Leicester]: Brockhampton Press, [1973].

Black Beauty. Abenteuer eines Pferdes. Stuttgart: Boje-Verlag, [1974]. **Note:** Translation, by Waltraude Callsen, of the Brockhampton Press, 1973 edition, with introduction by Susan Chitty and illustrations by Victor Ambrus.

Black Beauty. Adapted from the classic novel by Anna Sewell. New York: Marvel Comics Group, 1976. **Note:** Comic book format, 'Presented by Stan Lee. Adapted by Naunerle Farr. Illustrated by Rudy Nebres.'

Black Beauty: his Grooms and Companions. The Autobiography of a Horse. Translated from the original equine, by Anna Sewell. [London: David Paradine Developments Limited, 1977]. **Note:** Facsimile reprint of the London, Jarrold & Sons, 1877 edition, limited to 100 copies. Boxed, bound in leather, each copy autographed by Lucinda Prior-Palmer.

Black Beauty and Other Horse Stories. Edited by Paul J. Horowitz and Lily Owens. New York: Avenel Books, [1980]. **Note:** Described as a facsimile of 'the 1898 edition, complete with its charming graphic decorations and has been chosen because it is the finest Victorian edition currently available', p. viii.

Black Beauty: the Autobiography of a Horse. By Anna Sewell. Illustrated by John Spiers. New York: Wanderer Books, published by Simon & Schuster, [1982].

Black Beauty. [London]: Cathay Books, [1984?]. **Note:** Illustrated by Elaine Keenan.

Black Beauty ... Illustrated by Martin Knowelden with line drawings by Francis Mosely. London: Beehive Books, Orgis Publishing Limited; and Minneapolis: Kaleidoscope Books, 1986.

Black Beauty ... With illustrations by Lucy Kemp-Welch. New York: Children's Classics: a division of dilithium Press, Ltd, distributed by Crown Publishers, [1986]. **Note:** Foreword by Ellen S. Shapiro.

Black Beauty ... Newly illustrated by Charles Keeping. London: Victor Gollancz, 1988.

Sequels and related publications

This chronological list includes several titles described as sequels but which seem to have no relevance whatever to *Black Beauty* beyond title, or humane theme.

'Dowse, the Gypsy.' *Temple Bar*, vol. 5, 1885. Reprinted in *The Story Teller*, vol. 5, March 1886. Interpreted by at least one American library as extracted from *Black Beauty* because one of the horses in the story is named thus.

Our Gold Mine at Hollyhurst . . . A Prize Story of Massachusetts. Gold Mine Series no. 1. Boston: American Humane Education Society, 1893. One of the results of George T. Angell's promotion of stories with the humane theme to continue the influence of *Black Beauty*.

The Strike at Shane's: a Sequel to 'Black Beauty'. A Prize Story of Indiana. Chicago: A. Flanagan Company, [©1893, by The American Humane Education Society]. Possibly Gold Mine Series no. 2.

Four Months in New Hampshire: A Story of Love and Dumb Animals. Gold Mine Series no. 3. Sequel to *Black Beauty*. A prize story of New Hampshire. Written for, and revised, copyrighted, and published by the American Humane Education Society. Boston, [1894].

Son of Black Beauty. By Phyllis Briggs. London: Thames Publishing Company, [1954]. Publisher's note: 'In this book the art of the storyteller has been enlisted to produce what Black Beauty the horse could not – a son. This happy idea has enabled Phyllis Briggs to write a story in the same fine tradition as Anna Sewell's much-loved classic.'

Black Velvet. By Christine Pullein-Thompson. Illustrated by Elisabeth Grant. (Black Beauty's Clan series.) London: Brockhampton Press, 1975.

Black Ebony. By Josephine Pullein-Thompson. Illustrated by Elisabeth Grant. (Black Beauty's Clan series.) London: Brockhampton Press, 1975.

Black Princess. By Diana Pullein-Thompson. Illustrated by Elisabeth Grant. (Black Beauty's Clan series.) London: Brockhampton Press, 1975.

Black Beauty's Clan. By Josephine, Diana and Christine Pullein-Thompson. Illustrated by Elisabeth Grant. New York: McGraw-Hill Book Company, [©1975]. Includes: 'Black Ebony', 'Black Princess', and 'Black Velvet'.

Black Beauty's Family. By Josephine, Diana and Christine Pullein-Thompson. Illustrated by Elisabeth Grant. New York: McGraw-Hill Book Company, [©1978]. Includes: 'Nightshade', 'Black Romany', and 'Blossom'.

Black Beauty's Family. By Christine, Diana, and Josephine Pullein-Thompson. Illustrated by Elisabeth Grant. (Black Beauty's Clan series.) London: Hodder & Stoughton, 1980.

Black Nightshade. By Josephine Pullein-Thompson. Illustrated by Elisabeth Grant. (Black Beauty's Clan series.) London: Hodder & Stoughton, [1978, 1980].

Black Beauty Grows Up. Adapted by I. M. Richardson. Illustrated by Karen Milone. (Adventures of Black Beauty.) Mahwah, NJ: Troll Associates, 1983. Abridged version of Part I of the original novel.

Black Beauty and the Runaway Horse. Adapted by I. M. Richardson. (Adventures of Black Beauty.) Mahwah, NJ: Troll Associates, 1983. Abridged version of Part II of the novel.

The Courage of Black Beauty. Adapted by I. M. Richardson. Illustrated by Karen Milone. (Adventures of Black Beauty.) Mahwah, NJ: Troll Associates, 1983. Abridged version of Part III of the novel.

Beauty Finds a Home. Adapted by I. M. Richardson. (Adventures of Black Beauty.) Mahwah, NJ: Troll Associates, 1983. Abridged version of Part IV of the novel.

Beauty and Vicky. Novelisation by Andrea Hanson based on 'The Adventures of Black Beauty' television series. New York: Random House, [©1984].

Films, plays, recordings, collectables

This chronologically arranged list includes films, filmstrips, sound recordings and statuary. Spin-off products continue to be produced. The list is incomplete, but suggests the extent and nature of collectables confronting the Black Beauty aficionado. Most of the well-known film and television versions use the name of the horse, the richly described family lives portrayed in the novel, and the social contrasts as the basis of newly hatched plots. Much of the sorrow, misery and cruelty is not depicted in the intense manner of the novel.

FILMS, PLAYS AND TELEVISION

Black Beauty. Hepworth Company, 1906. Motion picture, 449 feet. Similarity to the Sewell novel in title only, descriptions indicate an approximately seven-minute street scene featuring a horse retrieving a hat for a gentleman.

Black Beauty. Vitagraph Picture Corporation, 1921. Motion picture, 7 reels. Directed by David Smith. Starred Jean Paige.

Black Beauty. Monogram Picture Corporation, 1933. Motion picture, 7 reels. Directed by Phil Rosen. Starred Alexander Kirkland and Esther Ralston. Apparently the first sound version.

Black Beauty: an Inspiring Play in One Act based on Anna Sewell's Immortal Novel. By Grace Barney. New York: Samuel French, 1942. 'We feel sure that this play should be presented in every school, church and high school in America'; cf. pref., p. 4. The horse never appears on the stage, and the play, rather stilted, is more a genteel parlour drama.

Black Beauty. 20th Century Fox, 1946. Motion picture, 76 minutes. Directed by Max Nosseck. Starred Mona Freeman and Richard Denning. Re-plotted version about a little girl and her love for her horse.

Black Beauty. Paramount Pictures, 1971. 106 minutes. Directed by James Hill. Starred Mark Lester, Walter Slezak, Ursula Glas and Peter Lee Lawrence. Described by one film guide as 'Classic story of king of wild horses who couldn't be tamed'!

The Adventures of Black Beauty. London Weekend Television, 1972. Distributed by Freemantle Corporation. Executive producers Paul Knight and Sidney Cole. Television version.

Black Beauty. Universal Studios [made for television], 1978. Starred Martin Milner and Kristoffer Tabori. First shown in five hour-long episodes, later in two parts over four hours.

Black Beauty. [New York: Paula Green, 1986?]. Video cassette of 1972 British serialisation by London Weekend Television.

RECORDS AND TAPES

The Story of Black Beauty. Based on the Book by Anna Sewell. See the pictures, hear the record, read the book. Walt Disney Productions, Burbank, Calif., Disneyland Vista Records, ©1966. 24 pp. illus. pamphlet and 7½″ 33.3 r.p.m. long playing record. (A Disneyland Record and Book, 318.)

The Story and Songs of Black Beauty. Based on the Book by Anna Sewell. Narrated by Robie Lester. Music by Camarata. [Burbank, Calif.?], Walt Disney Productions, ©1966. 12″ 33.3 r.p.m. long playing record with 11 pp. text in album. (A Disneyland Record, 3938.) Dust jacket and pamphlet design and illustrations by Al White.

464

Claire Bloom. Anna Sewell. Black Beauty. An Abridgement of the Novel Read by Claire Bloom. New York: Caedmon, ©1970. (Caedmon TC 1322.) 12" 33.3 r.p.m. long playing record. Jacket notes by Barbara Holdridge.

The Adventures of Black Beauty and the Story of Aladdin and his Wonderful Lamp. New York: Cosmo Recording Co., Record Guild of America, [n.d., 197–?]. (Simon Says series, M-30.) 12" 33.3 r.p.m. long playing record. Black Beauty: words by Jane Fradkin, music by Ron Howard, lyrics by Jane Fradkin. Aladdin: written and produced by Henry Tobias and David Ormont.

The Passage Players. Black Beauty. Dramatized in Story and Song and Sound Effects. [n.p.], ©1978. 12" 33.3 r.p.m. long playing record.

Black Beauty by Anna Sewell. Four 90 minute cassettes. [n.p., 1987?]. Classic books on cassettes. Narrated by Flo Gibson. Four cassette tapes in plastic box.

Black Beauty by Anna Sewell. Read by: Martin Blaine. [Pasadena, Calif.: Cassette Book Library, [1983?]]. Produced by Audio Book Company, Van Nuys, Calif. Two cassette tapes in paper wrapper, both numbered 827.

Hayley Mills Reads Black Beauty. [By] Anna Sewell. Abridged by Sam Curtis. Downsview, Ontario: Listen for Pleasure Ltd, ©1978, 1981. Produced by Graham Goodwin. Two cassette tapes in paper wrapper.

FILMSTRIPS

Black Beauty. (Best loved books series.) Filmfax Productions. Released by Universal Educational and Visual Arts, 1971. Filmstrip, 1 roll, coloured. 35 mm.

Black Beauty. Learning kit. [Filmstrip]. Paramount Pictures Corporation, made by Ealing Films. Wilmette, Ill.: Films Inc., 1976. Three rolls, coloured 3 mm film, and three cassettes 49 minutes, with teacher's guide, 15 activity cards and paperback copy of the book. Edited from the Paramount film of 1971.

COLLECTABLES

The statues listed below are the only ones the editors could identify, but there may be more which have survived without the Black Beauty identity. It is hard to believe that these are the only ones. Communication with British and American model horse collecting societies has not brought any more to light.

Black Beauty and foal on base. Earthenware figures designed by Graham Tonge. Beswick, Royal Doulton, [1972–3]. 10 inches high.

Black Beauty. Plastic figure, shown galloping. Wayne, N.J.: Breyer Animal Creations, [1979]. 8 inches high.

Black Beauty, his family and friends. Four plastic figures: Black Beauty, Duchess, Merrylegs and Ginger. Chicago: Breyer Animal Creations, [1980]. Box (9½ × 6½ × 7½ inches).

Black Beauty. Black porcelain bisque figure designed by Pamela du Boulay. Philadelphia: Franklin Mint, [1985]. 8½ inches high × 11 inches long.

466

Further reading and works consulted

Angell, George T. *Autobiographical Sketches and Personal Recollections*. Boston: American Humane Education Society, [1908?].

Baker, Margaret. *Anna Sewell and Black Beauty*. London: George Harrap, 1956.

Blount, Margaret. *Animal Land: Creatures of Children's Fiction*. New York: William Morrow, 1975.

Brereton, J. M. *The Horse in War*. Newton Abbot: David & Charles, and New York: Arco, 1976.

Carpenter, Humphrey. *Secret Gardens: a Study of the Golden Age of Children's Literature*. Boston: Houghton Mifflin, 1985.

Chambers, Alden. 'Letter from England: a Hope for Benefit.' *The Horn Book*, 53 (1977): 356–60.

Chitty, Susan. *The Woman who Wrote Black Beauty: a Life of Anna Sewell*. London: Hodder & Stoughton, 1971.

Dent, Anthony A. 'Miss Sewell of Norfolk.' *East Anglian Magazine*, 15/16 (1956): 542–7.

Doré, Gustave, and Jerrold, Blanchard. *London: a Pilgrimage*. New York: David & Charles, 1968 (reprint of London: Grant, 1872 original).

Ginger, Dawn D. 'Black Beauty.' *New Zealand Horse and Pony*, 19 (April 1978): 3–5.

Gordon, W. J. *The Horse World of London*. London: Religious Tract Society, 1893.

Grimshaw, Anne. *The Horse: a Bibliography of British Books 1851–1976*. London: The Library Association, 1982.

Harrison, Brian. 'Animals and the State in 19th Century England.' *English Historical Review*, 58 (1973): 786–820.

Huggett, Frank. *Carriages at Eight*. New York: Charles Scribner's Sons, and London: Lutterworth, 1979.

Jenkinson, Augustus John. *What Do Boys and Girls Read?* 2nd edn. London: Methuen, 1946.

Lansbury, Coral. *The Old Brown Dog: Women, Workers, and Vivisection in Edwardian England*. Madison, Wis.: University of Wisconsin Press, 1985.

McNulty, Faith. 'Children's Books for Christmas.' *New Yorker*, 61 (1 Dec. 1985): 137–47.

Mitchell, Sally. *The Dictionary of British Equestrian Artists*. [Woodbridge, Suffolk]: Antique Collectors' Club, [1985].

Niven, Charles D. *The History of the Humane Movement*. London: Johnson, [1967].

Opie, Peter. 'The Future of Children's Books Lies in the Past.' *Bookseller*, no. 3751 (12 Nov. 1977): 2812–13.

Our Dumb Animals (monthly), edited by George T. Angell. Boston, 1892–4 issues.

Padel, Ruth. 'Saddled with Ginger: Women, Men and Horses.' *Encounter*, 55:5 (November 1980): 45–54.

Pivirotto, Peg. 'The Author of *Black Beauty*.' *American Horseman*, 3 (March 1973): 19.

Ritvo, Harriet. *The Animal Estate*. Cambridge, Mass.: Harvard University Press, 1987.

Sayers, Francis Clarke. 'Walt Disney Accused.' *The Horn Book*, 41 (Dec. 1965): 602–11.

Sidney, Samuel. *Book of the Horse*. 1st edn. London: Cassell, 1874.

Sobel, Dava. 'The Truth about *Black Beauty*.' *Omni*, 9:6 (March 1987): 27.

Starrett, Vincent. '*Black Beauty* and its Author', in his *Buried Caesars: Essays in Literary Appreciation*. Chicago: Covici–McGee, 1923, pp. 205–23.

Stibbs, Andrew. '*Black Beauty*: Tales My Mother Told Me.' *Children's Literature in Education*, 22 (Autumn 1976): 128–34.

Turner, James. *Reckoning with the Beast: Animals, Pain, and Humanity in the Victorian Mind*. London and Baltimore: Johns Hopkins Press, [1980].

Walrond, Sallie. *Encyclopaedia of Driving*. Macclesfield: Horse Drawn Carriages, 1974.

Whitehead, Frank. *Children's Reading Interests*. London: Evans/ Methuen Educational, [1975].